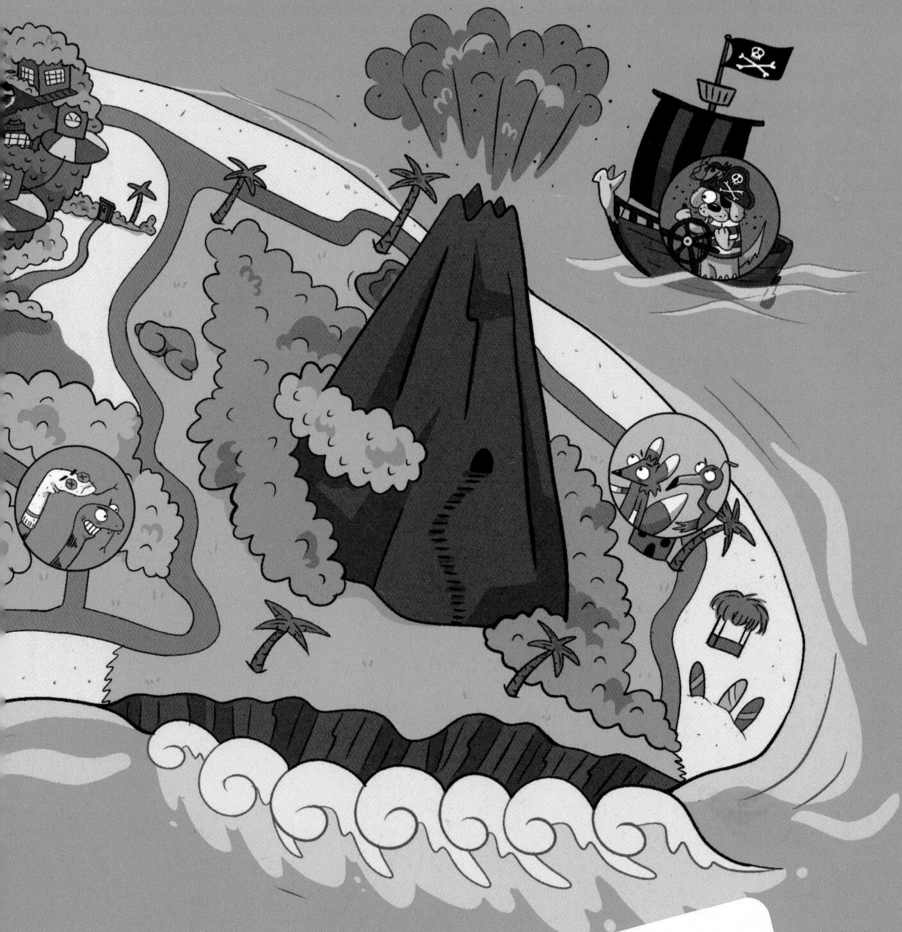

THE LEGEND OF GN E

Marks the Spot	The Dr
Pirates	Palm Tree
Sea Monster	Secret Cave

SLOTH SLEUTH

THE LEGEND OF GNAWFACE

By Cyndi Marko

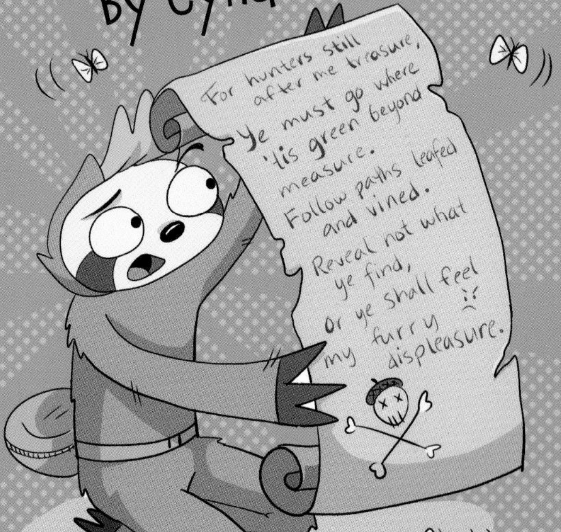
For hunters still
after me treasure,
Ye must go where
'tis green beyond
measure.
Follow paths leafed
and vined.
Reveal not what
ye find,
Or ye shall feel
my furry
displeasure.

Clarion Books
Imprints of HarperCollins*Publishers*

HARPER alley

Clarion Books is an imprint of HarperCollins Publishers.
HarperAlley is an imprint of HarperCollins Publishers.

The Legend of Gnawface
 For information address HarperCollins Children's Books, a division of HarperCollins Publishers, 195 Broadway, New York, NY 10007.
www.harperalley.com

ISBN 978-0-35-844894-5

Colors by Jessica Lome
Lettering by Natalie Fondriest
The artist used Clip Studio to create the digital illustrations for this book.

23 24 25 26 27 GPS 10 9 8 7 6 5 4 3 2 1

First Edition

THE PREAMBLE (BECAUSE NOBODY LIKES PROLOGUES EXCEPT FOR LIBRARIAN ANDREWS)

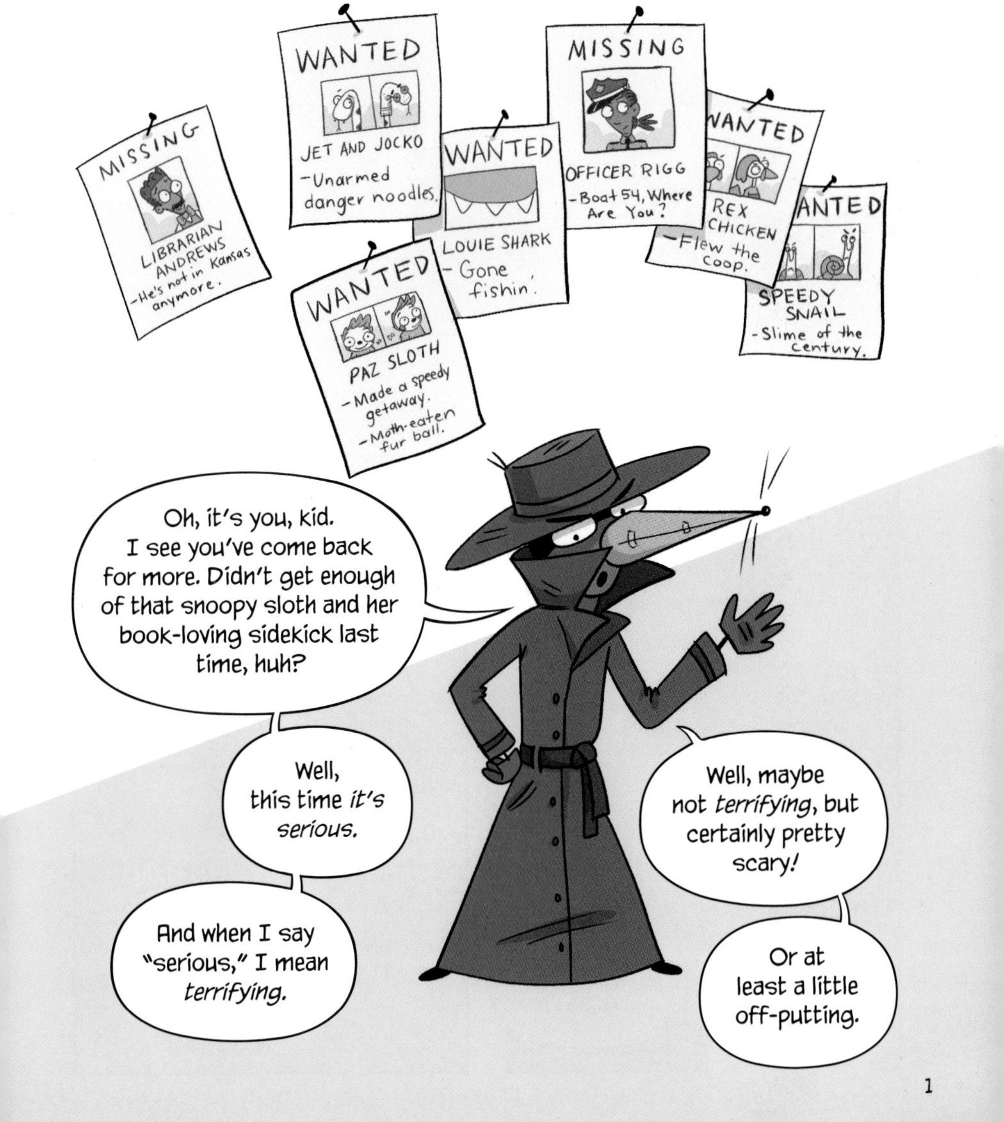
MISSING
LIBRARIAN ANDREWS
-He's not in Kansas anymore.
WANTED
JET AND JOCKO
-Unarmed danger noodles.
WANTED
PAZ SLOTH
-Made a speedy getaway.
-Moth-eaten fur ball.
WANTED
LOUIE SHARK
-Gone fishin'.
MISSING
OFFICER RIGG
-Boat 54, Where Are You?
WANTED
REX CHICKEN
-Flew the coop.
WANTED
SPEEDY SNAIL
-Slime of the century.
Oh, it's you, kid. I see you've come back for more. Didn't get enough of that snoopy sloth and her book-loving sidekick last time, huh?
Well, this time *it's serious.*
And when I say "serious," I mean *terrifying.*
Well, maybe not *terrifying*, but certainly pretty scary!
Or at least a little off-putting.

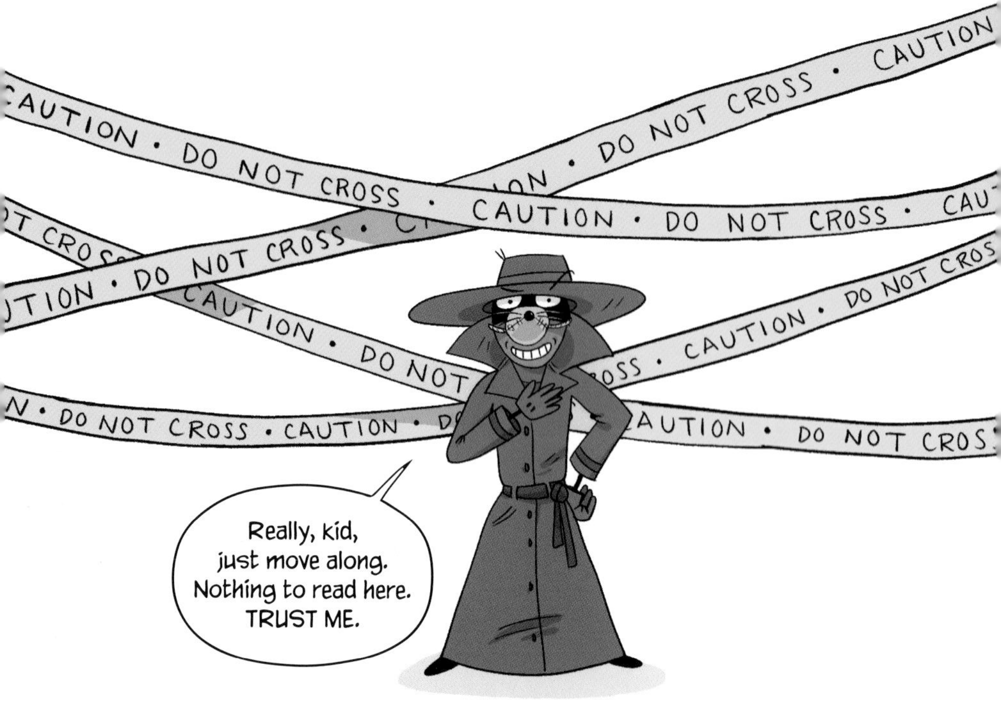
CAUTION • DO NOT CROSS • CAUTION • DO NOT CROSS
Really, kid, just move along. Nothing to read here. TRUST ME.

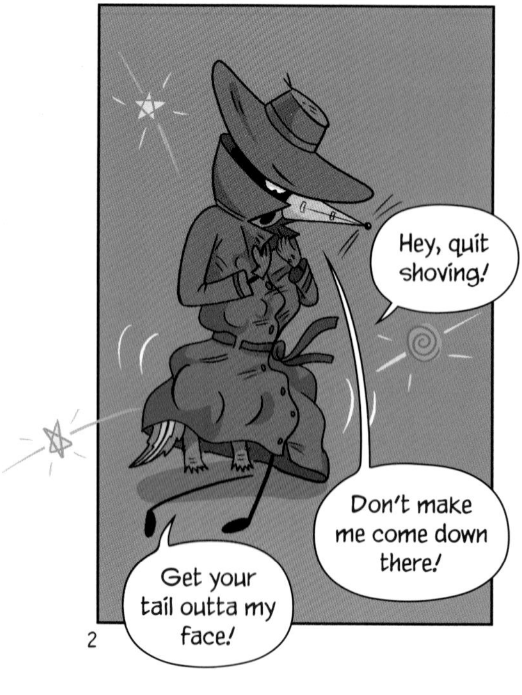
Hey, quit shoving!
Don't make me come down there!
Get your tail outta my face!

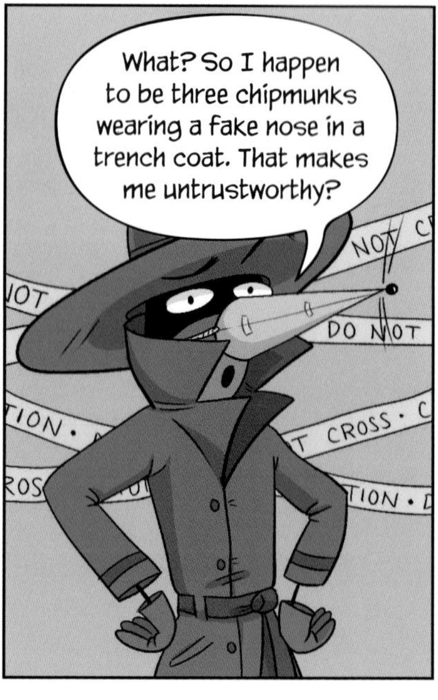
What? So I happen to be three chipmunks wearing a fake nose in a trench coat. That makes me untrustworthy?

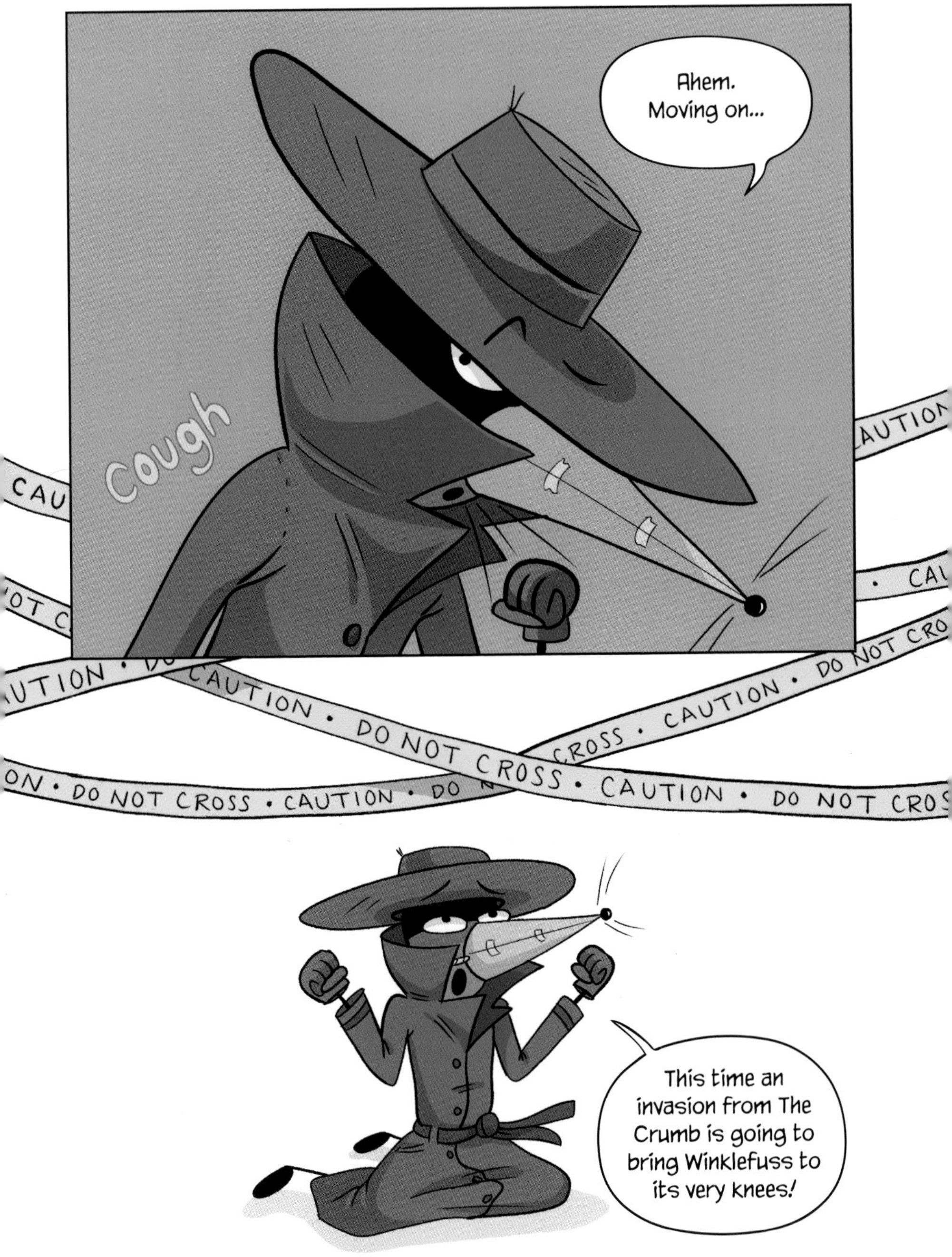
Ahem.
Moving on...
Cough
CAUTION • DO NOT CROSS • CAUTION • DO NOT CROSS
This time an invasion from The Crumb is going to bring Winklefuss to its very knees!

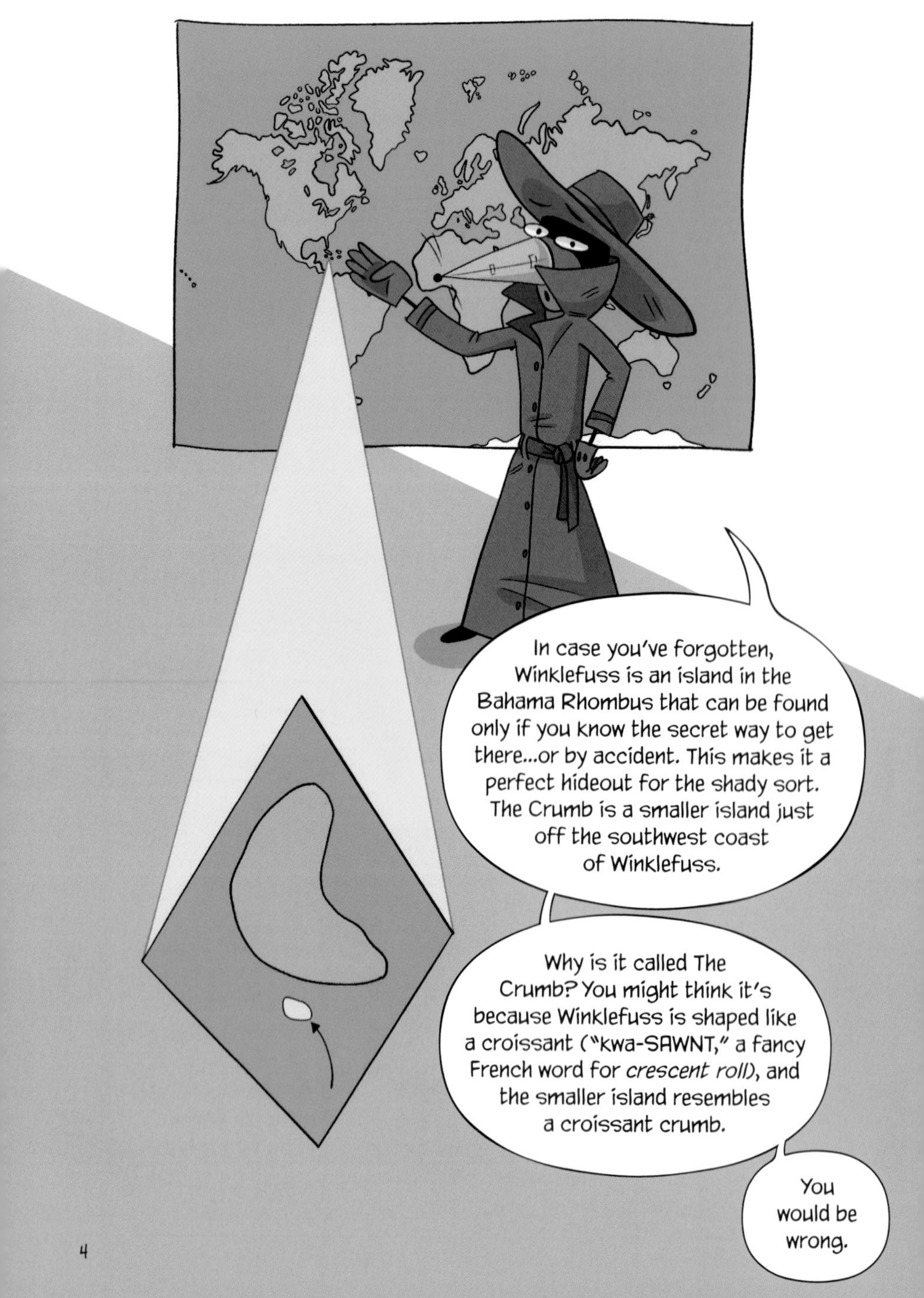
In case you've forgotten, Winklefuss is an island in the Bahama Rhombus that can be found only if you know the secret way to get there...or by accident. This makes it a perfect hideout for the shady sort. The Crumb is a smaller island just off the southwest coast of Winklefuss.
Why is it called The Crumb? You might think it's because Winklefuss is shaped like a croissant ("kwa-SAWNT," a fancy French word for *crescent roll*), and the smaller island resembles a croissant crumb.
You would be wrong.

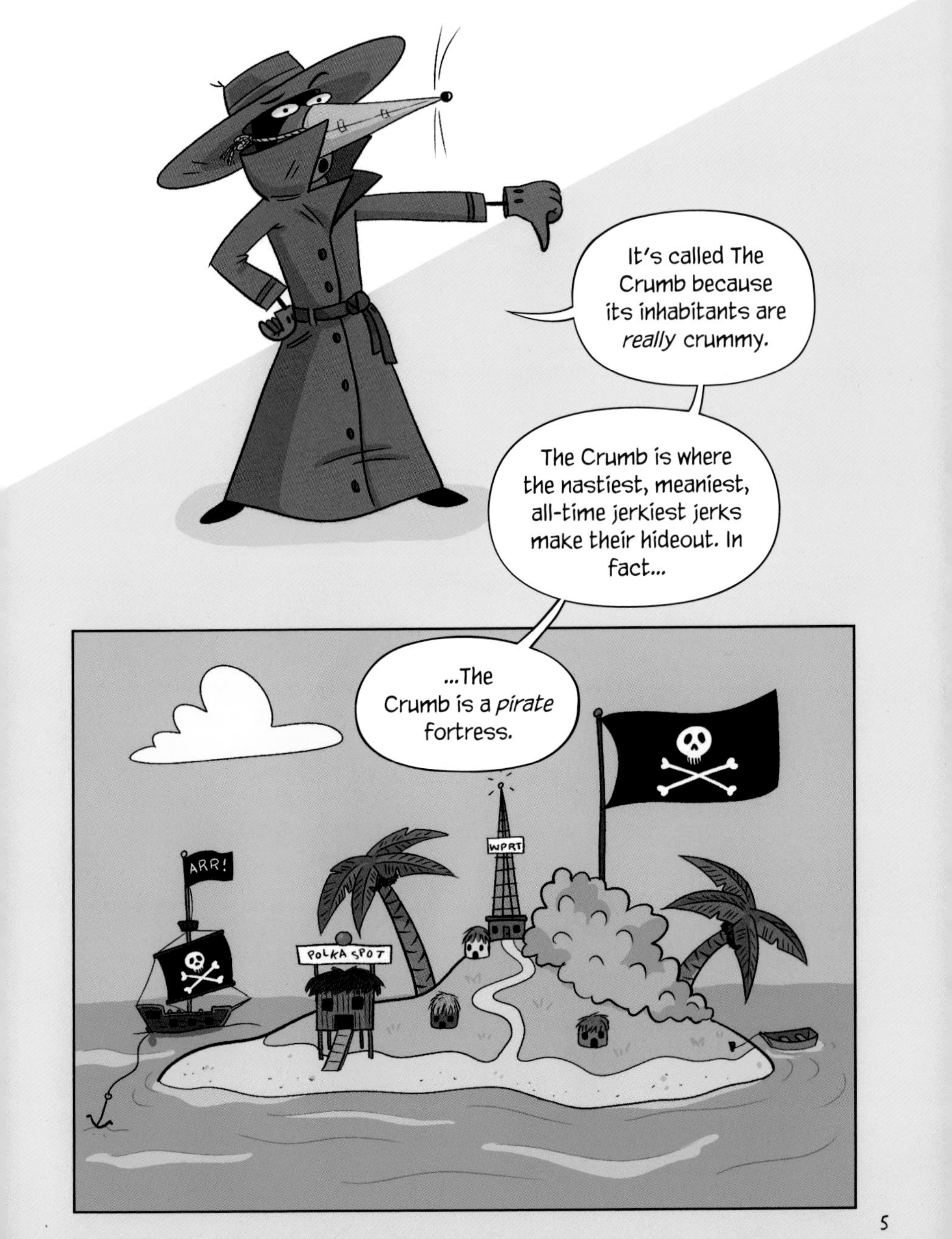
It's called The Crumb because its inhabitants are *really* crummy.
The Crumb is where the nastiest, meaniest, all-time jerkiest jerks make their hideout. In fact...
...The Crumb is a *pirate* fortress.
ARR!
POLKA SPOT
WPRT

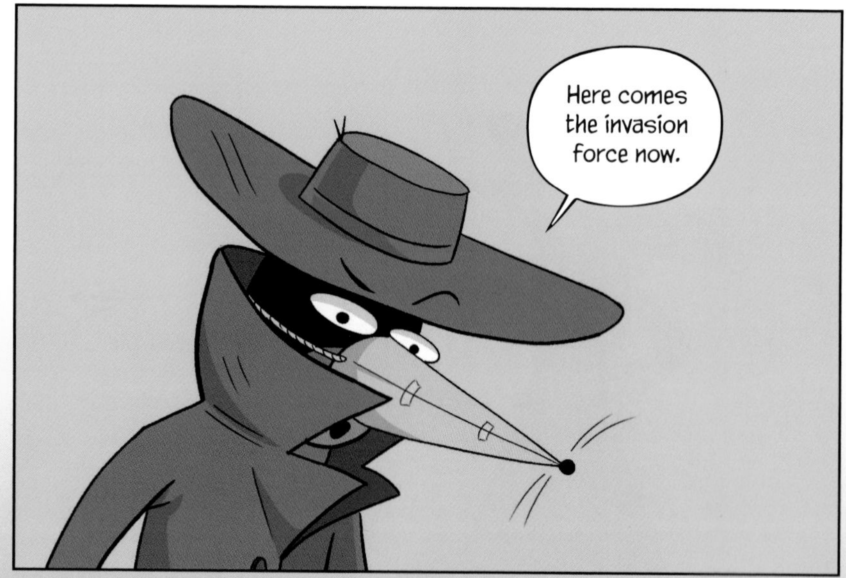
Here comes the invasion force now.

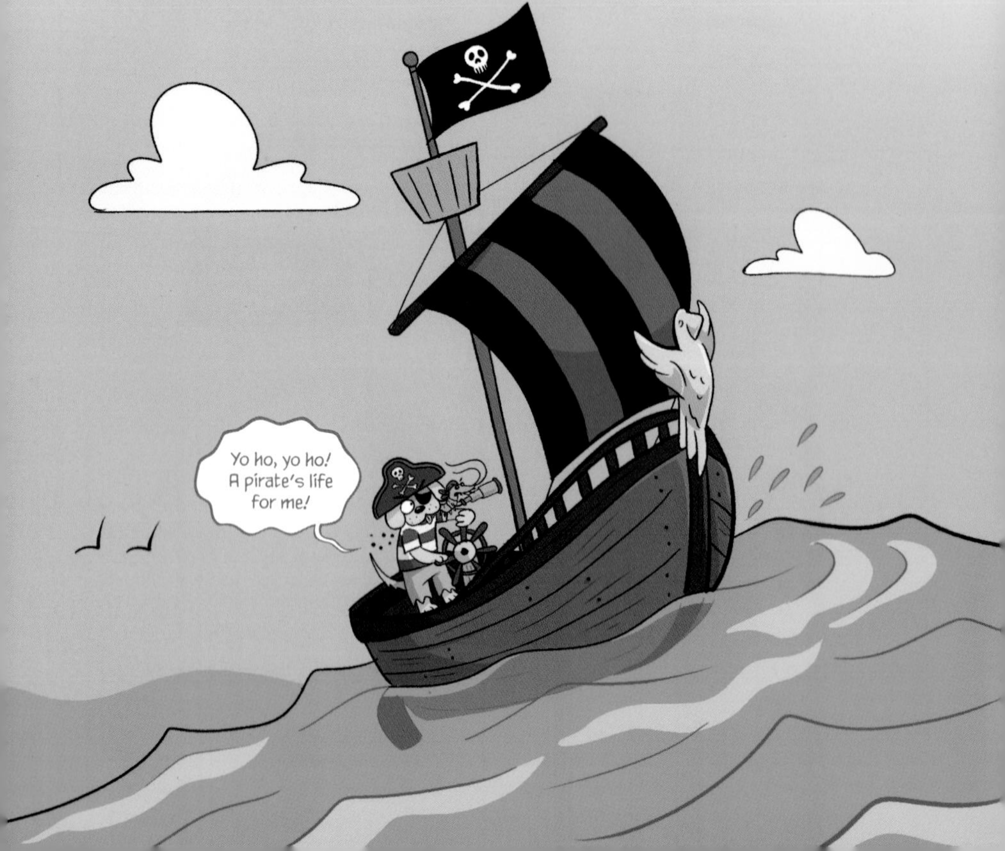
Yo ho, yo ho! A pirate's life for me!

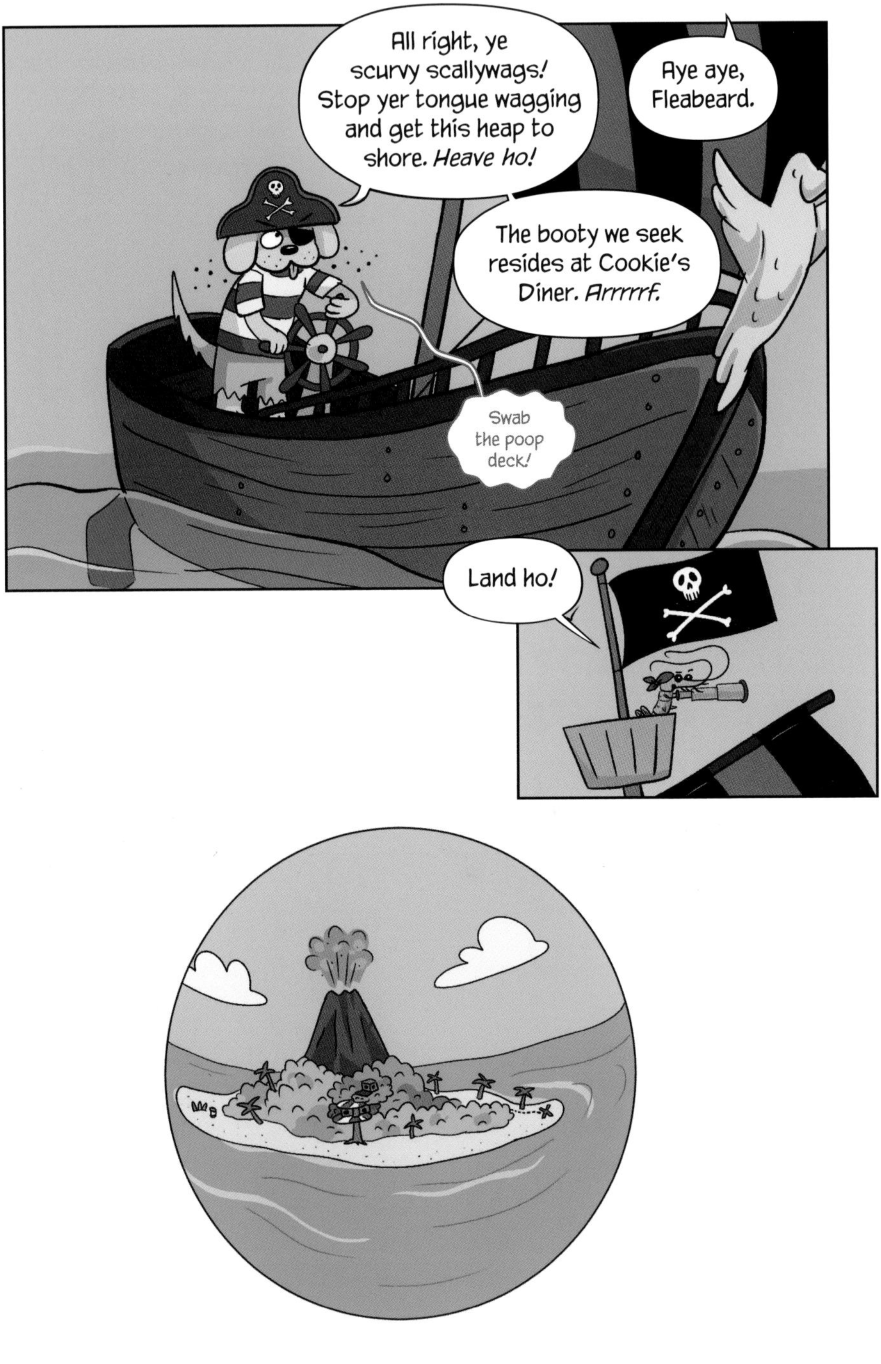
All right, ye scurvy scallywags! Stop yer tongue wagging and get this heap to shore. *Heave ho!*
Aye aye, Fleabeard.
The booty we seek resides at Cookie's Diner. *Arrrrrf.*
Swab the poop deck!
Land ho!

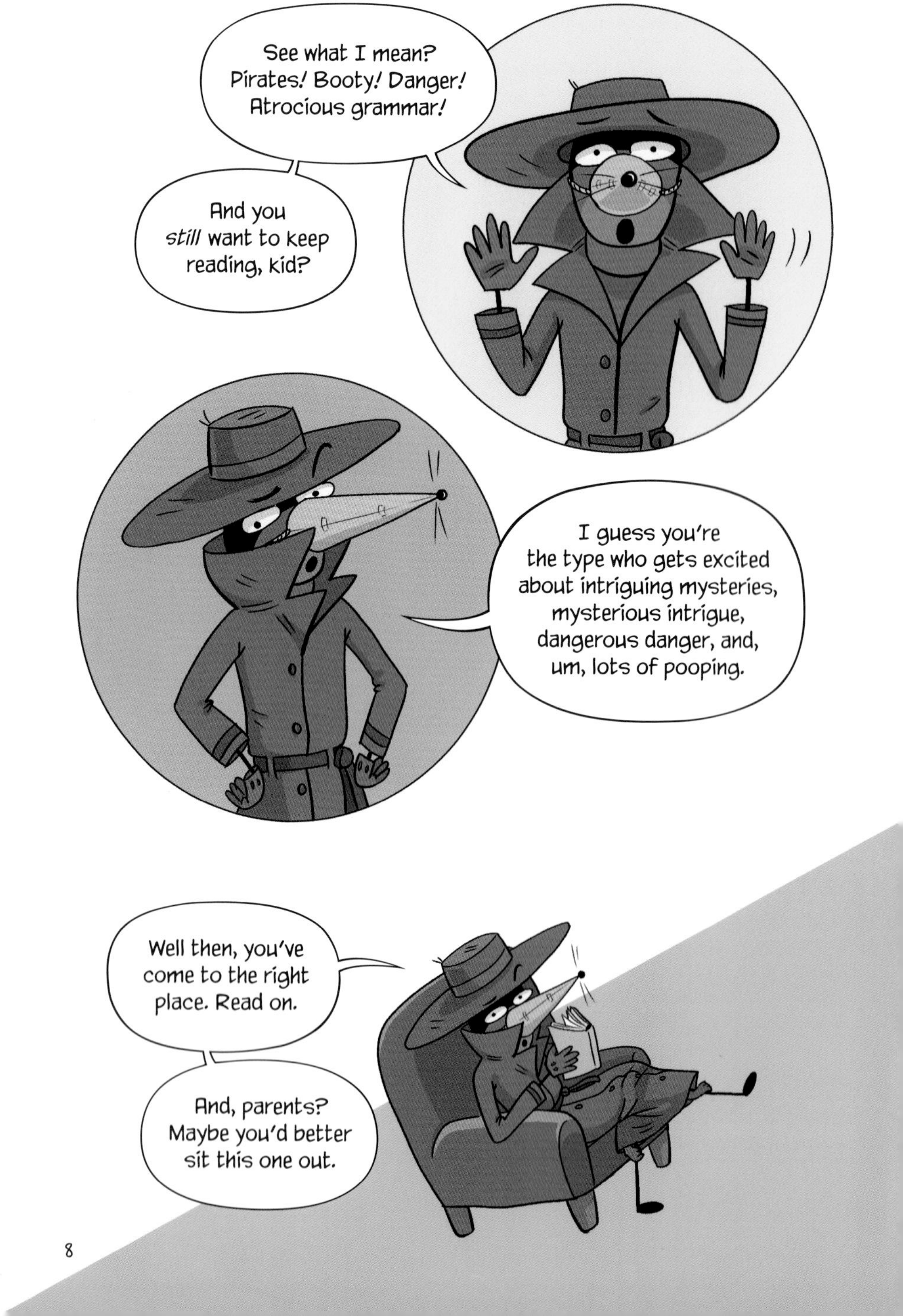
See what I mean? Pirates! Booty! Danger! Atrocious grammar!
And you *still* want to keep reading, kid?
I guess you're the type who gets excited about intriguing mysteries, mysterious intrigue, dangerous danger, and, um, lots of pooping.
Well then, you've come to the right place. Read on.
And, parents? Maybe you'd better sit this one out.

CHAPTER 1

MONDAY. BRIGHT AND EARLY. PAZ'S TREEHOUSE.

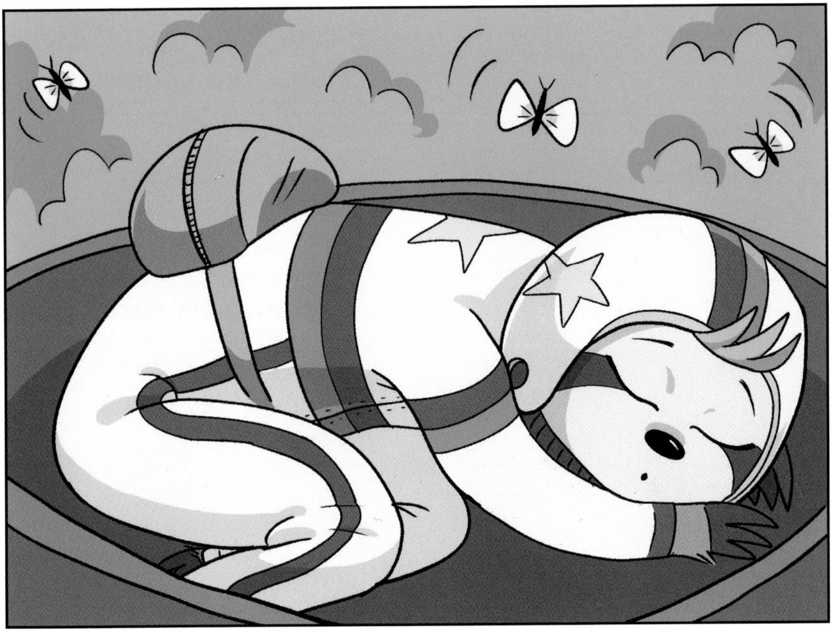

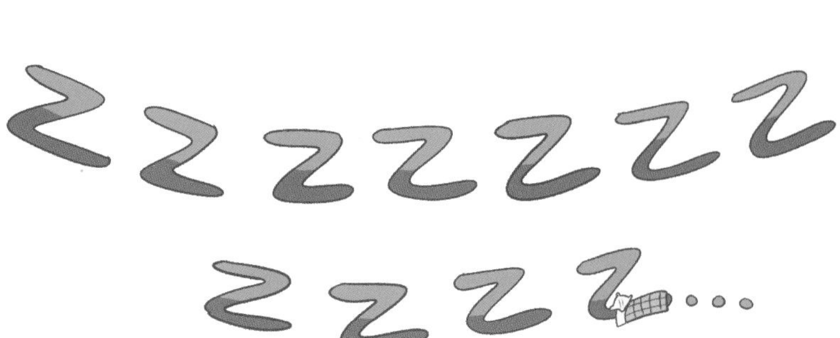
ZZZZZZZZ
ZZZZZ...

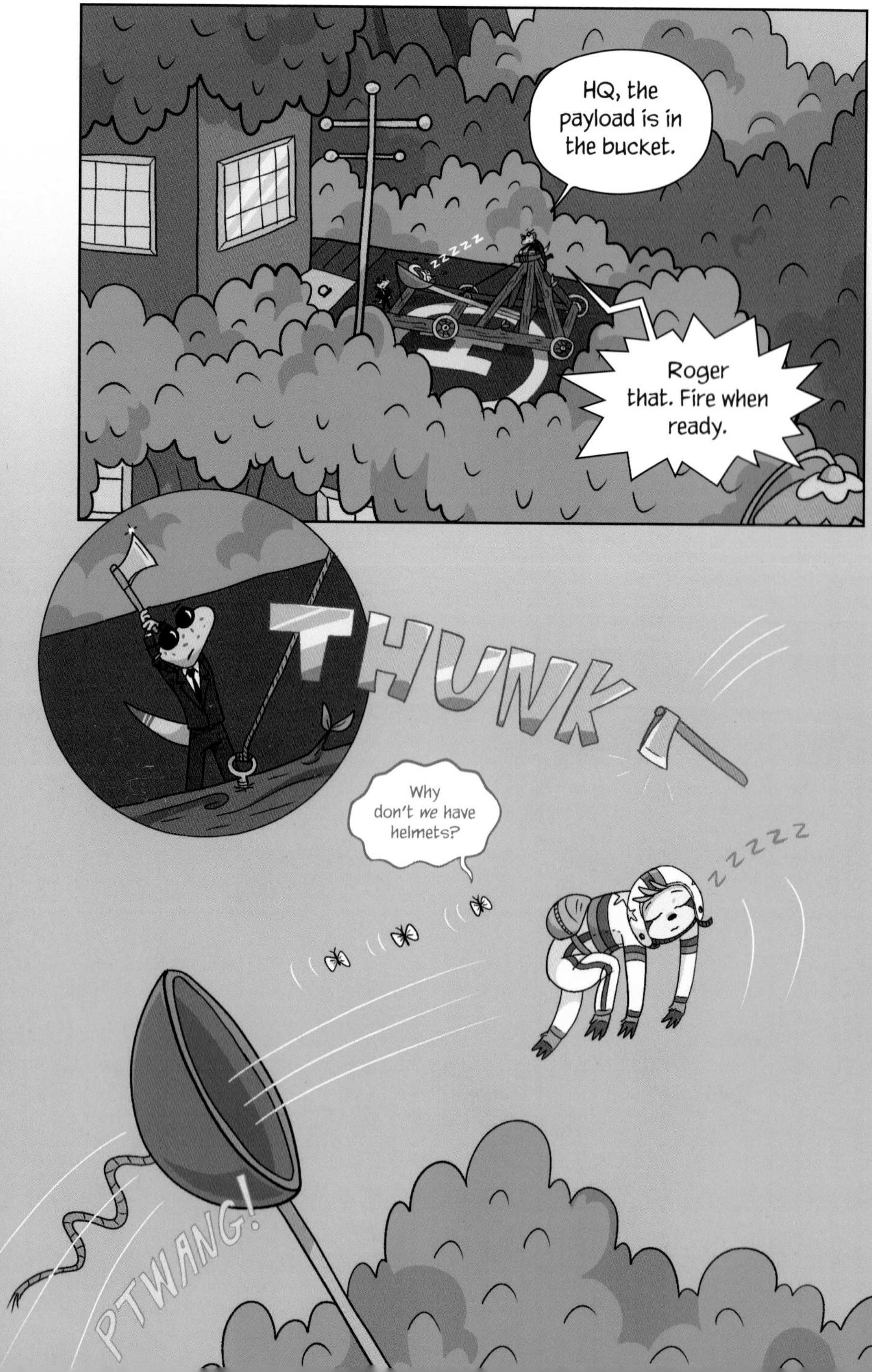
HQ, the payload is in the bucket.
Roger that. Fire when ready.
ZZZZZ
THUNK
Why don't we have helmets?
ZZZZZ
PTWANG!

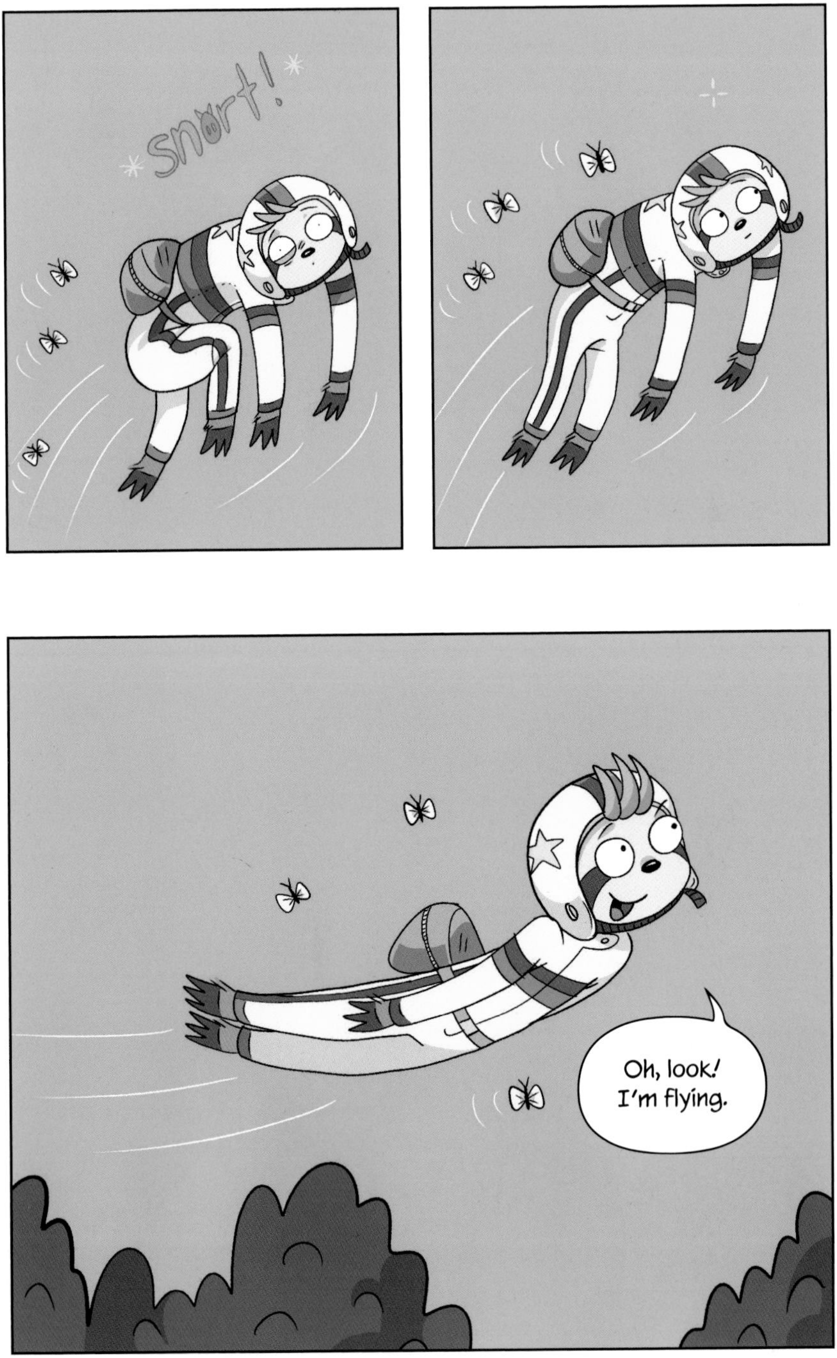
snort!
Oh, look!
I'm flying.

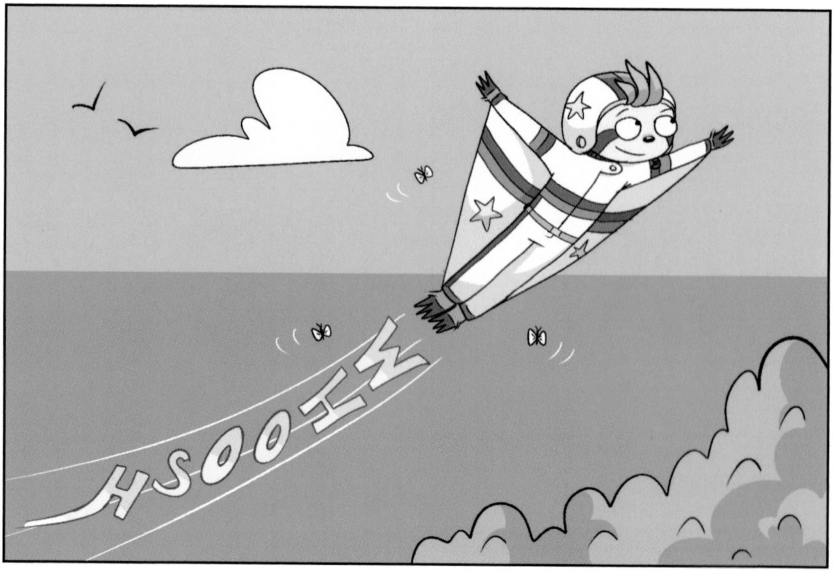
WHOOSH

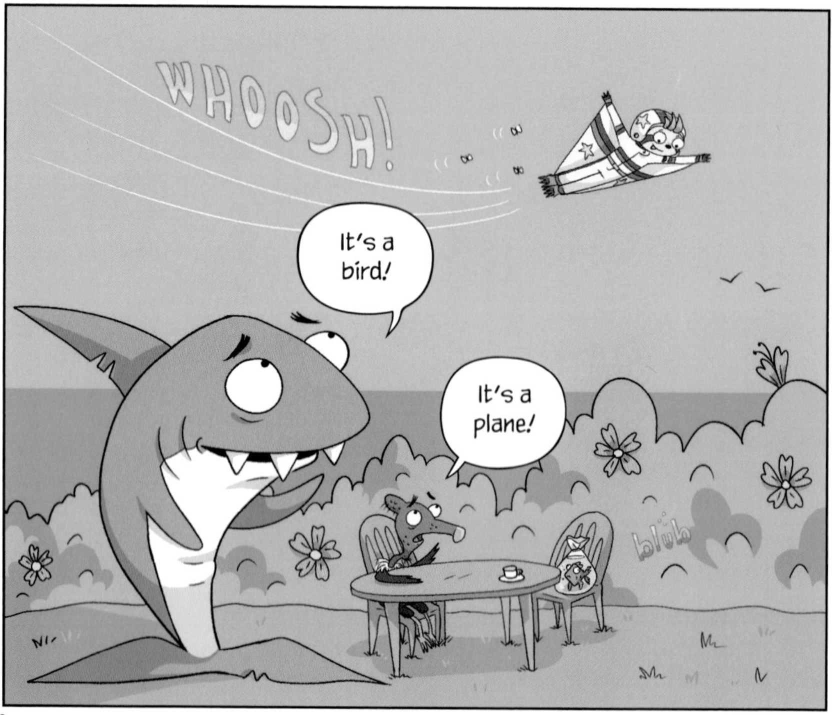
WHOOSH!
It's a bird!
It's a plane!
blub

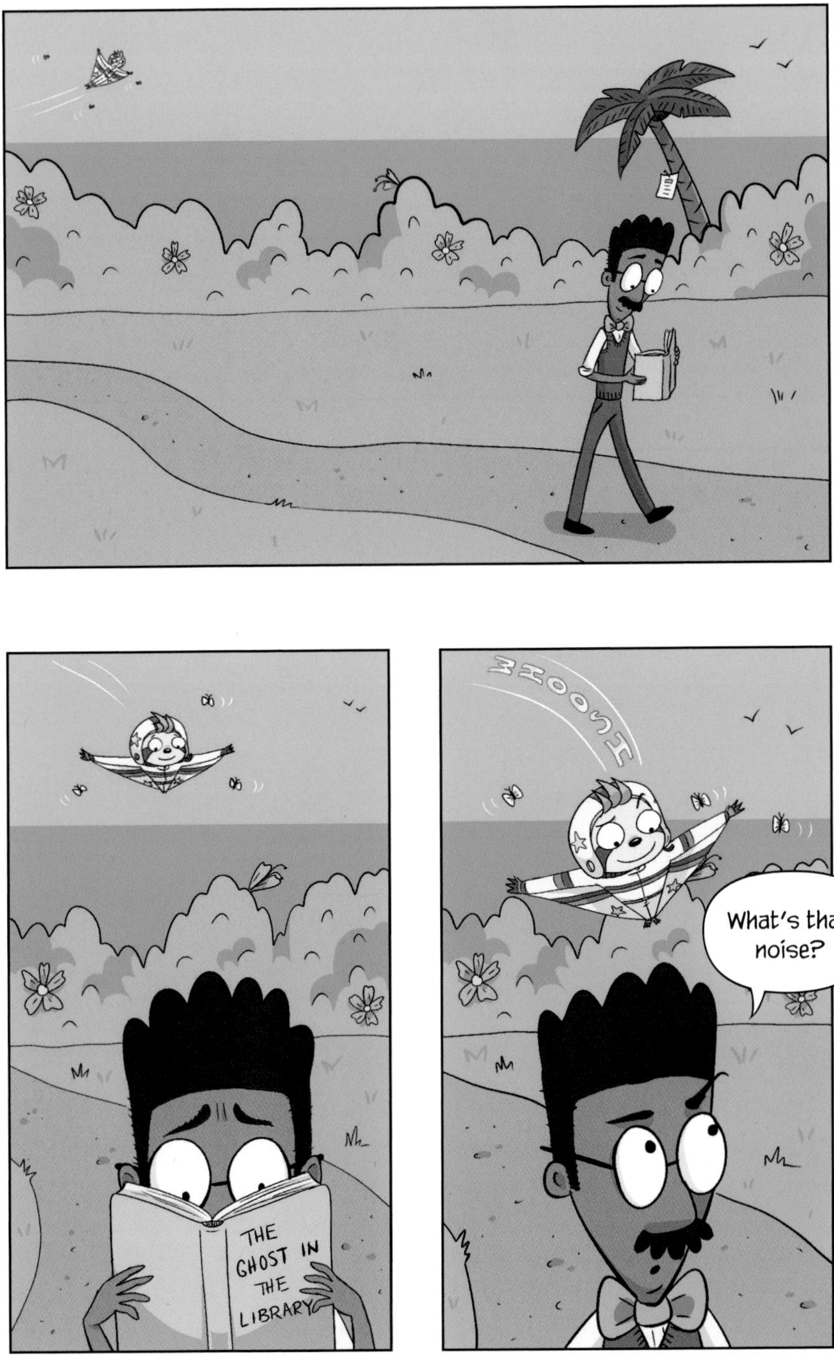
THE GHOST IN THE LIBRARY
What's that noise?

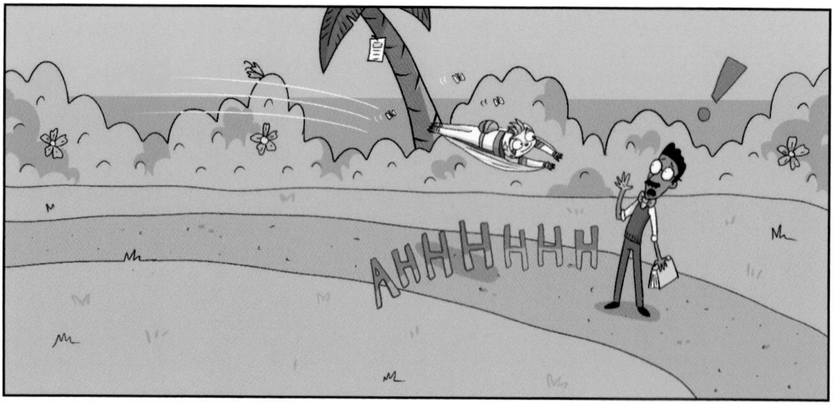
AHHHHHHH

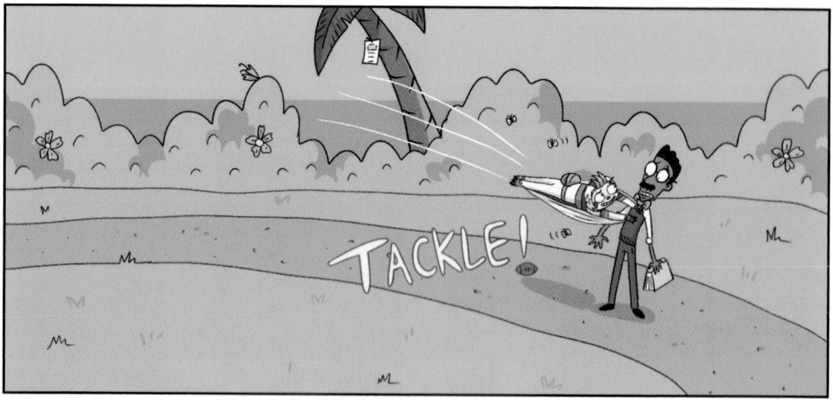
TACKLE!

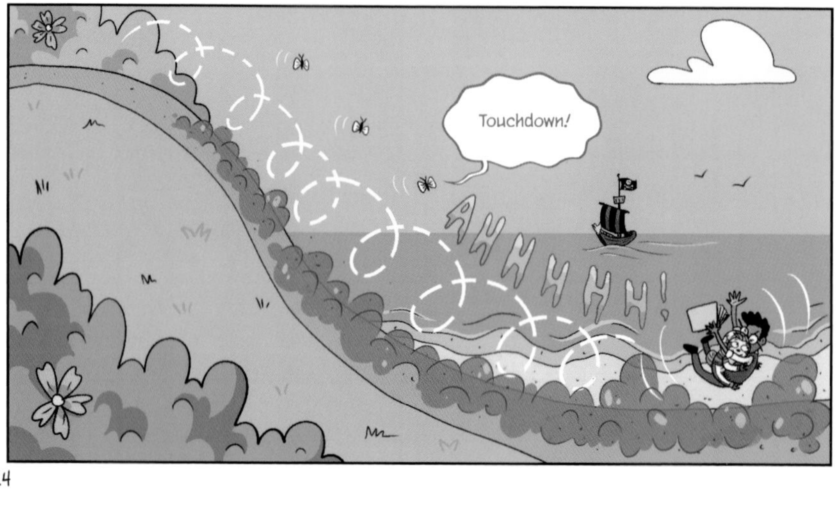
Touchdown!
AHHHHHH!

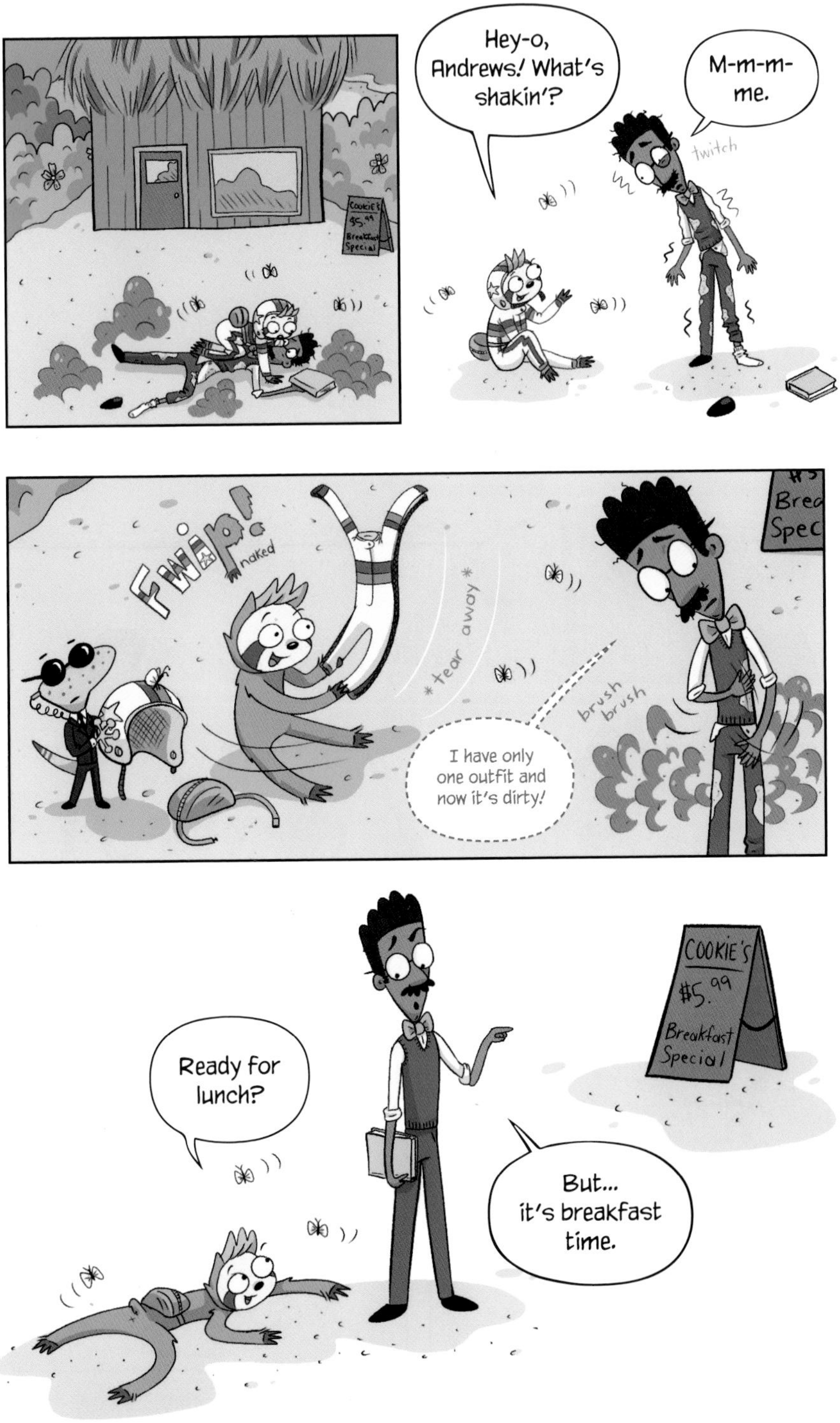
COOKIE'S
$5.99
Breakfast Special
Hey-o, Andrews! What's shakin'?
M-m-m-me.
twitch
FWIP!
naked
tear away
brush brush
I have only one outfit and now it's dirty!
COOKIE'S
$5.99
Breakfast Special
Ready for lunch?
But... it's breakfast time.

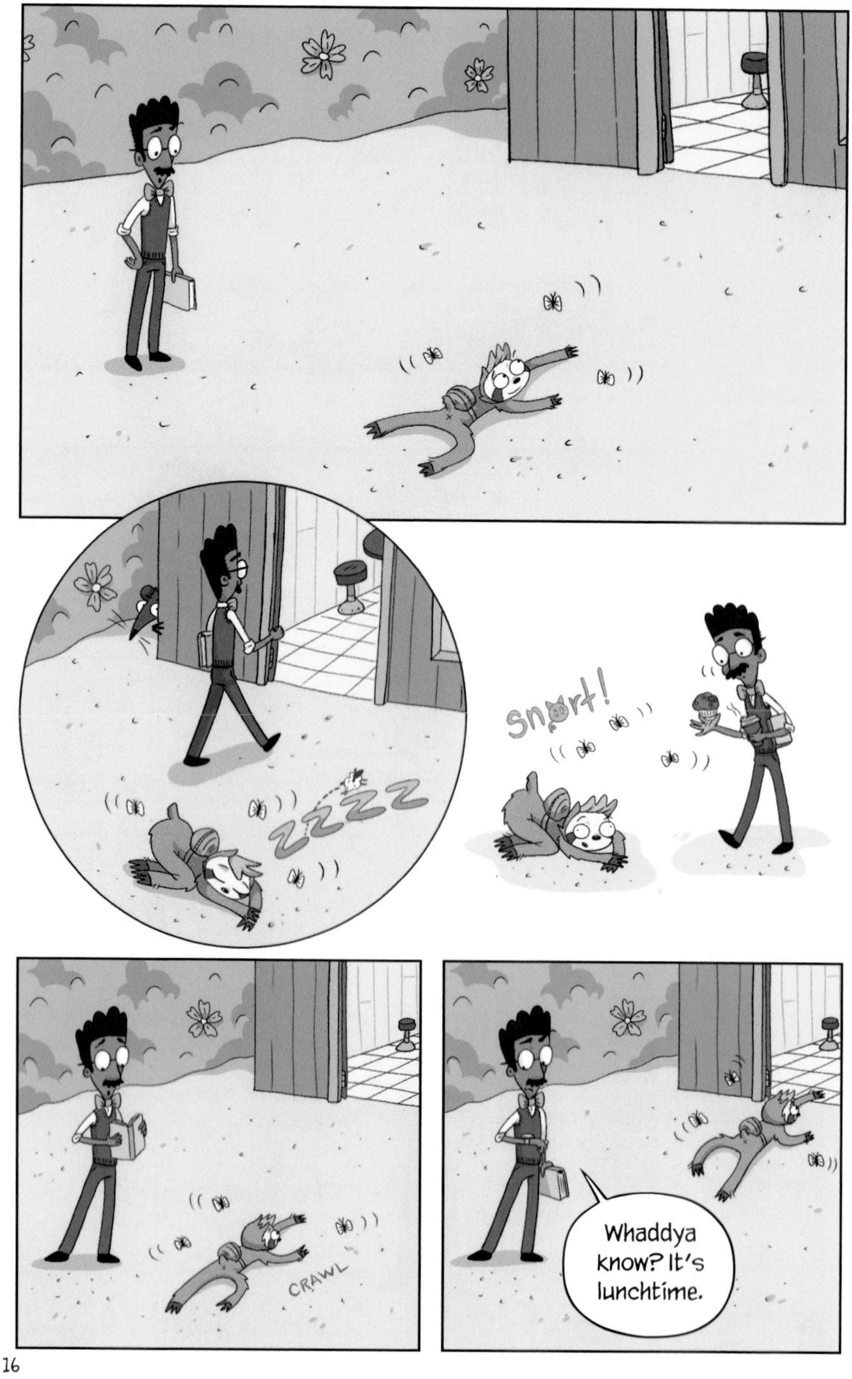
Snort!
ZZZZ
CRAWL
Whaddya know? It's lunchtime.

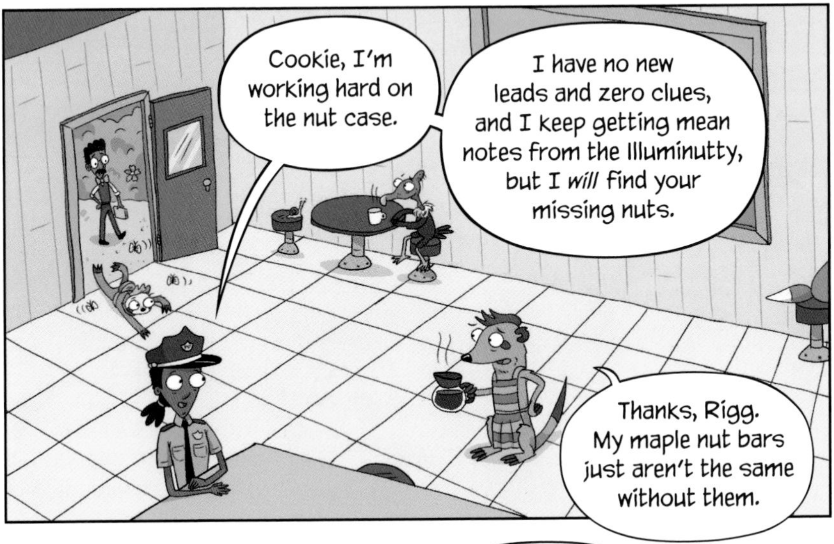
Cookie, I'm working hard on the nut case.
I have no new leads and zero clues, and I keep getting mean notes from the Illuminutty, but I *will* find your missing nuts.
Thanks, Rigg. My maple nut bars just aren't the same without them.

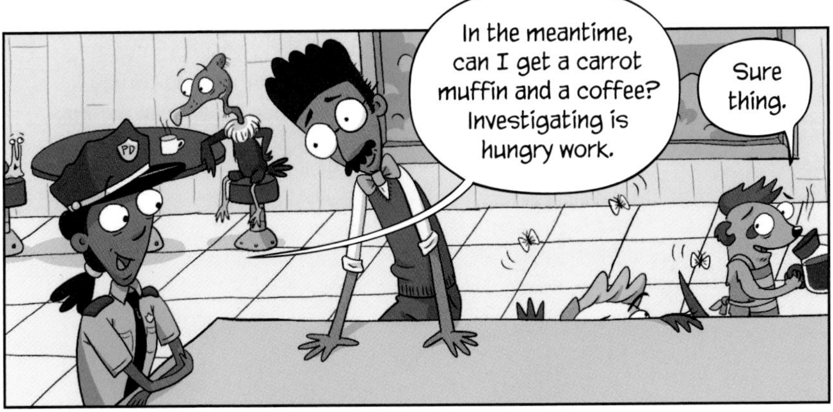
In the meantime, can I get a carrot muffin and a coffee? Investigating is hungry work.
Sure thing.

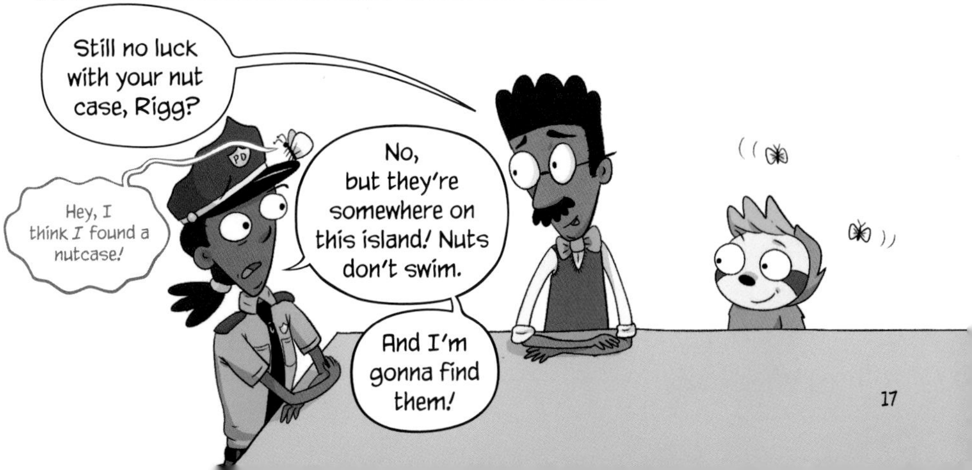
Still no luck with your nut case, Rigg?
Hey, I think *I* found a nutcase!
No, but they're somewhere on this island! Nuts don't swim.
And I'm gonna find them!

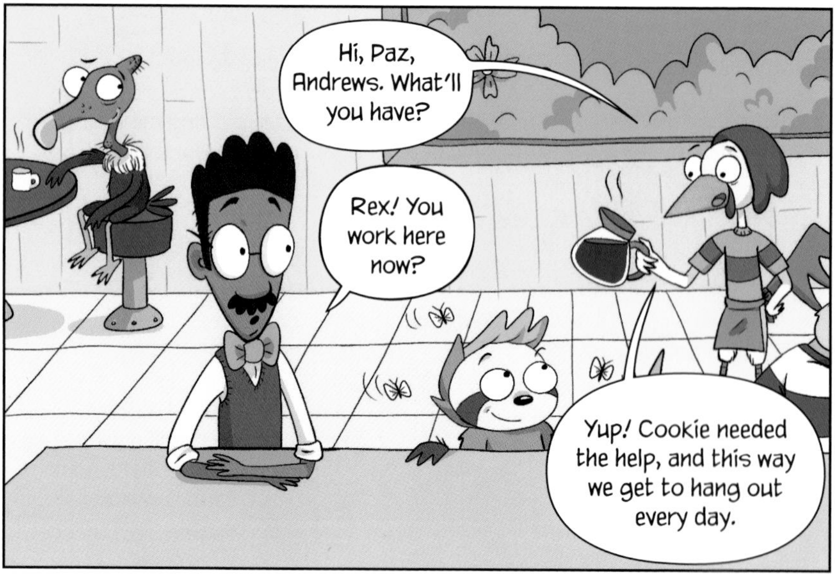
Hi, Paz, Andrews. What'll you have?
Rex! You work here now?
Yup! Cookie needed the help, and this way we get to hang out every day.

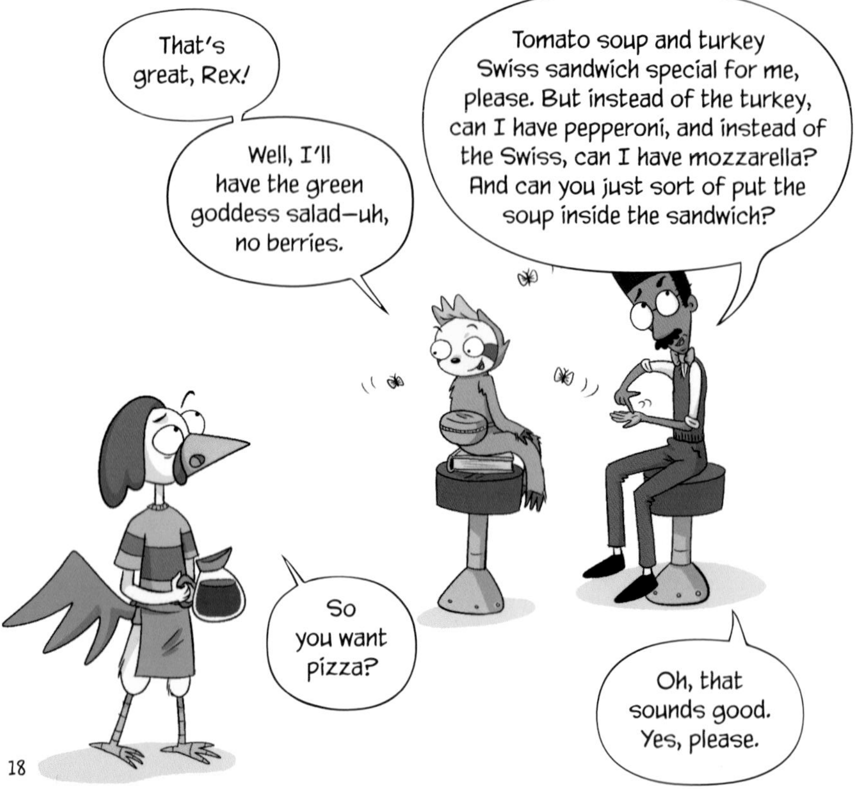
That's great, Rex!
Well, I'll have the green goddess salad—uh, no berries.
Tomato soup and turkey Swiss sandwich special for me, please. But instead of the turkey, can I have pepperoni, and instead of the Swiss, can I have mozzarella? And can you just sort of put the soup inside the sandwich?
So you want pizza?
Oh, that sounds good. Yes, please.

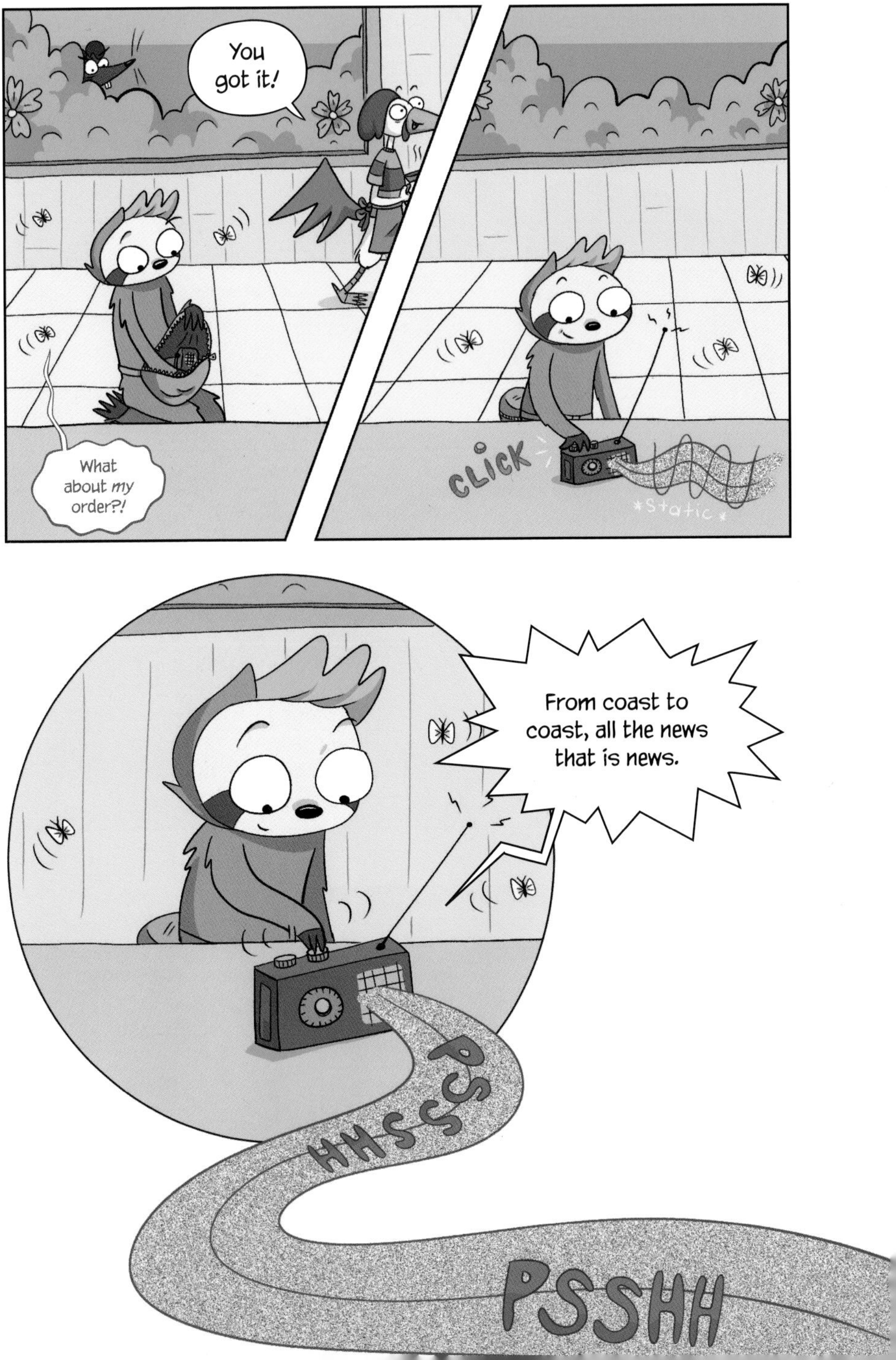
You got it!
What about *my* order?!
CLICK
Static
From coast to coast, all the news that is news.
PSSSHH
PSSHH

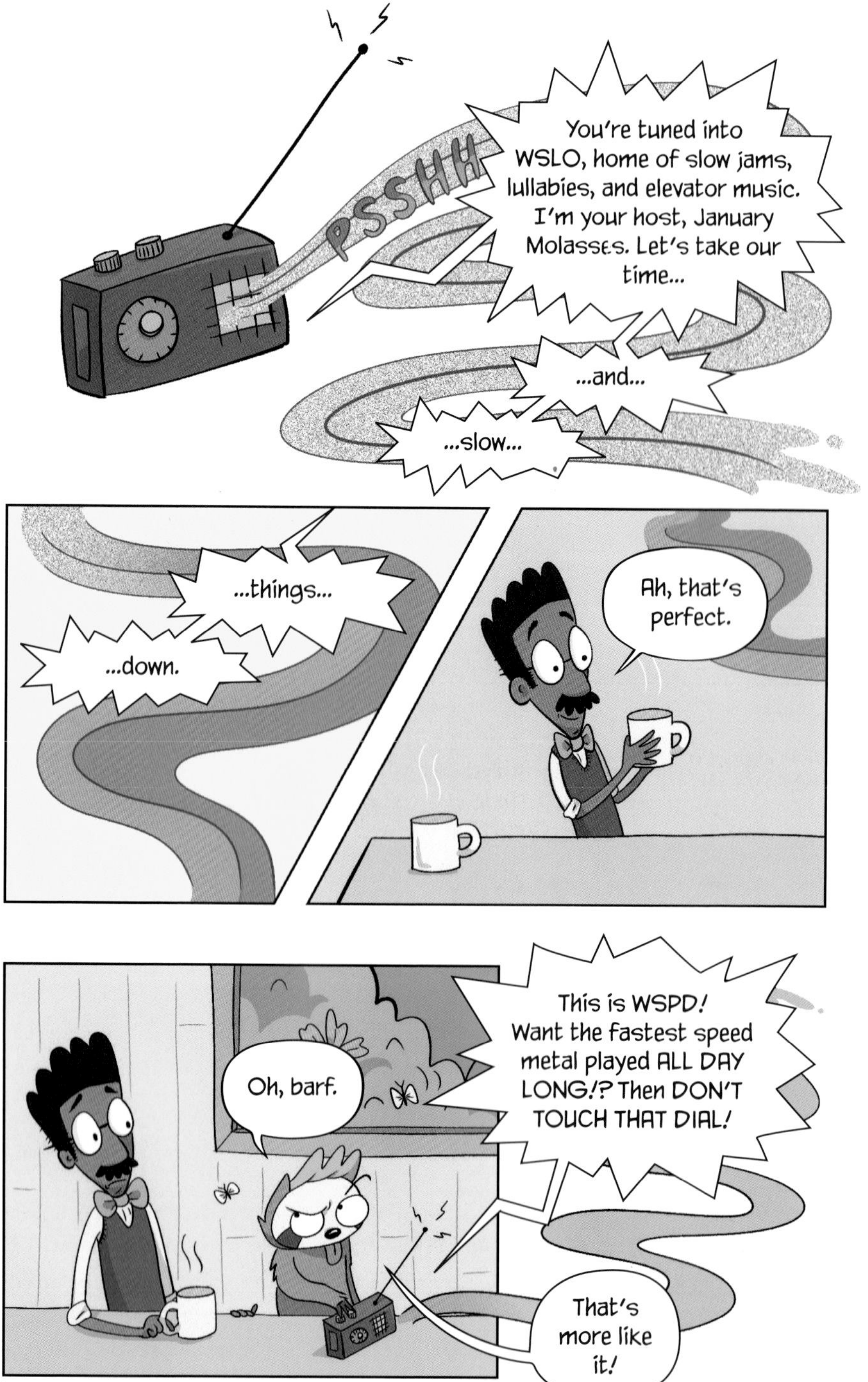
PSSHH
You're tuned into WSLO, home of slow jams, lullabies, and elevator music. I'm your host, January Molasses. Let's take our time...
...and...
...slow...
...things...
...down.
Ah, that's perfect.
This is WSPD! Want the fastest speed metal played ALL DAY LONG!? Then DON'T TOUCH THAT DIAL!
Oh, barf.
That's more like it!

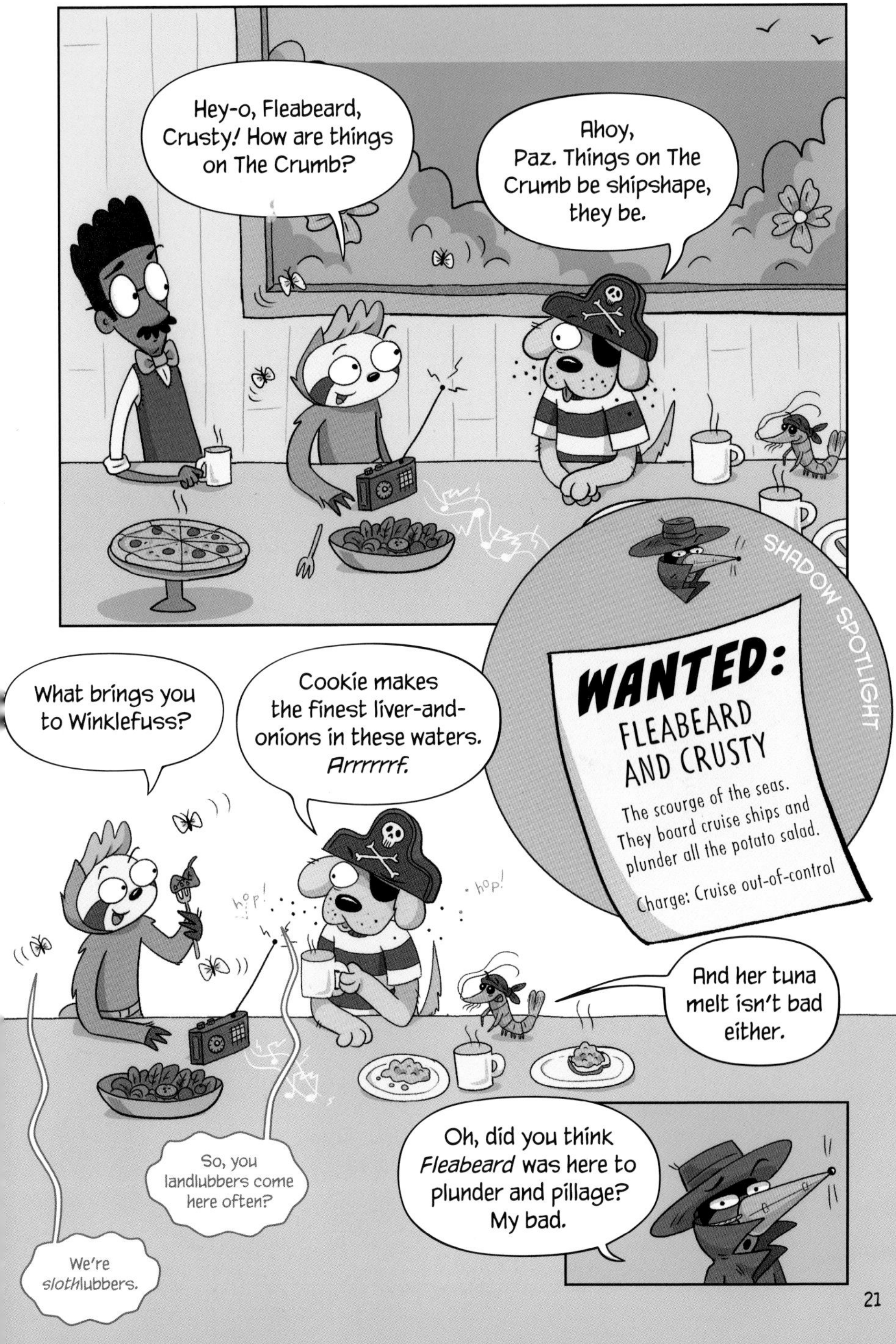

Hey-o, Fleabeard, Crusty! How are things on The Crumb?
Ahoy, Paz. Things on The Crumb be shipshape, they be.
SHADOW SPOTLIGHT
WANTED:
FLEABEARD AND CRUSTY
The scourge of the seas. They board cruise ships and plunder all the potato salad.
Charge: Cruise out-of-control
What brings you to Winklefuss?
Cookie makes the finest liver-and-onions in these waters. *Arrrrrrf.*
hop!
hop!
And her tuna melt isn't bad either.
So, you landlubbers come here often?
We're *sloth*lubbers.
Oh, did you think *Fleabeard* was here to plunder and pillage? My bad.

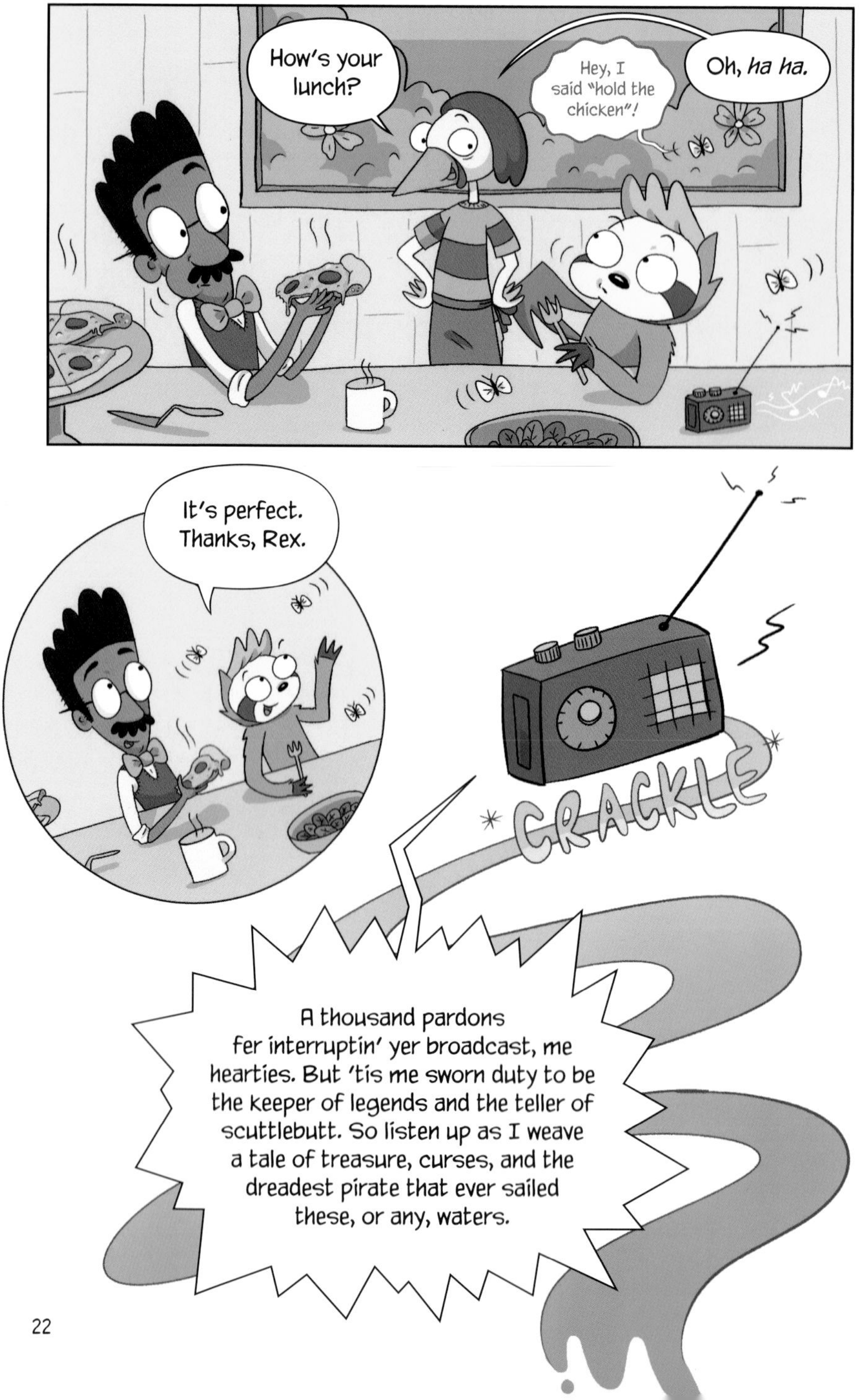
How's your lunch?
Hey, I said "hold the chicken"!
Oh, *ha ha.*
It's perfect. Thanks, Rex.
CRACKLE
A thousand pardons fer interruptin' yer broadcast, me hearties. But 'tis me sworn duty to be the keeper of legends and the teller of scuttlebutt. So listen up as I weave a tale of treasure, curses, and the dreadest pirate that ever sailed these, or any, waters.

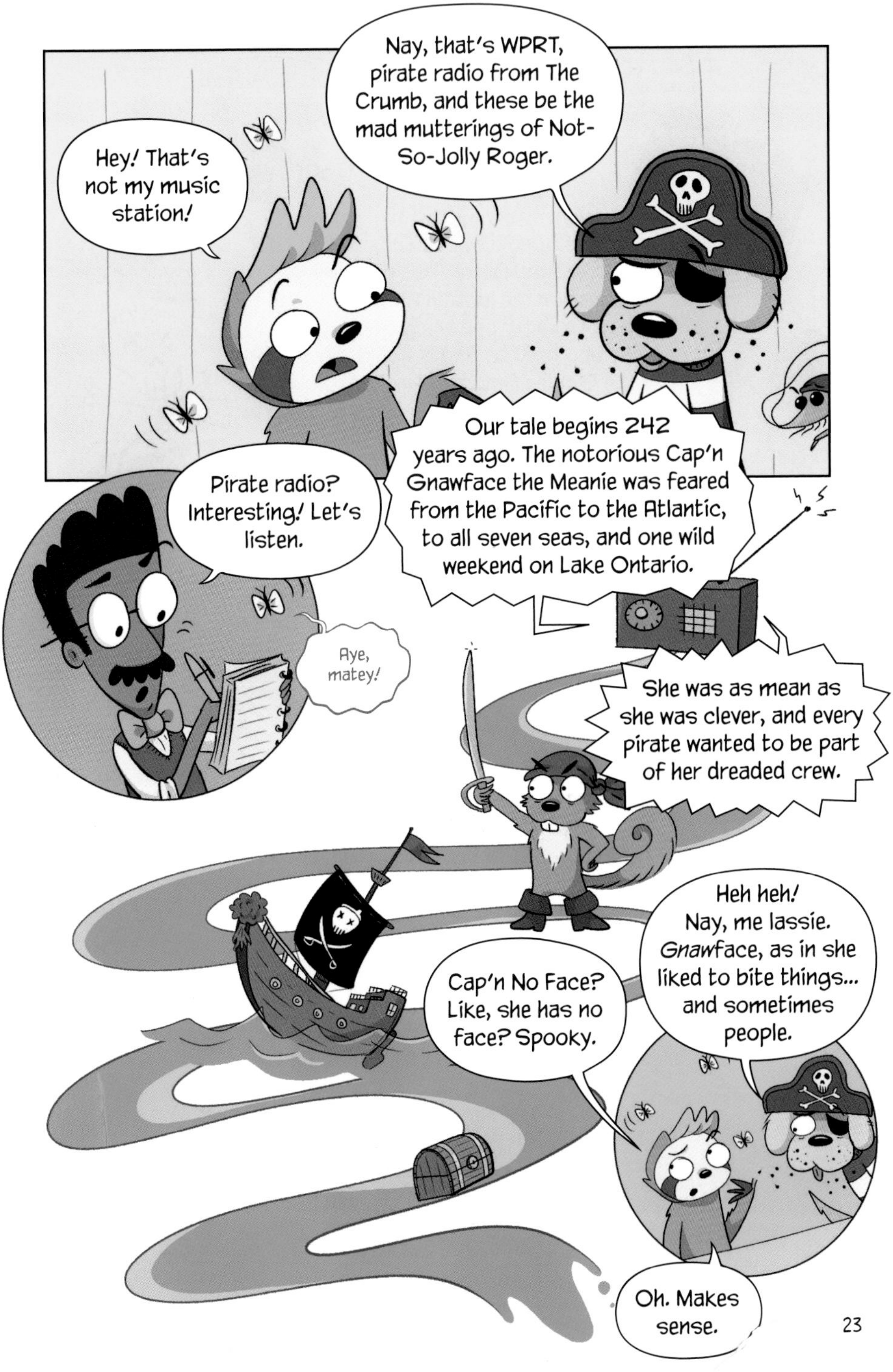
Hey! That's not my music station!
Nay, that's WPRT, pirate radio from The Crumb, and these be the mad mutterings of Not-So-Jolly Roger.
Pirate radio? Interesting! Let's listen.
Our tale begins 242 years ago. The notorious Cap'n Gnawface the Meanie was feared from the Pacific to the Atlantic, to all seven seas, and one wild weekend on Lake Ontario.
Aye, matey!
She was as mean as she was clever, and every pirate wanted to be part of her dreaded crew.
Cap'n No Face? Like, she has no face? Spooky.
Heh heh! Nay, me lassie. *Gnaw*face, as in she liked to bite things... and sometimes people.
Oh. Makes sense.

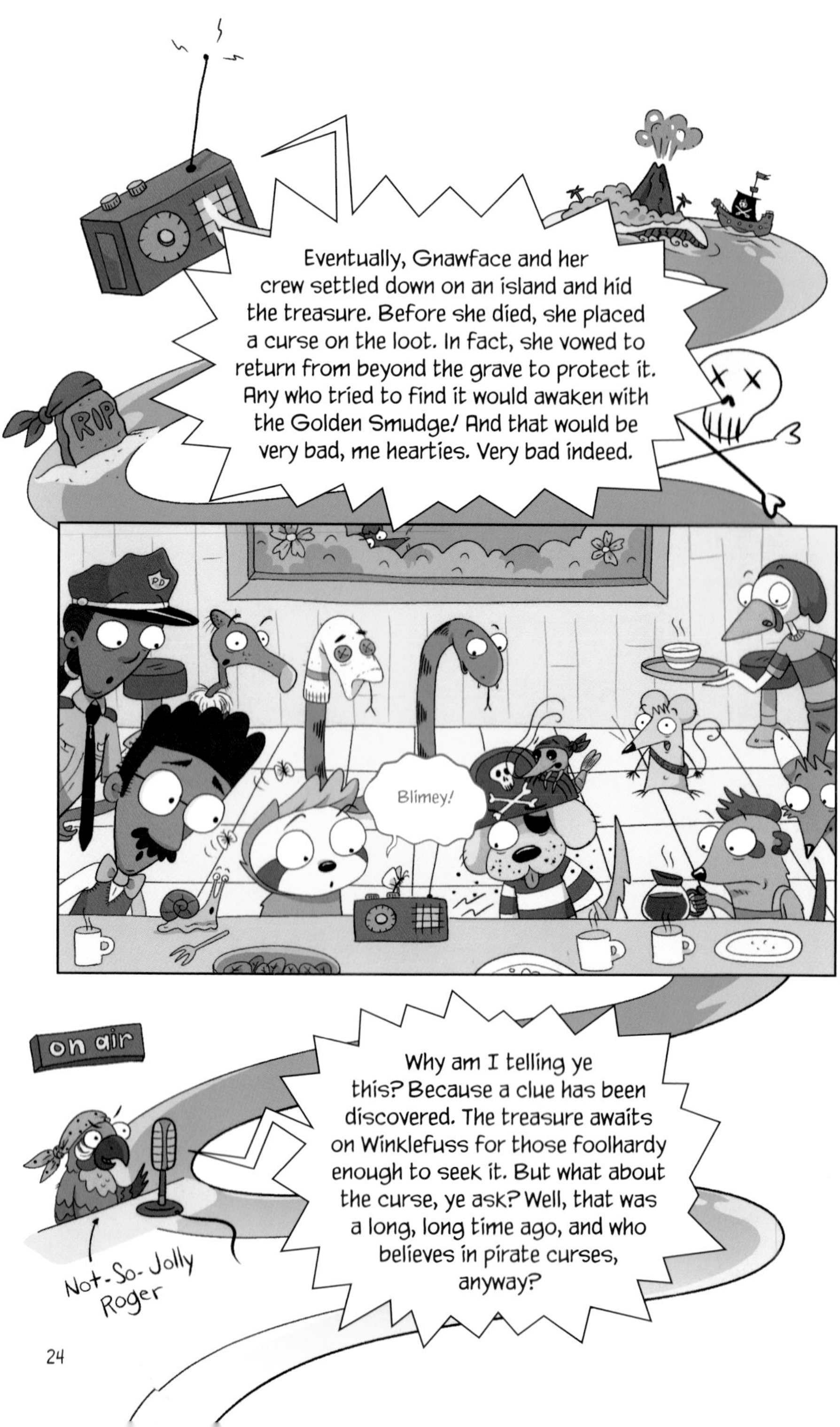
Eventually, Gnawface and her crew settled down on an island and hid the treasure. Before she died, she placed a curse on the loot. In fact, she vowed to return from beyond the grave to protect it. Any who tried to find it would awaken with the Golden Smudge! And that would be very bad, me hearties. Very bad indeed.
RIP
PD
Blimey!
on air
Why am I telling ye this? Because a clue has been discovered. The treasure awaits on Winklefuss for those foolhardy enough to seek it. But what about the curse, ye ask? Well, that was a long, long time ago, and who believes in pirate curses, anyway?
Not-So-Jolly Roger

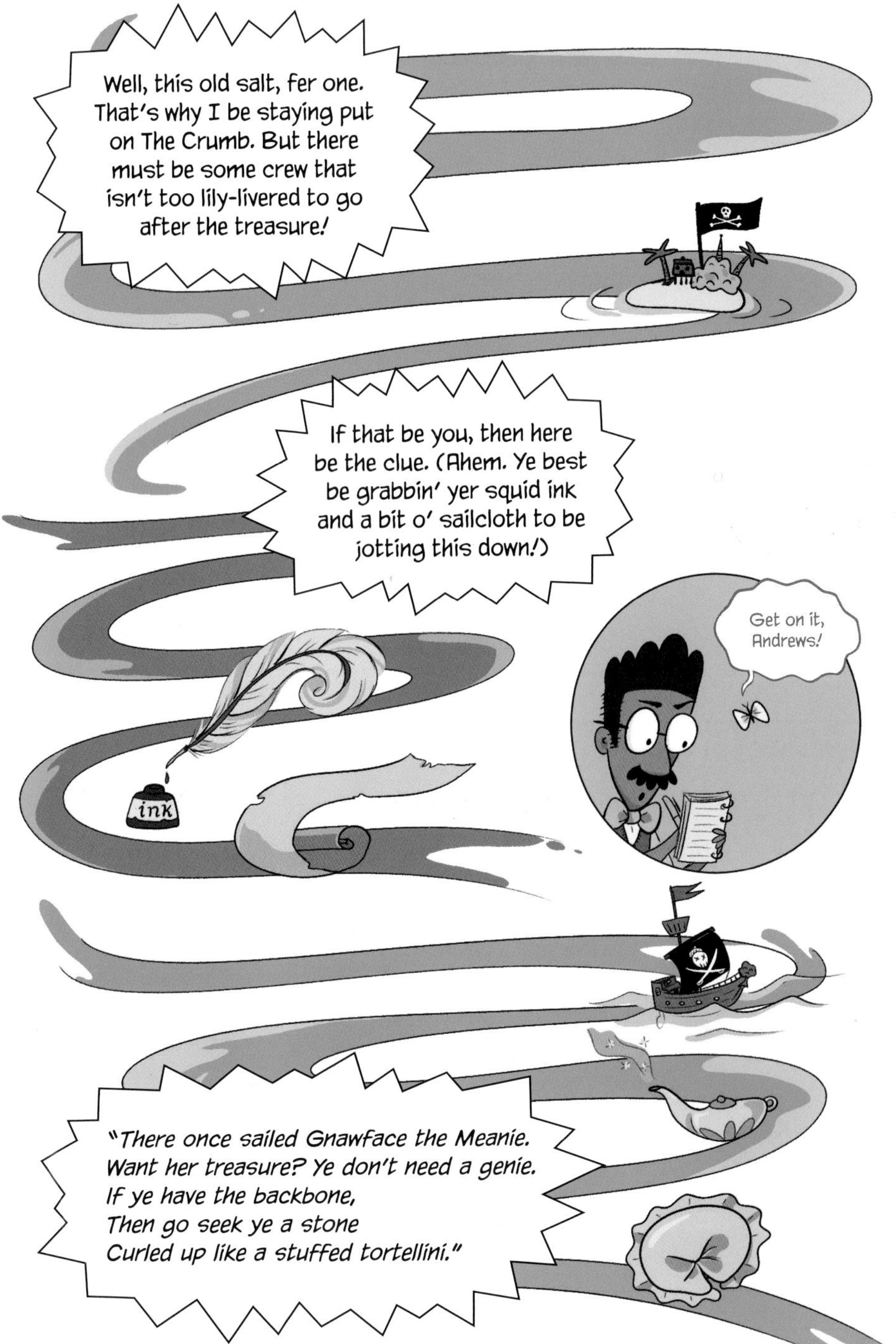
Well, this old salt, fer one. That's why I be staying put on The Crumb. But there must be some crew that isn't too lily-livered to go after the treasure!
If that be you, then here be the clue. (Ahem. Ye best be grabbin' yer squid ink and a bit o' sailcloth to be jotting this down!)
Get on it, Andrews!
ink
"There once sailed Gnawface the Meanie.
Want her treasure? Ye don't need a genie.
If ye have the backbone,
Then go seek ye a stone
Curled up like a stuffed tortellini."

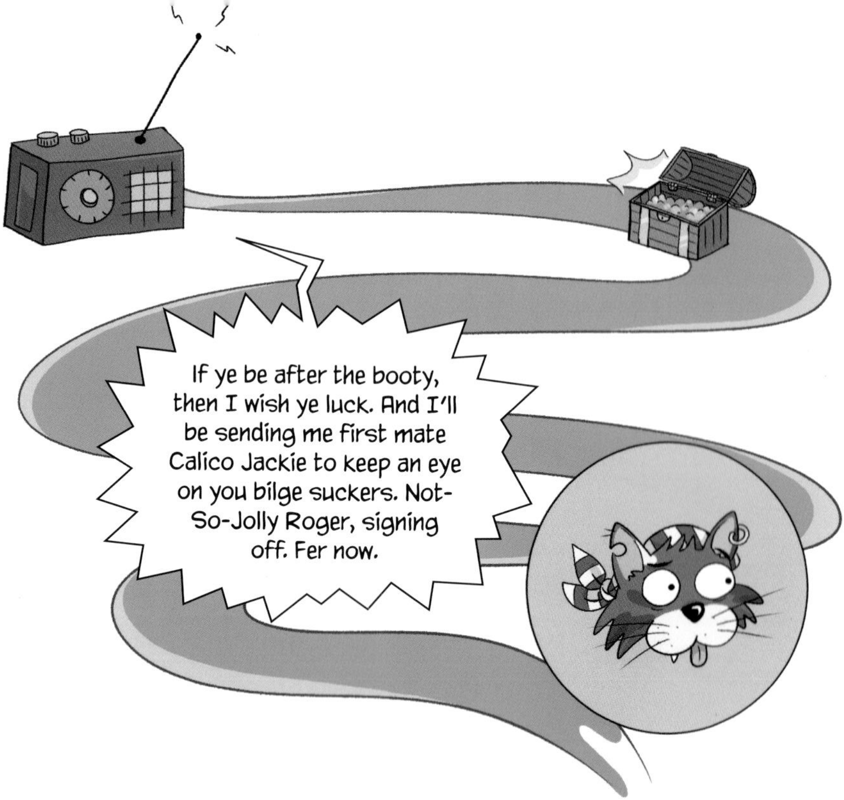
If ye be after the booty, then I wish ye luck. And I'll be sending me first mate Calico Jackie to keep an eye on you bilge suckers. Not-So-Jolly Roger, signing off. Fer now.

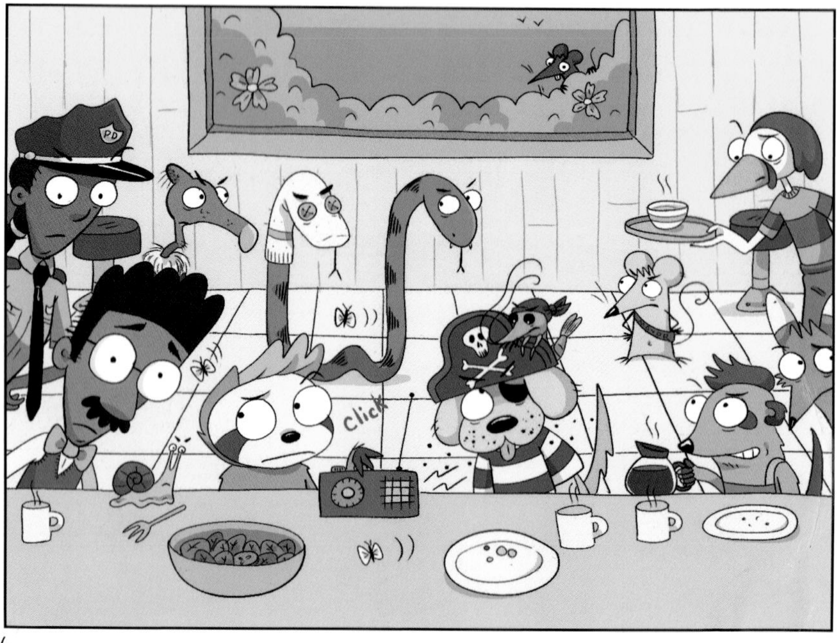
CLICK

CHAPTER 2

MONDAY. LUNCH RUSH.
SITTING IN STUNNED SILENCE AT COOKIE'S DINER.

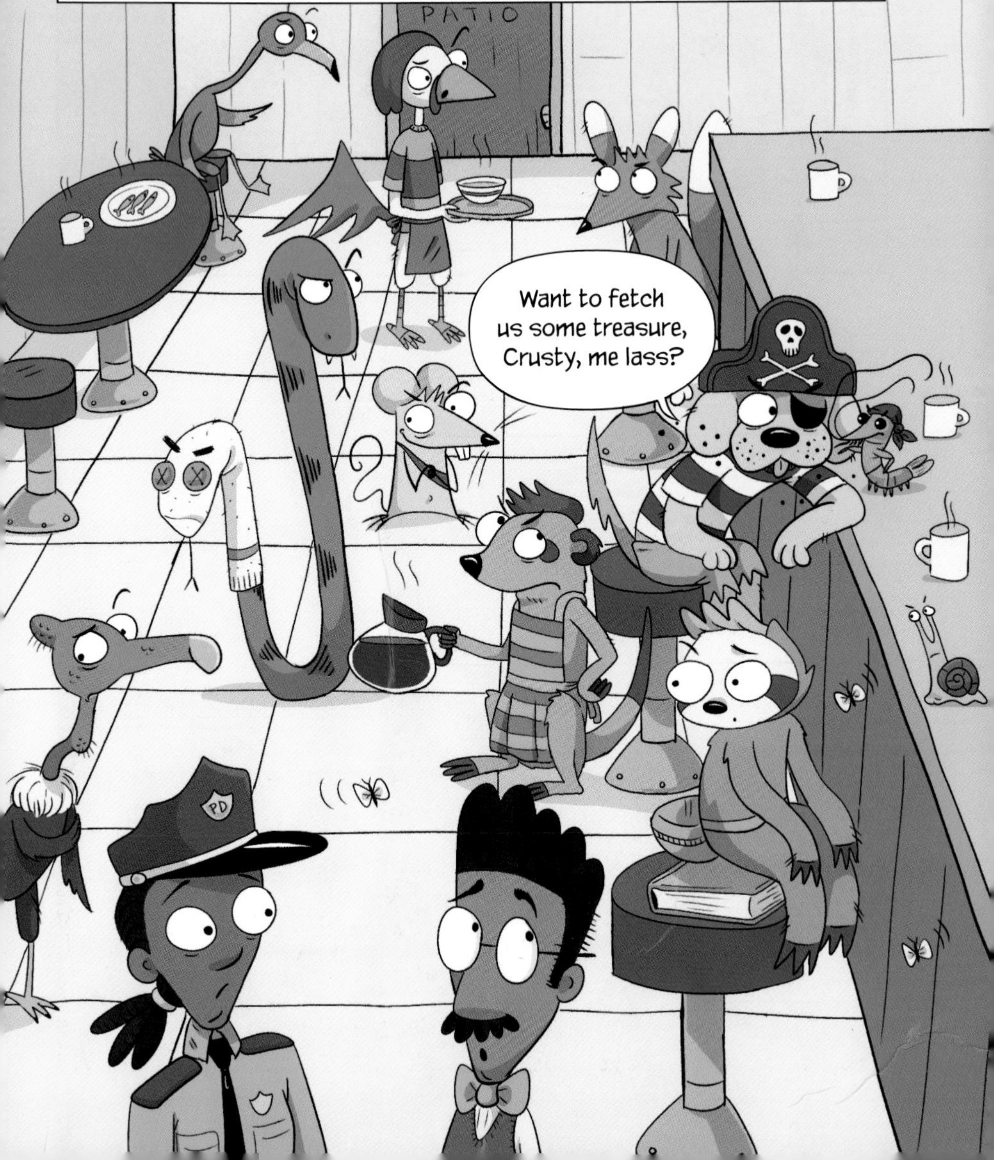
PATIO
Want to fetch us some treasure, Crusty, me lass?

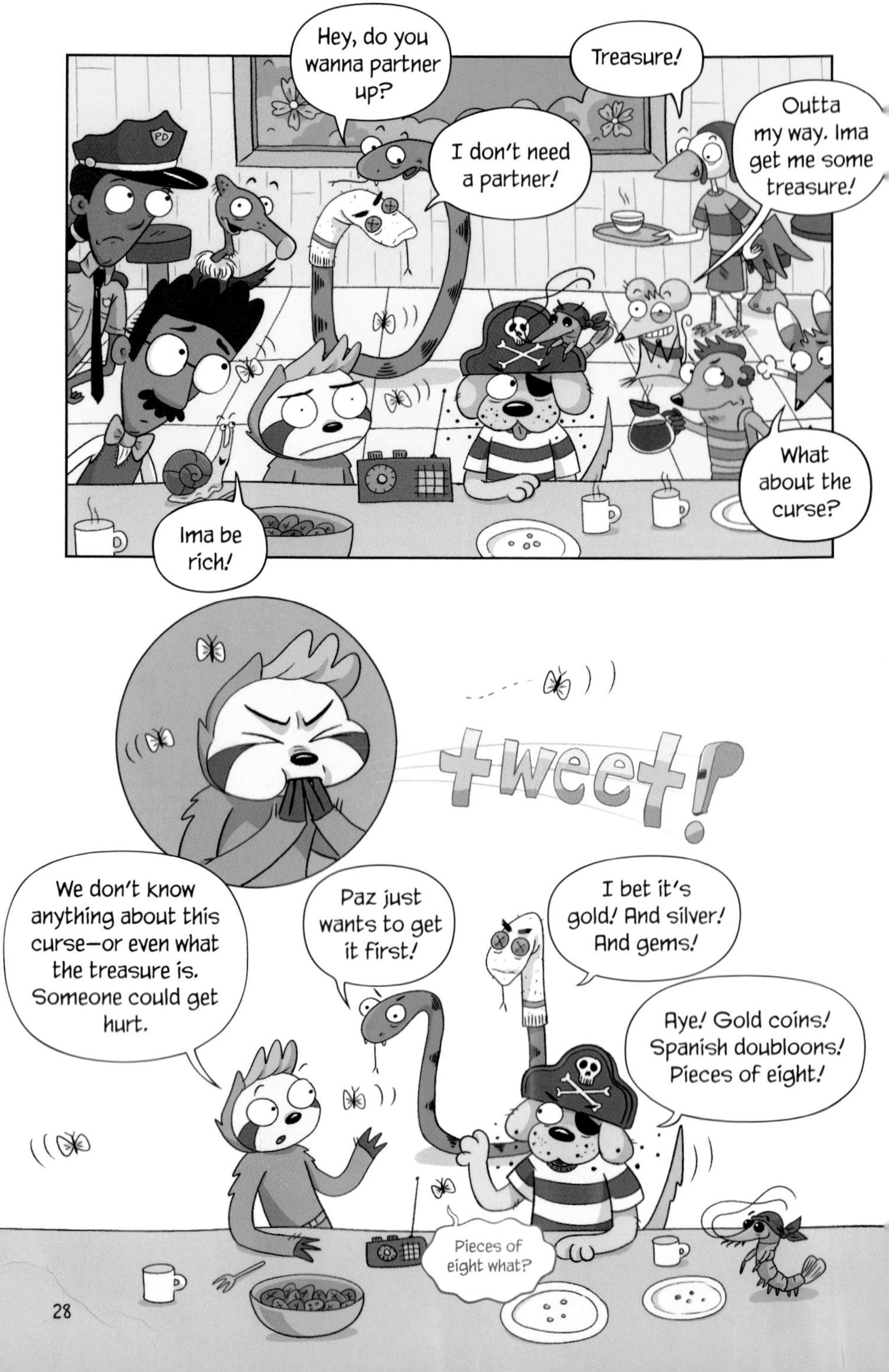
Hey, do you wanna partner up?
I don't need a partner!
Treasure!
Outta my way. Ima get me some treasure!
Ima be rich!
What about the curse?
tweet!
We don't know anything about this curse—or even what the treasure is. Someone could get hurt.
Paz just wants to get it first!
I bet it's gold! And silver! And gems!
Aye! Gold coins! Spanish doubloons! Pieces of eight!
Pieces of eight what?

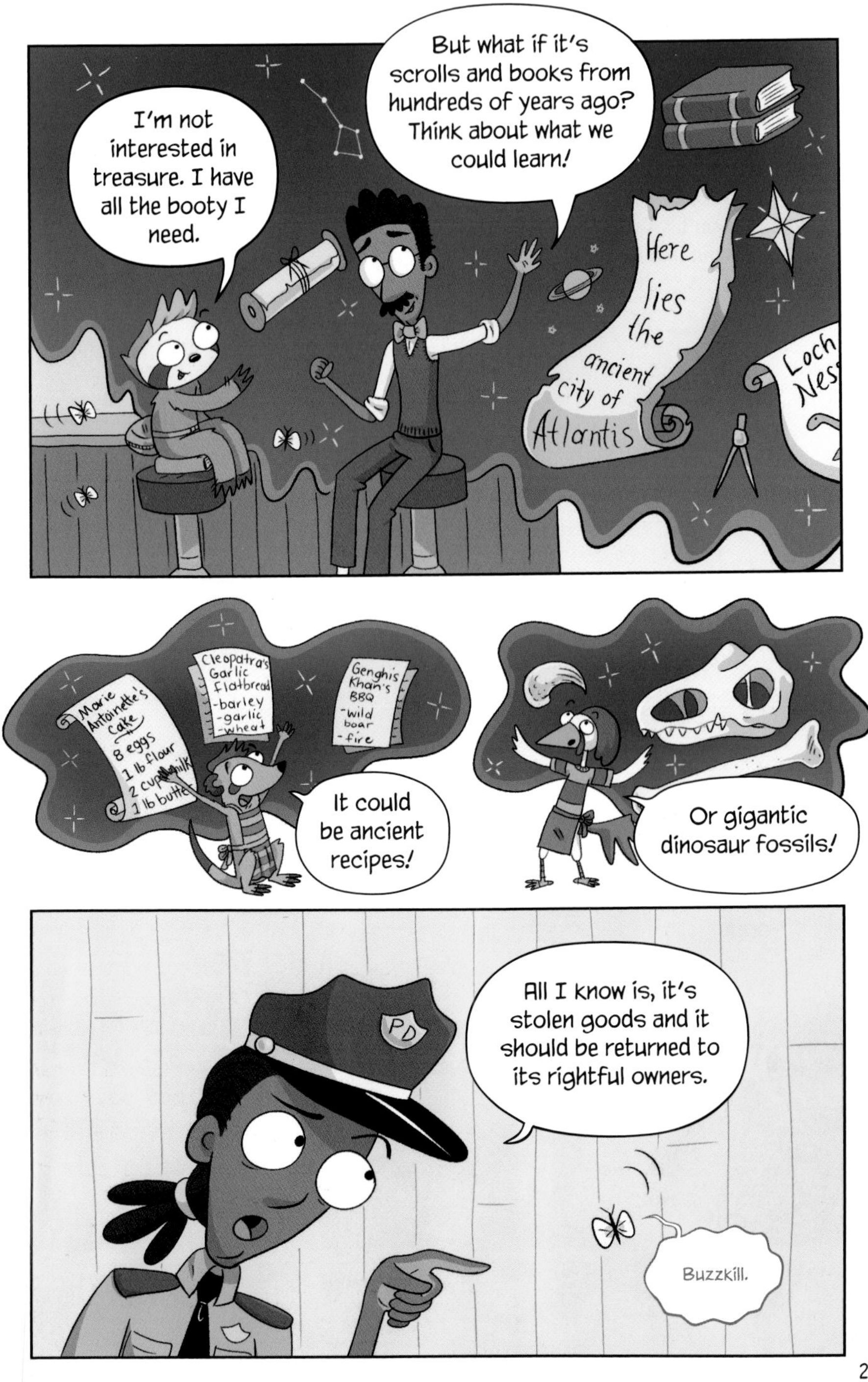
I'm not interested in treasure. I have all the booty I need.
But what if it's scrolls and books from hundreds of years ago? Think about what we could learn!
Here lies the ancient city of Atlantis
Loch Ness
Marie Antoinette's cake
8 eggs
1 lb flour
2 cup milk
1 lb butter
Cleopatra's Garlic Flatbread
-barley
-garlic
-wheat
Genghis Khan's BBQ
-wild boar
-fire
It could be ancient recipes!
Or gigantic dinosaur fossils!
PD
All I know is, it's stolen goods and it should be returned to its rightful owners.
Buzzkill.

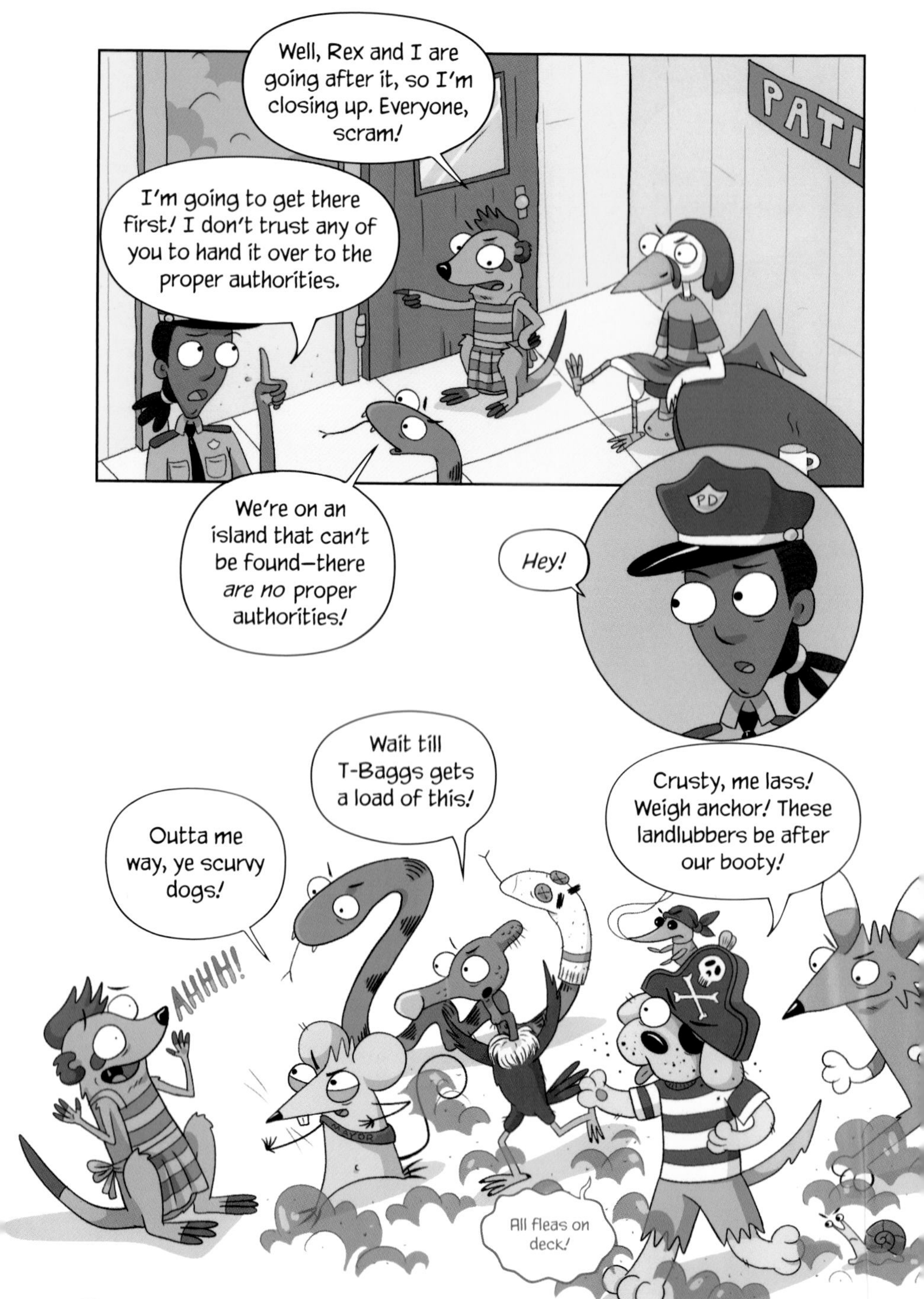
Well, Rex and I are going after it, so I'm closing up. Everyone, scram!
I'm going to get there first! I don't trust any of you to hand it over to the proper authorities.
We're on an island that can't be found—there *are no* proper authorities!
Hey!
Outta me way, ye scurvy dogs!
AHHH!
Wait till T-Baggs gets a load of this!
Crusty, me lass! Weigh anchor! These landlubbers be after our booty!
All fleas on deck!

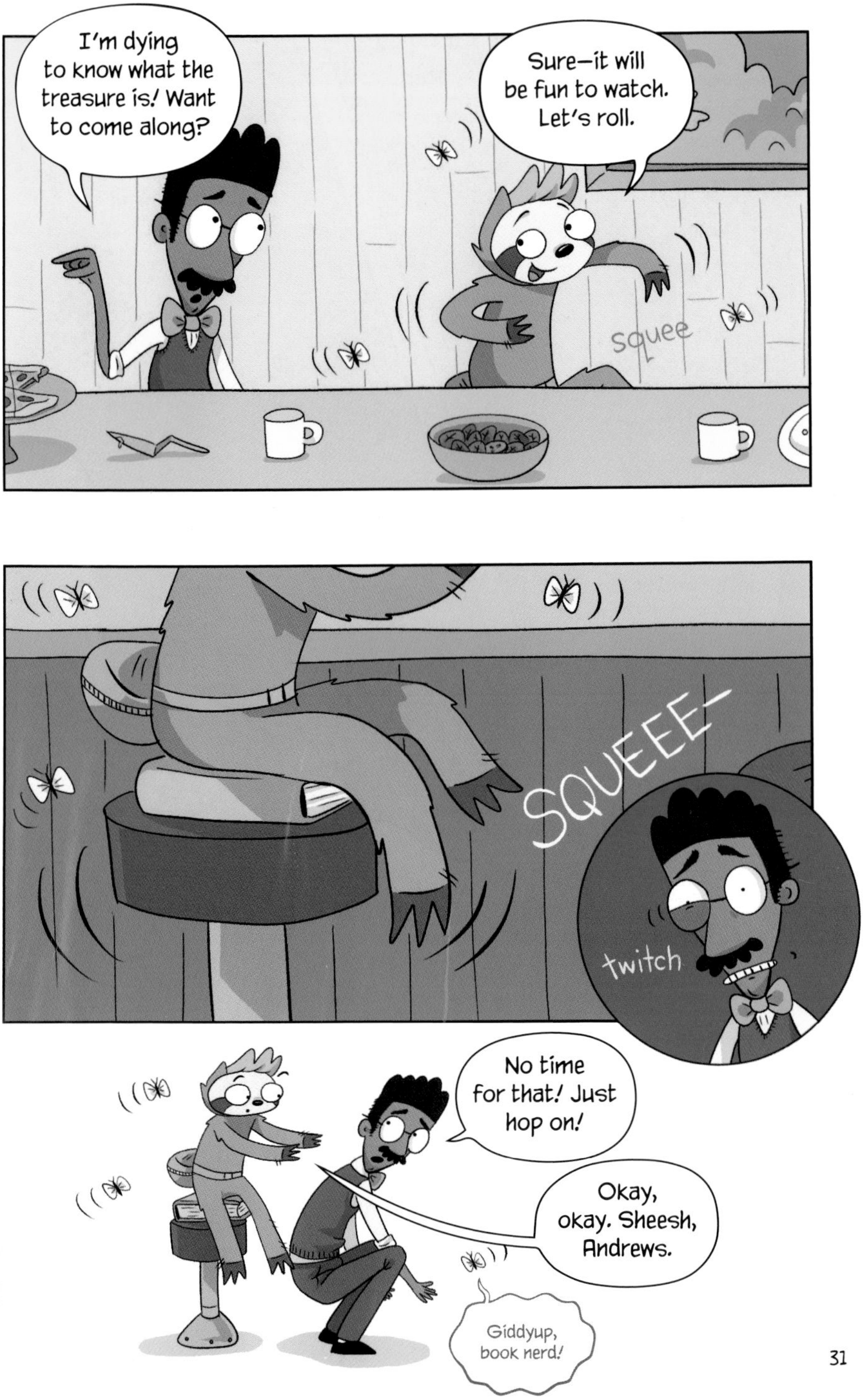
I'm dying to know what the treasure is! Want to come along?
Sure—it will be fun to watch. Let's roll.
squee
SQUEEE—
twitch
No time for that! Just hop on!
Okay, okay. Sheesh, Andrews.
Giddyup, book nerd!

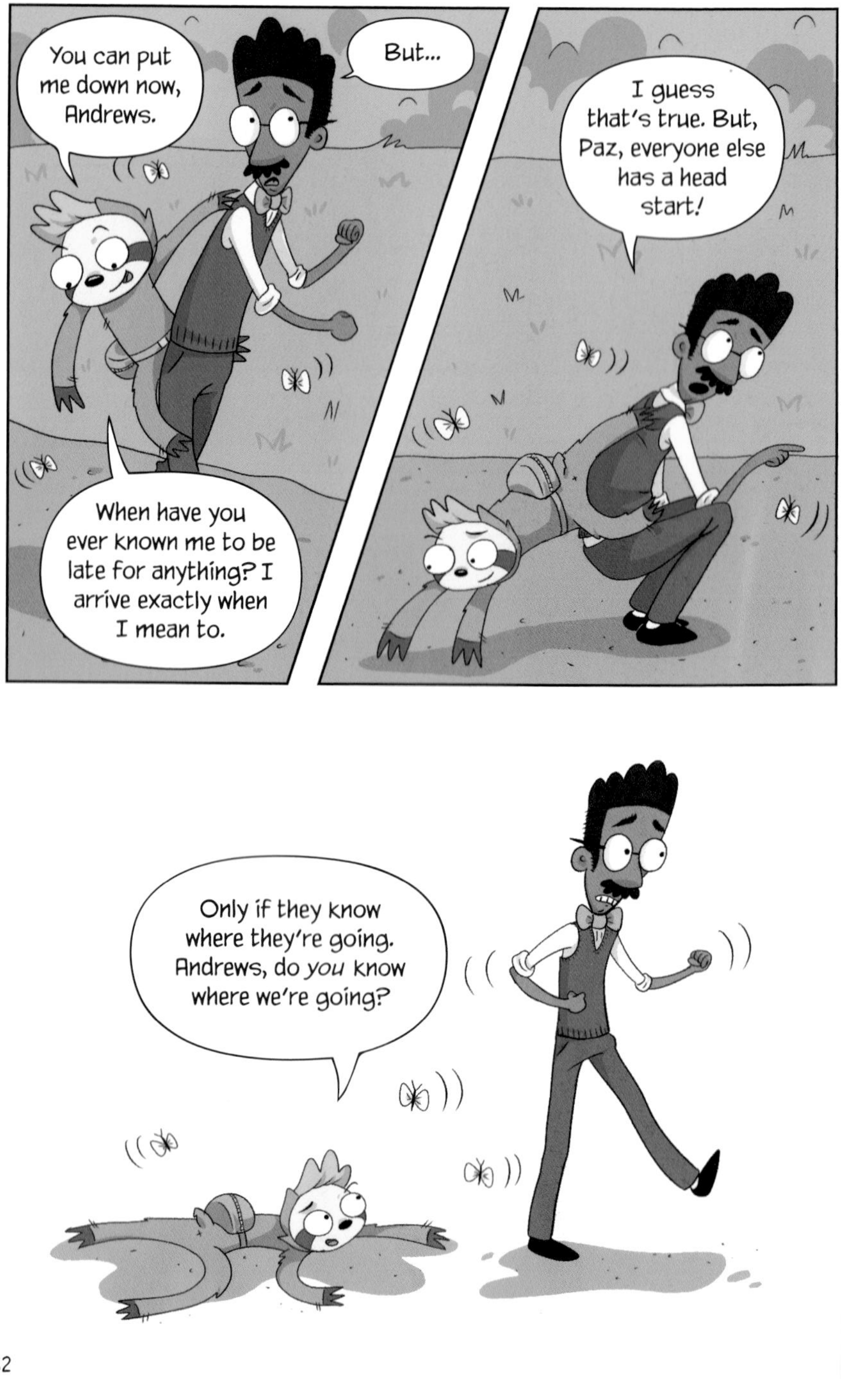
You can put me down now, Andrews.
But...
When have you ever known me to be late for anything? I arrive exactly when I mean to.
I guess that's true. But, Paz, everyone else has a head start!
Only if they know where they're going. Andrews, do *you* know where we're going?

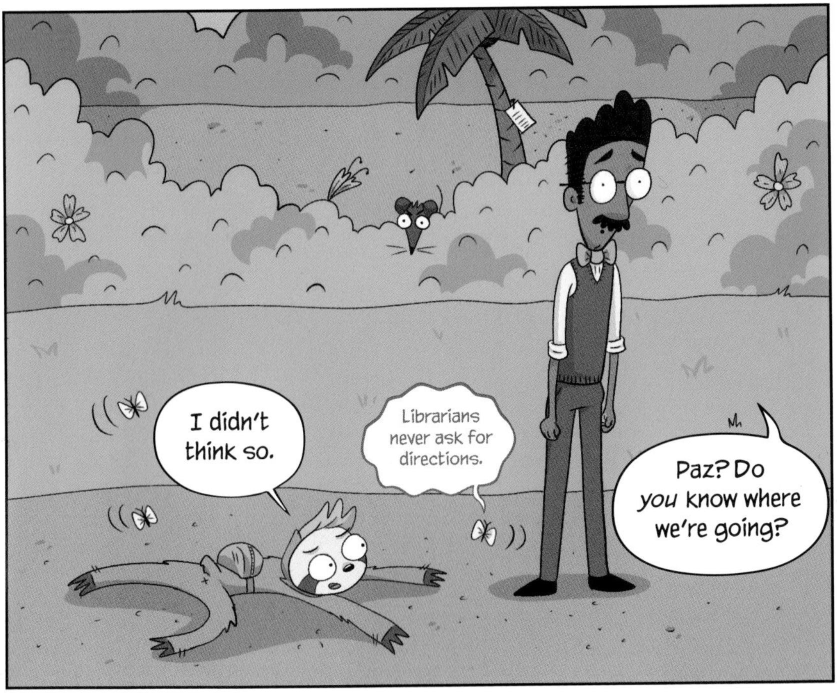
Paz? Do *you* know where we're going?
Librarians never ask for directions.
I didn't think so.

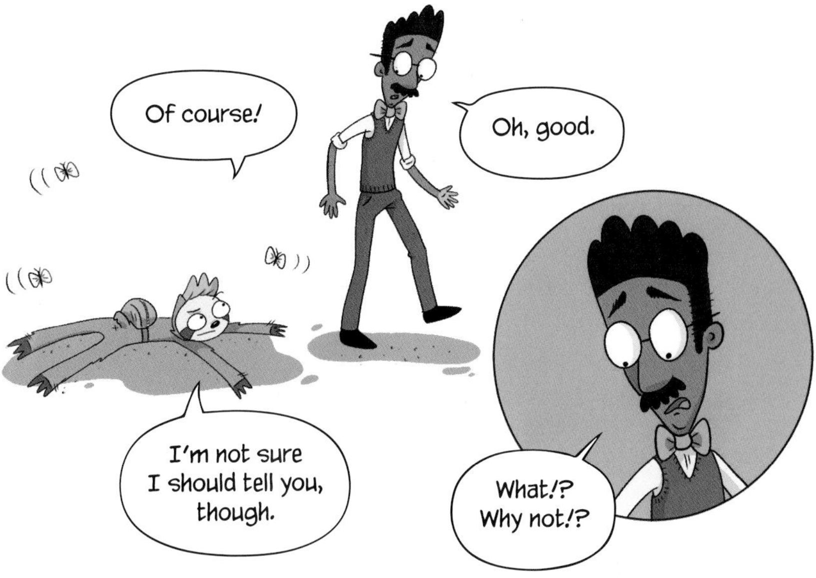
Of course!
Oh, good.
I'm not sure I should tell you, though.
What!? Why not!?

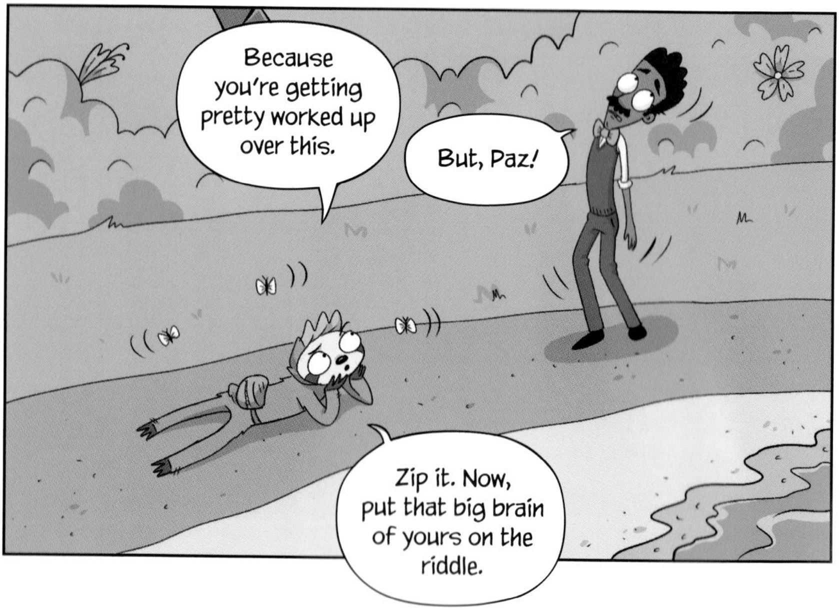
Because you're getting pretty worked up over this.
But, Paz!
Zip it. Now, put that big brain of yours on the riddle.

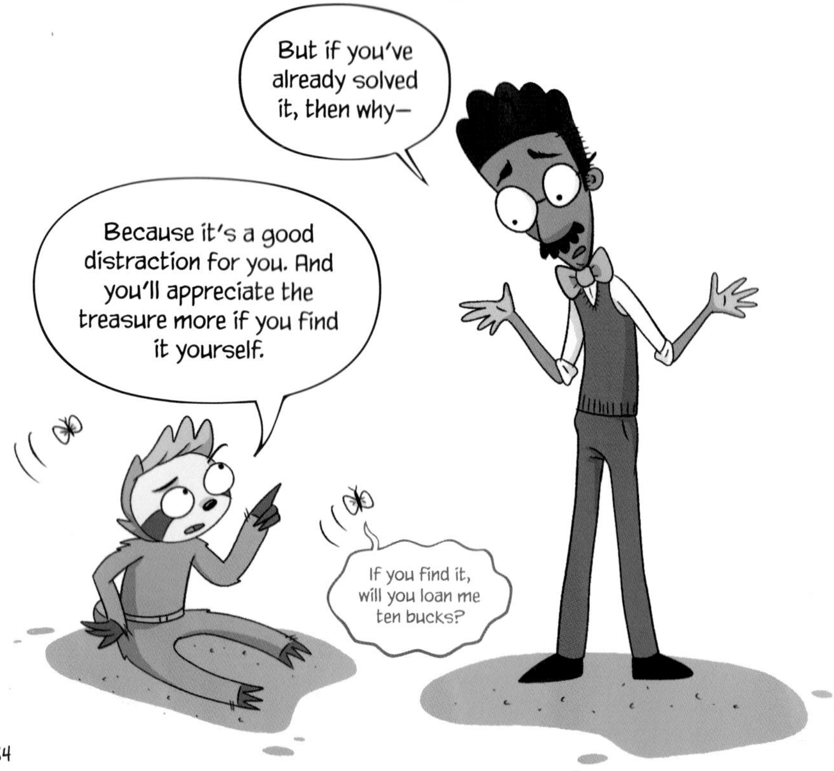
But if you've already solved it, then why—
Because it's a good distraction for you. And you'll appreciate the treasure more if you find it yourself.
If you find it, will you loan me ten bucks?

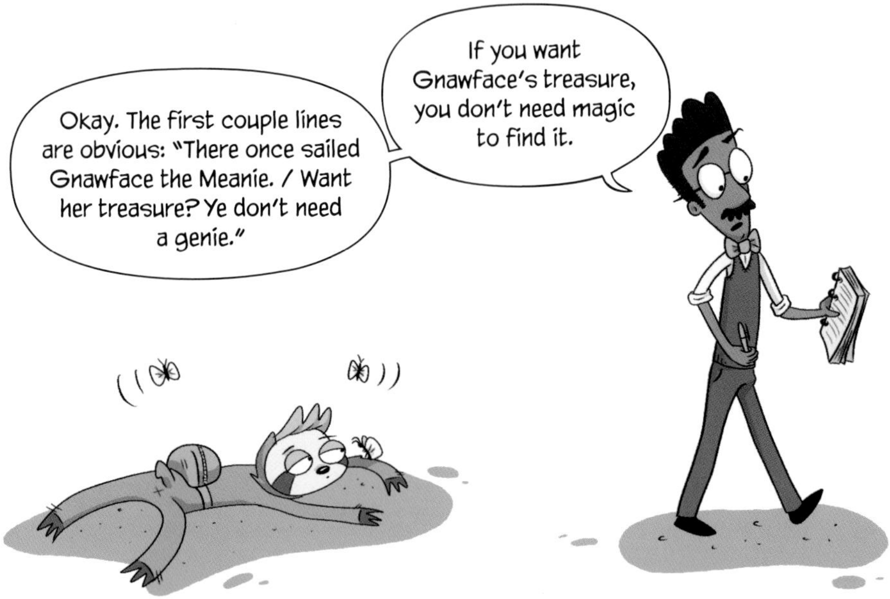
Okay. The first couple lines are obvious: "There once sailed Gnawface the Meanie. / Want her treasure? Ye don't need a genie."
If you want Gnawface's treasure, you don't need magic to find it.

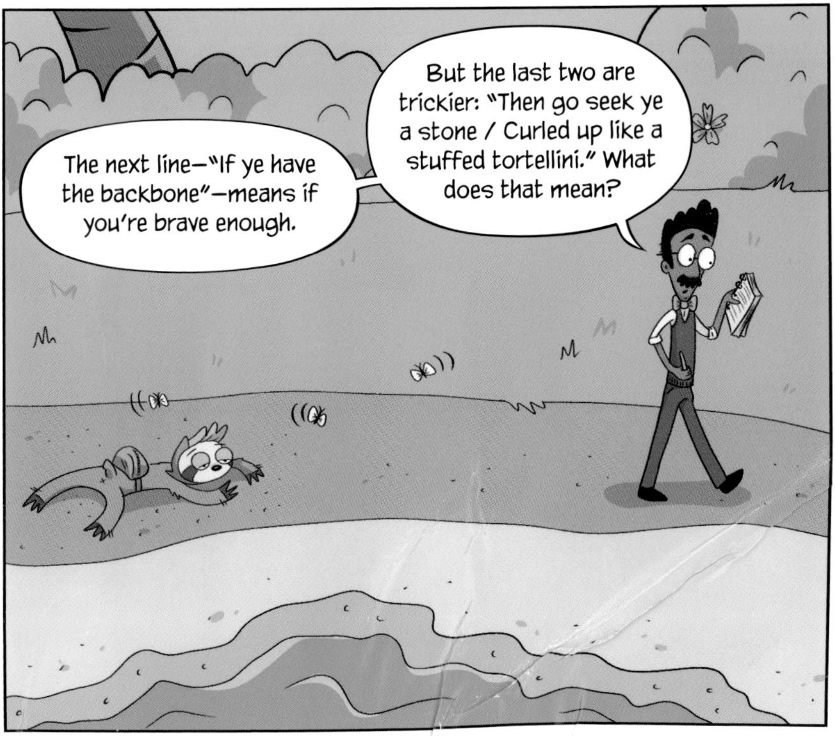
The next line—"If ye have the backbone"—means if you're brave enough.
But the last two are trickier: "Then go seek ye a stone / Curled up like a stuffed tortellini." What does that mean?

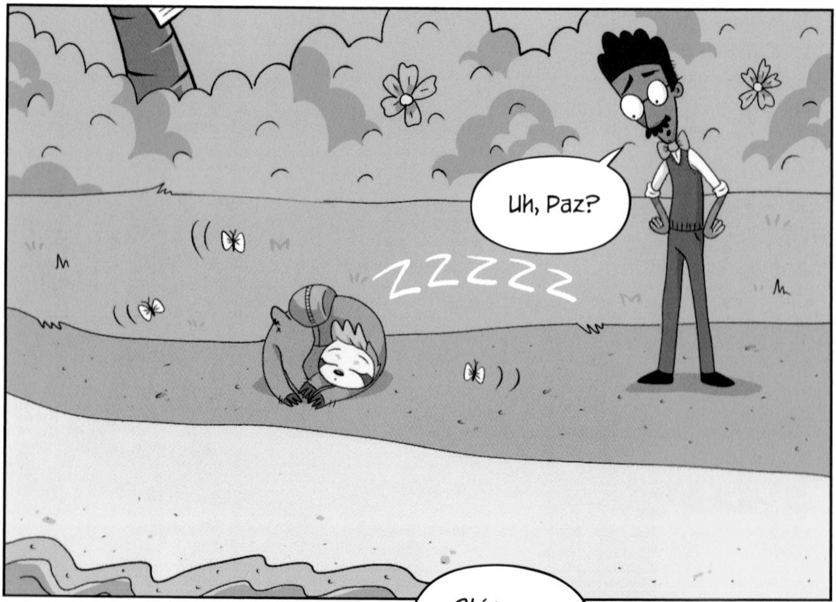
Uh, Paz?
ZZZZZ

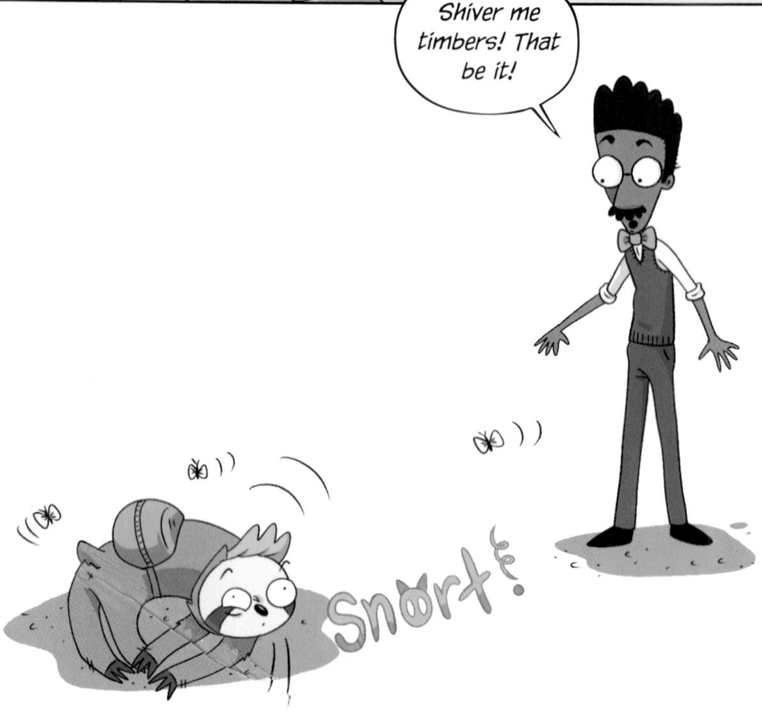
Shiver me timbers! That be it!
Snort!

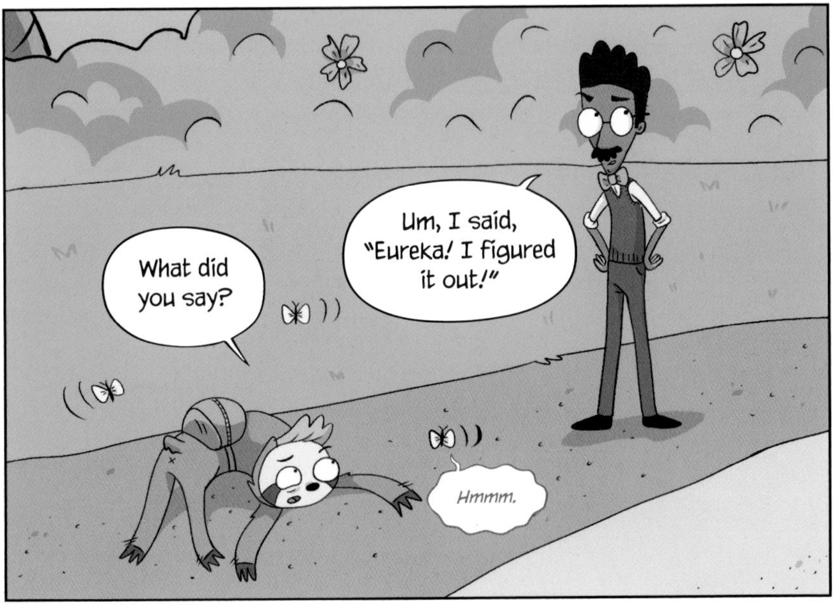
What did you say?
Um, I said, "Eureka! I figured it out!"
Hmmm.

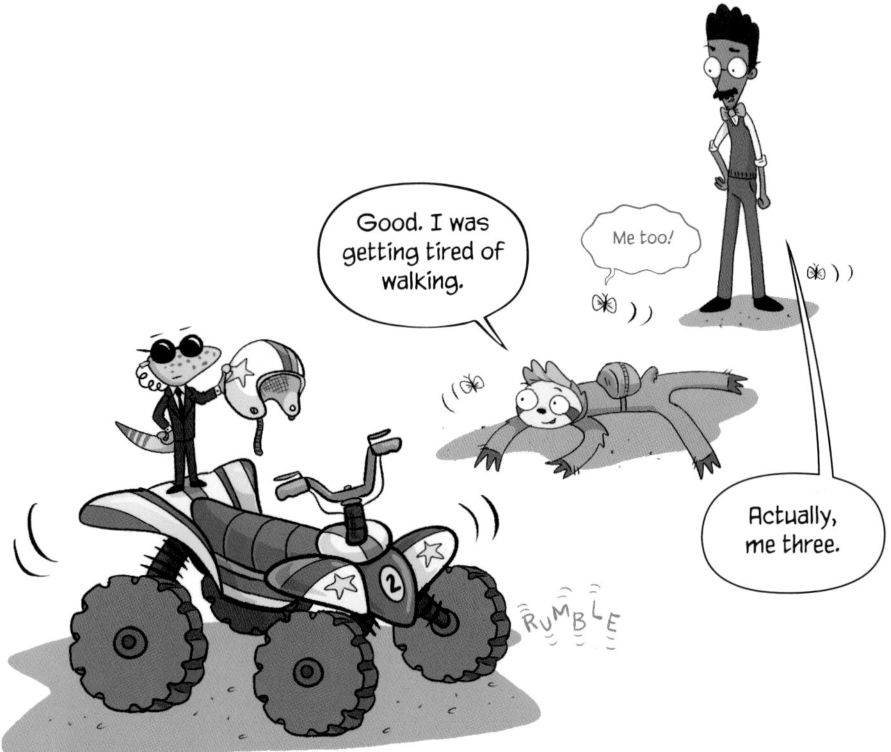
Good. I was getting tired of walking.
Me too!
Actually, me three.
RUMBLE

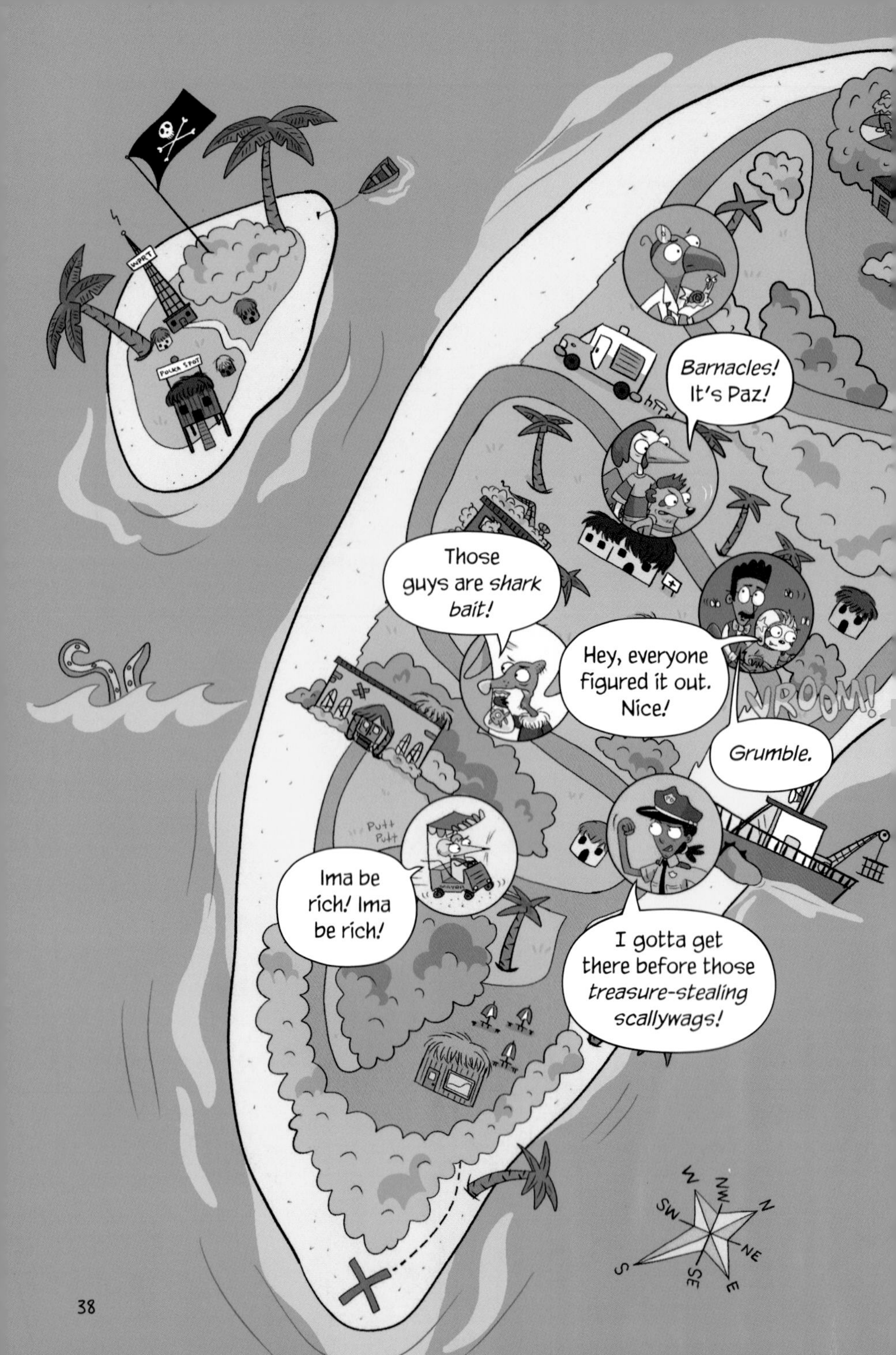
WPRT
POLKA SPOT
Barnacles! It's Paz!
Those guys are shark bait!
Hey, everyone figured it out. Nice!
VROOM!
Grumble.
Putt Putt
Ima be rich! Ima be rich!
I gotta get there before those treasure-stealing scallywags!
W
NW
N
NE
E
SE
S
SW

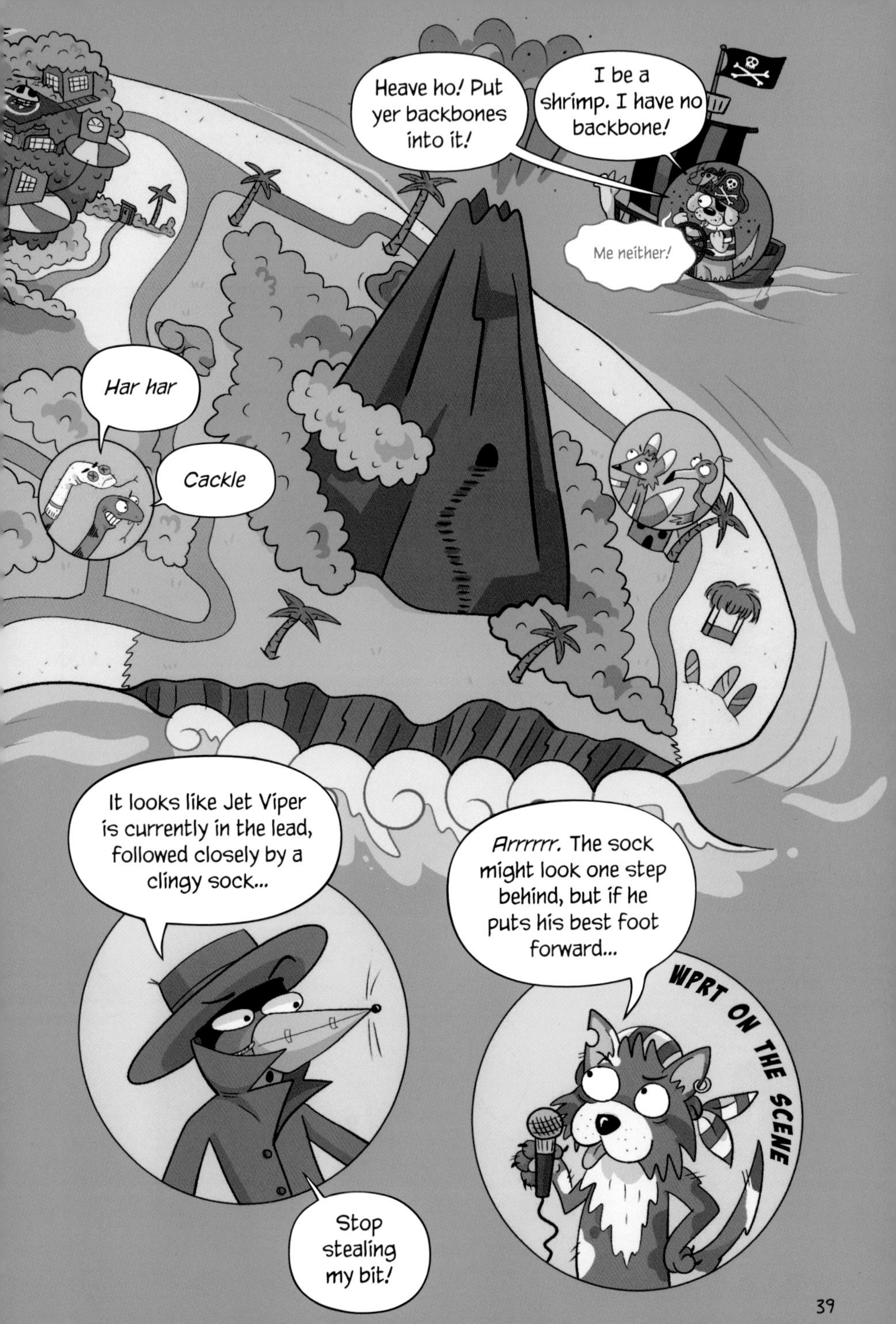
Heave ho! Put yer backbones into it!
I be a shrimp. I have no backbone!
Me neither!
Har har
Cackle
It looks like Jet Viper is currently in the lead, followed closely by a clingy sock...
Stop stealing my bit!
Arrrrrr. The sock might look one step behind, but if he puts his best foot forward...
WPRT ON THE SCENE

MONDAY. MIDAFTERNOON.
TREASURE HUNTING AT SLEEPING SLOTH ROCK.

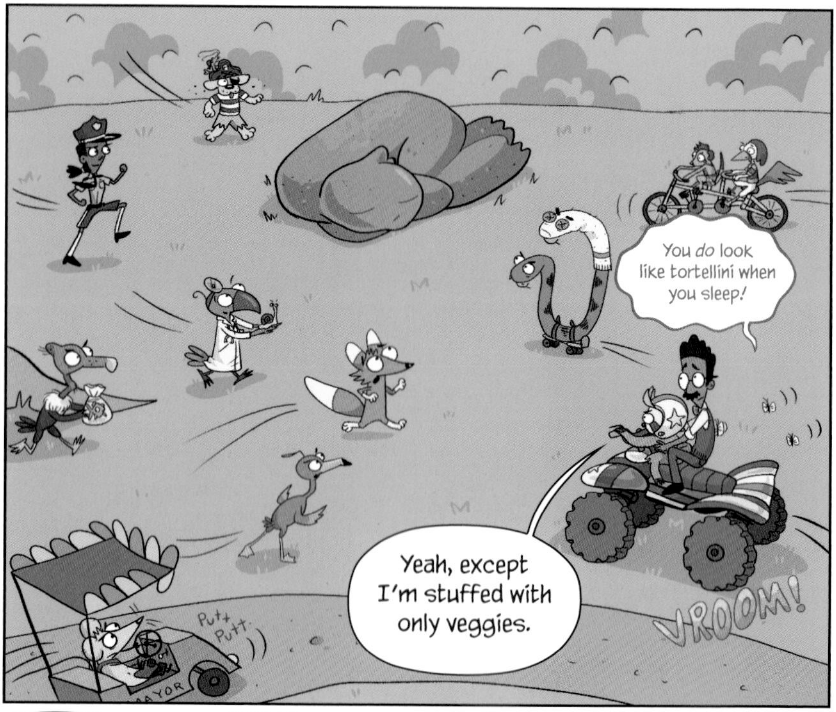

You *do* look like tortellini when you sleep!
Yeah, except I'm stuffed with only veggies.
VROOM!
Putt Putt
MAYOR

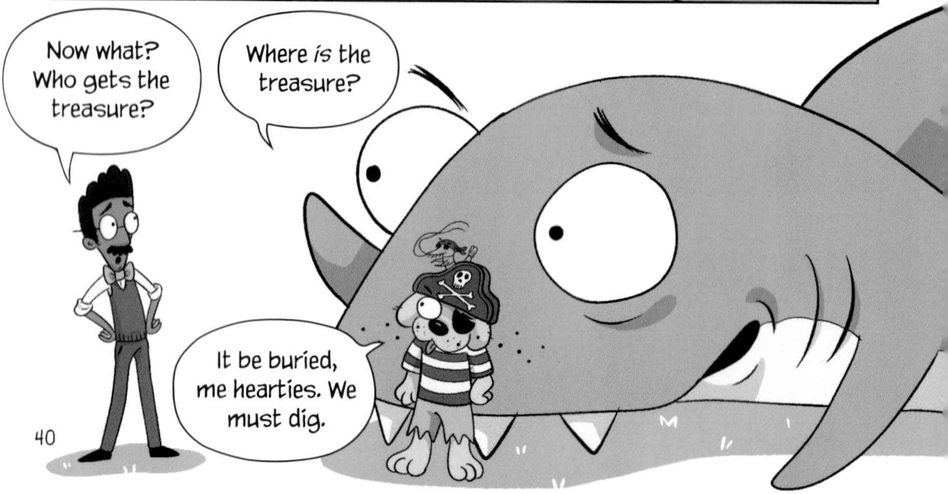

Now what? Who gets the treasure?
Where *is* the treasure?
It be buried, me hearties. We must dig.

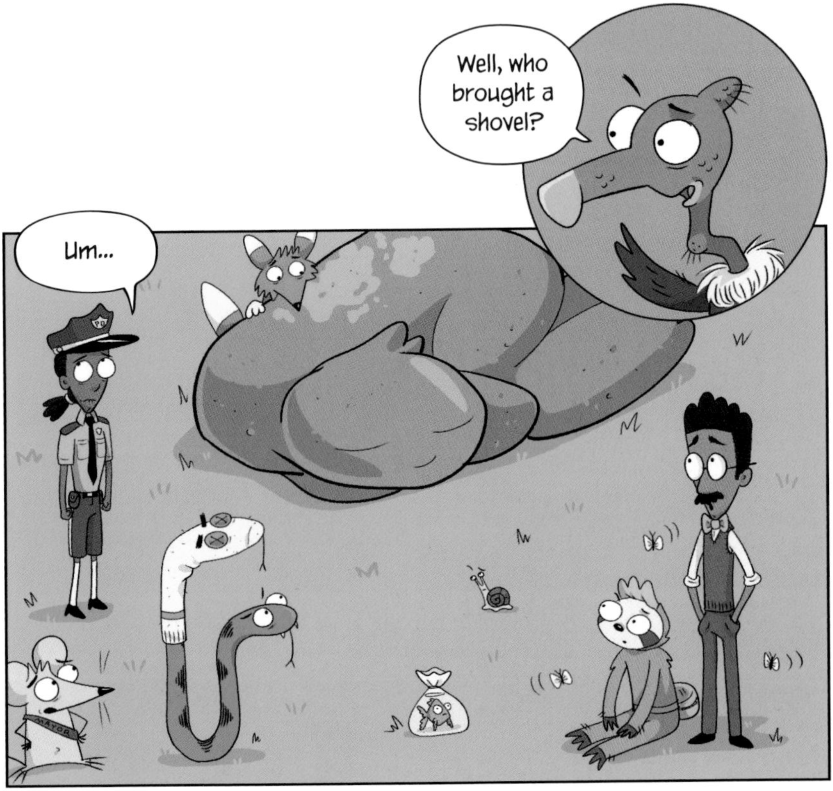
Well, who brought a shovel?
Um...

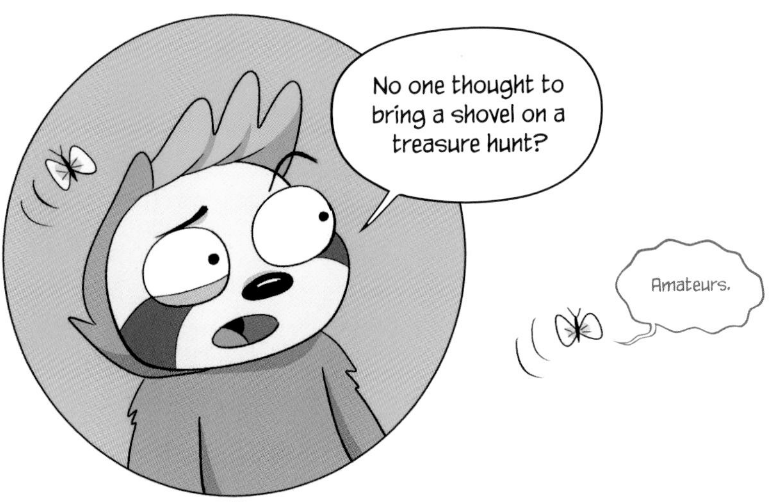
No one thought to bring a shovel on a treasure hunt?
Amateurs.

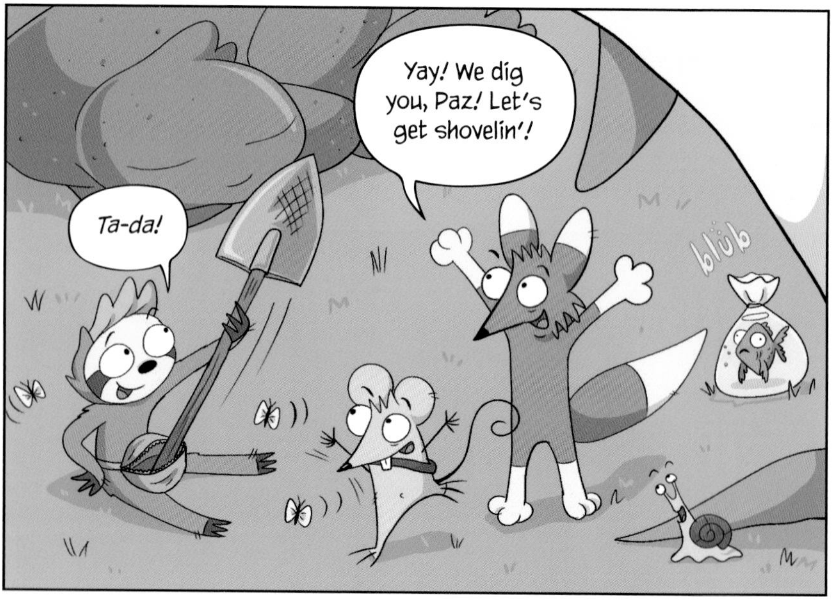

Ta-da!
Yay! We dig you, Paz! Let's get shovelin'!
blub

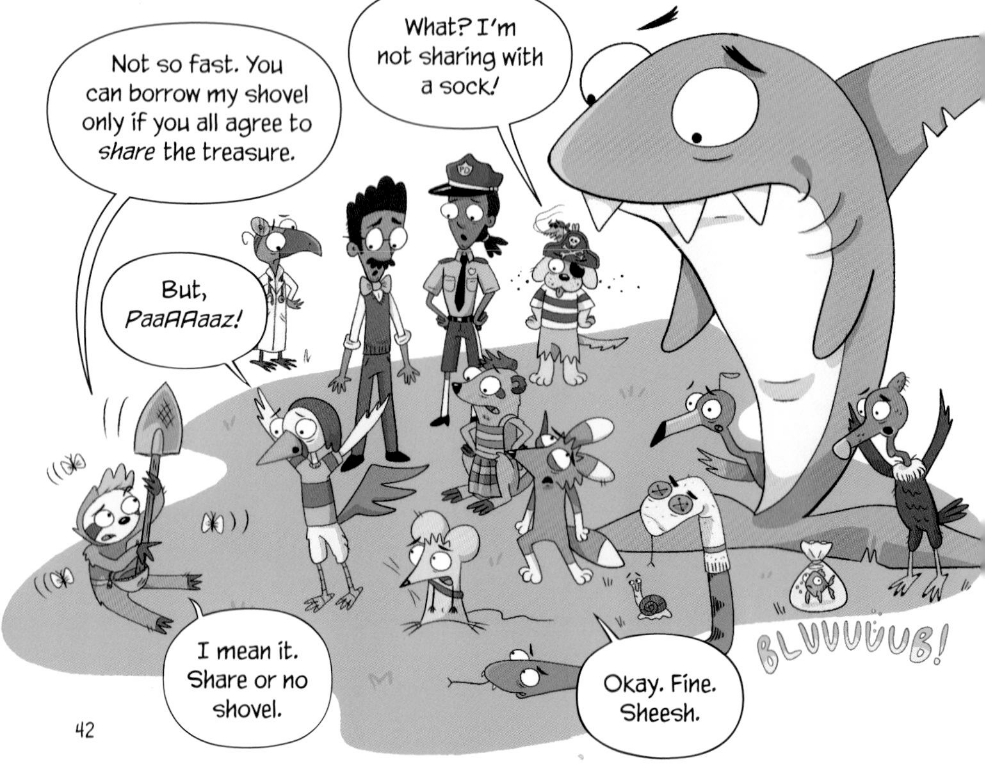

Not so fast. You can borrow my shovel only if you all agree to *share* the treasure.
What? I'm not sharing with a sock!
But, PaaAAaaz!
I mean it. Share or no shovel.
Okay. Fine. Sheesh.
BLUUUUUB!

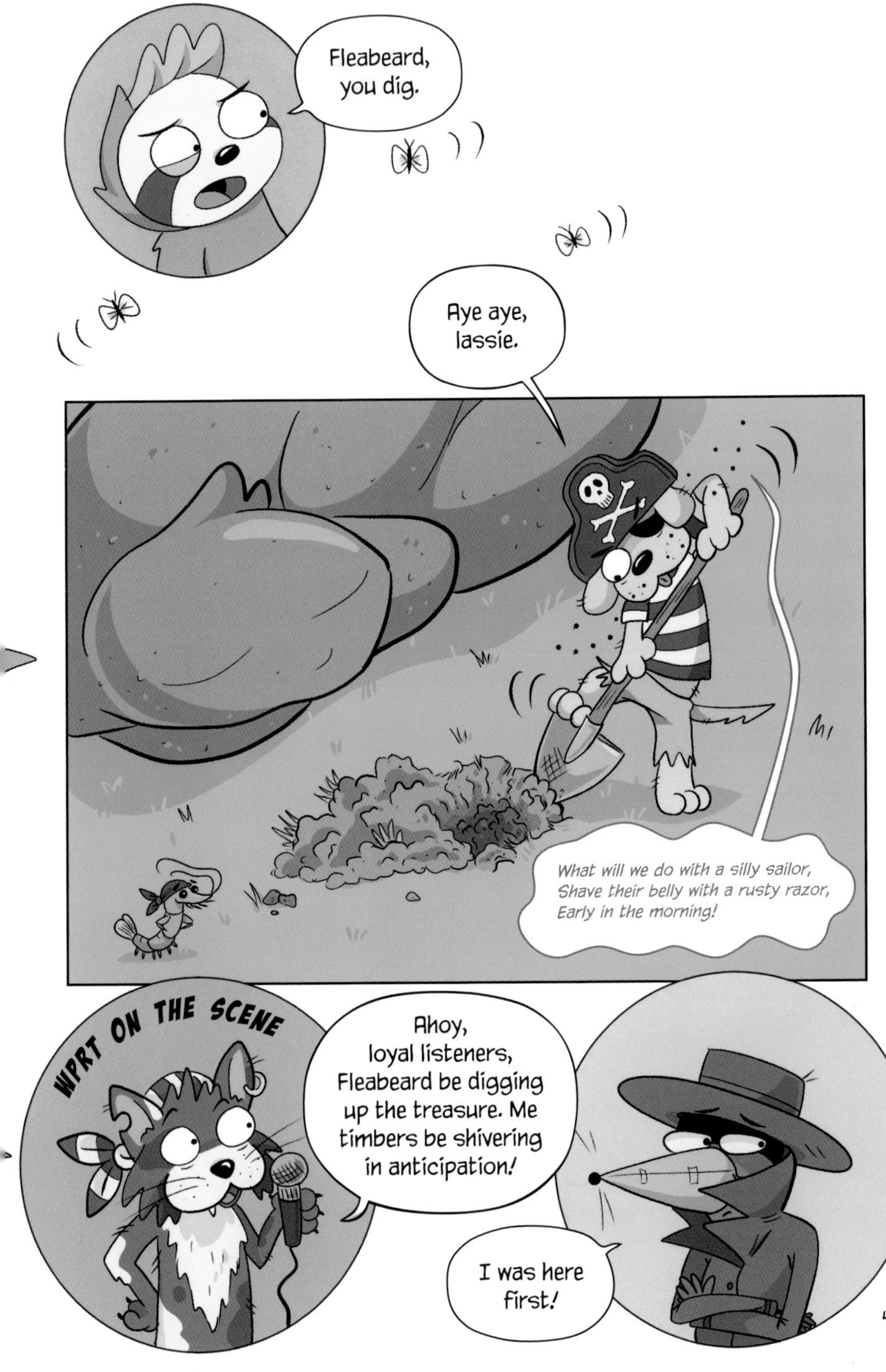
Fleabeard,
you dig.
Aye aye,
lassie.
What will we do with a silly sailor,
Shave their belly with a rusty razor,
Early in the morning!
WPRT ON THE SCENE
Ahoy,
loyal listeners,
Fleabeard be digging
up the treasure. Me
timbers be shivering
in anticipation!
I was here
first!

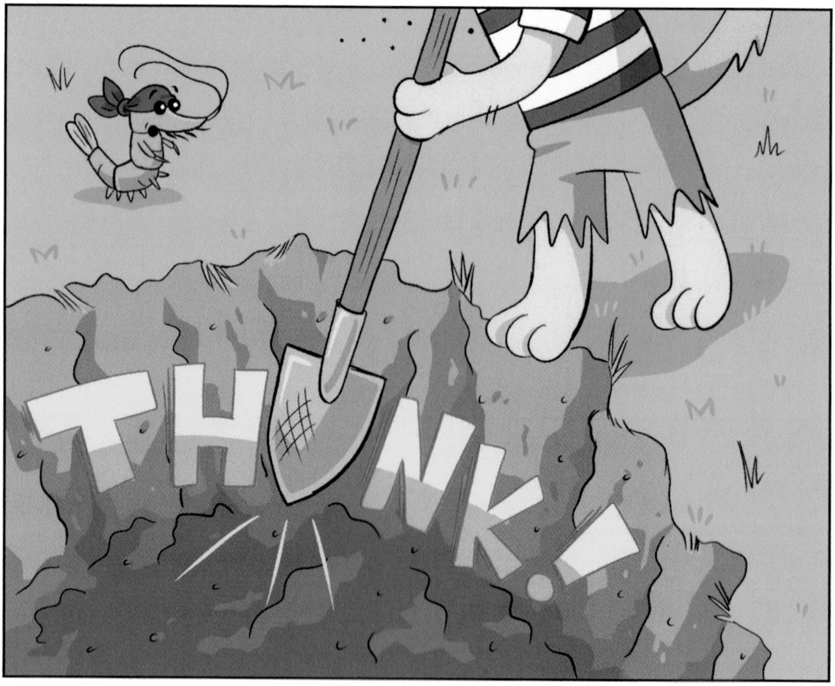
THUNK!

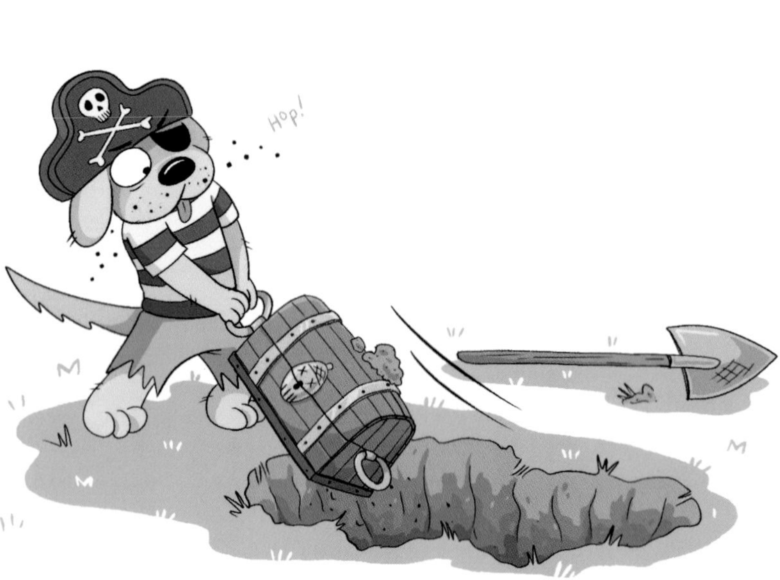
Hop!

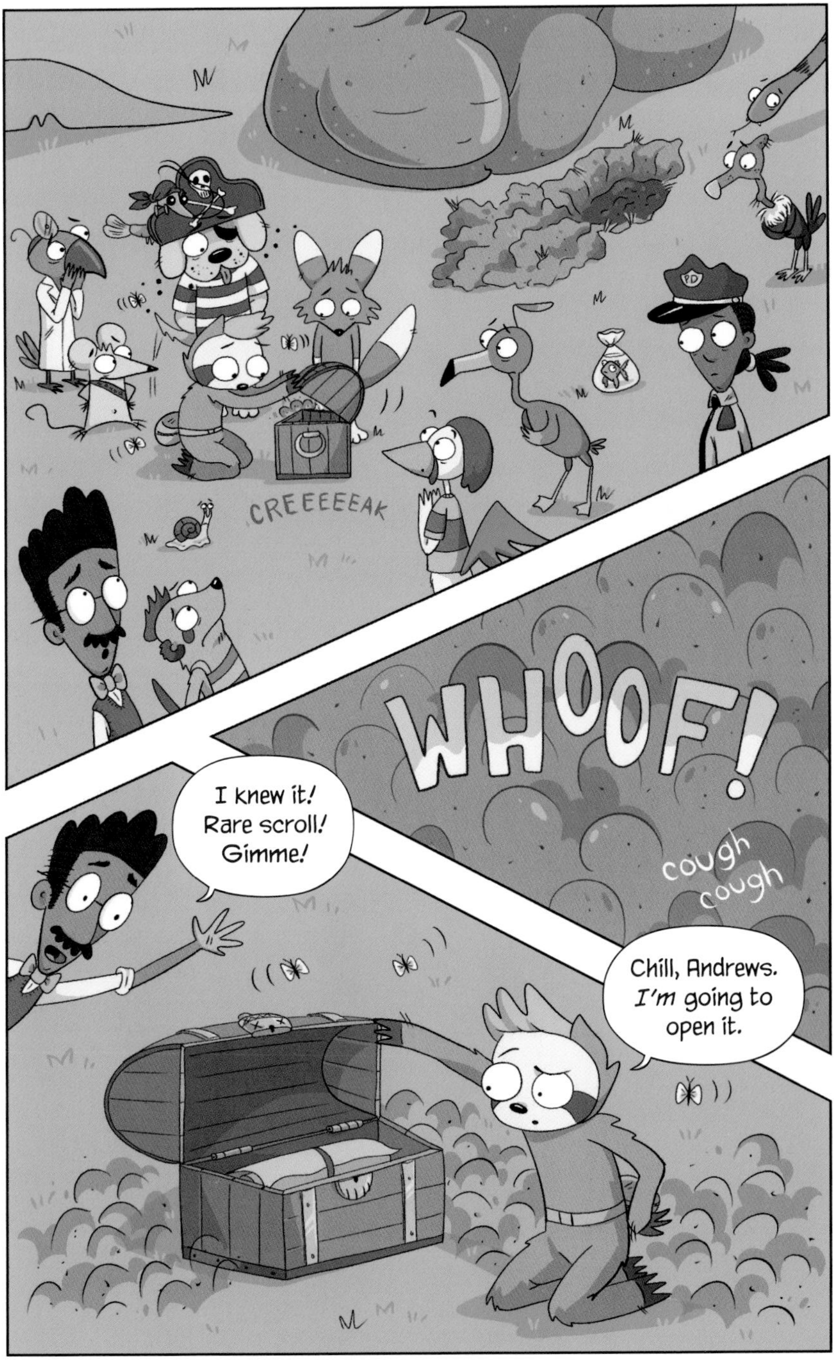
CREEEEEAK
WHOOF!
cough cough
I knew it! Rare scroll! Gimme!
Chill, Andrews. *I'm* going to open it.

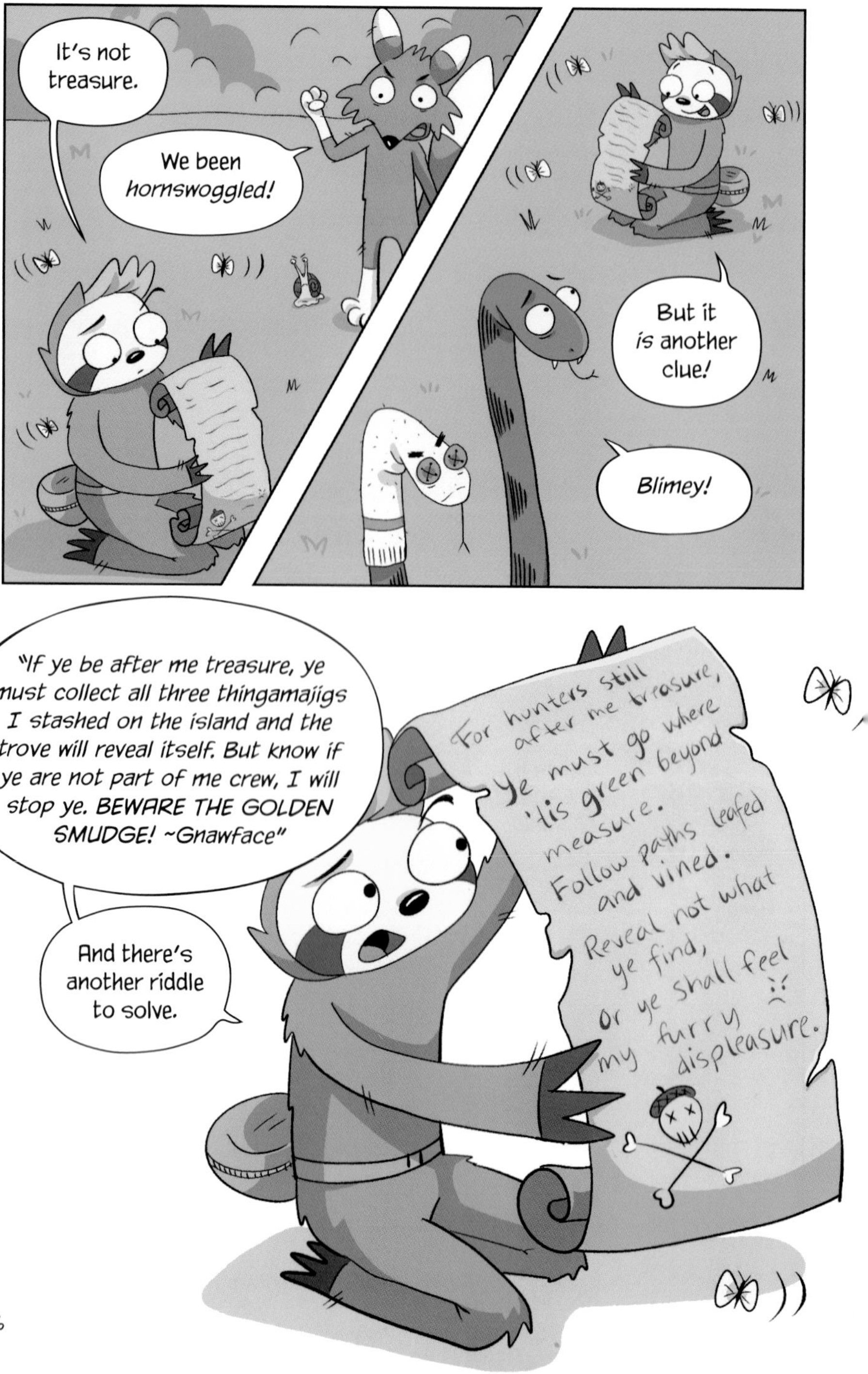
It's not treasure.
We been *hornswoggled!*
But it *is* another clue!
Blimey!
"If ye be after me treasure, ye must collect all three thingamajigs I stashed on the island and the trove will reveal itself. But know if ye are not part of me crew, I will stop ye. BEWARE THE GOLDEN SMUDGE! ~Gnawface"
For hunters still after me treasure, Ye must go where 'tis green beyond measure. Follow paths leafed and vined. Reveal not what ye find, or ye shall feel my furry displeasure.
And there's another riddle to solve.

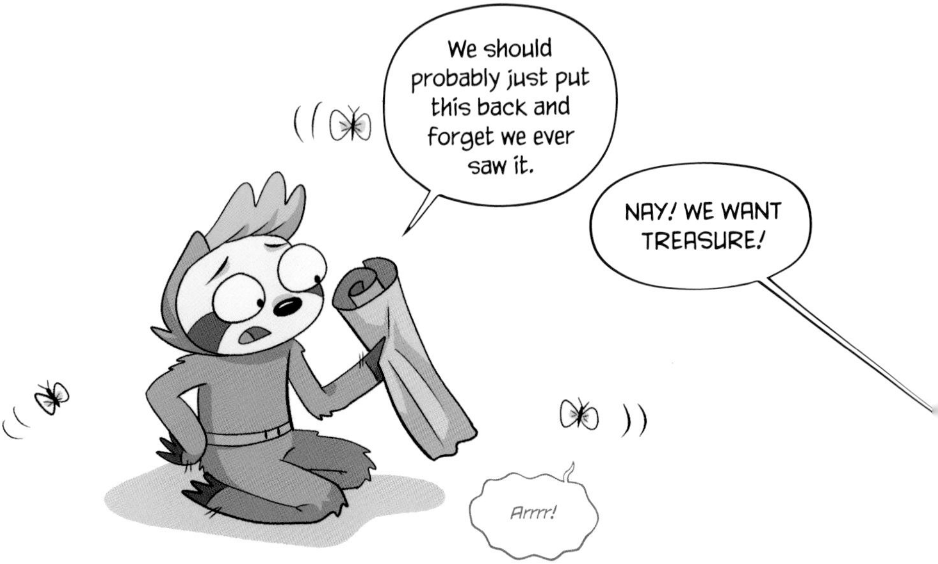
We should probably just put this back and forget we ever saw it.
NAY! WE WANT TREASURE!
Arrrr!

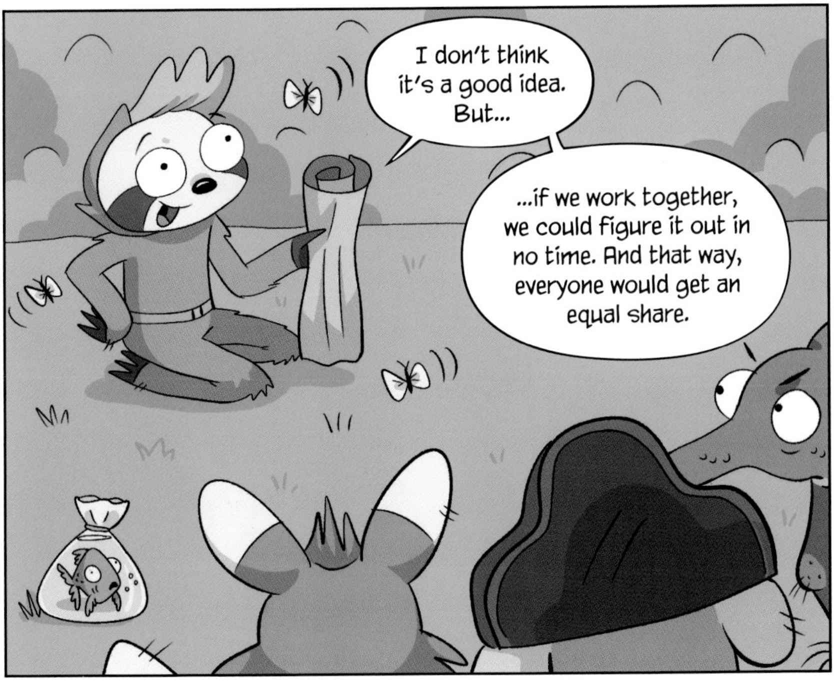
I don't think it's a good idea. But...
...if we work together, we could figure it out in no time. And that way, everyone would get an equal share.

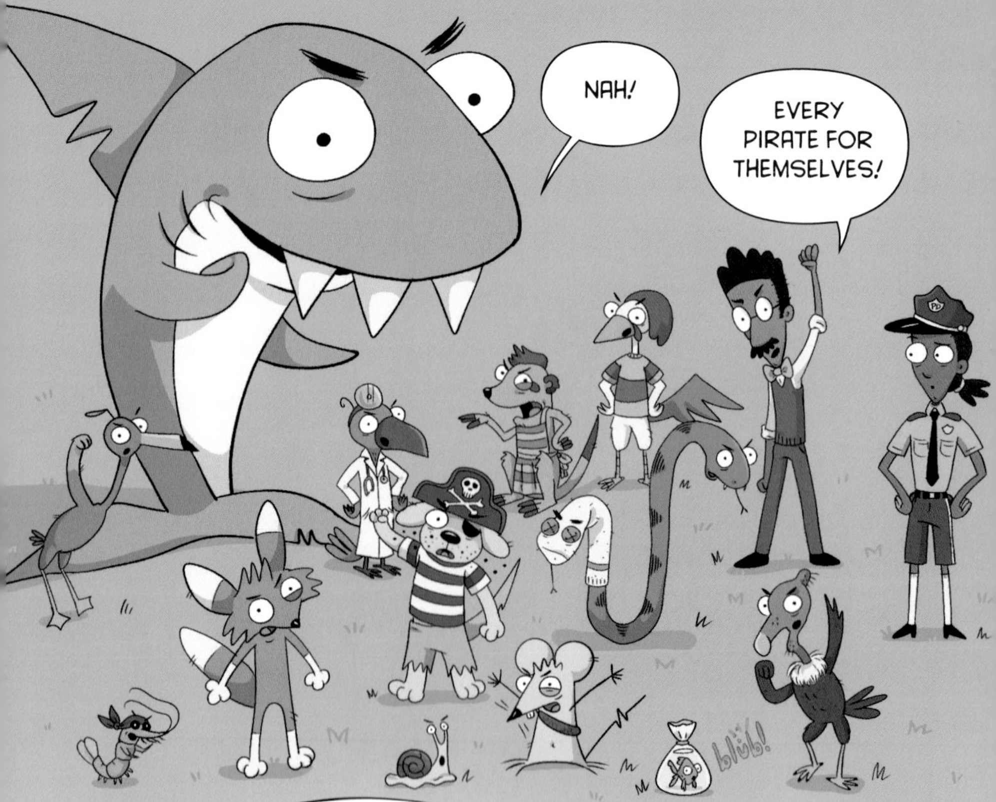
NAH!
EVERY PIRATE FOR THEMSELVES!
blub!

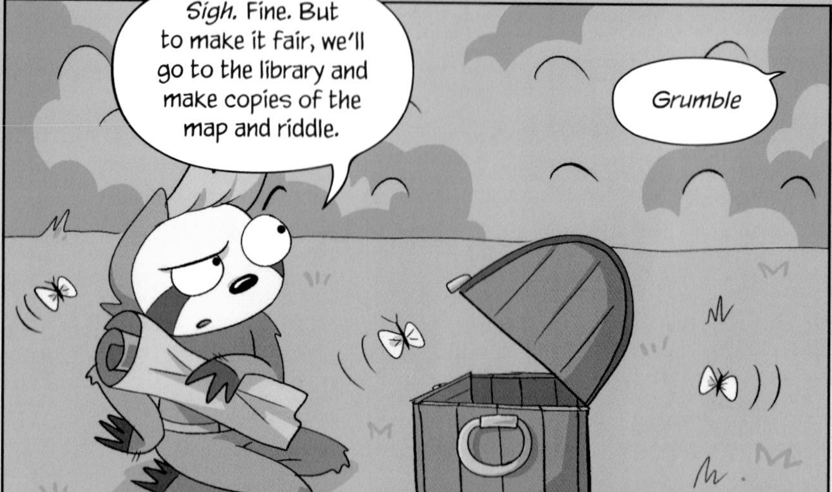
Sigh. Fine. But to make it fair, we'll go to the library and make copies of the map and riddle.
Grumble

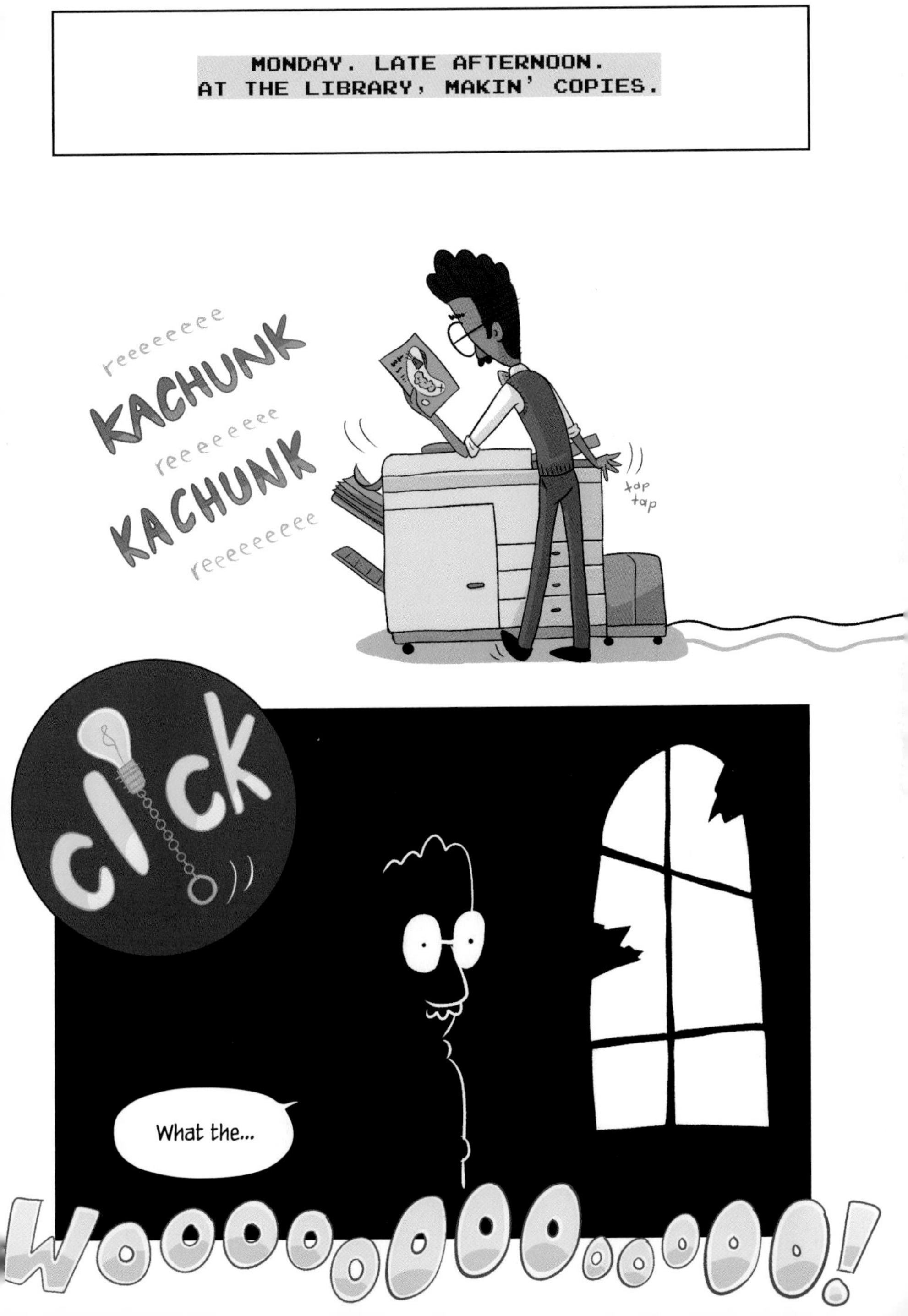
MONDAY. LATE AFTERNOON.
AT THE LIBRARY, MAKIN' COPIES.
reeeeeeeee
KACHUNK
reeeeeeeee
KACHUNK
reeeeeeeee
tap tap
click
What the...
WOOOOOOOO...OOOO!

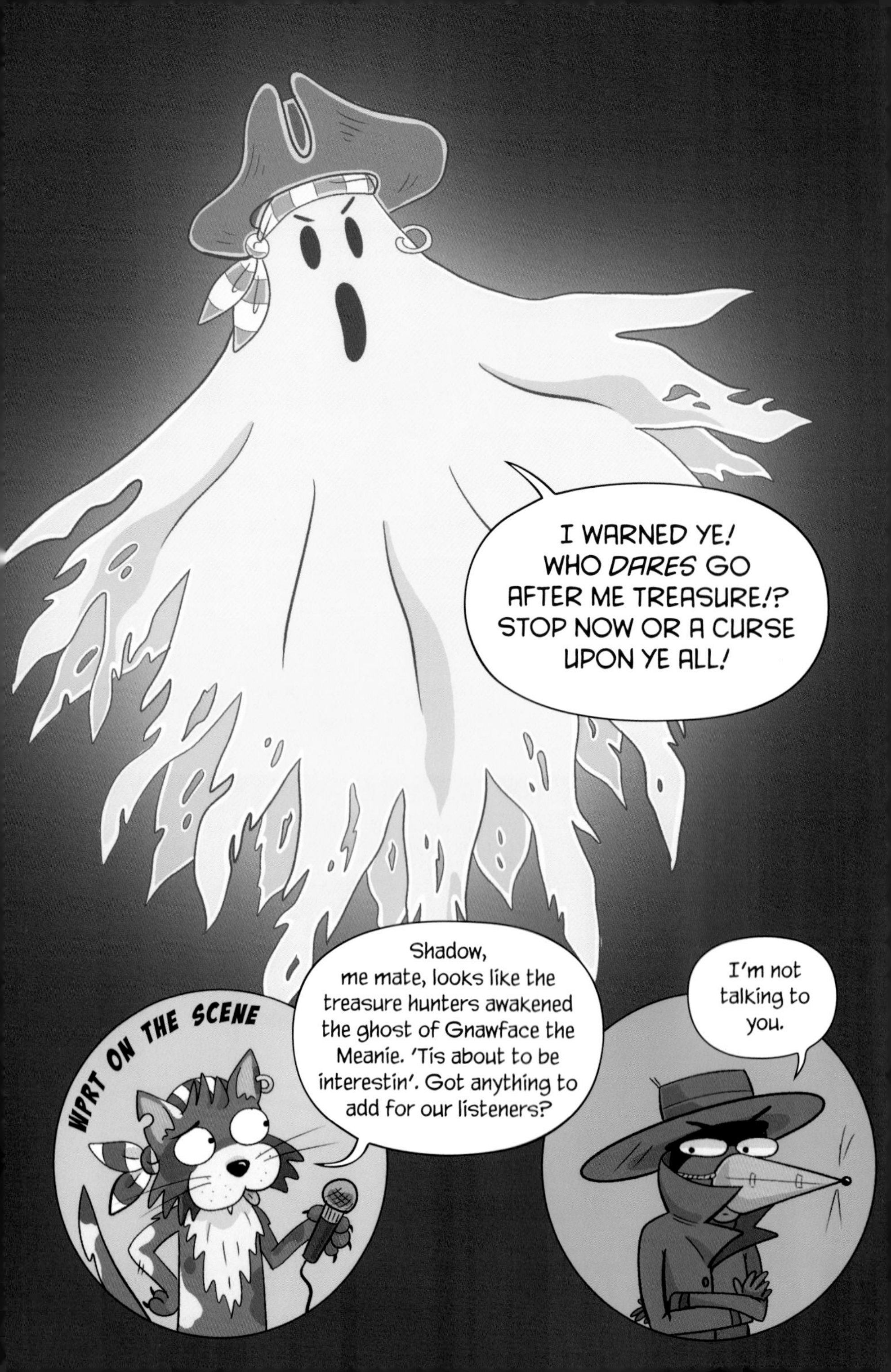
I WARNED YE! WHO *DARES* GO AFTER ME TREASURE!? STOP NOW OR A CURSE UPON YE ALL!
WPRT ON THE SCENE
Shadow, me mate, looks like the treasure hunters awakened the ghost of Gnawface the Meanie. 'Tis about to be interestin'. Got anything to add for our listeners?
I'm not talking to you.

CHAPTER 3

MONDAY. LATER AFTERNOON.
COWERING IN THE DARK FROM A GHOST.

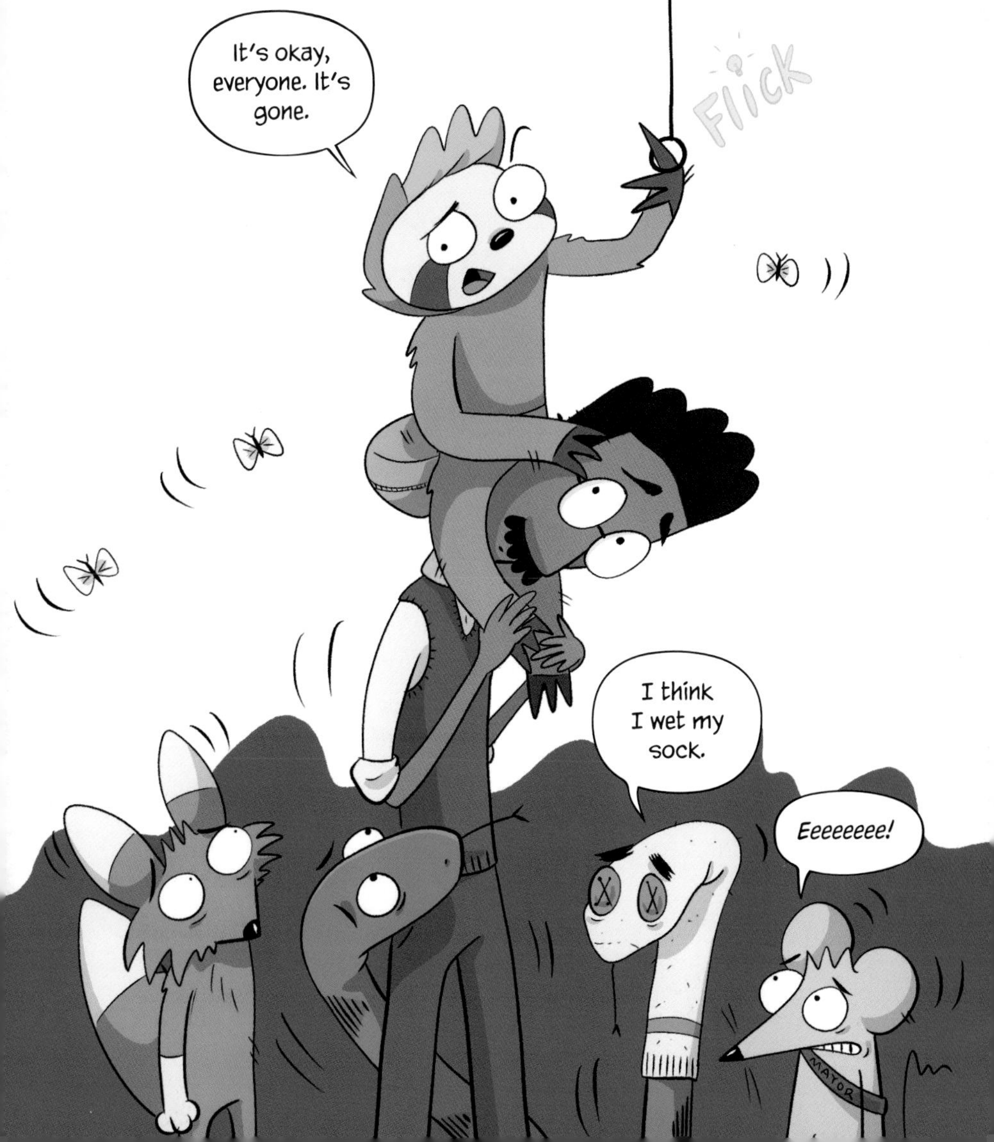
It's okay, everyone. It's gone.
Flick
I think I wet my sock.
Eeeeeeee!
MATOR

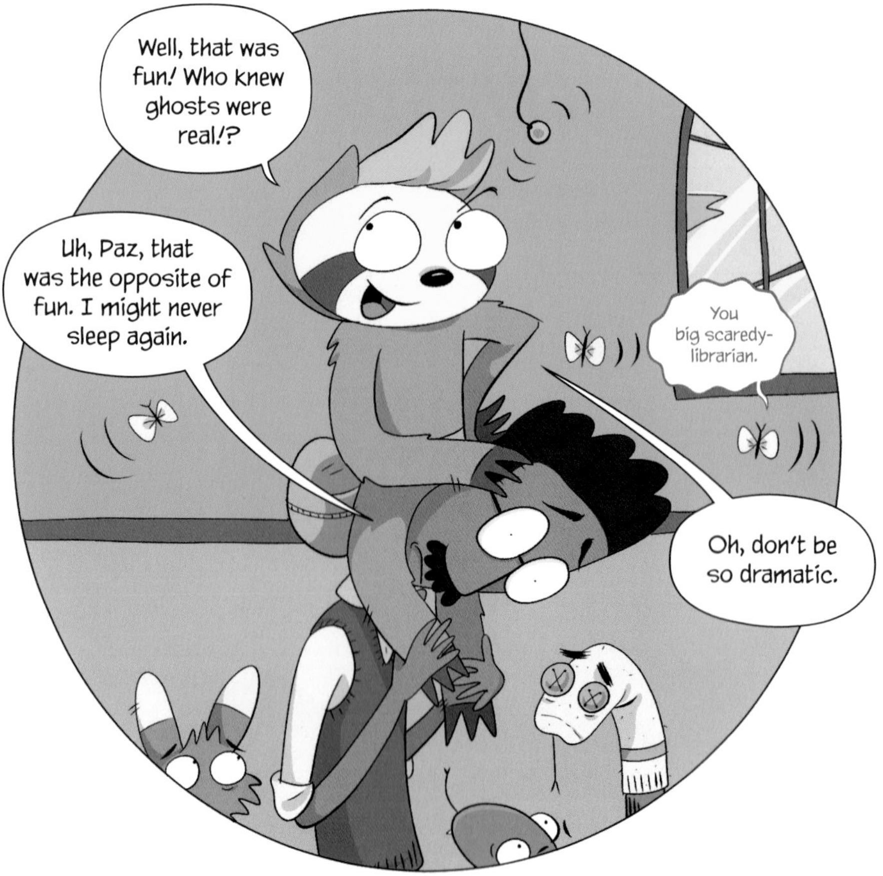
Well, that was fun! Who knew ghosts were real!?
Uh, Paz, that was the opposite of fun. I might never sleep again.
Oh, don't be so dramatic.
You big scaredy-librarian.

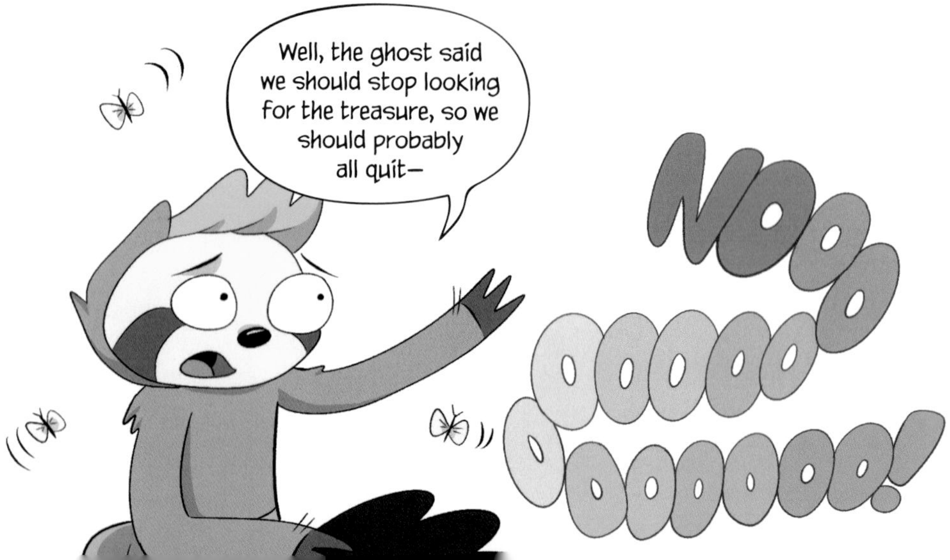
Well, the ghost said we should stop looking for the treasure, so we should probably all quit—
NOOOOOOOOOOOOOOOOOOO!

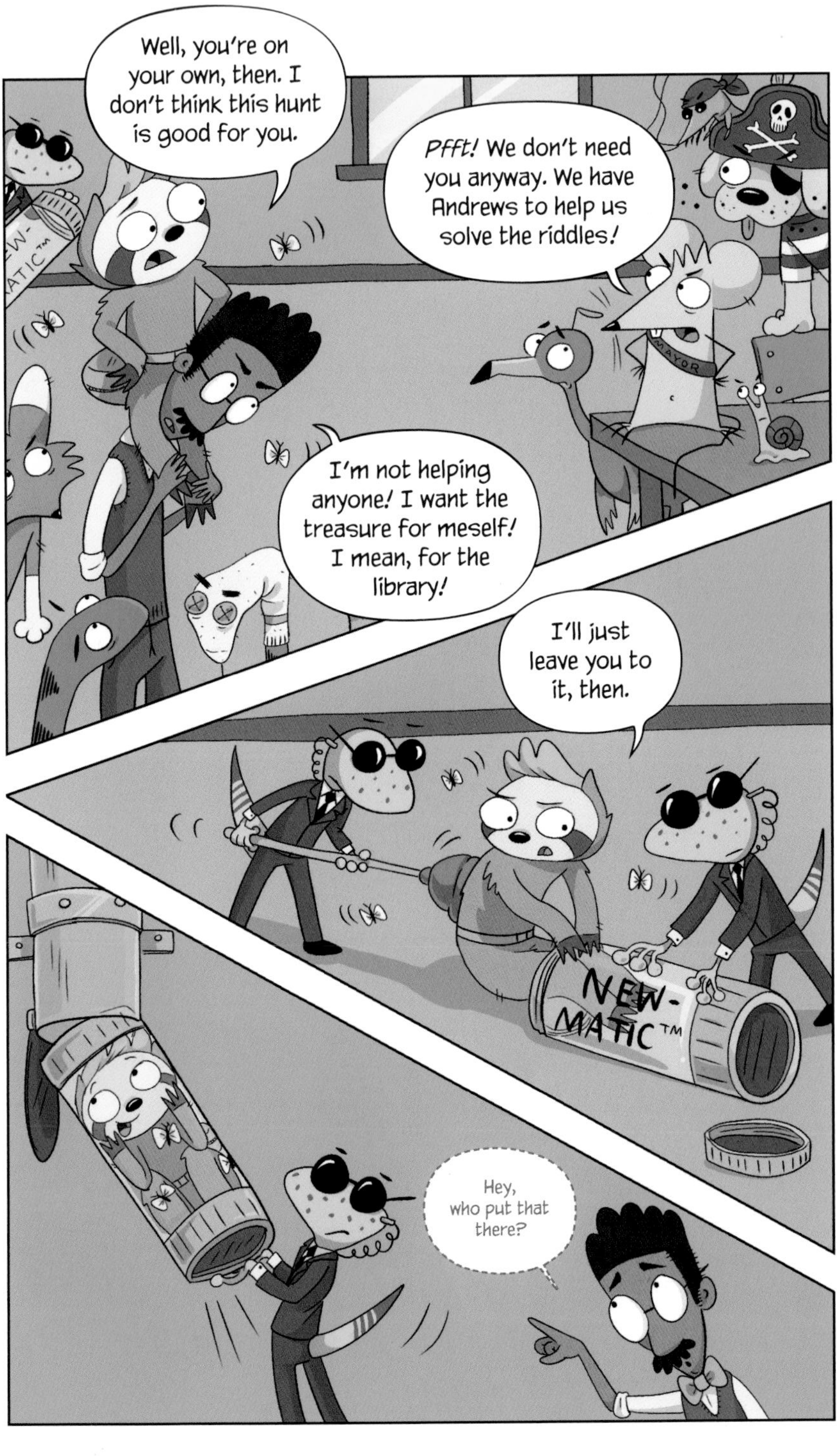
Well, you're on your own, then. I don't think this hunt is good for you.
Pfft! We don't need you anyway. We have Andrews to help us solve the riddles!
MAYOR
I'm not helping anyone! I want the treasure for meself! I mean, for the library!
I'll just leave you to it, then.
NEW-MATIC™
Hey, who put that there?

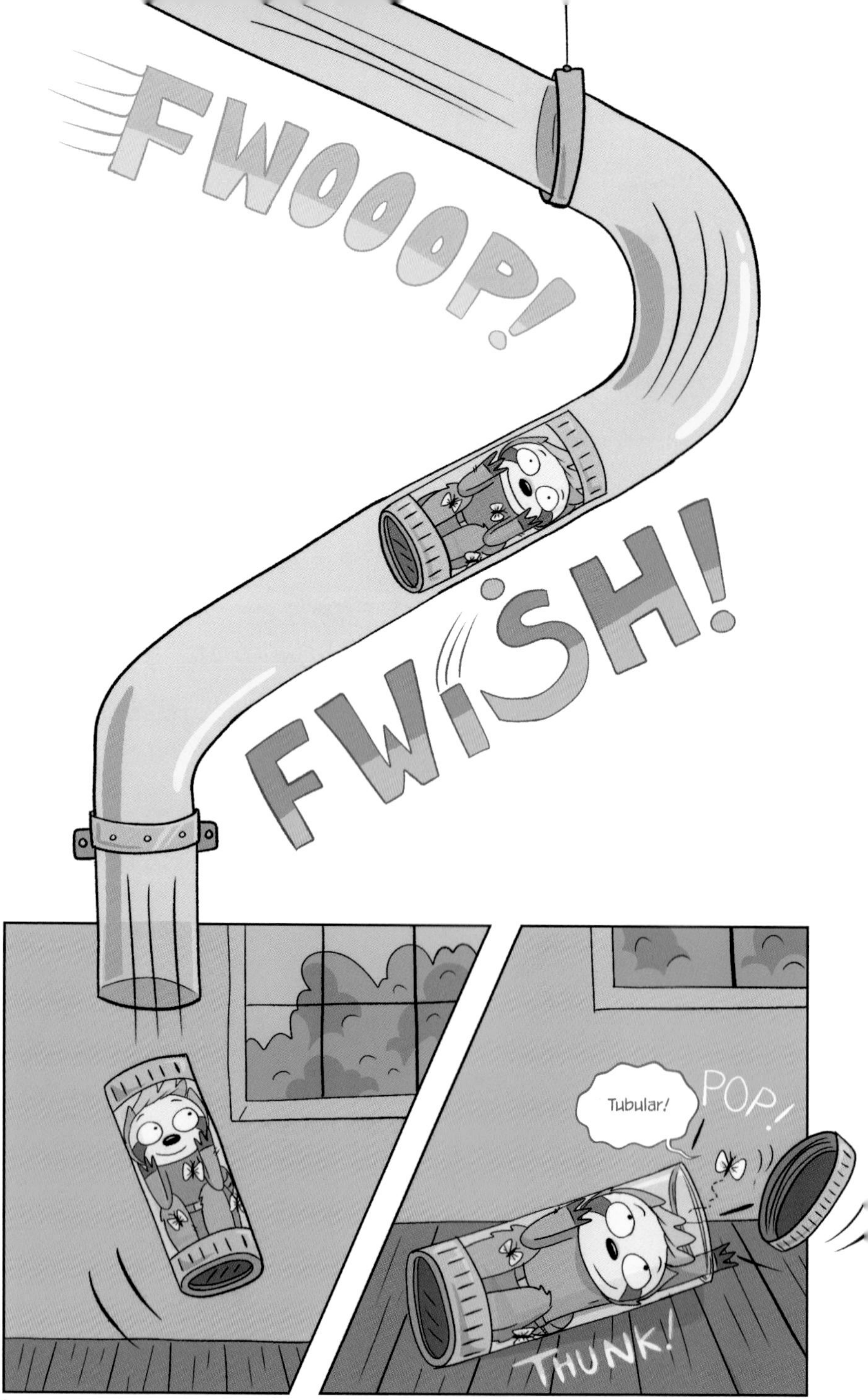
FWOOOP!
FWISH!
Tubular!
POP!
THUNK!

YAWN!

Stretch!

YAWN. I guess things will be quiet for the next few days while everyone looks for treasure

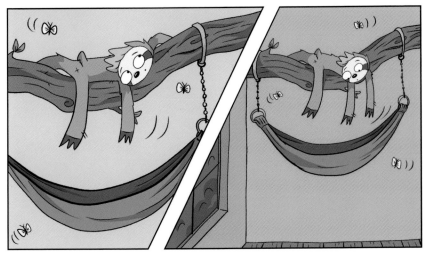

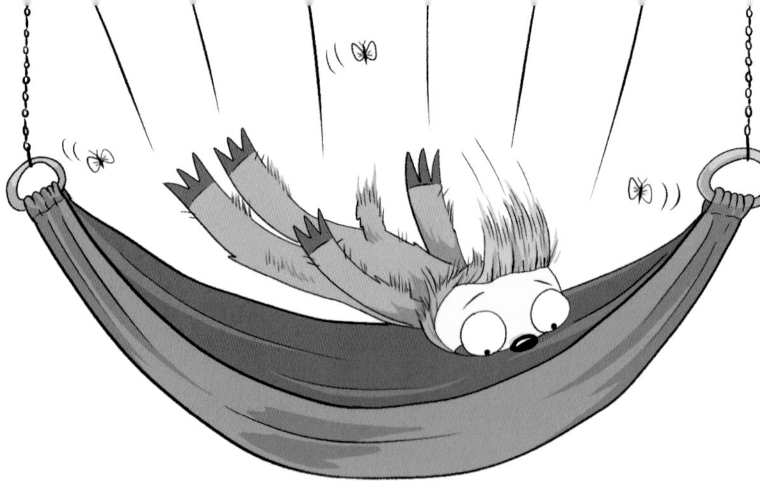

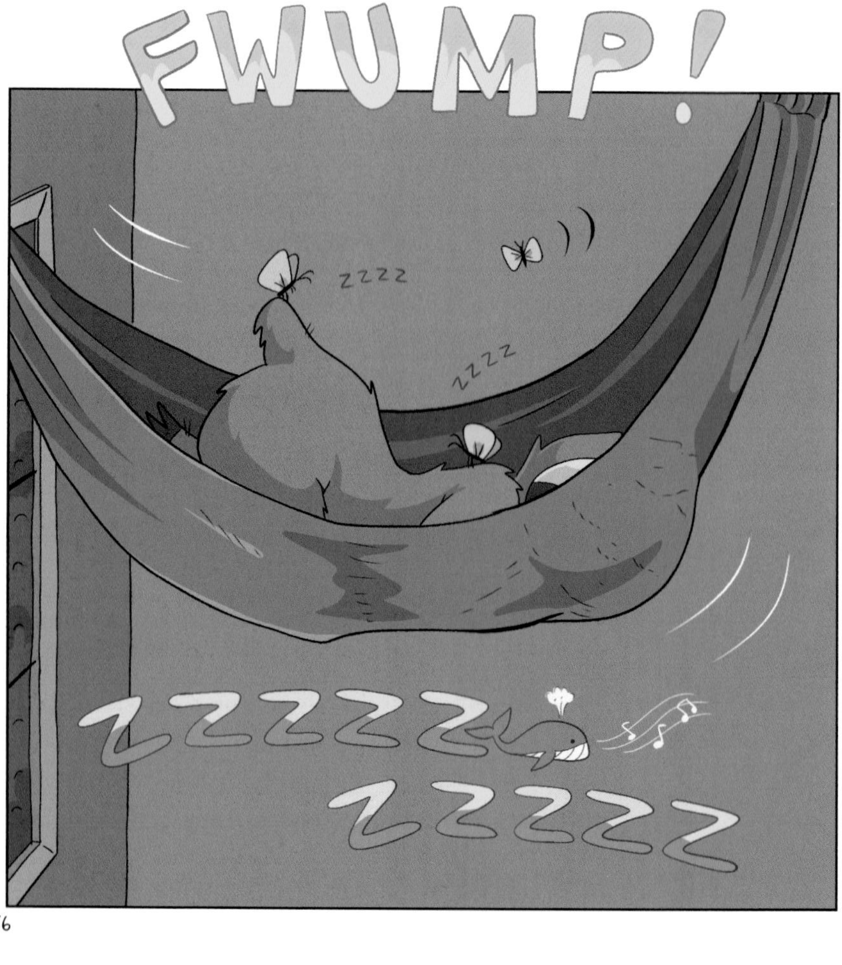
FWUMP!
ZZZZ
ZZZZ
ZZZZZ
ZZZZZ

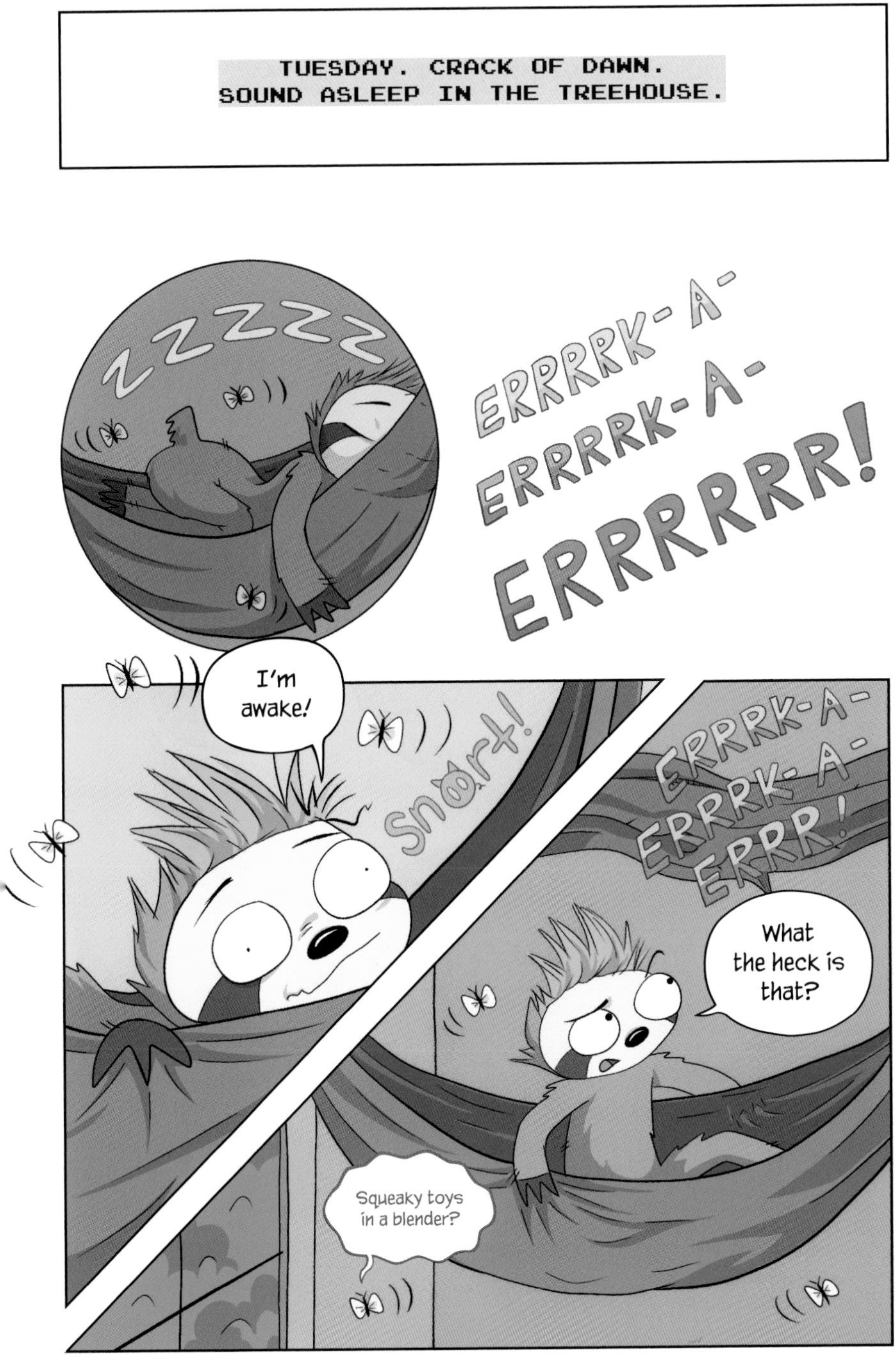
TUESDAY. CRACK OF DAWN.
SOUND ASLEEP IN THE TREEHOUSE.
ZZZZZ
ERRRRK-A-
ERRRRK-A-
ERRRRRR!
I'm awake!
Snort!
ERRRK-A-
ERRRK-A-
ERRR!
What the heck is that?
Squeaky toys in a blender?

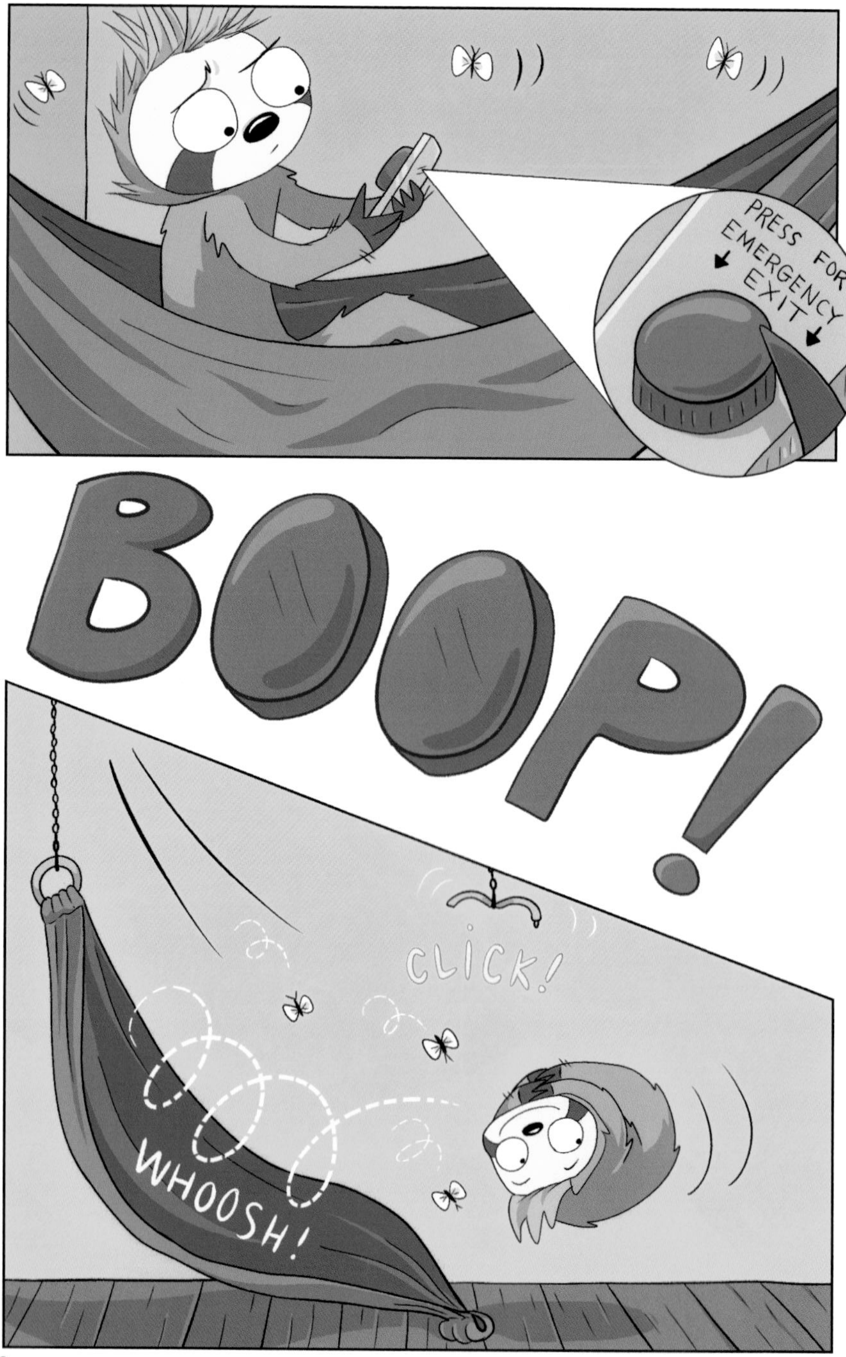
PRESS FOR EMERGENCY EXIT
BOOP!
CLICK!
WHOOSH!

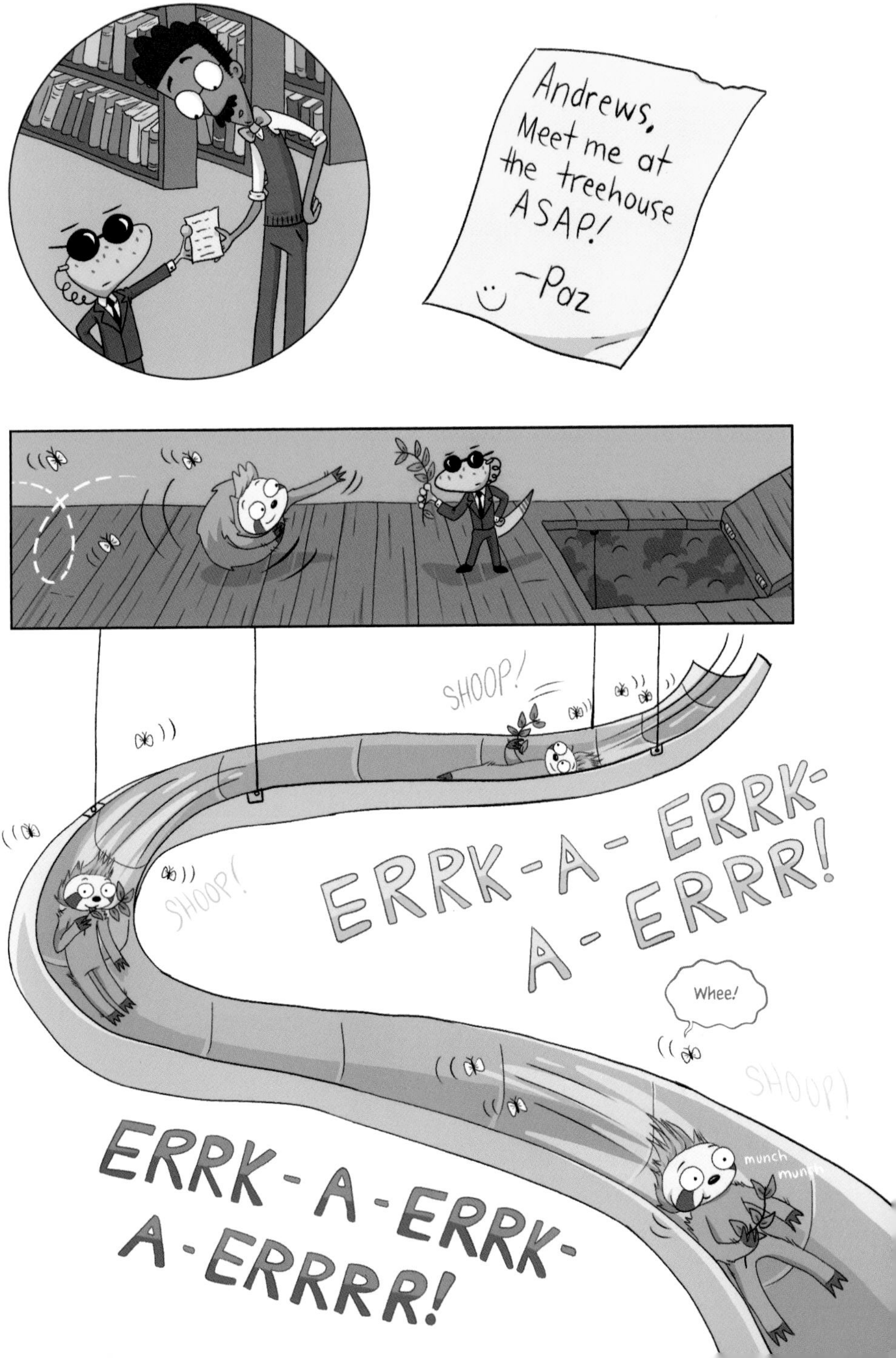

Andrews,
Meet me at
the treehouse
ASAP!
-Paz
SHOOP!
SHOOP!
ERRK-A-ERRK-
A-ERRR!
Whee!
SHOOP!
ERRK-A-ERRK-
A-ERRRRR!
munch
munch

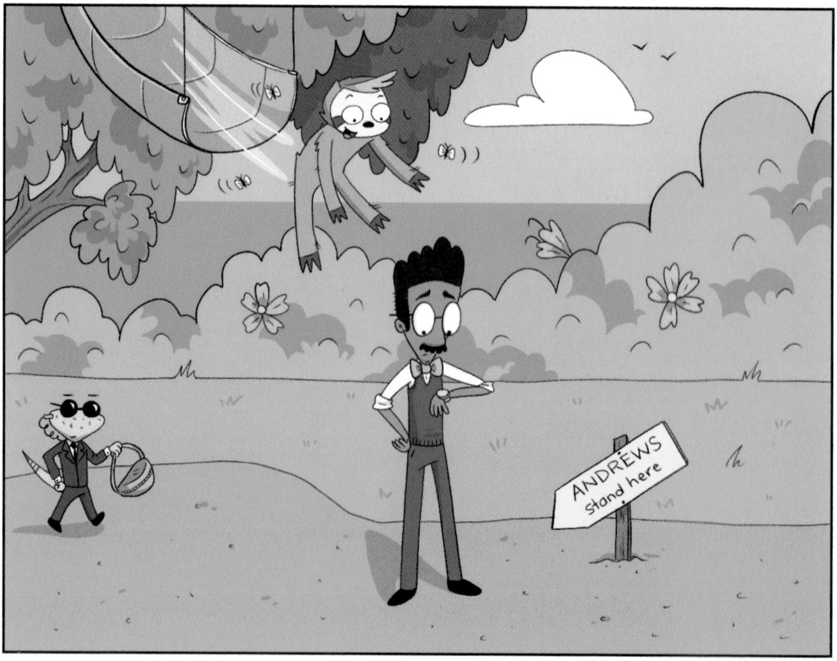
ANDREWS
stand here

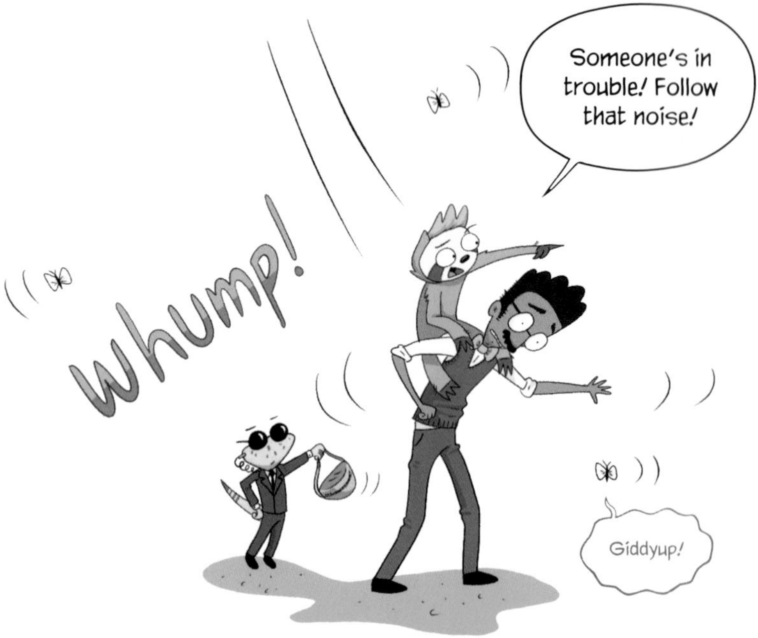
Someone's in trouble! Follow that noise!
whump!
Giddyup!

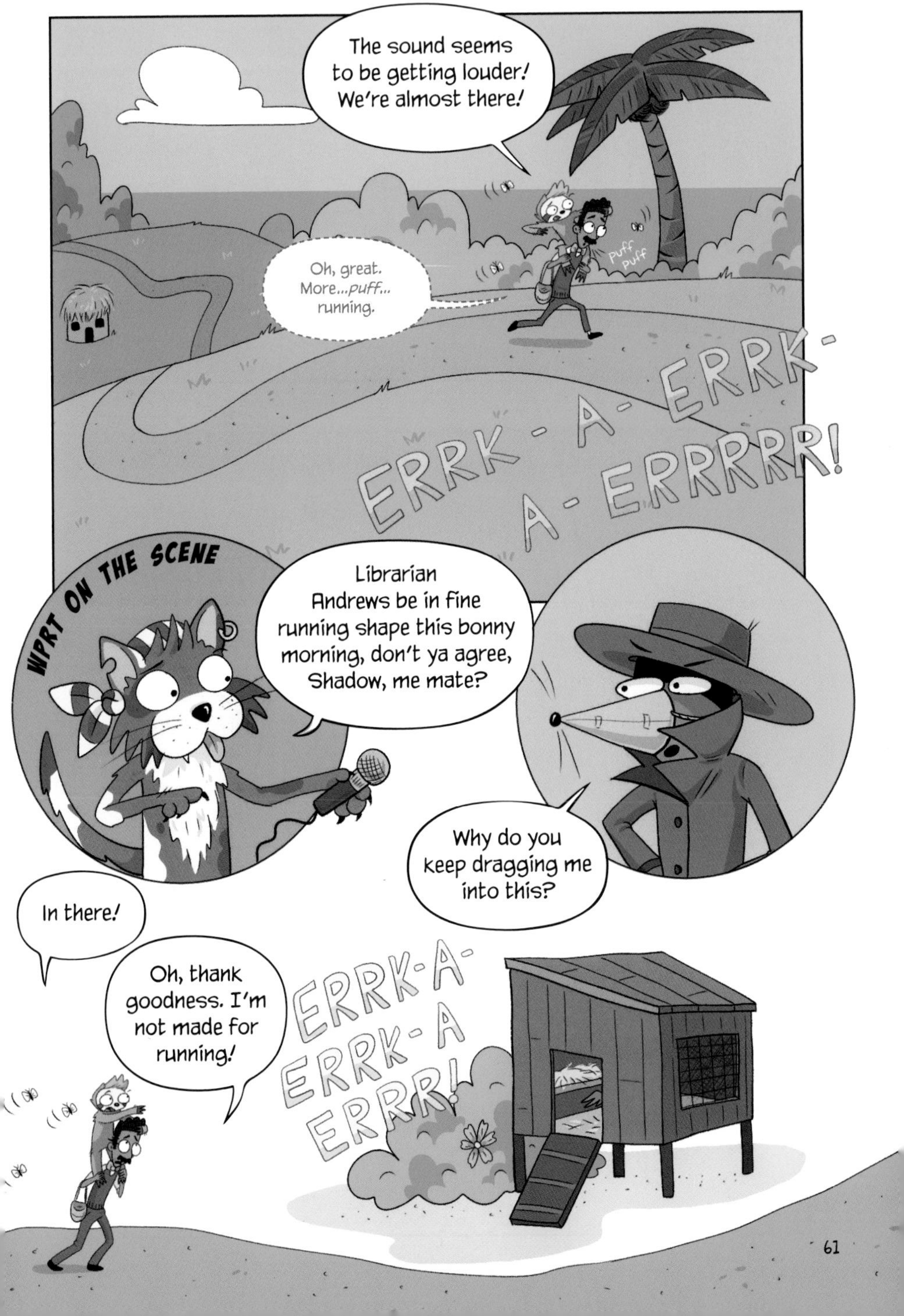
The sound seems to be getting louder! We're almost there!
Oh, great. More...*puff*... running.
puff puff
ERRK - A - ERRK - A - ERRRRRR!
WPRT ON THE SCENE
Librarian Andrews be in fine running shape this bonny morning, don't ya agree, Shadow, me mate?
Why do you keep dragging me into this?
In there!
Oh, thank goodness. I'm not made for running!
ERRK-A-ERRK-A ERRR!

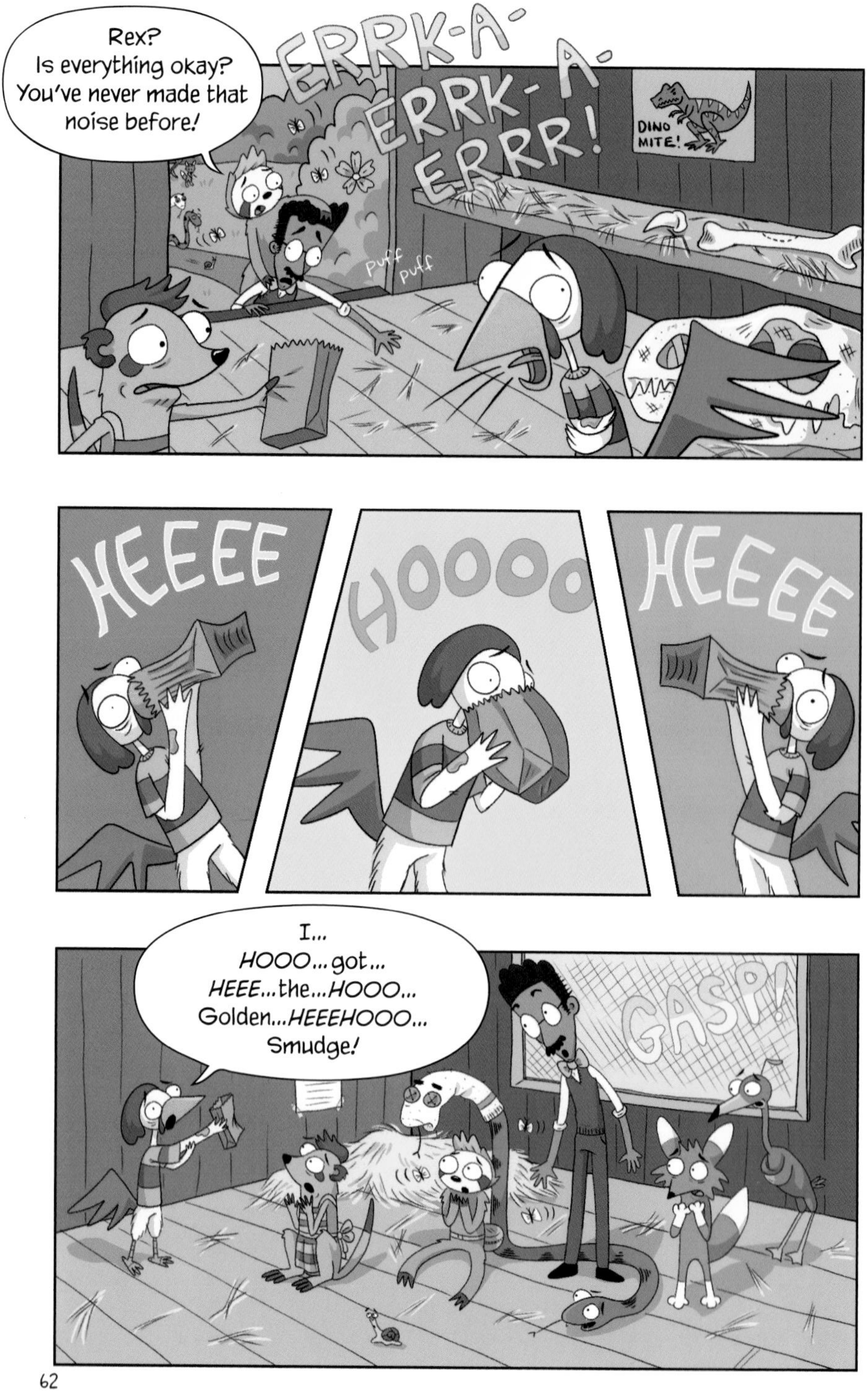
Rex? Is everything okay? You've never made that noise before!
ERRK-A-ERRK-A-ERRR!
DINO MITE!
puff puff
HEEEE
HOOOO
HEEEE
I... HOOO...got... HEEE...the...HOOO... Golden...HEEEHOOO... Smudge!
GASP!

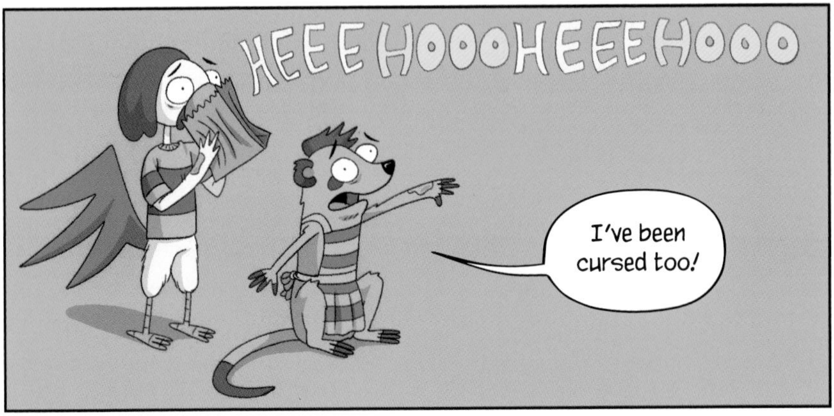
HEEEHOOOHEEEHOOO
I've been cursed too!

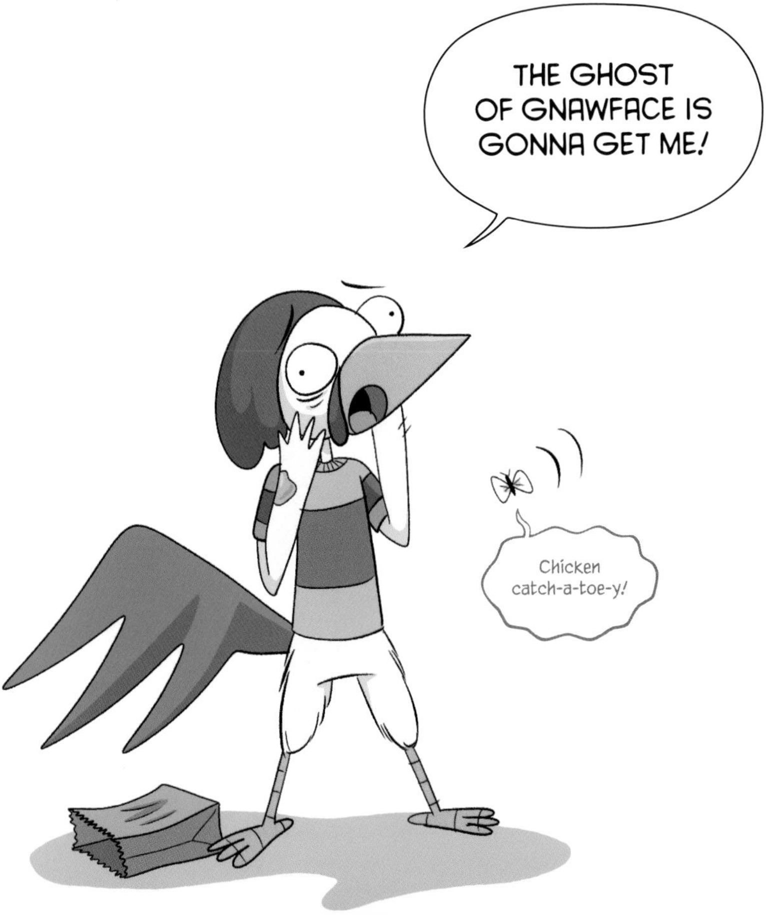
THE GHOST OF GNAWFACE IS GONNA GET ME!
Chicken catch-a-toe-y!

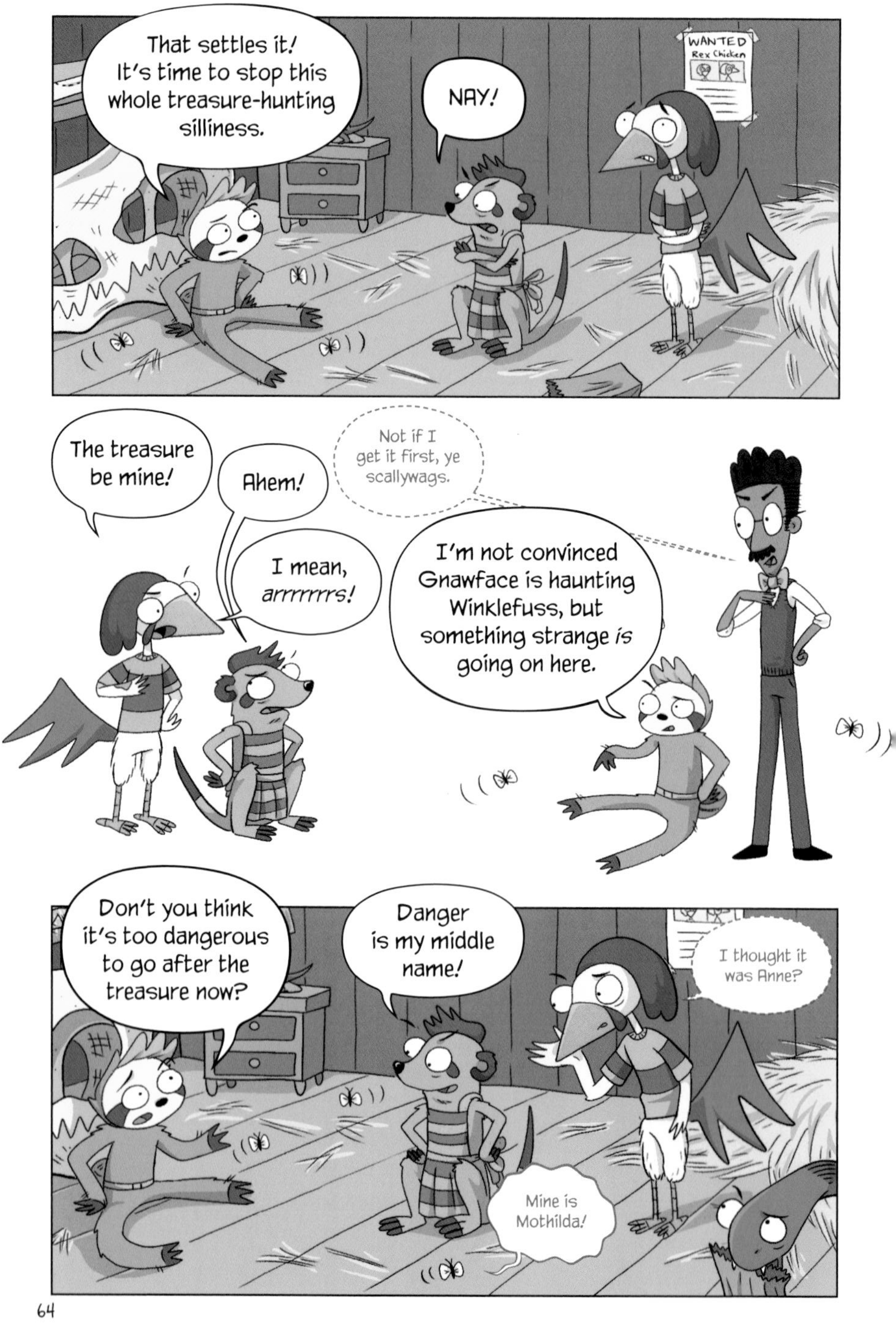
That settles it! It's time to stop this whole treasure-hunting silliness.
NAY!
WANTED
Rex Chicken
The treasure be mine!
Ahem!
I mean, *arrrrrrrs!*
Not if I get it first, ye scallywags.
I'm not convinced Gnawface is haunting Winklefuss, but something strange *is* going on here.
Don't you think it's too dangerous to go after the treasure now?
Danger is my middle name!
I thought it was Anne?
Mine is Mothilda!

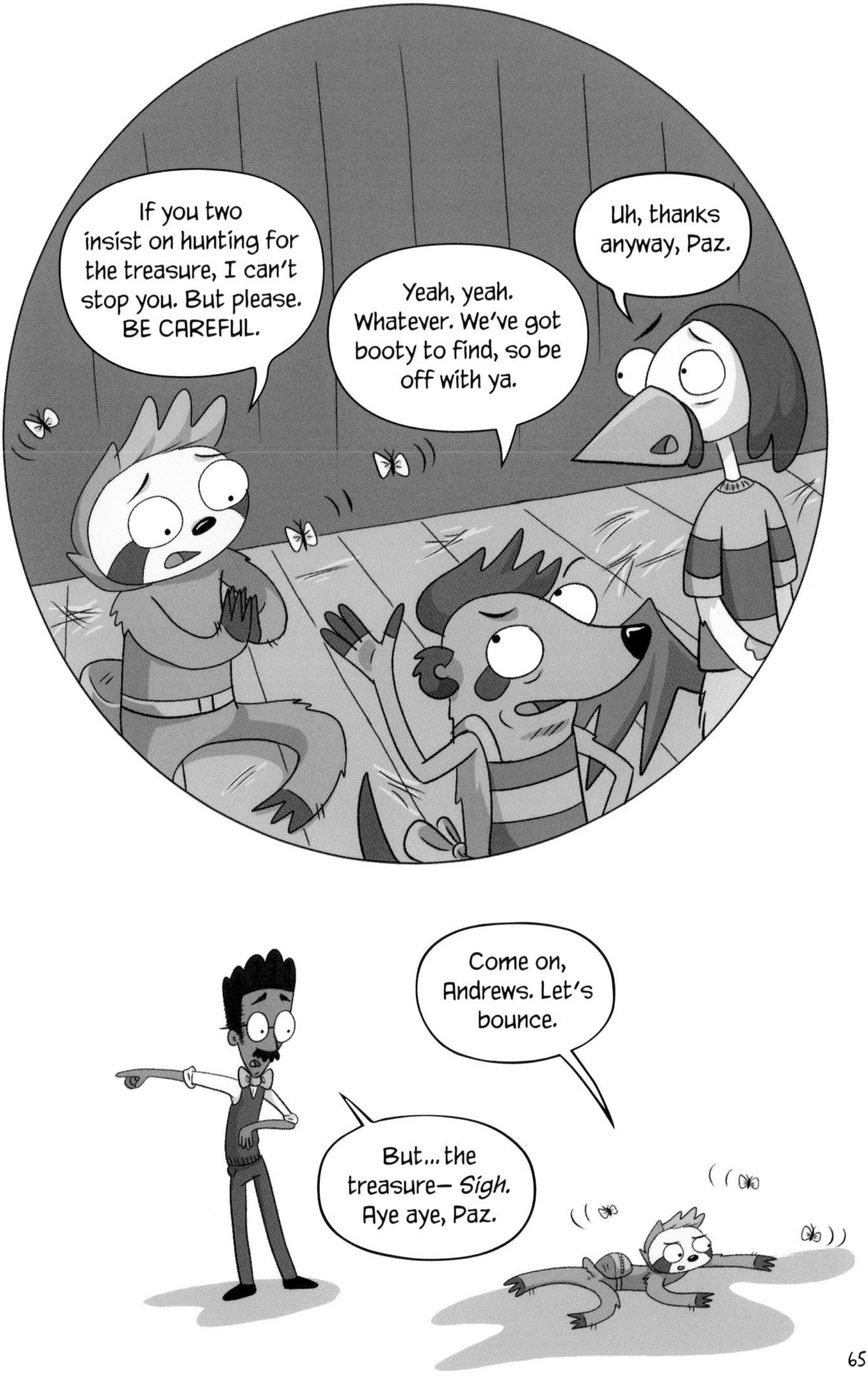
If you two insist on hunting for the treasure, I can't stop you. But please. BE CAREFUL.
Yeah, yeah. Whatever. We've got booty to find, so be off with ya.
Uh, thanks anyway, Paz.
Come on, Andrews. Let's bounce.
But... the treasure— *Sigh.* Aye aye, Paz.

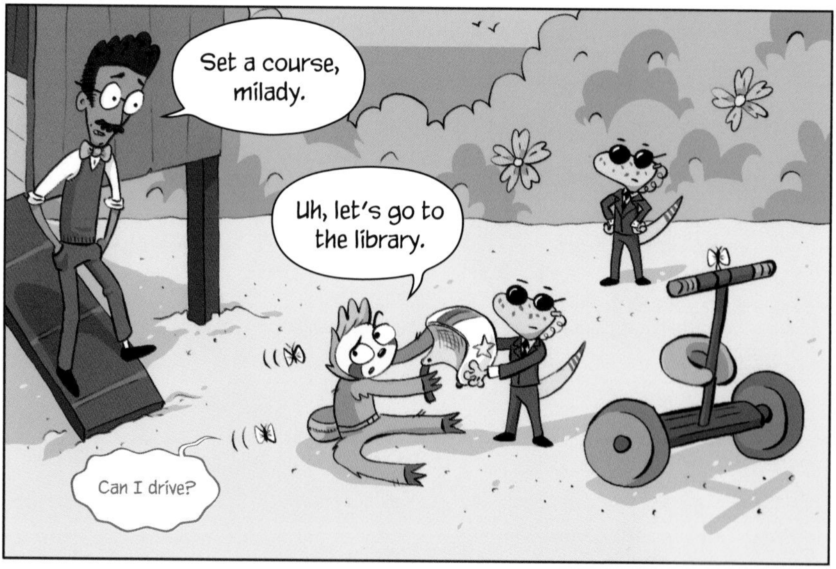
Set a course, milady.
Uh, let's go to the library.
Can I drive?

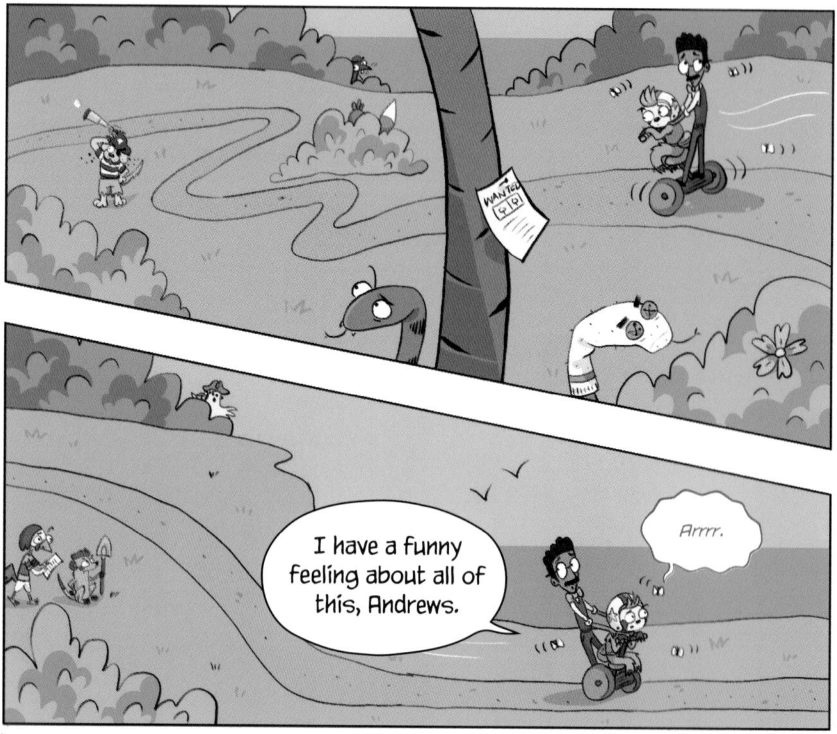
I have a funny feeling about all of this, Andrews.
Arrrr.

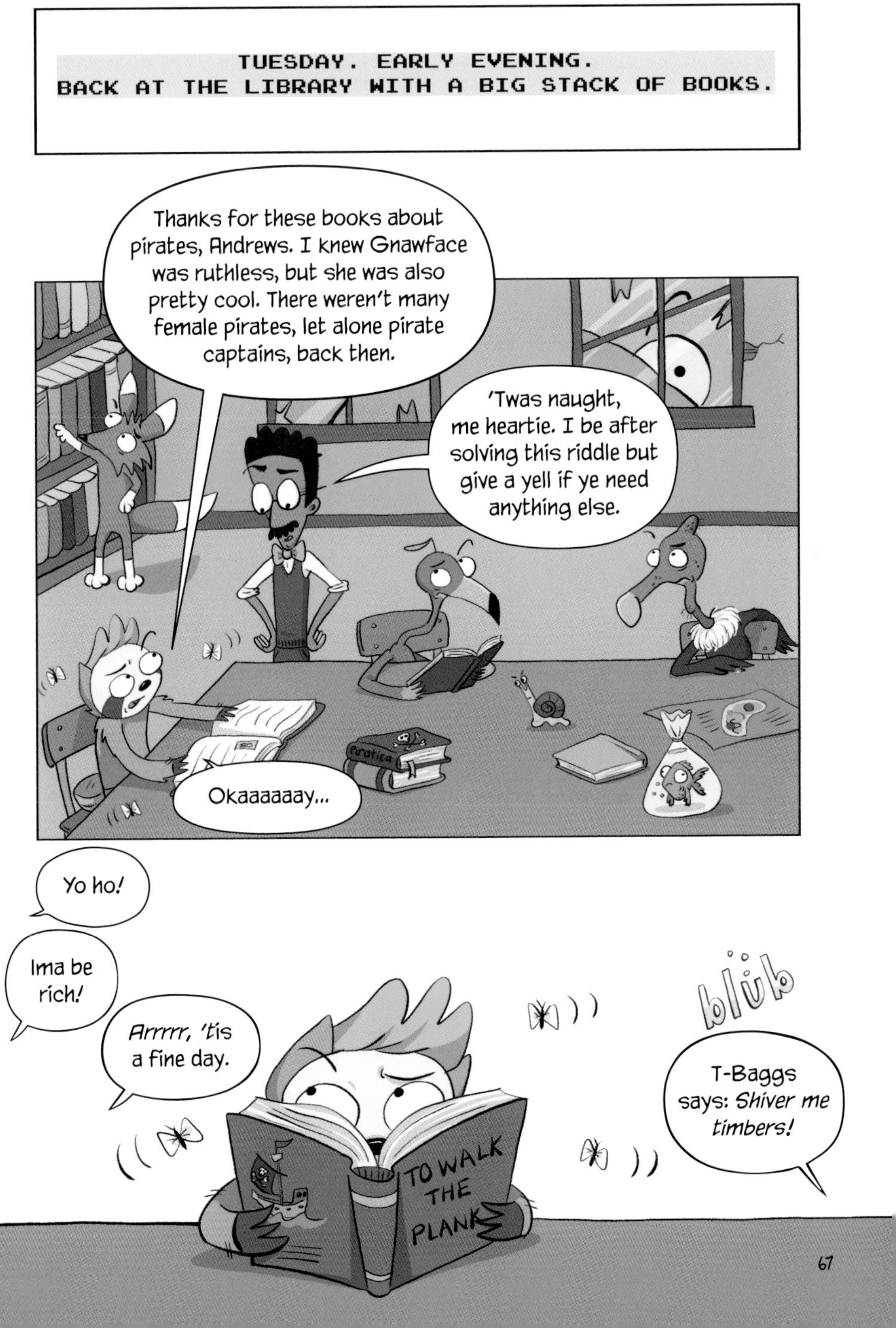
TUESDAY. EARLY EVENING.
BACK AT THE LIBRARY WITH A BIG STACK OF BOOKS.
Thanks for these books about pirates, Andrews. I knew Gnawface was ruthless, but she was also pretty cool. There weren't many female pirates, let alone pirate captains, back then.
'Twas naught, me heartie. I be after solving this riddle but give a yell if ye need anything else.
Piratica
Okaaaaaay...
Yo ho!
Ima be rich!
Arrrrr, 'tis a fine day.
blub
T-Baggs says: *Shiver me timbers!*
TO WALK THE PLANK

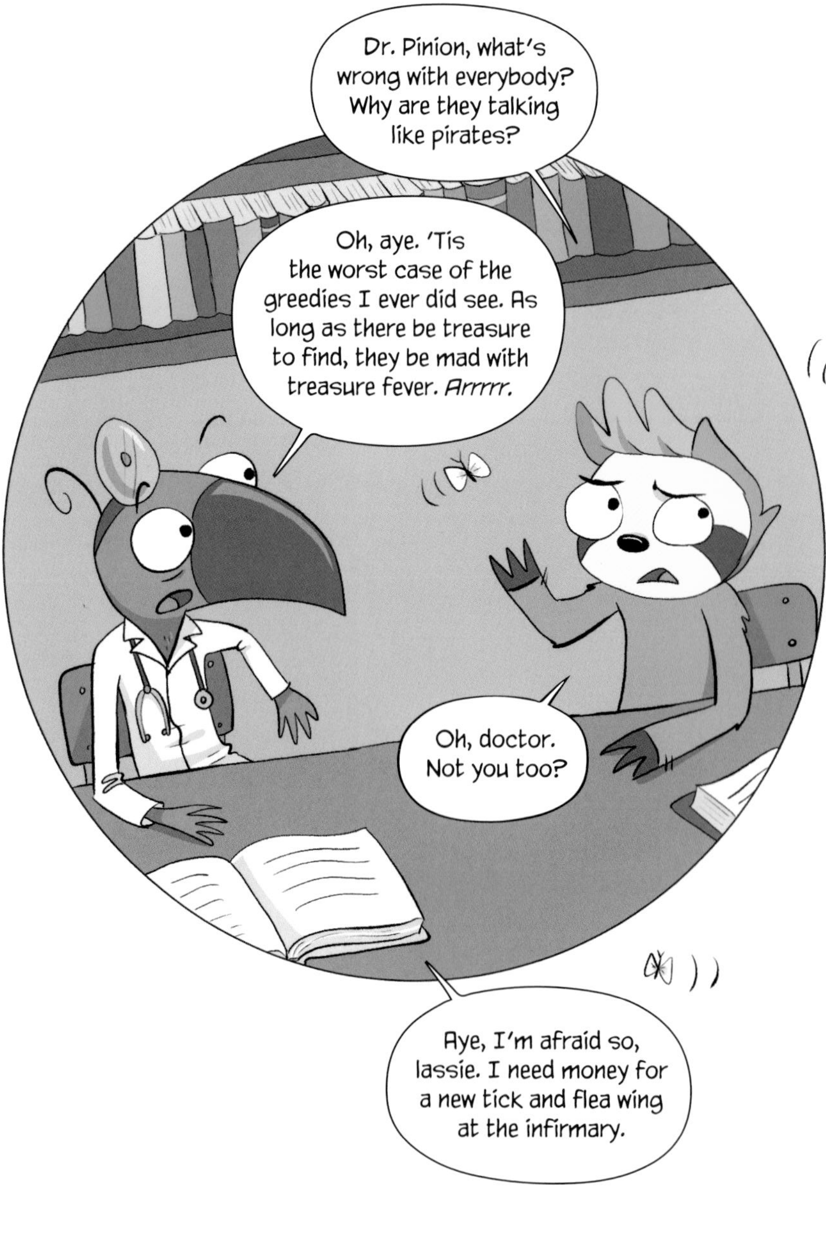
Dr. Pinion, what's wrong with everybody? Why are they talking like pirates?
Oh, aye. 'Tis the worst case of the greedies I ever did see. As long as there be treasure to find, they be mad with treasure fever. *Arrrrr.*
Oh, doctor. Not you too?
Aye, I'm afraid so, lassie. I need money for a new tick and flea wing at the infirmary.

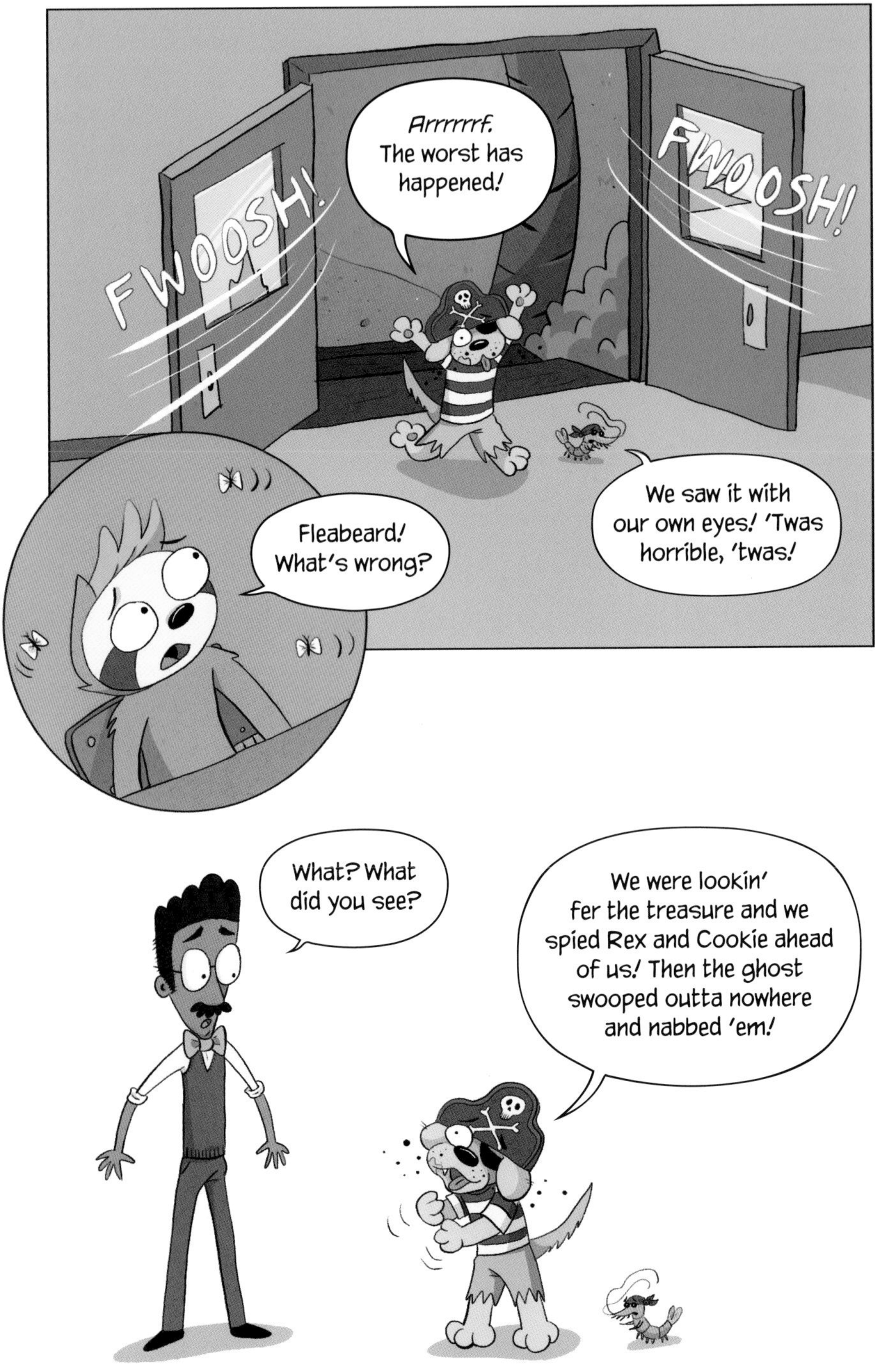
FWOOSH!
Arrrrrrf.
The worst has happened!
FWOOSH!
Fleabeard! What's wrong?
We saw it with our own eyes! 'Twas horrible, 'twas!
What? What did you see?
We were lookin' fer the treasure and we spied Rex and Cookie ahead of us! Then the ghost swooped outta nowhere and nabbed 'em!

CHAPTER 4

TUESDAY. SCARY O'CLOCK.
SHAKING LIKE LEAVES IN THE LIBRARY.

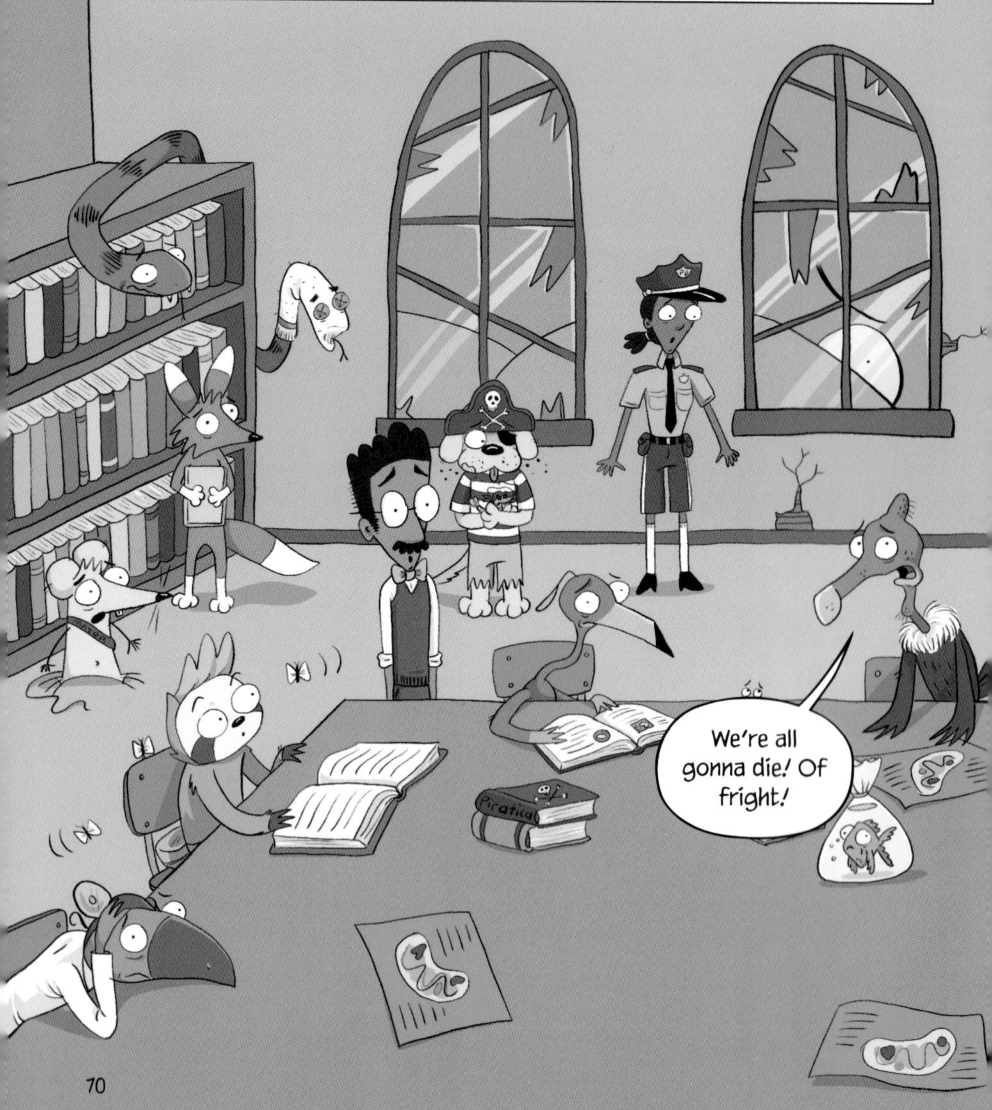
We're all gonna die! Of fright!
Piratical

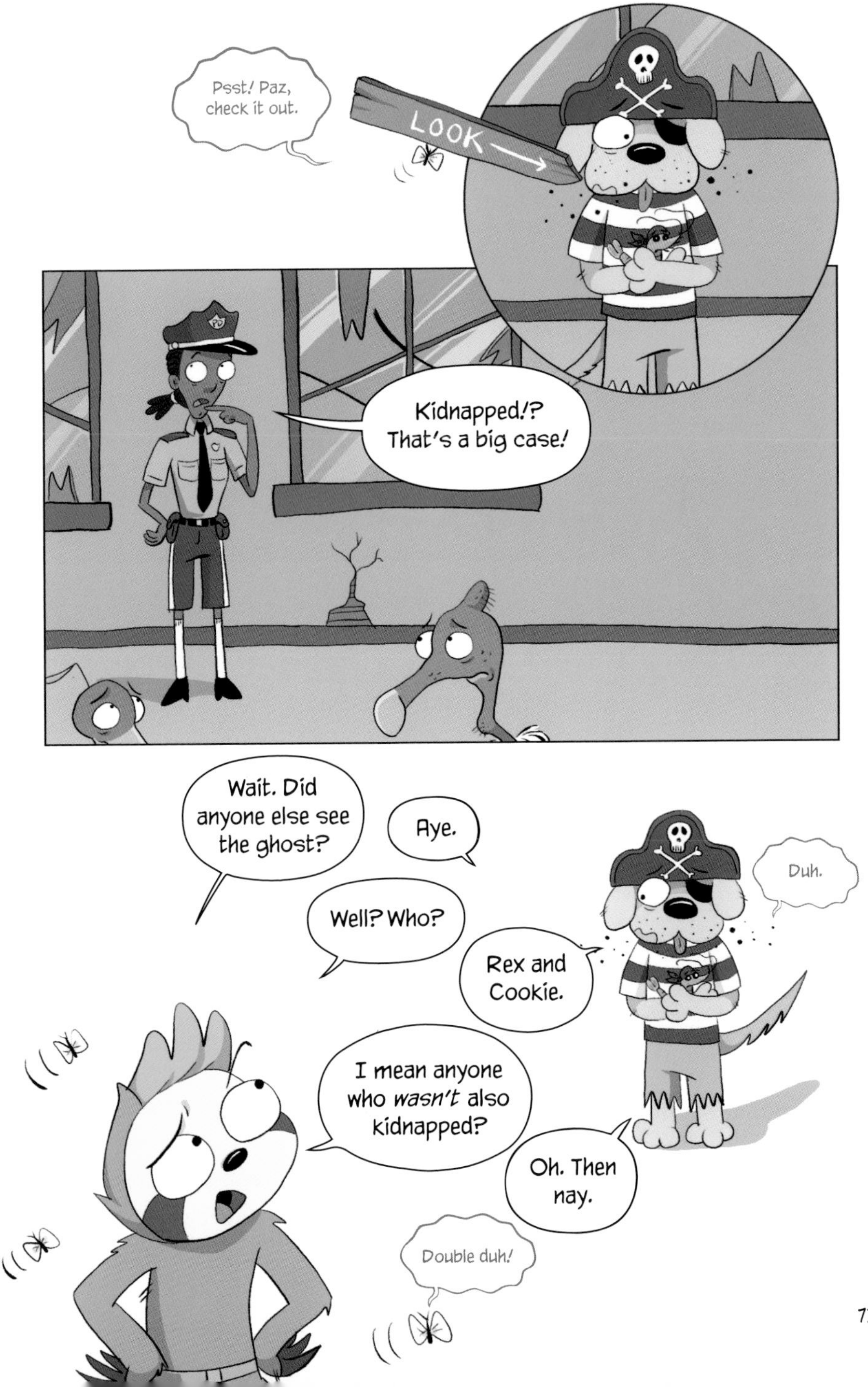

Psst! Paz, check it out.
LOOK
Kidnapped!? That's a big case!
Wait. Did anyone else see the ghost?
Aye.
Duh.
Well? Who?
Rex and Cookie.
I mean anyone who *wasn't* also kidnapped?
Oh. Then nay.
Double duh!

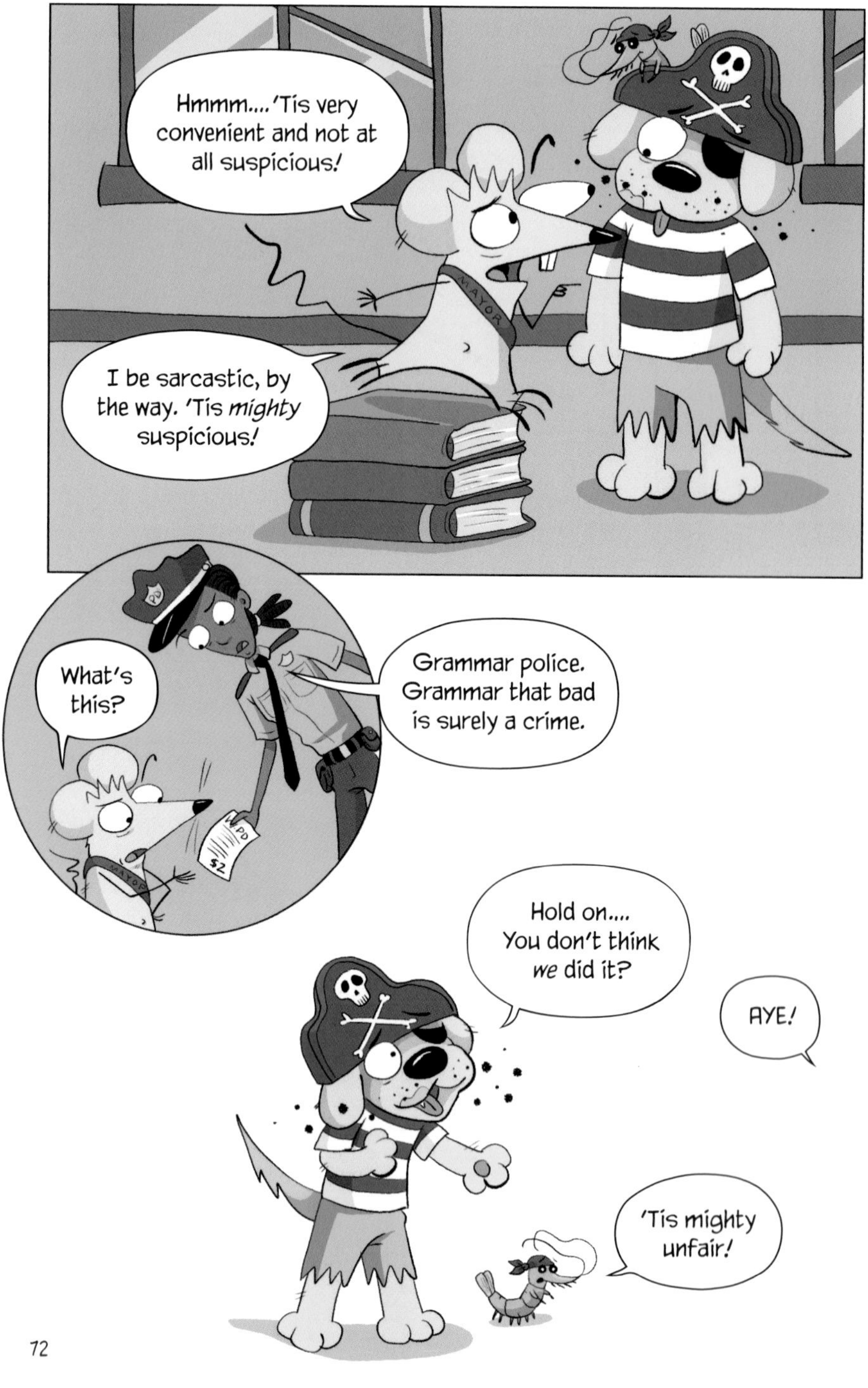
Hmmm....'Tis very convenient and not at all suspicious!
I be sarcastic, by the way. 'Tis *mighty* suspicious!
What's this?
Grammar police. Grammar that bad is surely a crime.
Hold on.... You don't think *we* did it?
AYE!
'Tis mighty unfair!

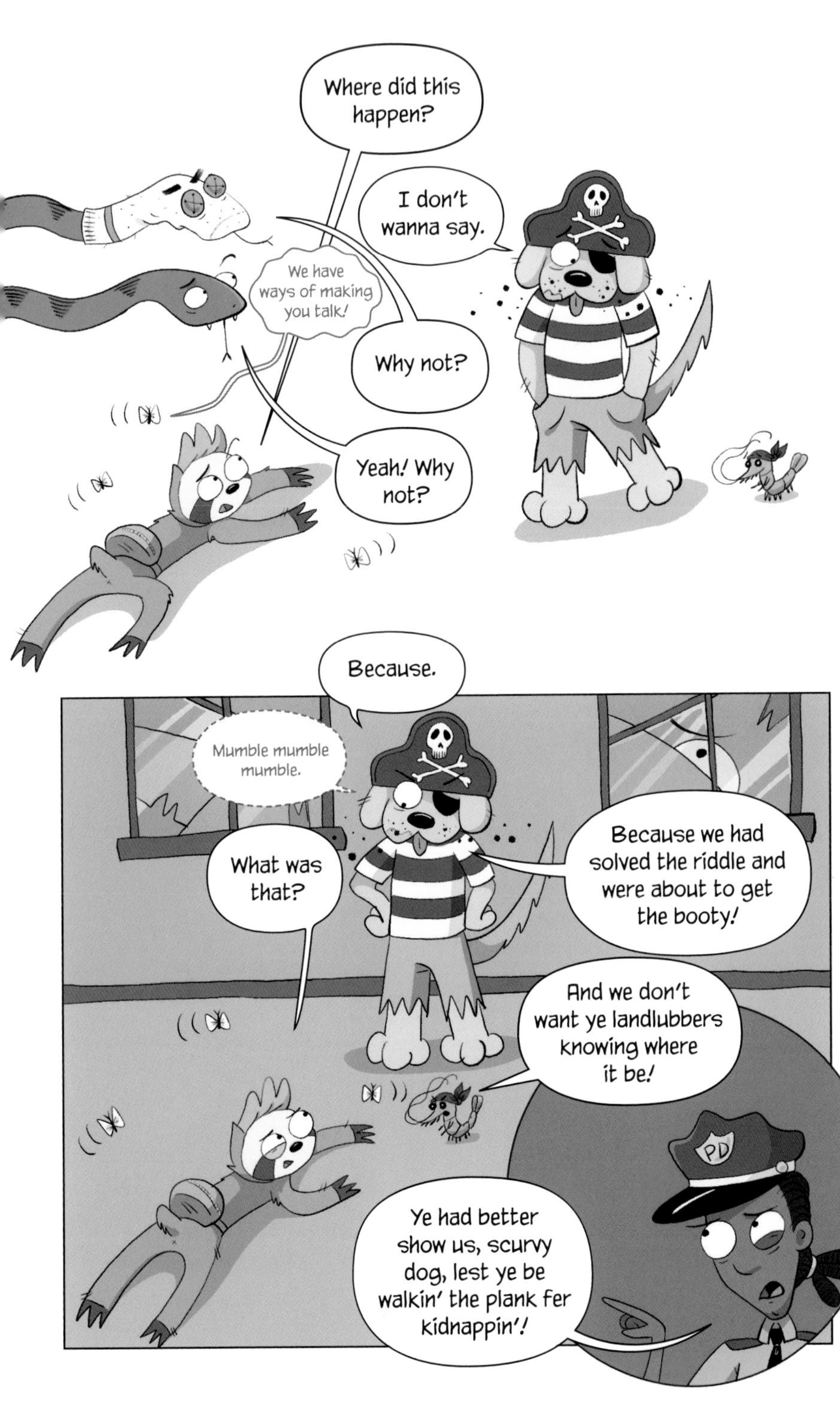
Where did this happen?
I don't wanna say.
We have ways of making you talk!
Why not?
Yeah! Why not?
Because.
Mumble mumble mumble.
What was that?
Because we had solved the riddle and were about to get the booty!
And we don't want ye landlubbers knowing where it be!
Ye had better show us, scurvy dog, lest ye be walkin' the plank fer kidnappin'!
PD

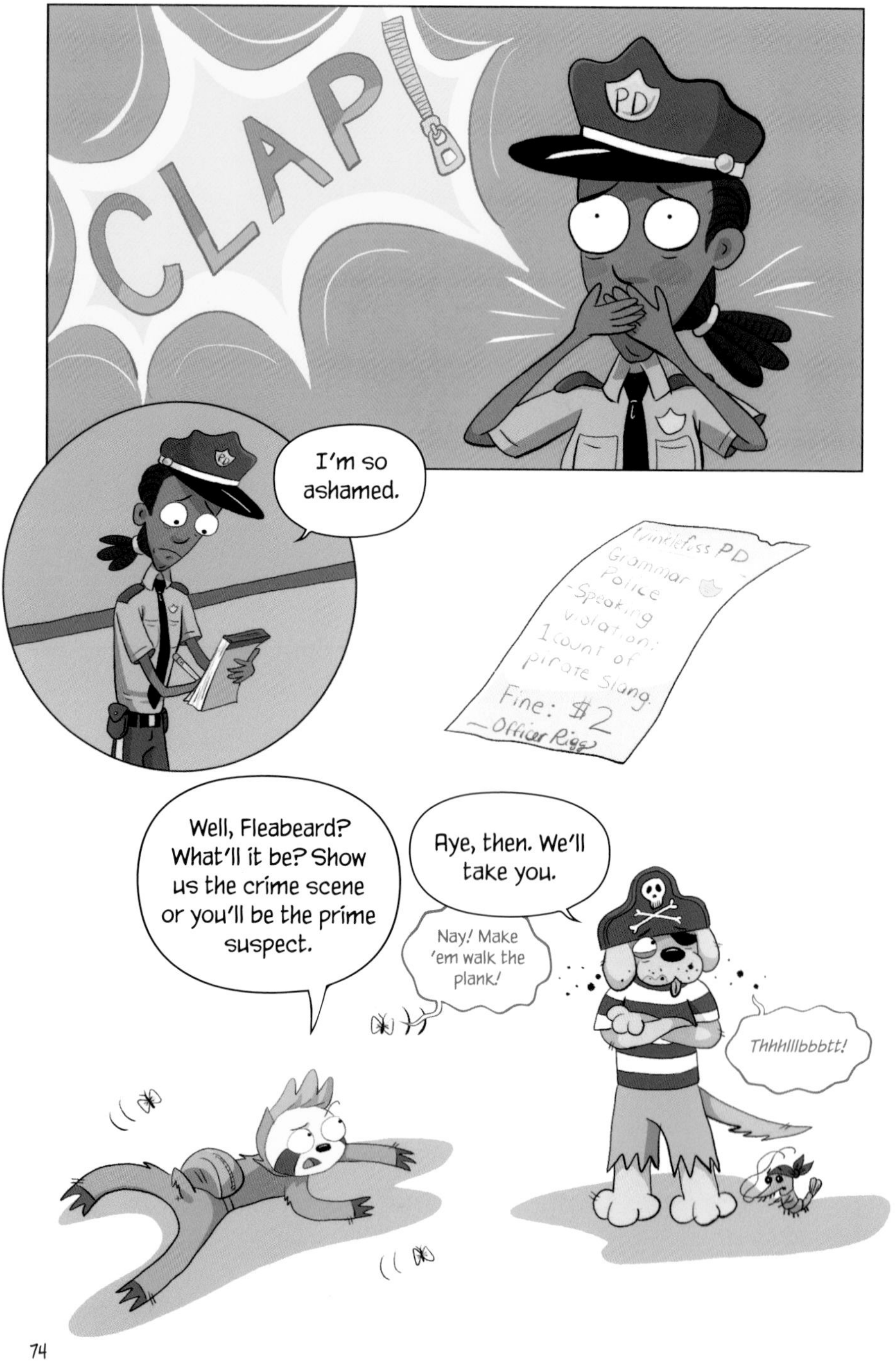
CLAP!
I'm so ashamed.
Twinklefoss PD Grammar Police
-Speaking violation: 1 count of pirate slang.
Fine: $2
—Officer Rigg
Well, Fleabeard? What'll it be? Show us the crime scene or you'll be the prime suspect.
Aye, then. We'll take you.
Nay! Make 'em walk the plank!
Thhhlllbbbtt!

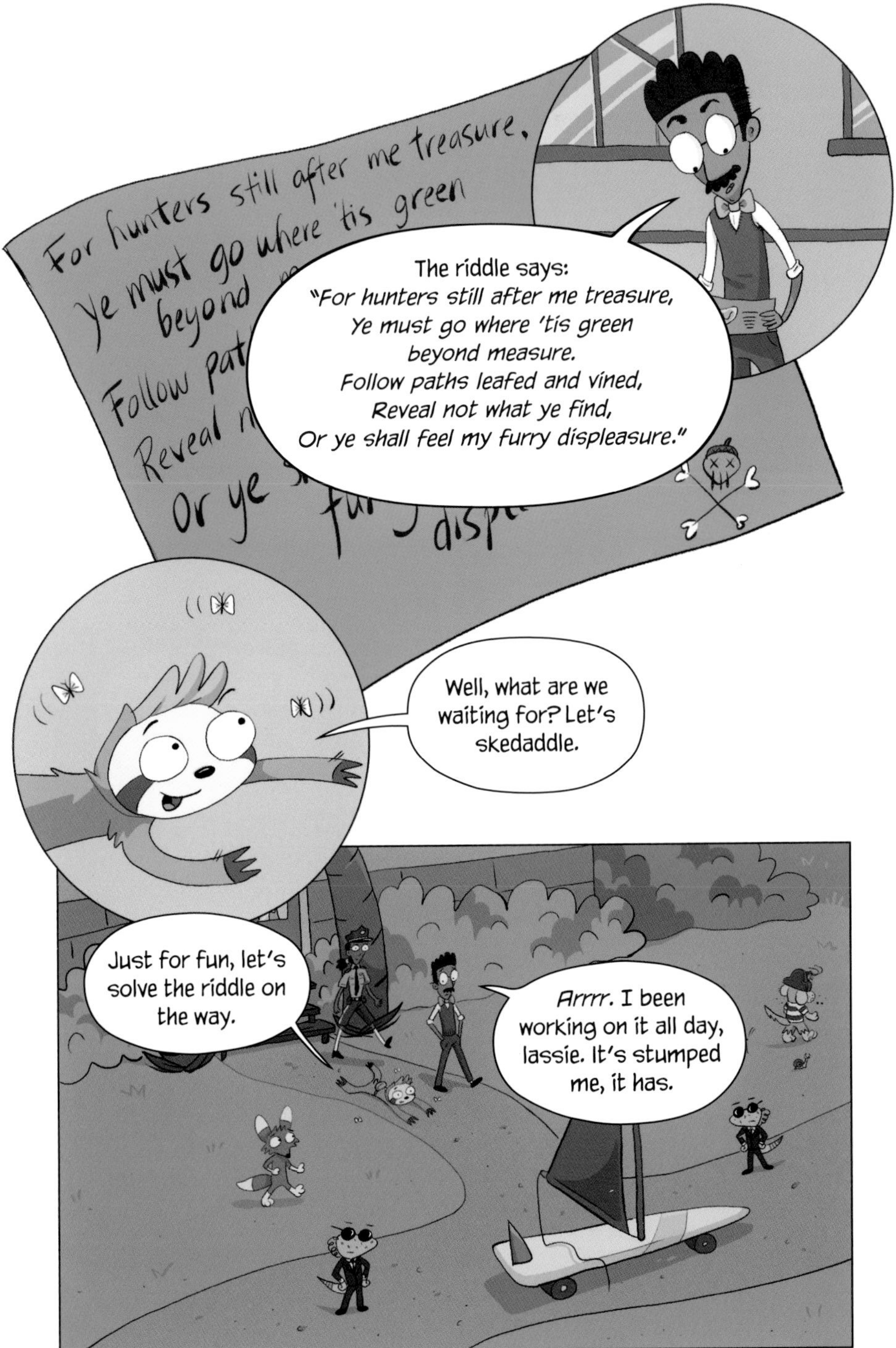
For hunters still after me treasure,
Ye must go where 'tis green
The riddle says:
"For hunters still after me treasure,
Ye must go where 'tis green
beyond measure.
Follow paths leafed and vined,
Reveal not what ye find,
Or ye shall feel my furry displeasure."
Well, what are we waiting for? Let's skedaddle.
Just for fun, let's solve the riddle on the way.
Arrrr. I been working on it all day, lassie. It's stumped me, it has.

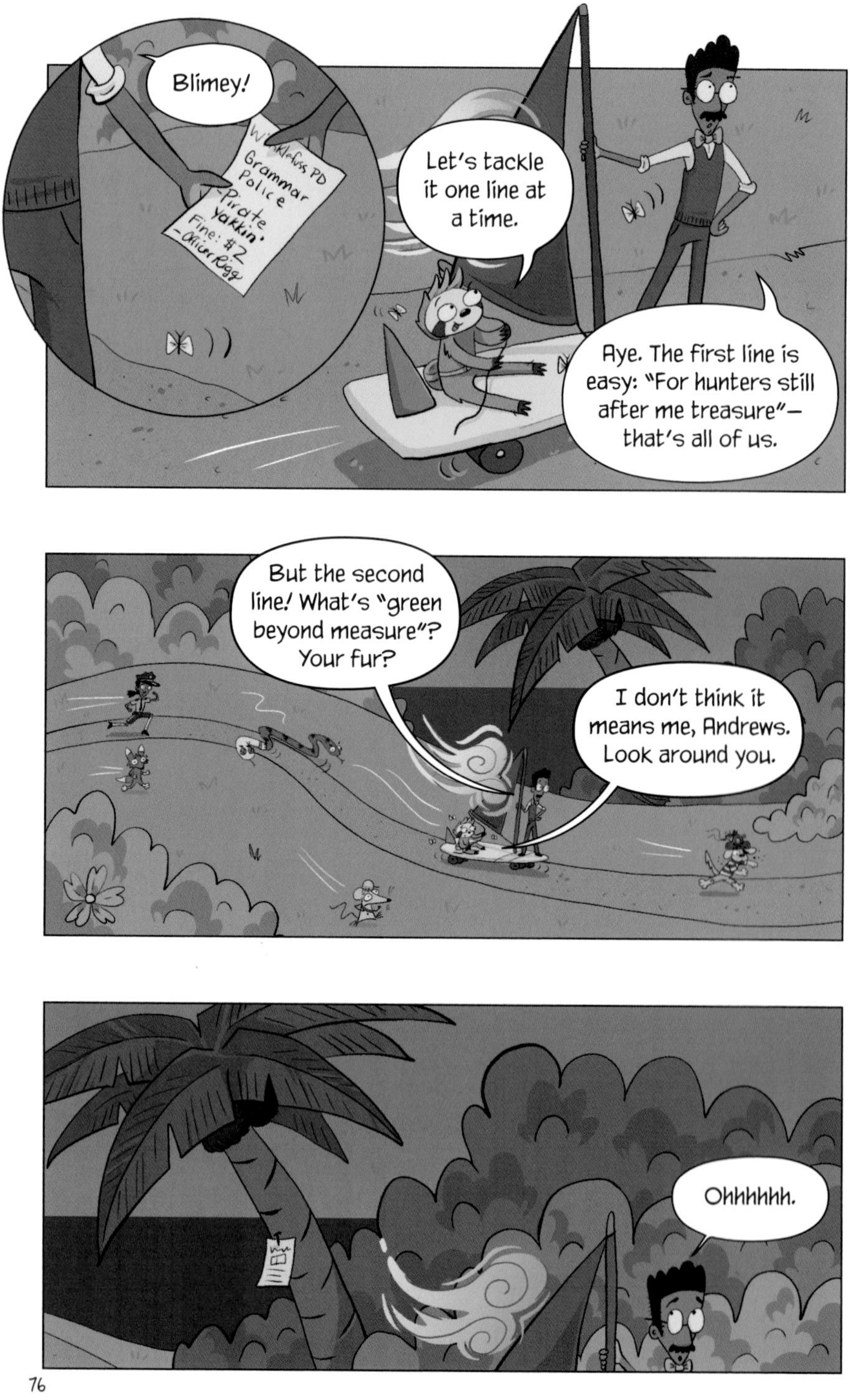
Blimey!
Winklefuss PD
Grammar Police
-Pirate Yakkin'
Fine: $2
-Officer Rigg
Let's tackle it one line at a time.
Aye. The first line is easy: "For hunters still after me treasure"— that's all of us.
But the second line! What's "green beyond measure"? Your fur?
I don't think it means me, Andrews. Look around you.
Ohhhhhh.

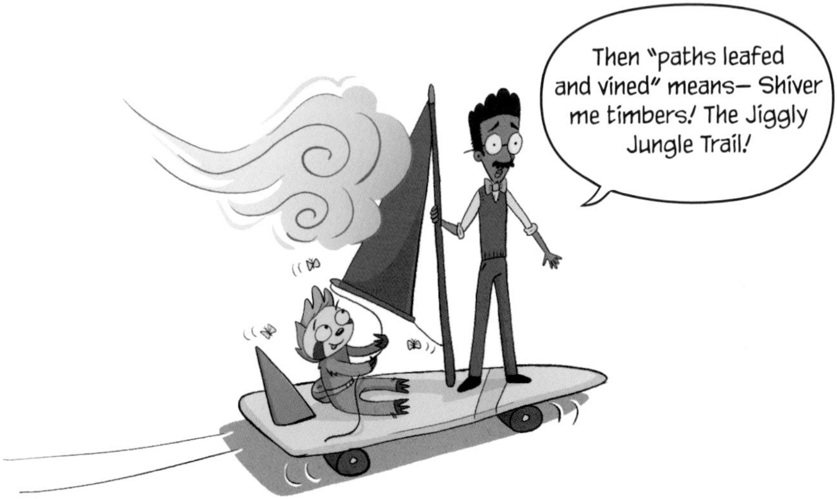
Then "paths leafed and vined" means— Shiver me timbers! The Jiggly Jungle Trail!

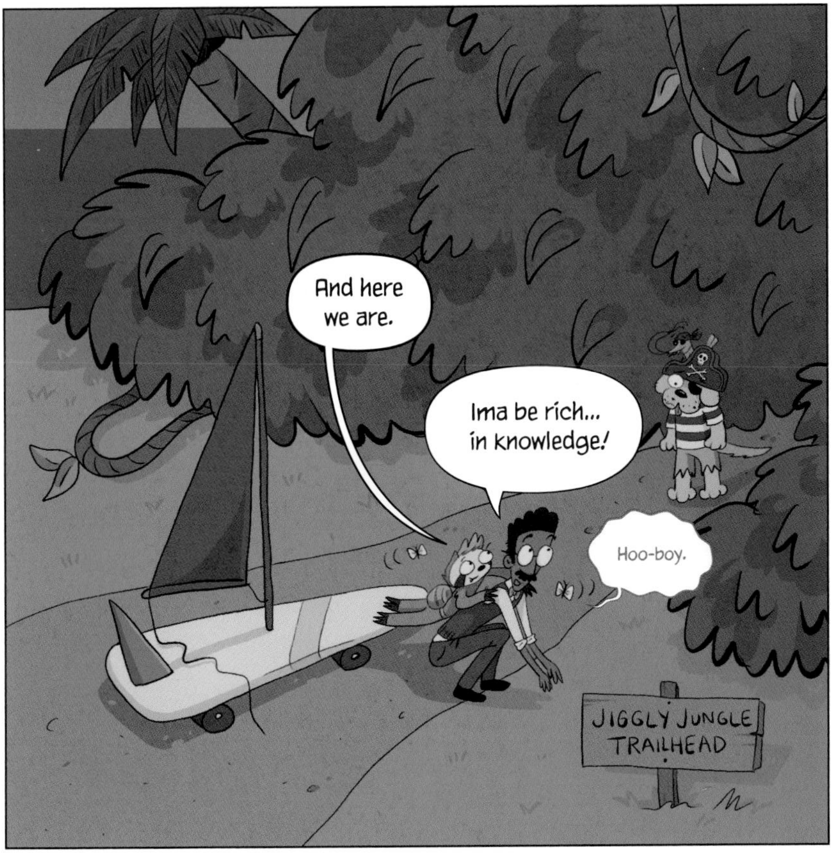
And here we are.
Ima be rich... in knowledge!
Hoo-boy.
JIGGLY JUNGLE TRAILHEAD

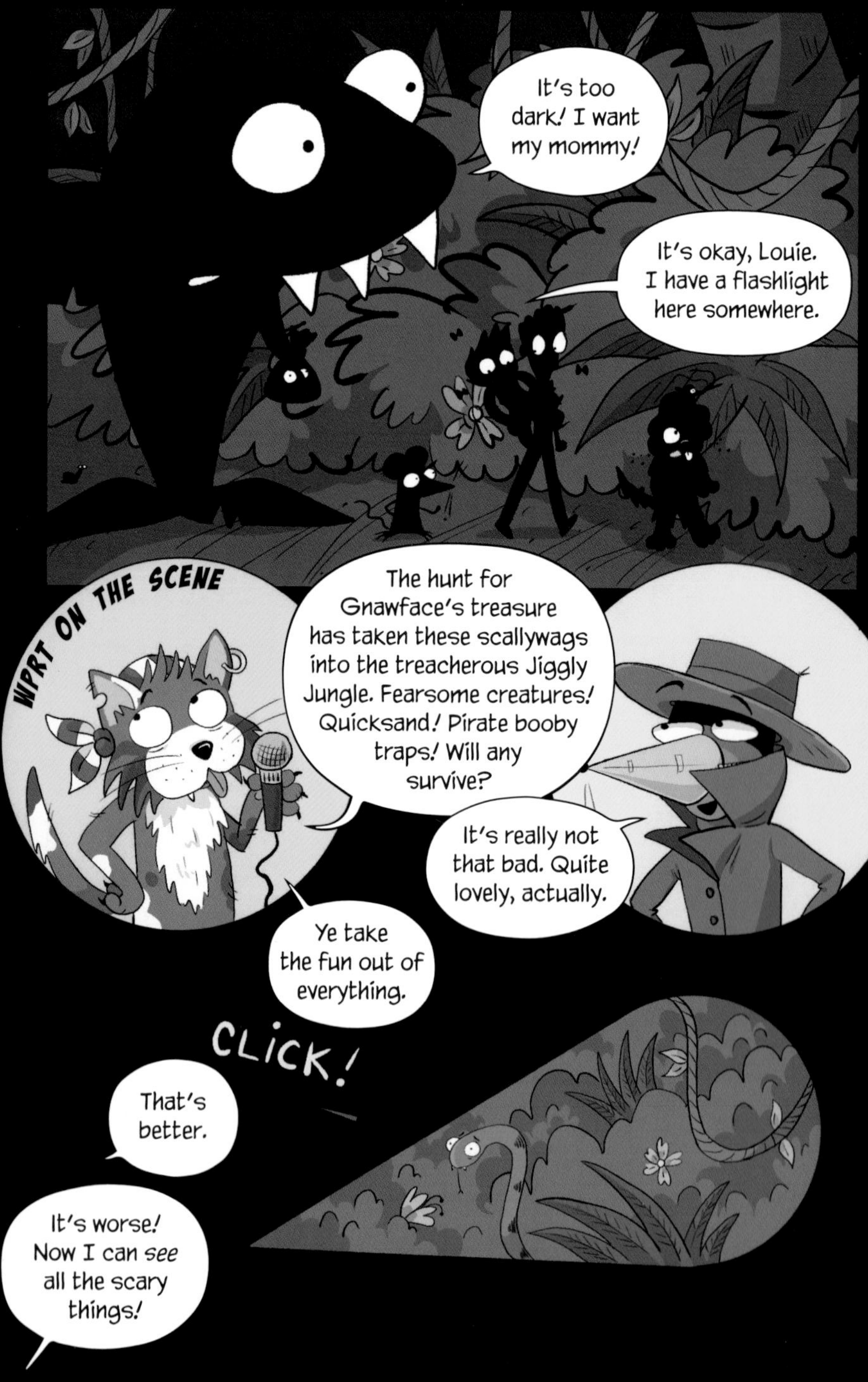
It's too dark! I want my mommy!
It's okay, Louie. I have a flashlight here somewhere.
WPRT ON THE SCENE
The hunt for Gnawface's treasure has taken these scallywags into the treacherous Jiggly Jungle. Fearsome creatures! Quicksand! Pirate booby traps! Will any survive?
It's really not that bad. Quite lovely, actually.
Ye take the fun out of everything.
CLICK!
That's better.
It's worse! Now I can *see* all the scary things!

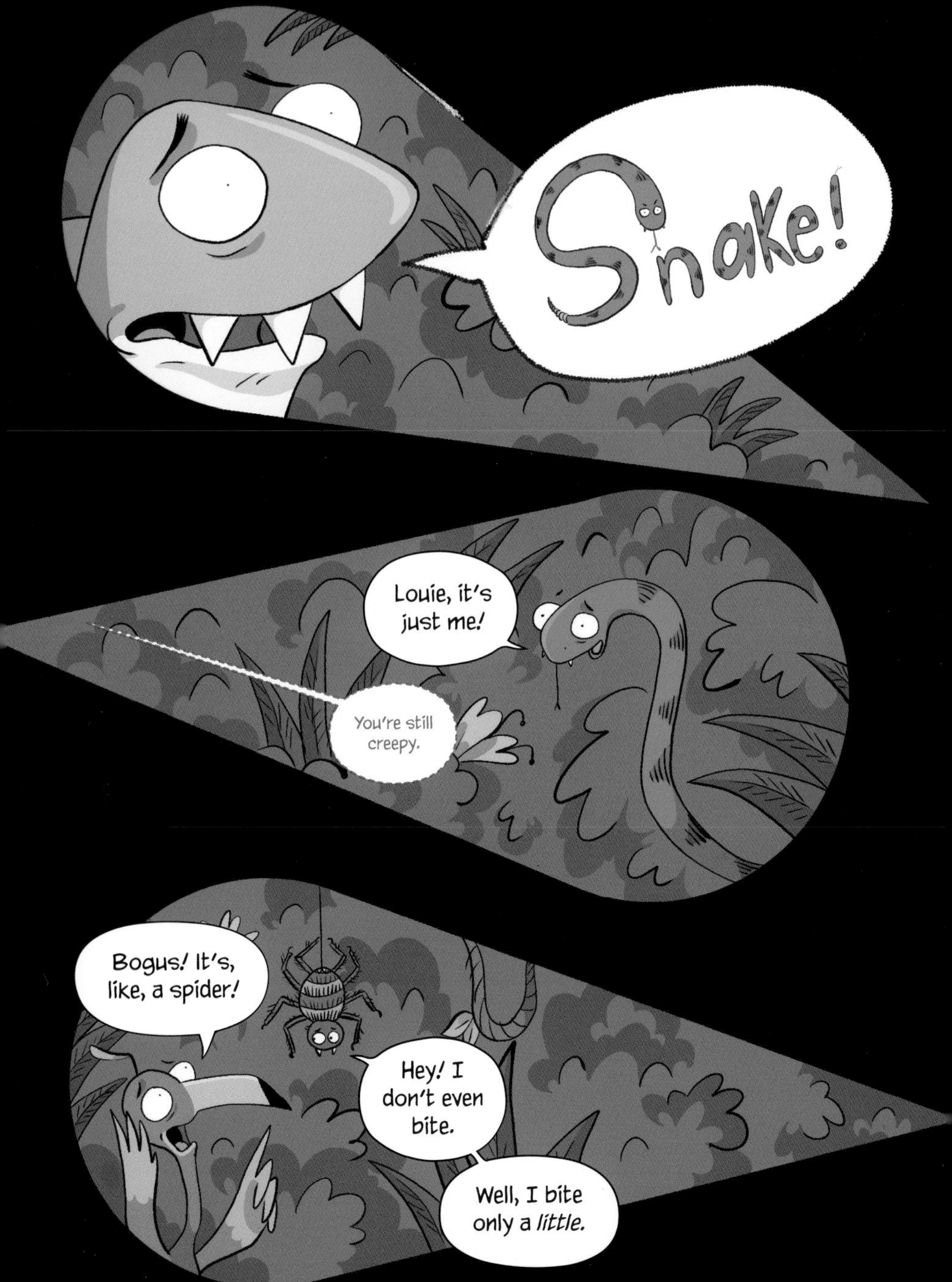

Snake!
Louie, it's just me!
You're still creepy.
Bogus! It's, like, a spider!
Hey! I don't even bite.
Well, I bite only a *little.*

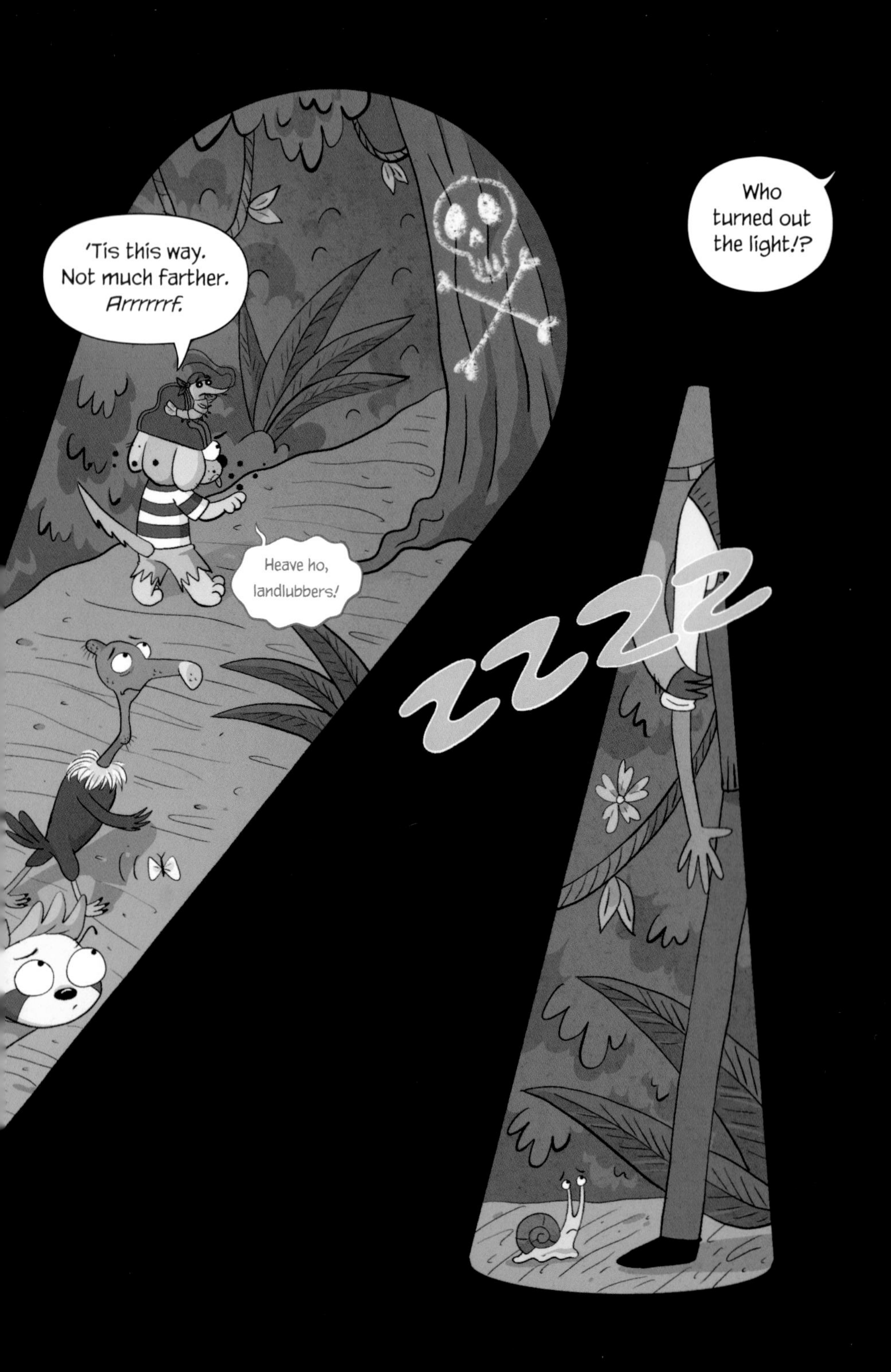
'Tis this way. Not much farther. *Arrrrrrf.*
Heave ho, landlubbers!
Who turned out the light!?
ZZZZ

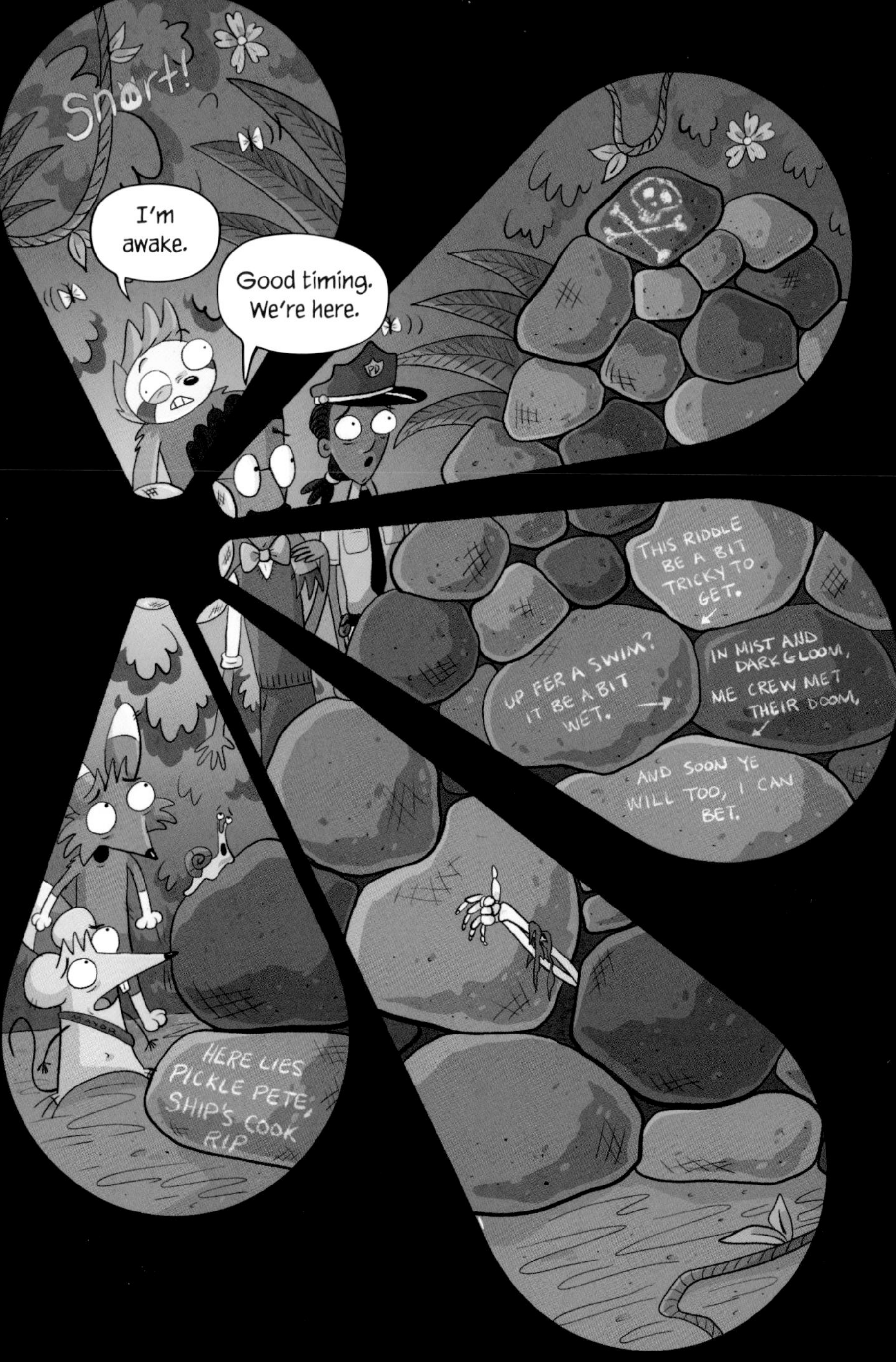
Snort!
I'm awake.
Good timing. We're here.
THIS RIDDLE BE A BIT TRICKY TO GET.
UP FER A SWIM? IT BE A BIT WET.
IN MIST AND DARK GLOOM, ME CREW MET THEIR DOOM,
AND SOON YE WILL TOO, I CAN BET.
HERE LIES PICKLE PETE, SHIP'S COOK RIP

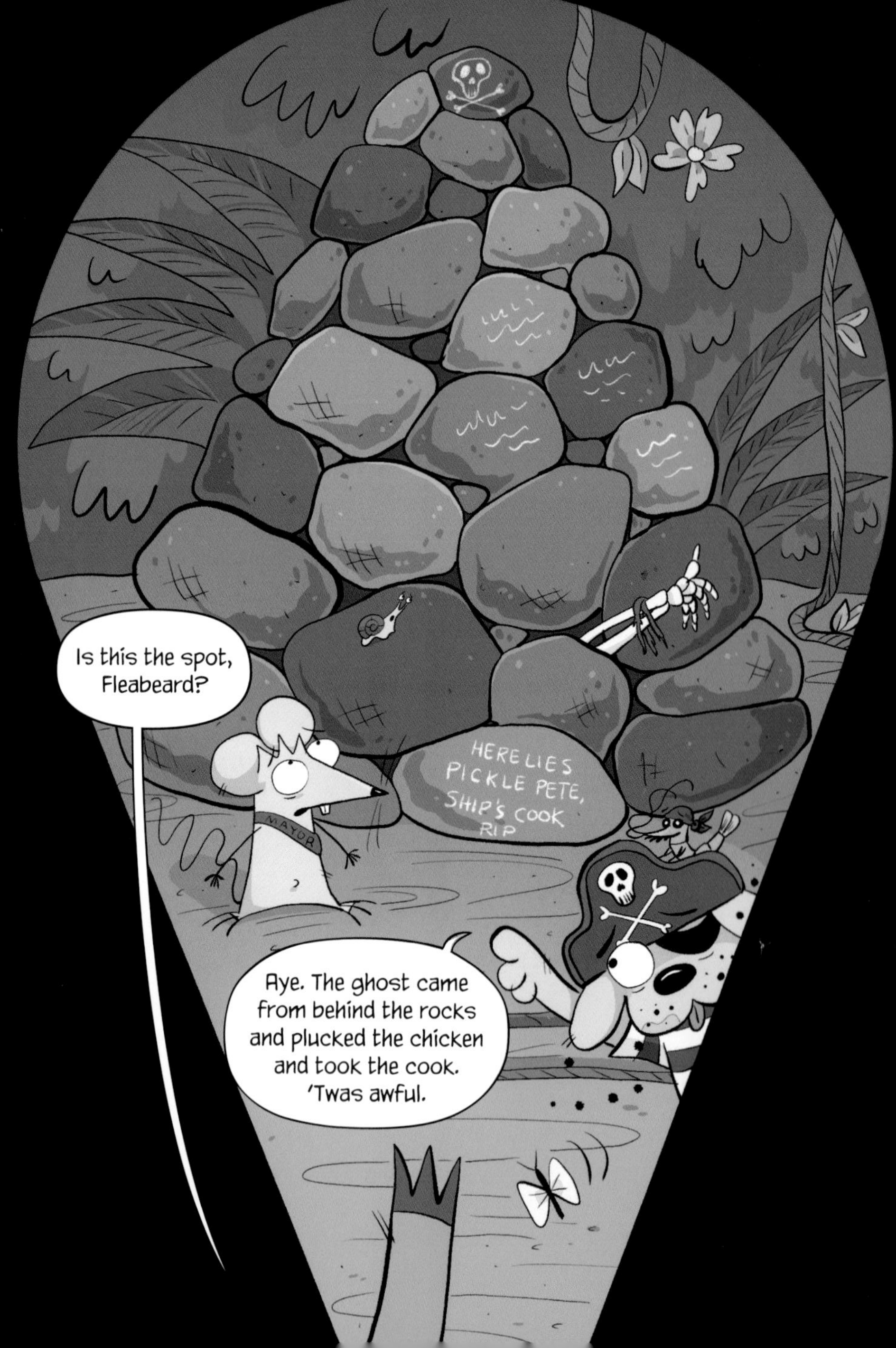
Is this the spot, Fleabeard?
HERE LIES PICKLE PETE, SHIP'S COOK RIP
MAYOR
Aye. The ghost came from behind the rocks and plucked the chicken and took the cook. 'Twas awful.

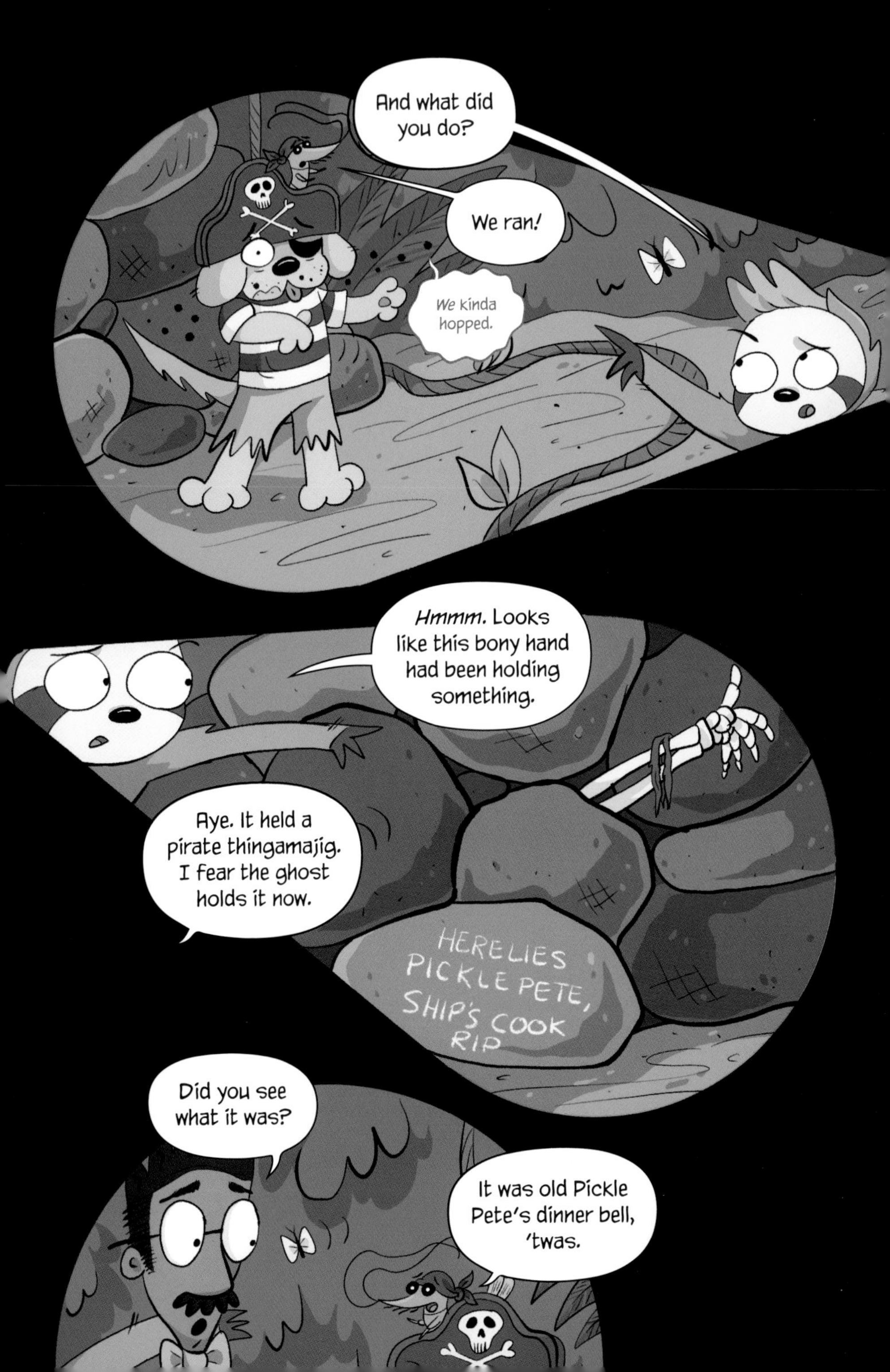
And what did you do?
We ran!
We kinda hopped.
Hmmm. Looks like this bony hand had been holding something.
Aye. It held a pirate thingamajig. I fear the ghost holds it now.
HERE LIES PICKLE PETE, SHIP'S COOK RIP
Did you see what it was?
It was old Pickle Pete's dinner bell, 'twas.

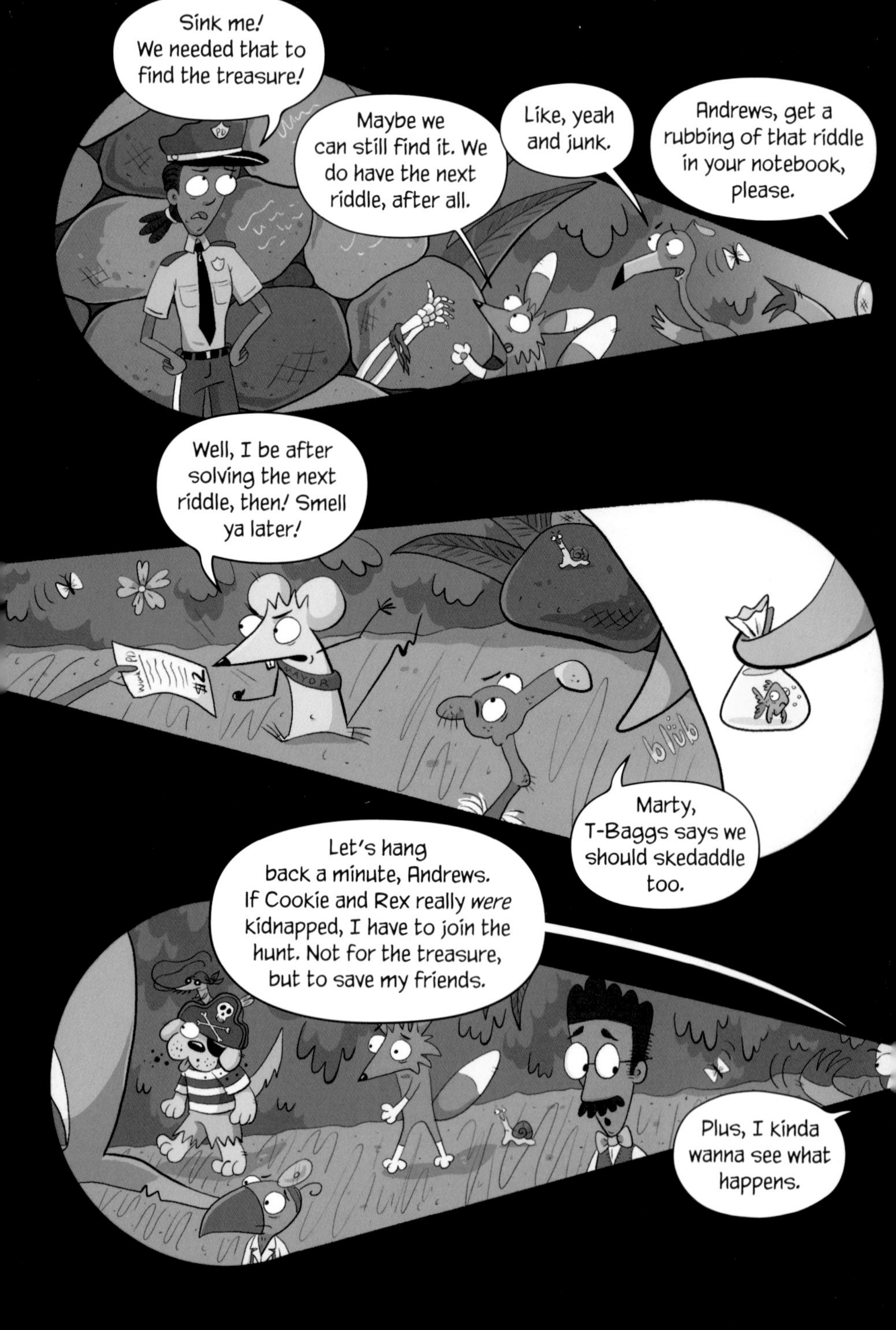
Sink me! We needed that to find the treasure!
Maybe we can still find it. We do have the next riddle, after all.
Like, yeah and junk.
Andrews, get a rubbing of that riddle in your notebook, please.
Well, I be after solving the next riddle, then! Smell ya later!
MAYOR
#2
blub
Marty, T-Baggs says we should skedaddle too.
Let's hang back a minute, Andrews. If Cookie and Rex really *were* kidnapped, I have to join the hunt. Not for the treasure, but to save my friends.
Plus, I kinda wanna see what happens.

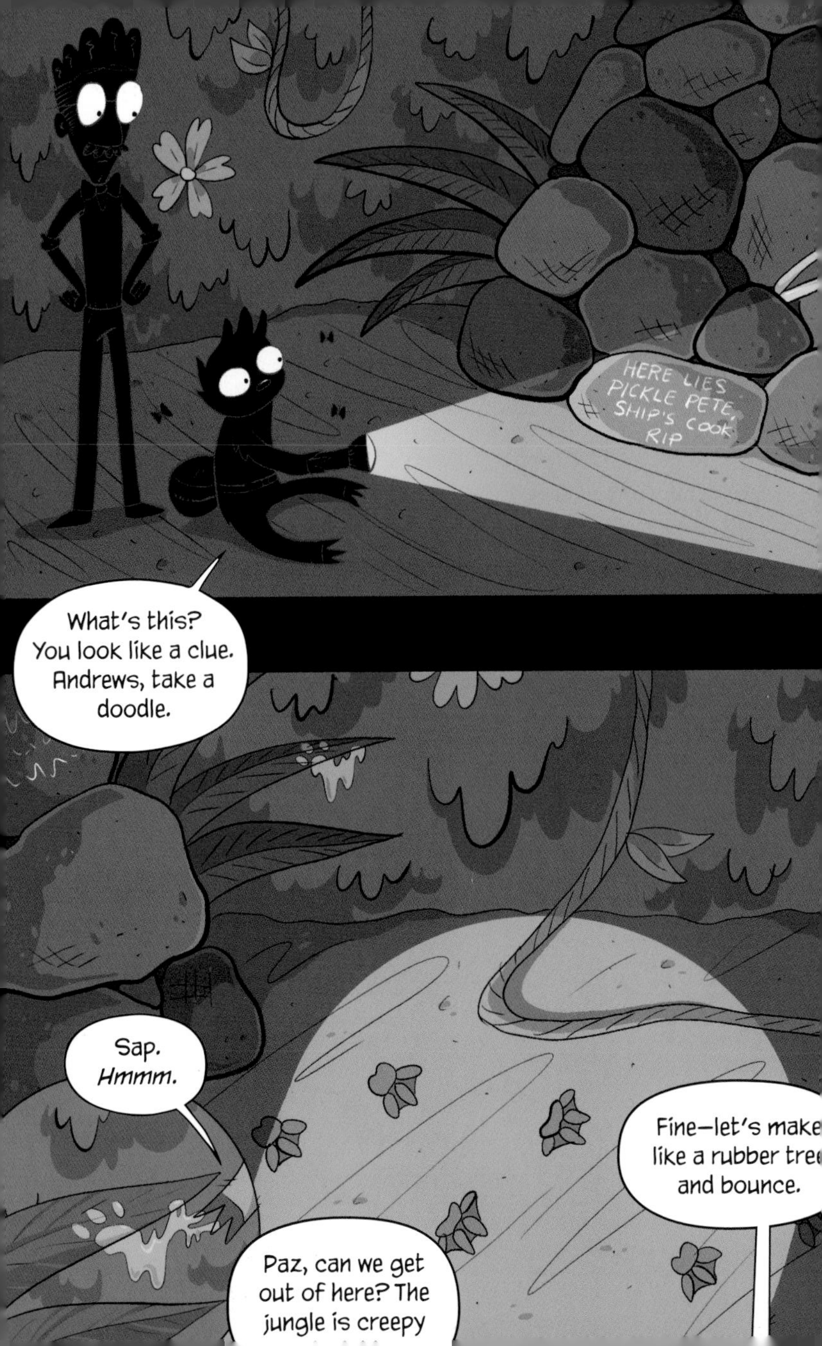
HERE LIES PICKLE PETE, SHIP'S COOK RIP
What's this? You look like a clue. Andrews, take a doodle.
Sap. *Hmmm.*
Fine—let's make like a rubber tree and bounce.
Paz, can we get out of here? The jungle is creepy

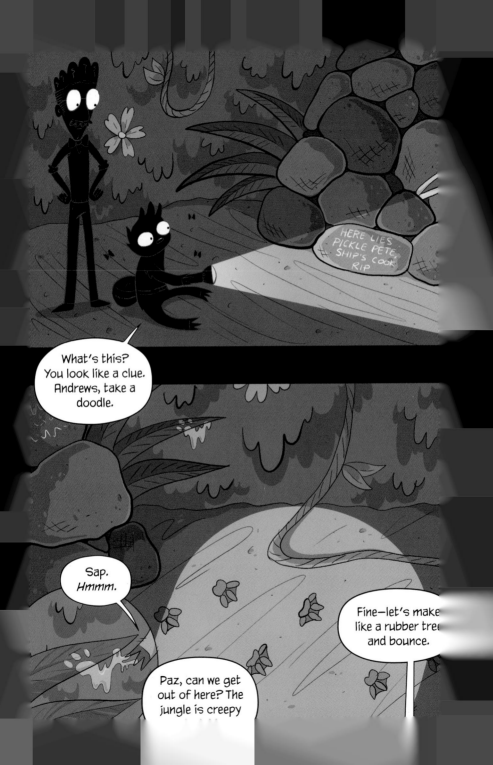

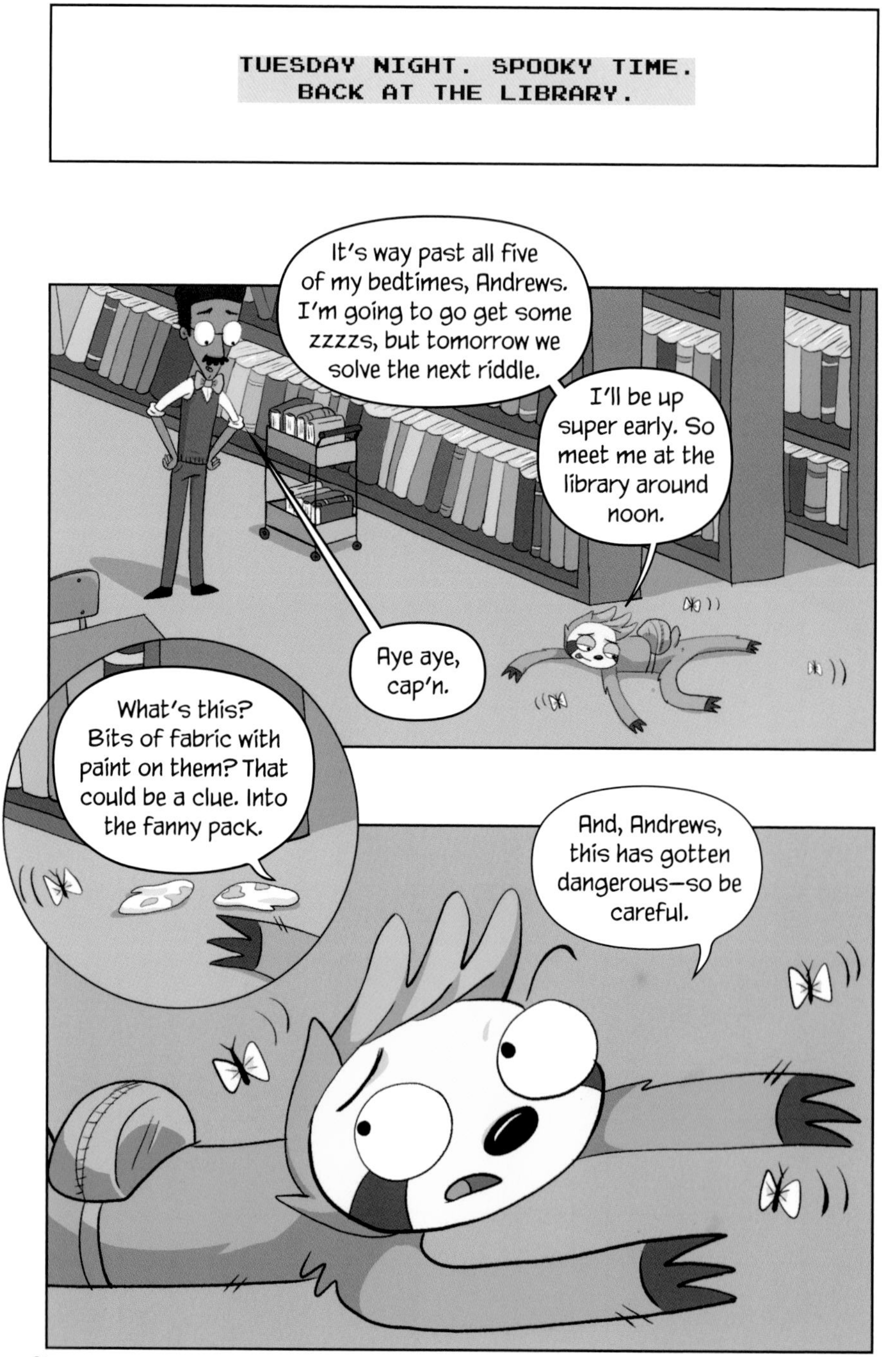
TUESDAY NIGHT. SPOOKY TIME.
BACK AT THE LIBRARY.
It's way past all five of my bedtimes, Andrews. I'm going to go get some zzzzs, but tomorrow we solve the next riddle.
I'll be up super early. So meet me at the library around noon.
Aye aye, cap'n.
What's this? Bits of fabric with paint on them? That could be a clue. Into the fanny pack.
And, Andrews, this has gotten dangerous—so be careful.

CHAPTER 5

WEDNESDAY. DARK AND EARLY.
WAKING UP IN THE TREEHOUSE.

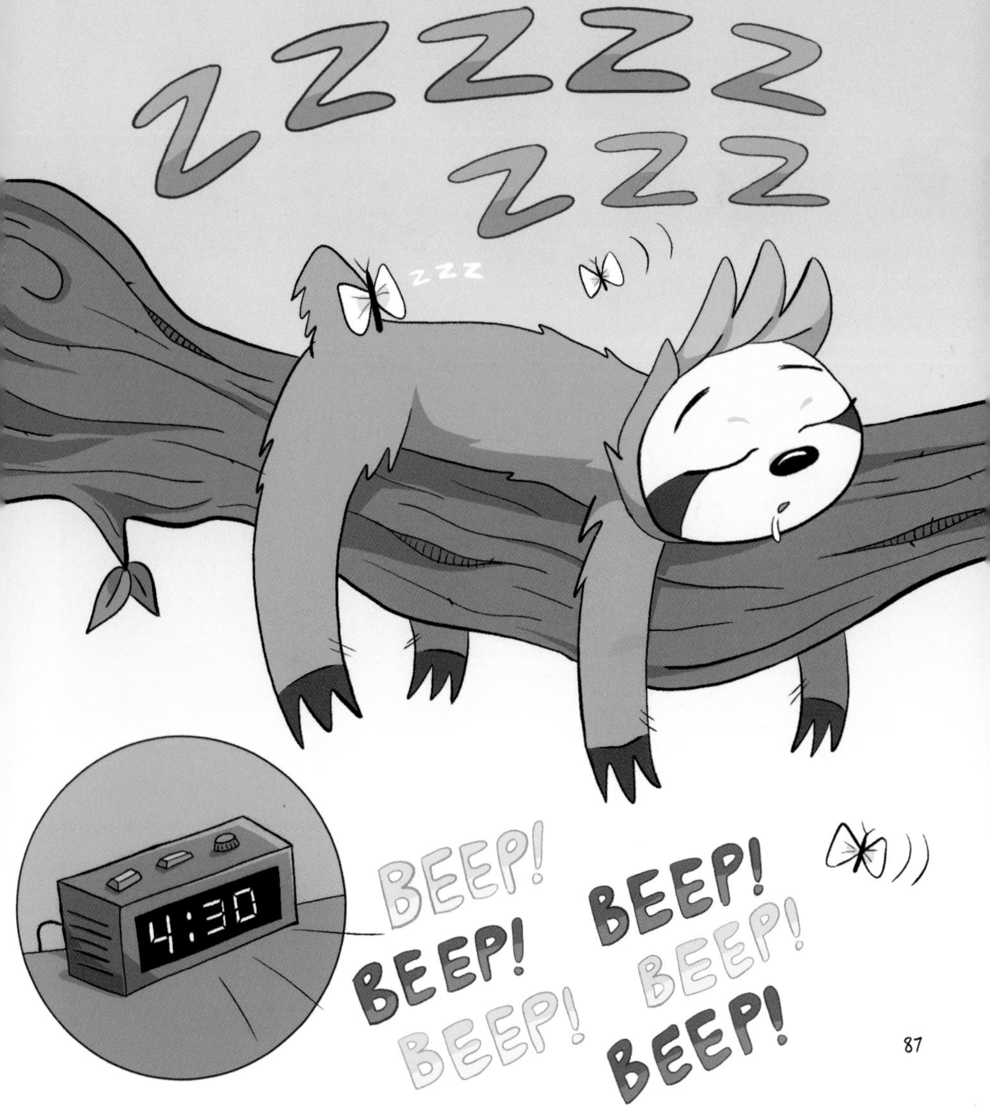
ZZZZZ
ZZZ
ZZZ
4:30
BEEP!
BEEP!
BEEP!
BEEP!
BEEP!
BEEP!
BEEP!

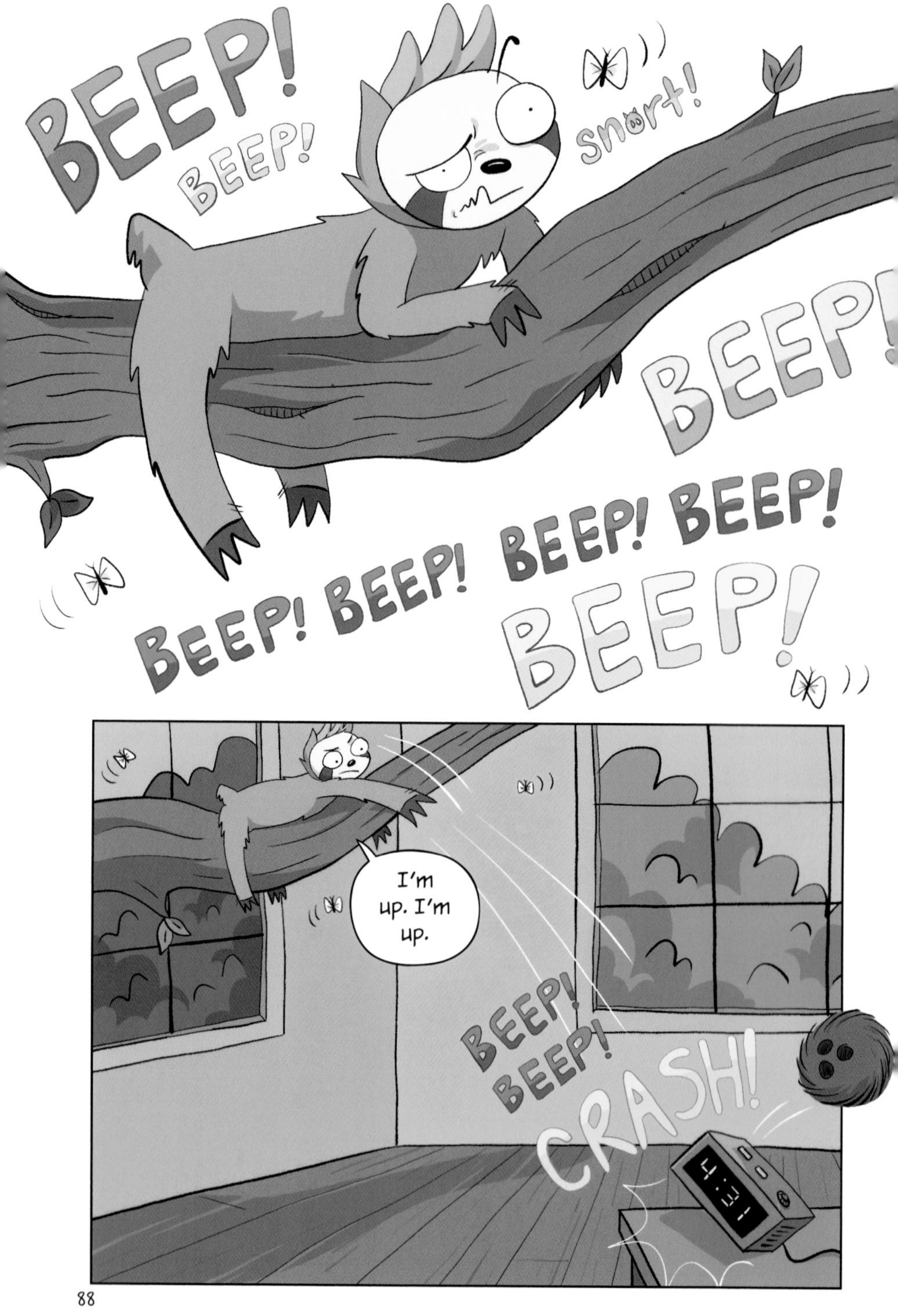
BEEP!
BEEP!
Snort!
BEEP!
BEEP! BEEP! BEEP! BEEP!
BEEP!
I'm up. I'm up.
BEEP!
BEEP!
CRASH!

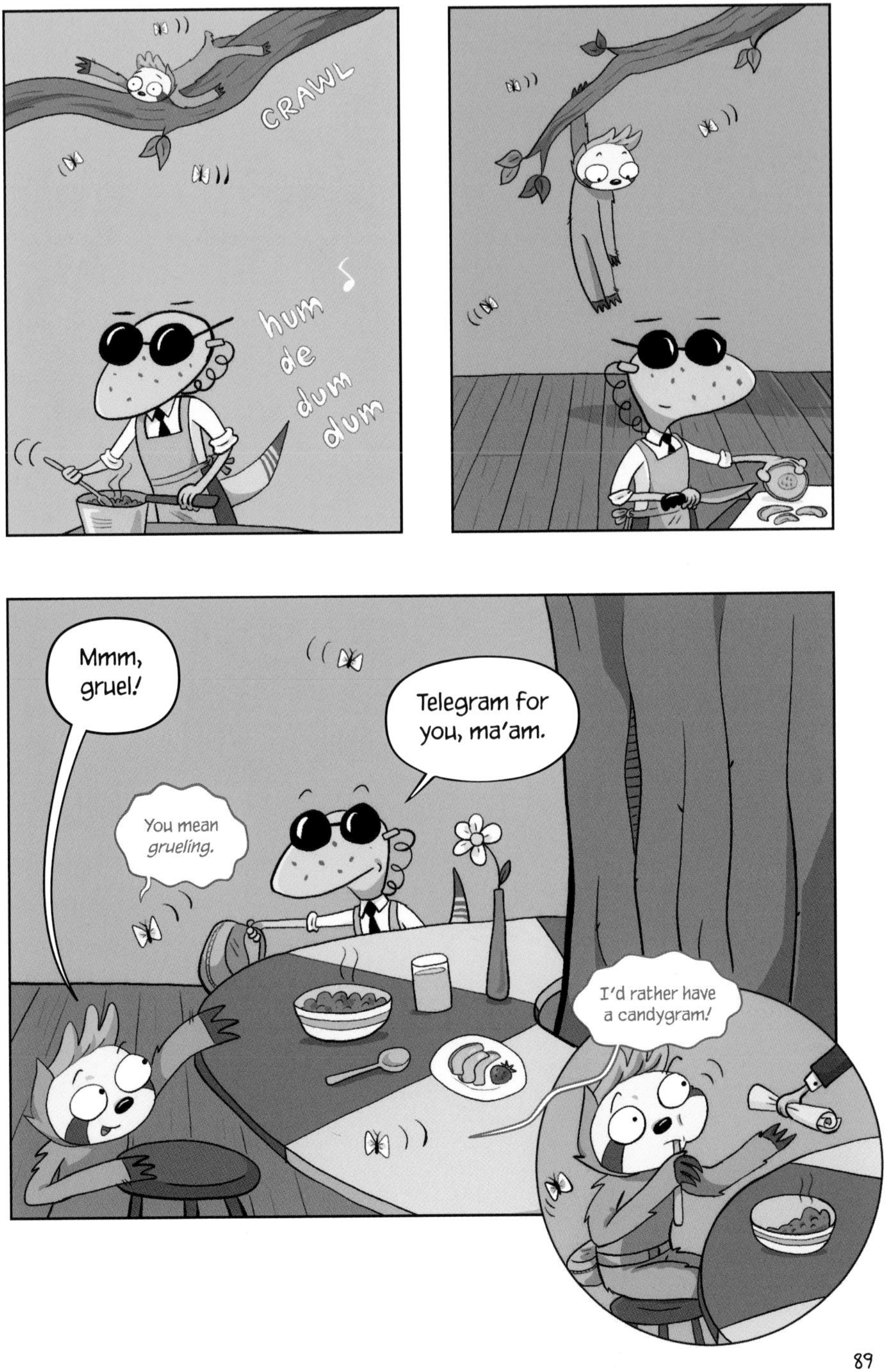
CRAWL
hum de dum dum
Mmm, gruel!
Telegram for you, ma'am.
You mean *grueling.*
I'd rather have a candygram!

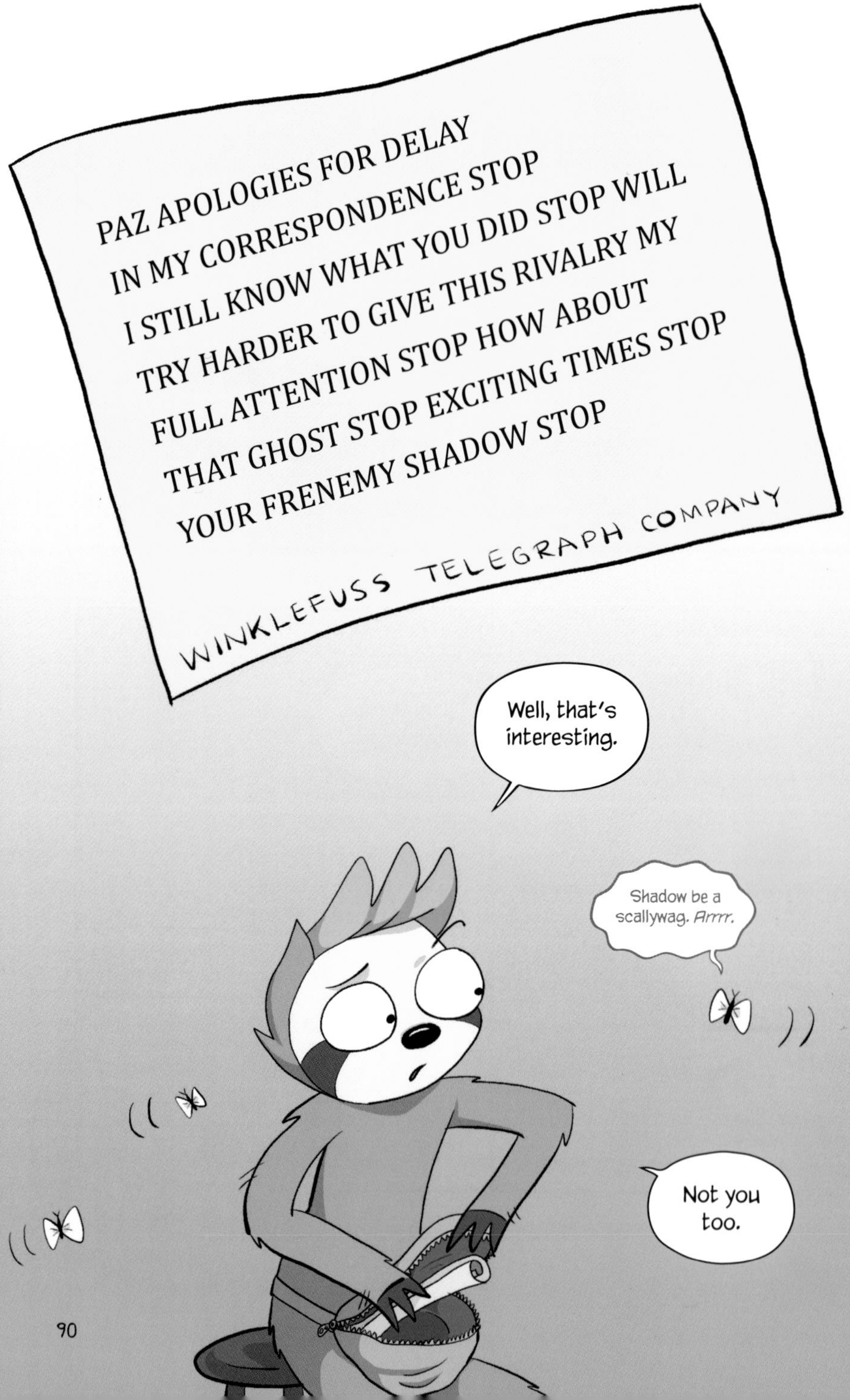
PAZ APOLOGIES FOR DELAY
IN MY CORRESPONDENCE STOP
I STILL KNOW WHAT YOU DID STOP WILL
TRY HARDER TO GIVE THIS RIVALRY MY
FULL ATTENTION STOP HOW ABOUT
THAT GHOST STOP EXCITING TIMES STOP
YOUR FRENEMY SHADOW STOP
WINKLEFUSS TELEGRAPH COMPANY
Well, that's interesting.
Shadow be a scallywag. *Arrrr.*
Not you too.

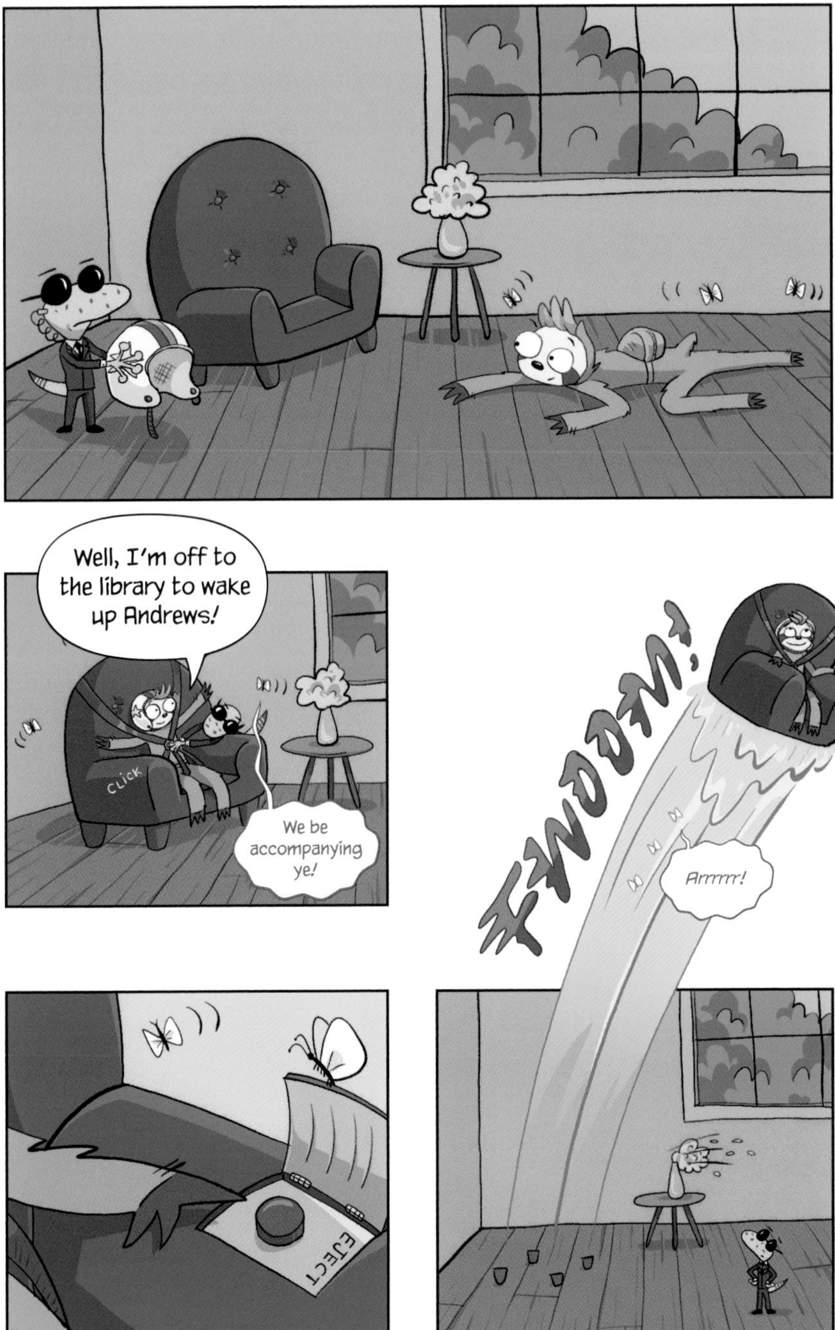

Well, I'm off to the library to wake up Andrews!
CLICK
We be accompanying ye!
FWOOM!
Arrrrrr!
EJECT

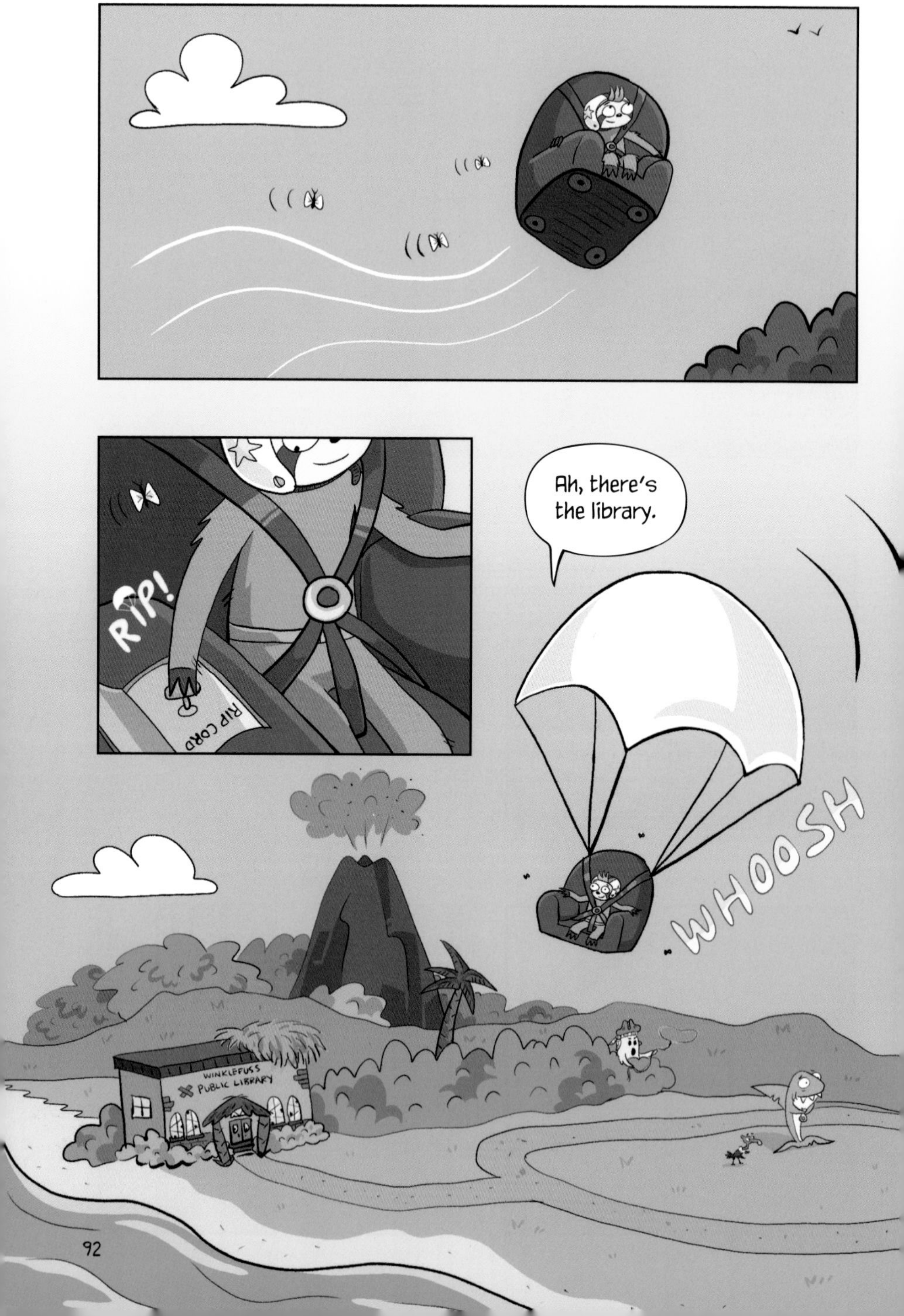
RIP!
RIP CORD
Ah, there's the library.
WHOOSH
WINKLEFUSS PUBLIC LIBRARY

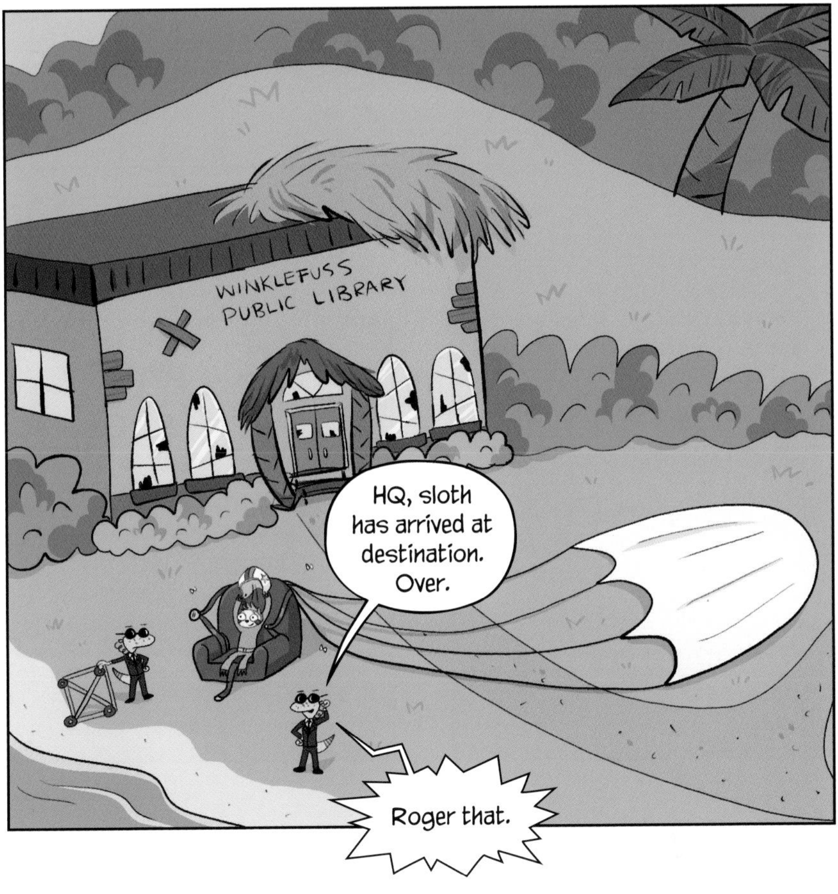
WINKLEFUSS PUBLIC LIBRARY
HQ, sloth has arrived at destination. Over.
Roger that.

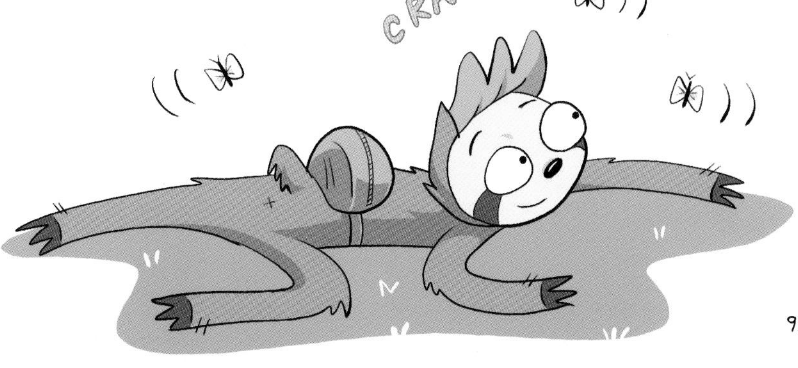
CRAWL

WEDNESDAY. SOMETIME LATER. IN THE STACKS.

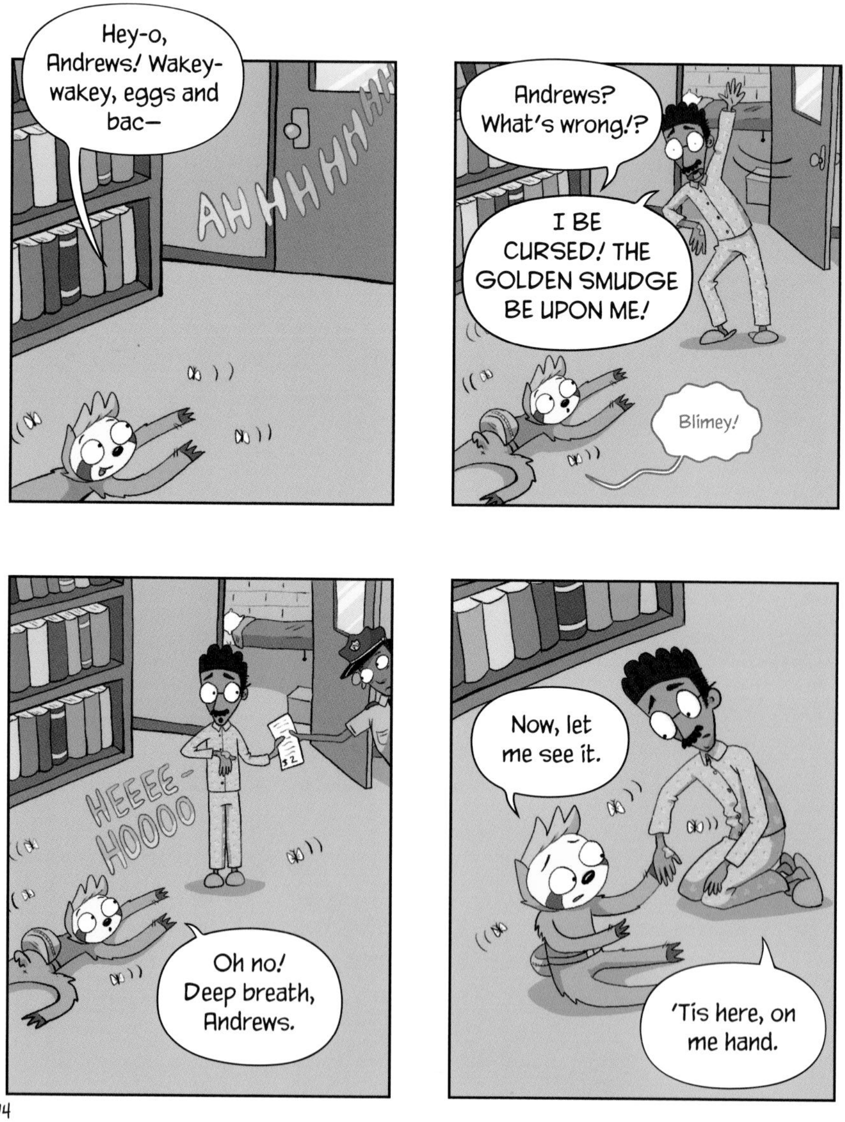
Hey-o, Andrews! Wakey-wakey, eggs and bac—
AHHHHHHH!
Andrews? What's wrong!?
I BE CURSED! THE GOLDEN SMUDGE BE UPON ME!
Blimey!
HEEEE-HOOOO
Oh no! Deep breath, Andrews.
Now, let me see it.
'Tis here, on me hand.

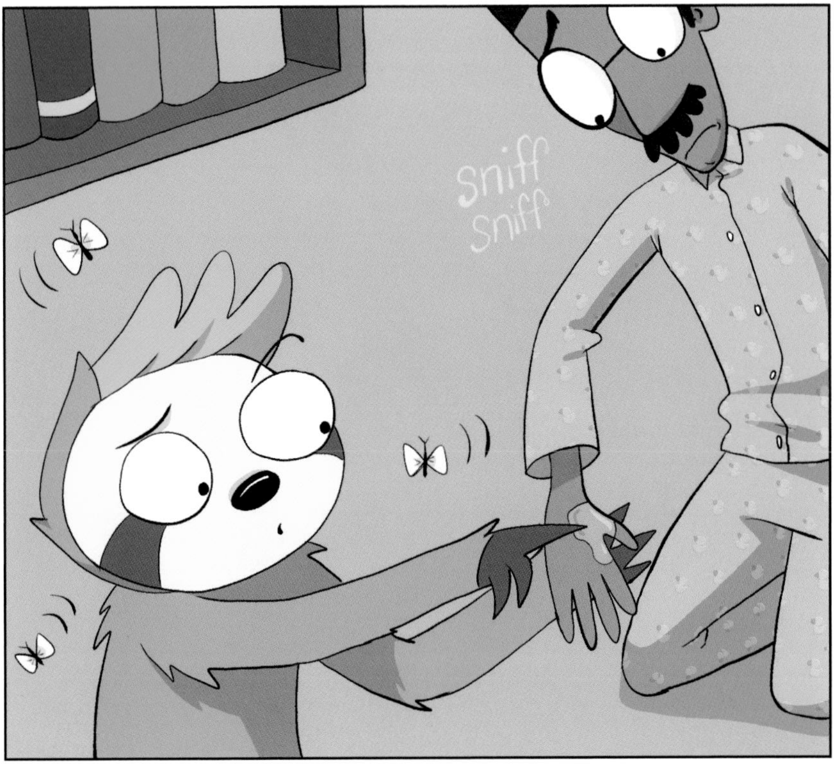
Sniff
Sniff

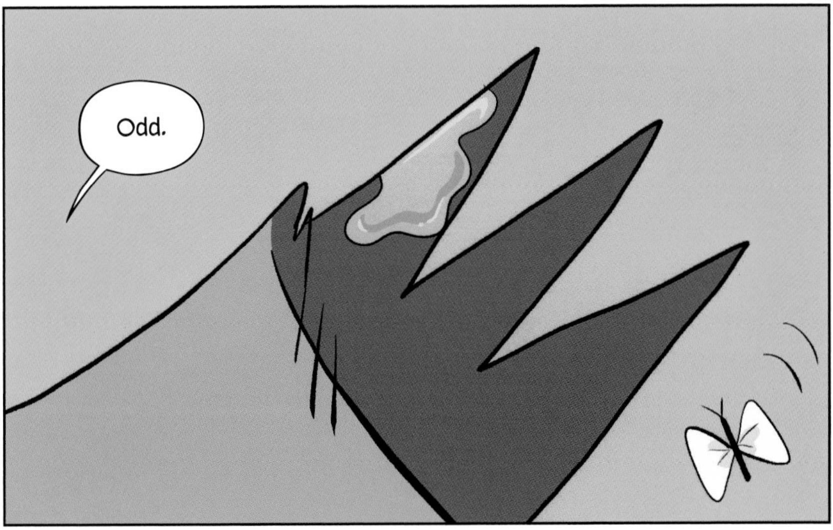
Odd.

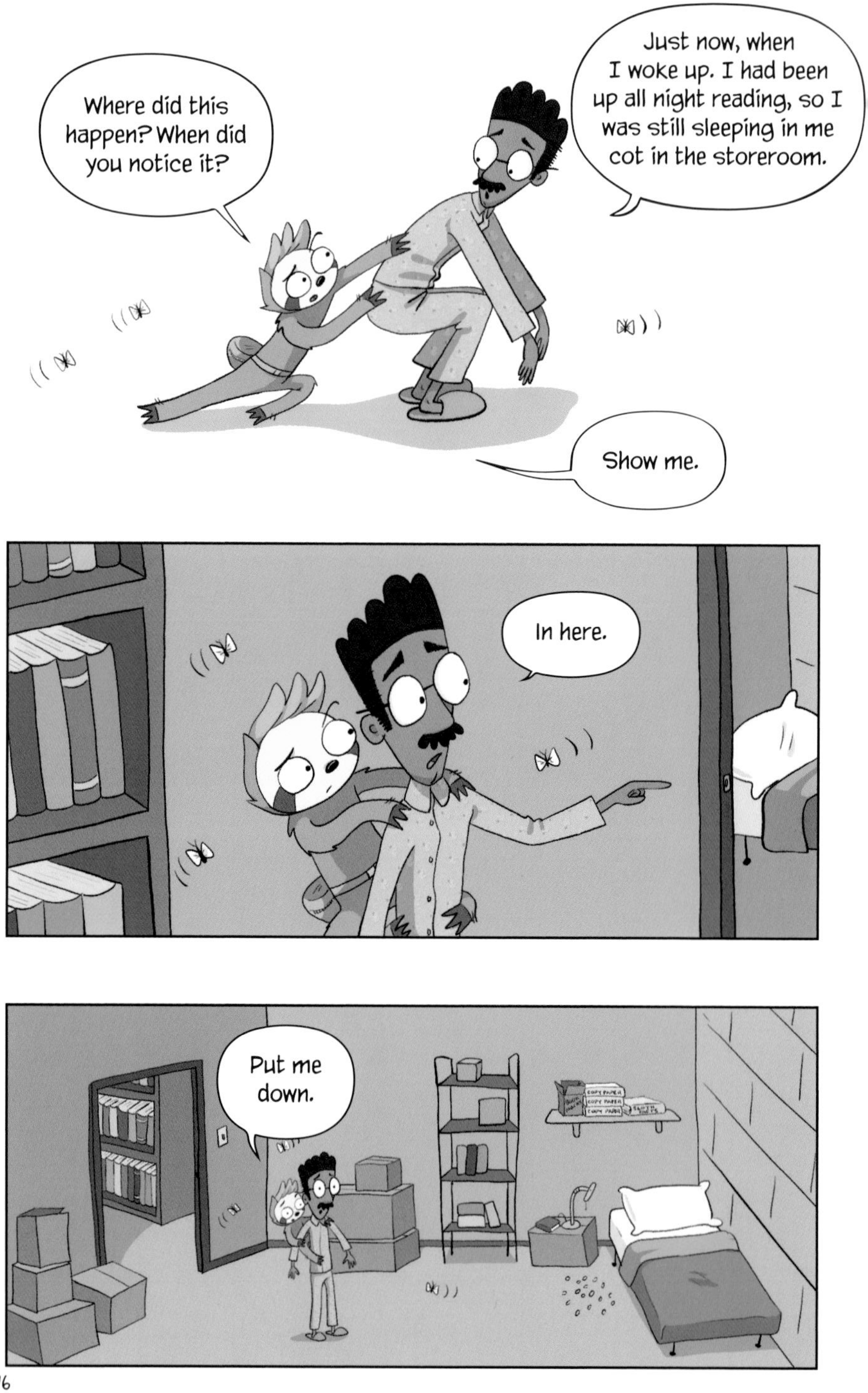
Where did this happen? When did you notice it?
Just now, when I woke up. I had been up all night reading, so I was still sleeping in me cot in the storeroom.
Show me.
In here.
Put me down.

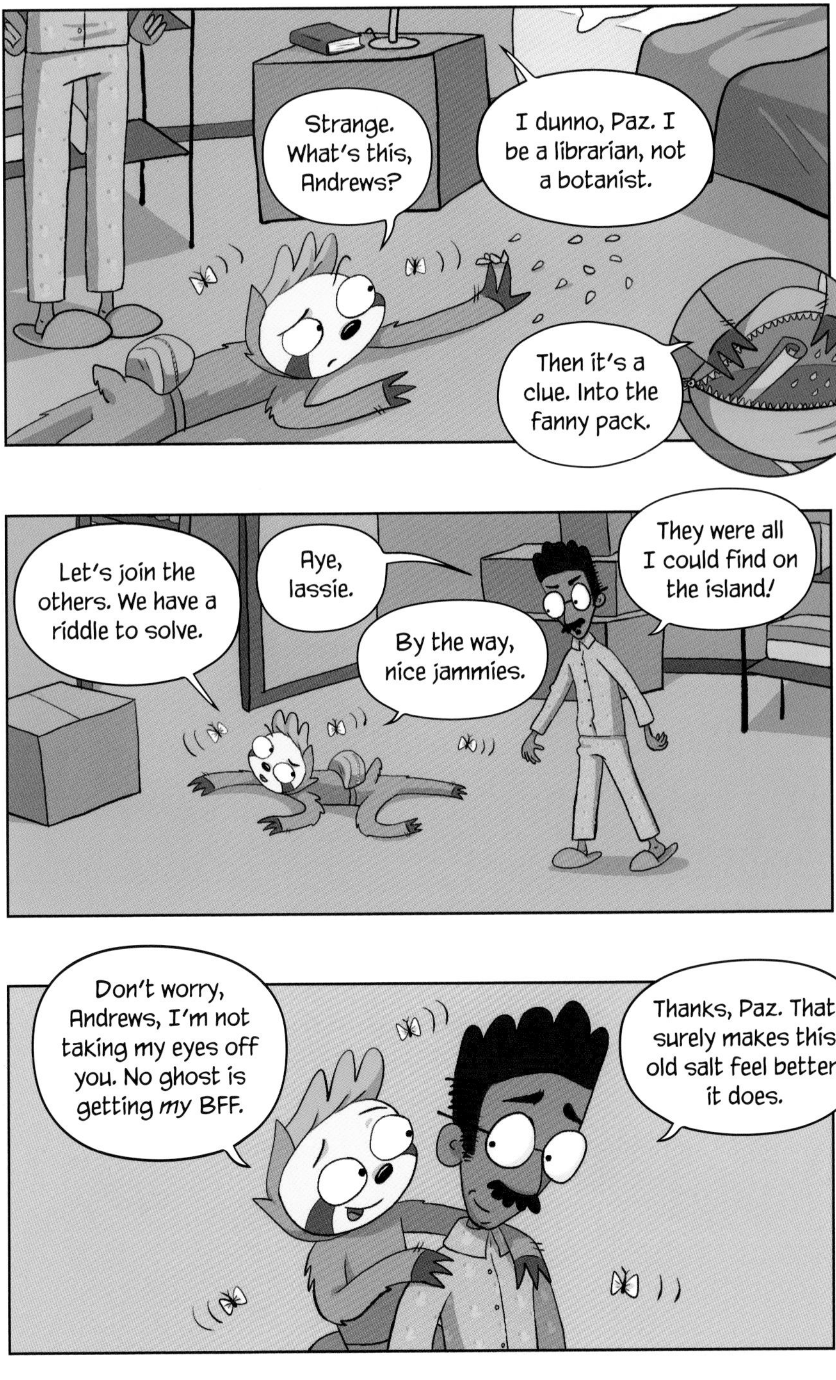
Strange. What's this, Andrews?
I dunno, Paz. I be a librarian, not a botanist.
Then it's a clue. Into the fanny pack.
Let's join the others. We have a riddle to solve.
Aye, lassie.
By the way, nice jammies.
They were all I could find on the island!
Don't worry, Andrews, I'm not taking my eyes off you. No ghost is getting *my* BFF.
Thanks, Paz. That surely makes this old salt feel better, it does.

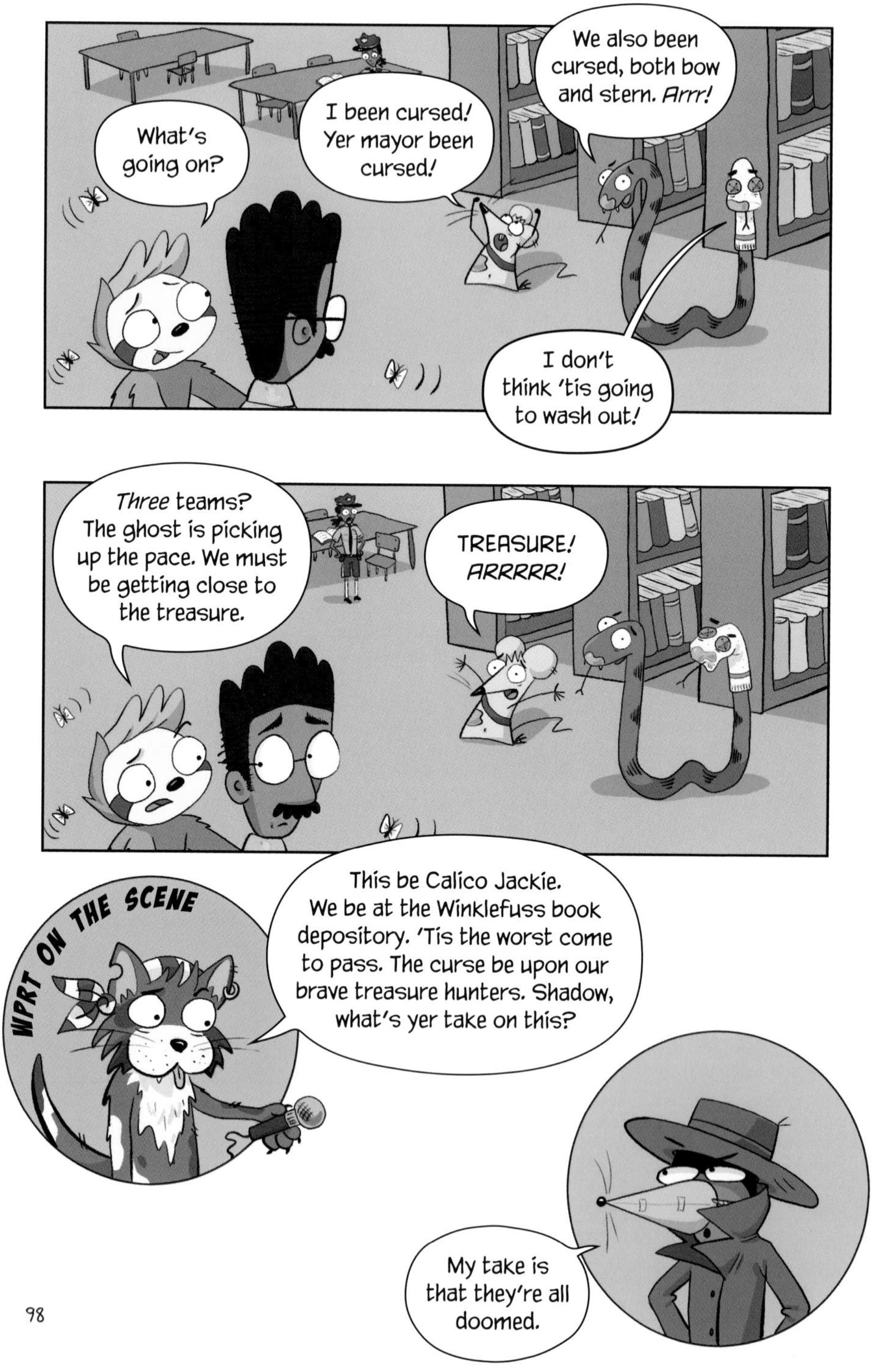
What's going on?
I been cursed! Yer mayor been cursed!
We also been cursed, both bow and stern. Arrr!
I don't think 'tis going to wash out!
Three teams? The ghost is picking up the pace. We must be getting close to the treasure.
TREASURE! ARRRRR!
WPRT ON THE SCENE
This be Calico Jackie. We be at the Winklefuss book depository. 'Tis the worst come to pass. The curse be upon our brave treasure hunters. Shadow, what's yer take on this?
My take is that they're all doomed.

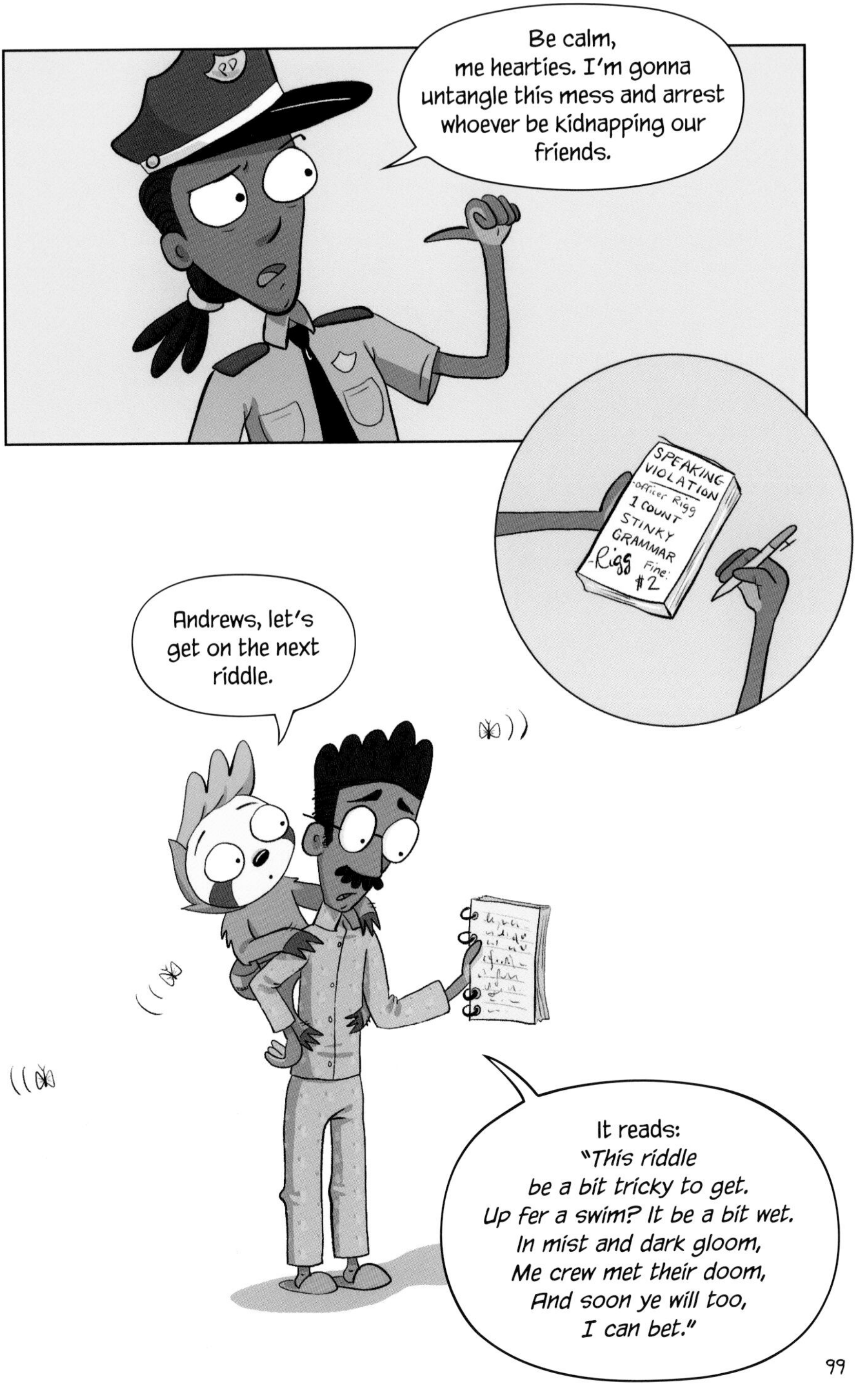
Be calm, me hearties. I'm gonna untangle this mess and arrest whoever be kidnapping our friends.
SPEAKING VIOLATION
-officer Rigg
1 COUNT STINKY GRAMMAR
-Rigg
Fine: #2
Andrews, let's get on the next riddle.
It reads: "This riddle be a bit tricky to get. Up fer a swim? It be a bit wet. In mist and dark gloom, Me crew met their doom, And soon ye will too, I can bet."

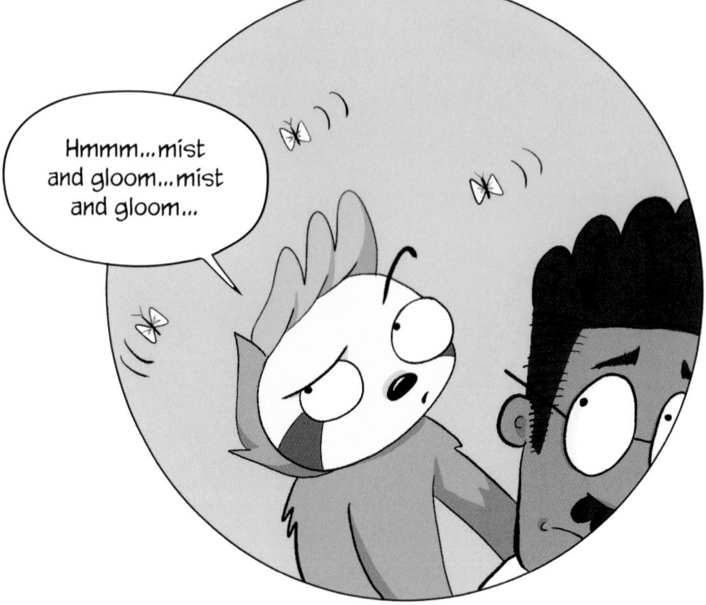
Hmmm...mist and gloom...mist and gloom...

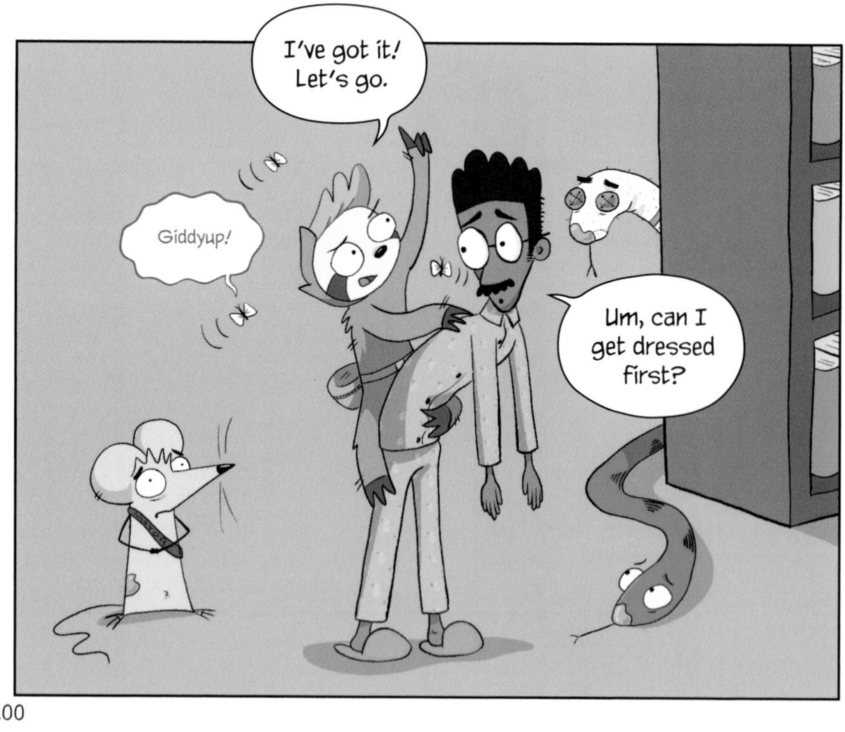
I've got it! Let's go.
Giddyup!
Um, can I get dressed first?

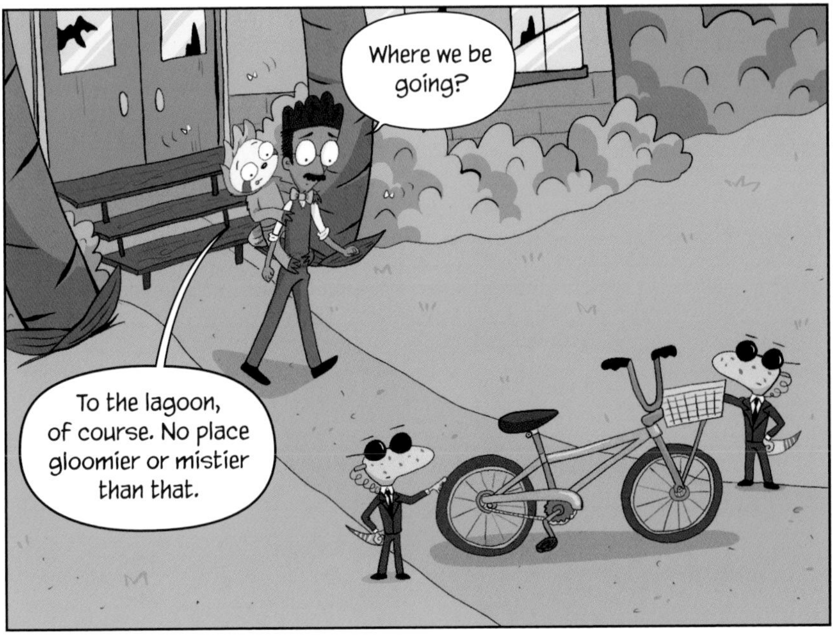
Where we be going?
To the lagoon, of course. No place gloomier or mistier than that.

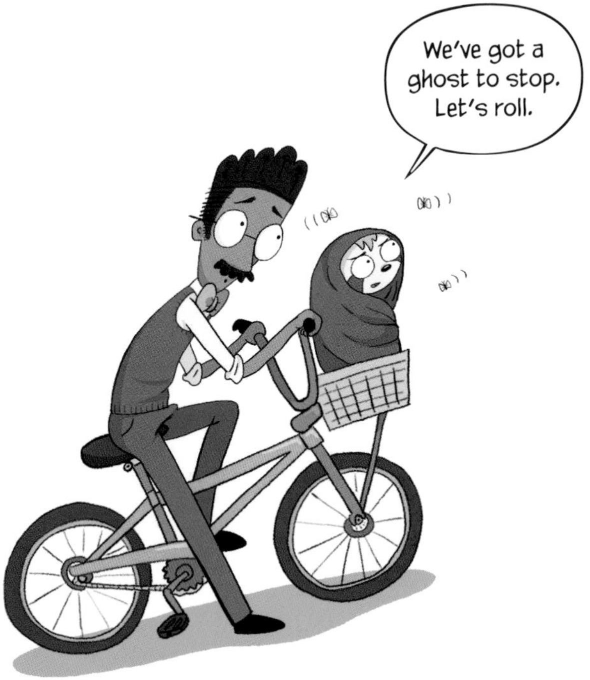
We've got a ghost to stop. Let's roll.

CHAPTER 6

WEDNESDAY. LATE AFTERNOON.
IN A BOAT ON THE LAGOON.

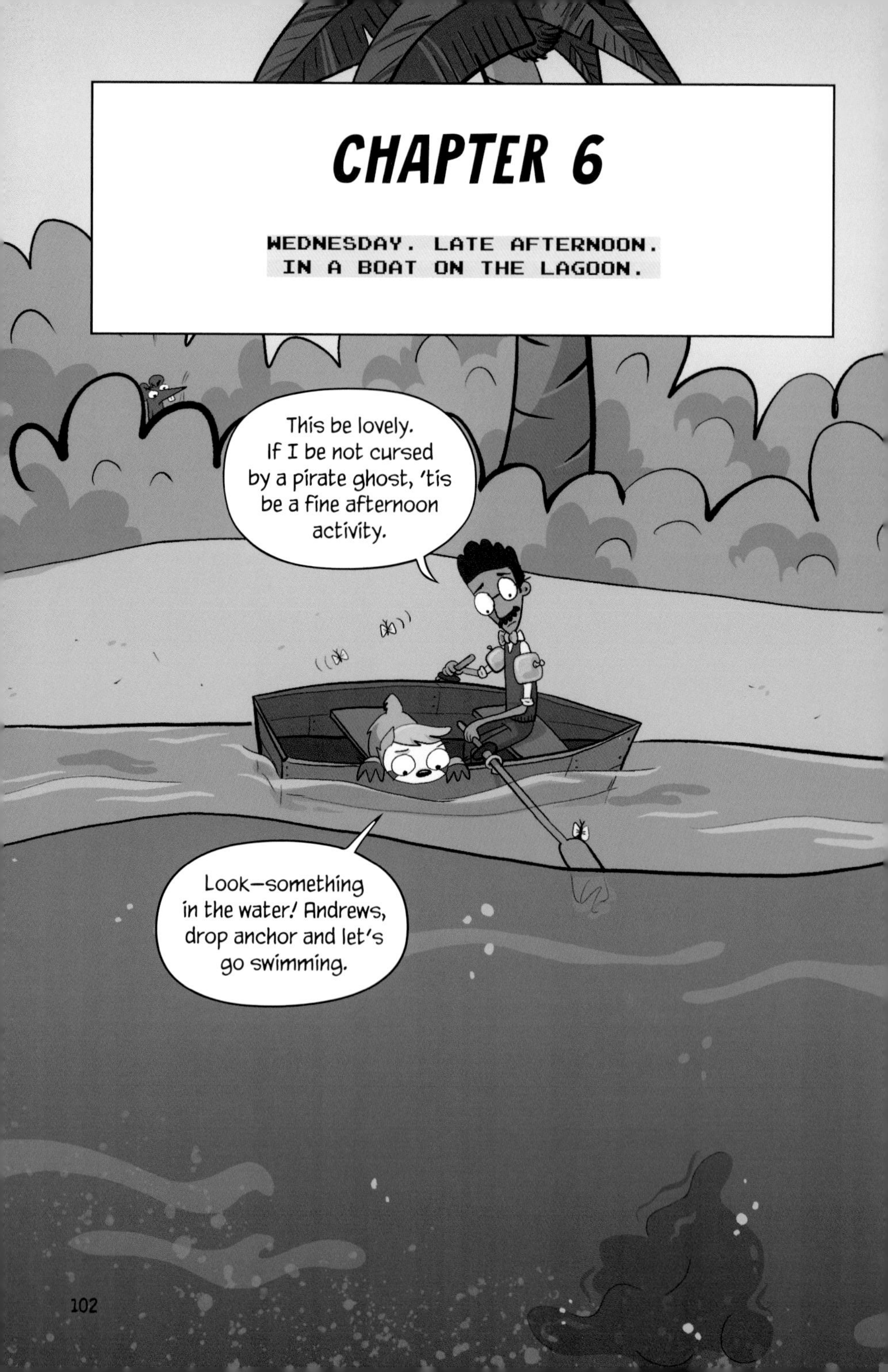
This be lovely. If I be not cursed by a pirate ghost, 'tis be a fine afternoon activity.
Look—something in the water! Andrews, drop anchor and let's go swimming.

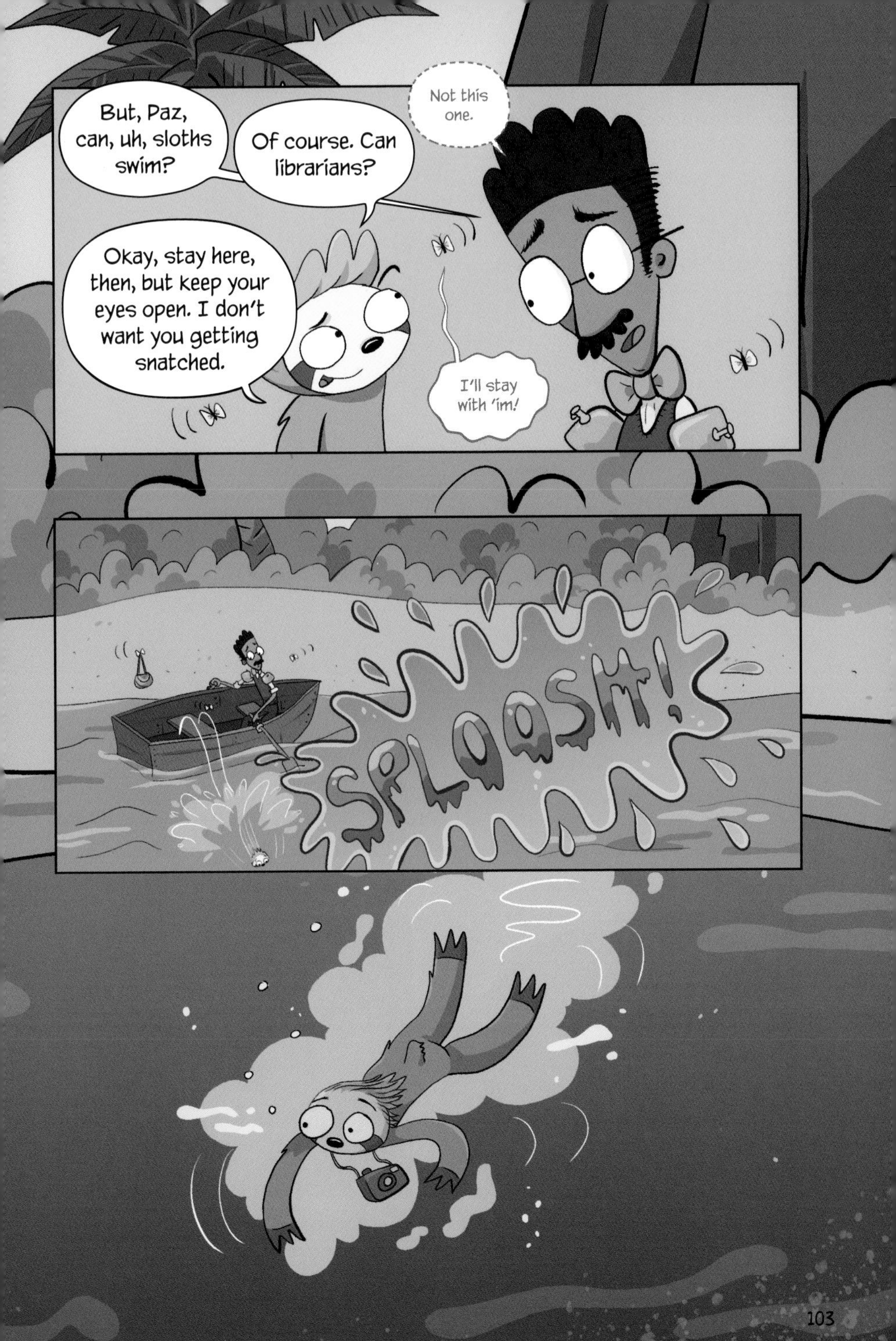
But, Paz, can, uh, sloths swim?
Of course. Can librarians?
Not this one.
Okay, stay here, then, but keep your eyes open. I don't want you getting snatched.
I'll stay with 'im!
SPLOOSH!

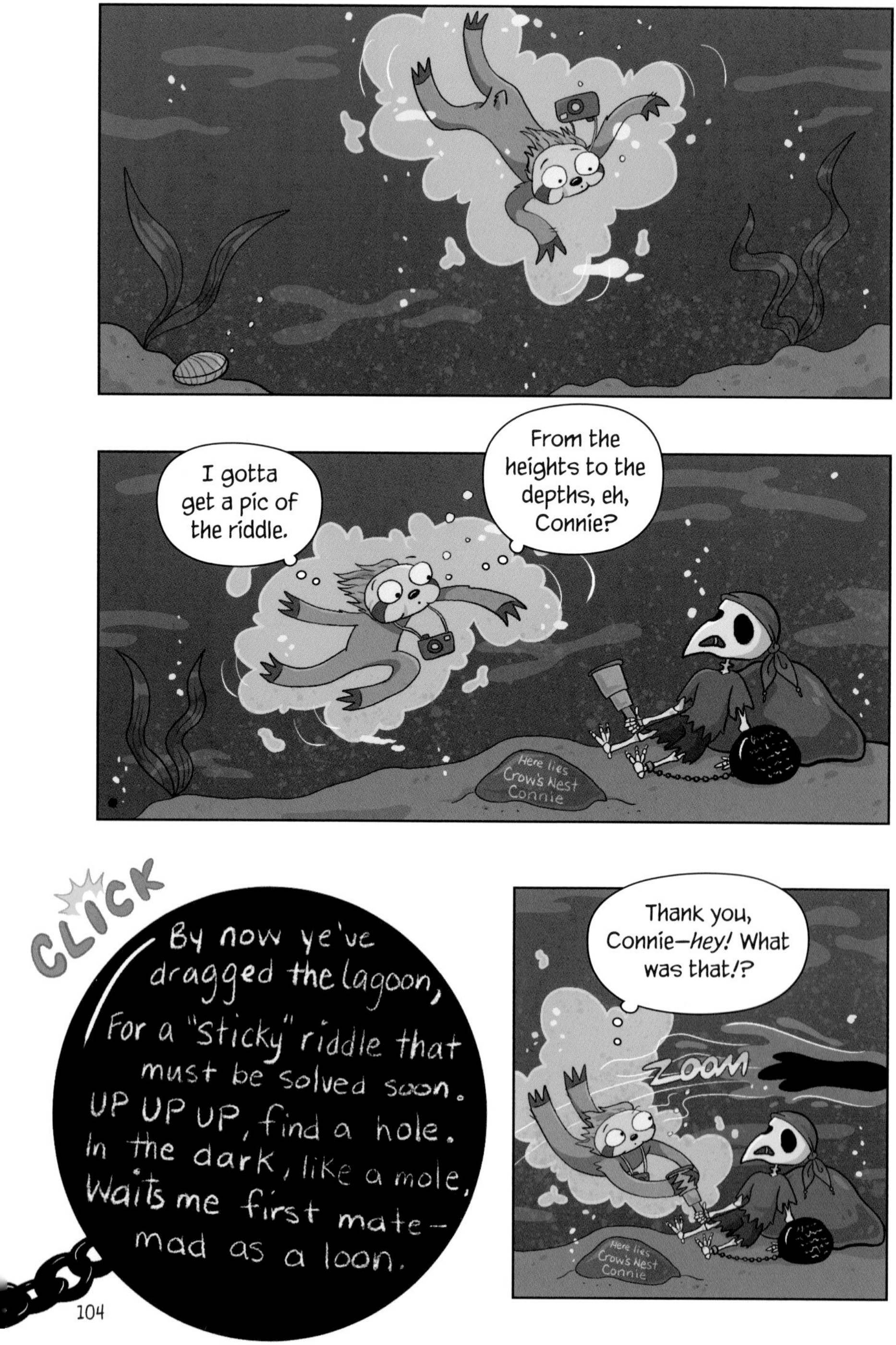
I gotta get a pic of the riddle.
From the heights to the depths, eh, Connie?
Here lies Crow's Nest Connie
CLICK
By now ye've dragged the lagoon,
For a "sticky" riddle that must be solved soon.
UP UP UP, find a hole.
In the dark, like a mole,
Waits me first mate—mad as a loon.
Thank you, Connie—*hey!* What was that*!?*
ZOOM
Here lies Crow's Nest Connie

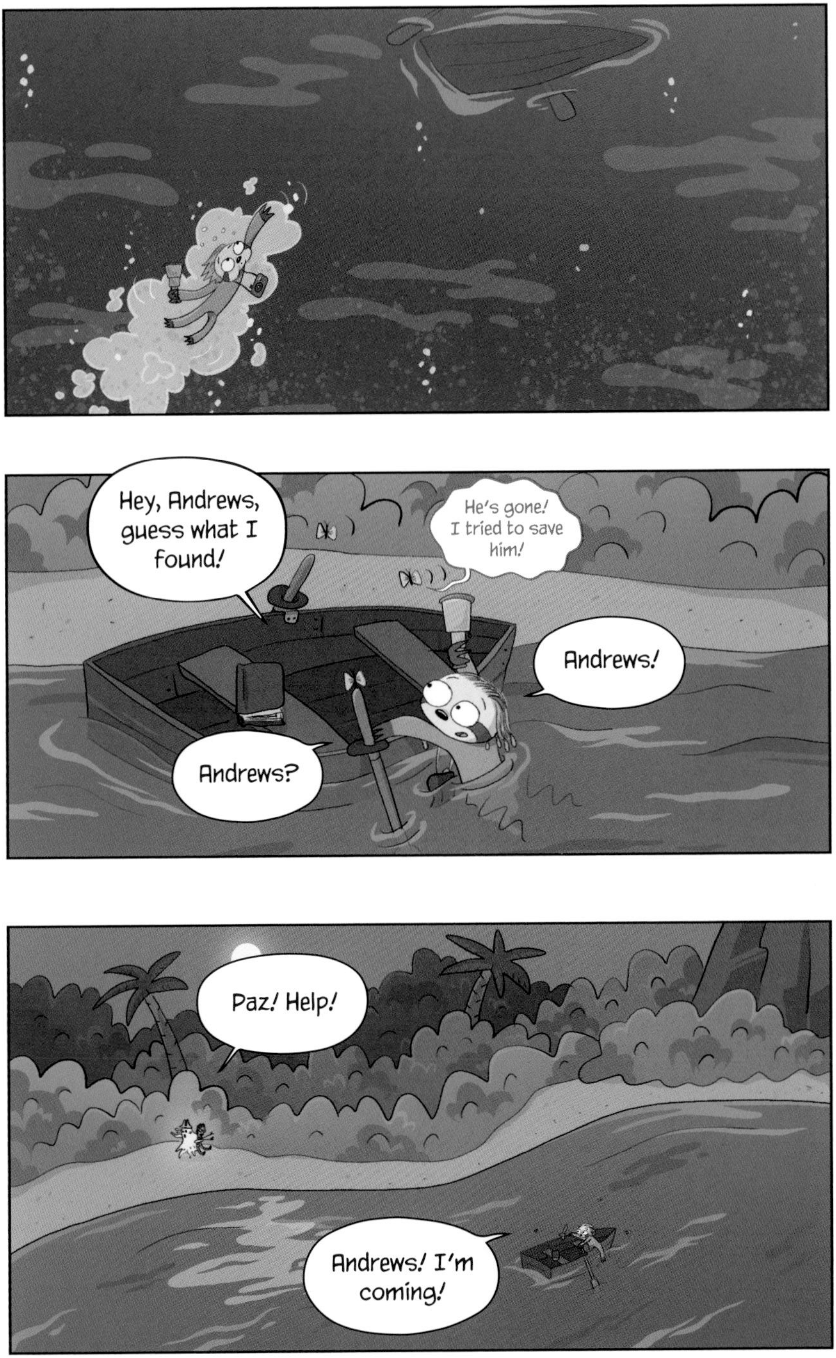
Hey, Andrews, guess what I found!
He's gone! I tried to save him!
Andrews!
Andrews?
Paz! Help!
Andrews! I'm coming!

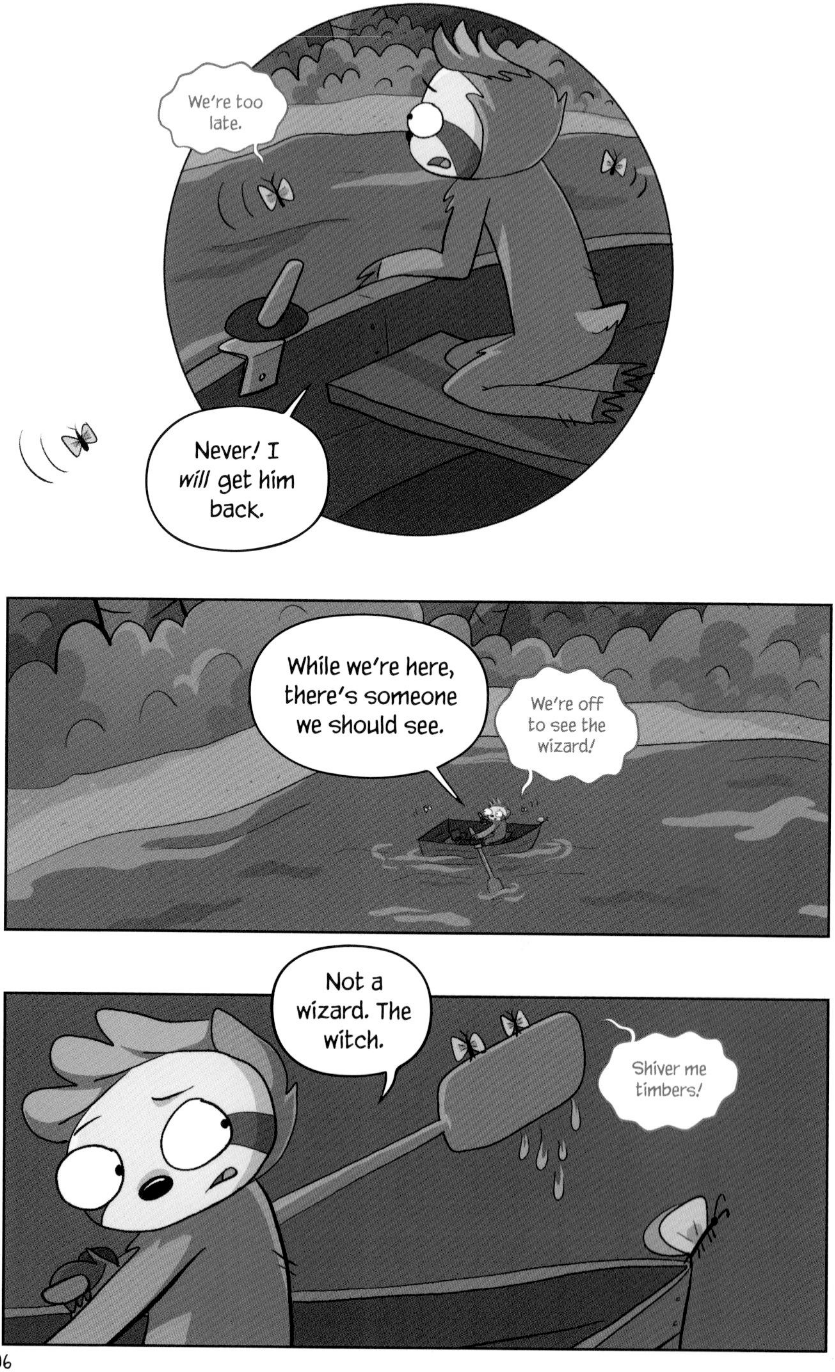
We're too late.
Never! I *will* get him back.
While we're here, there's someone we should see.
We're off to see the wizard!
Not a wizard. The witch.
Shiver me timbers!

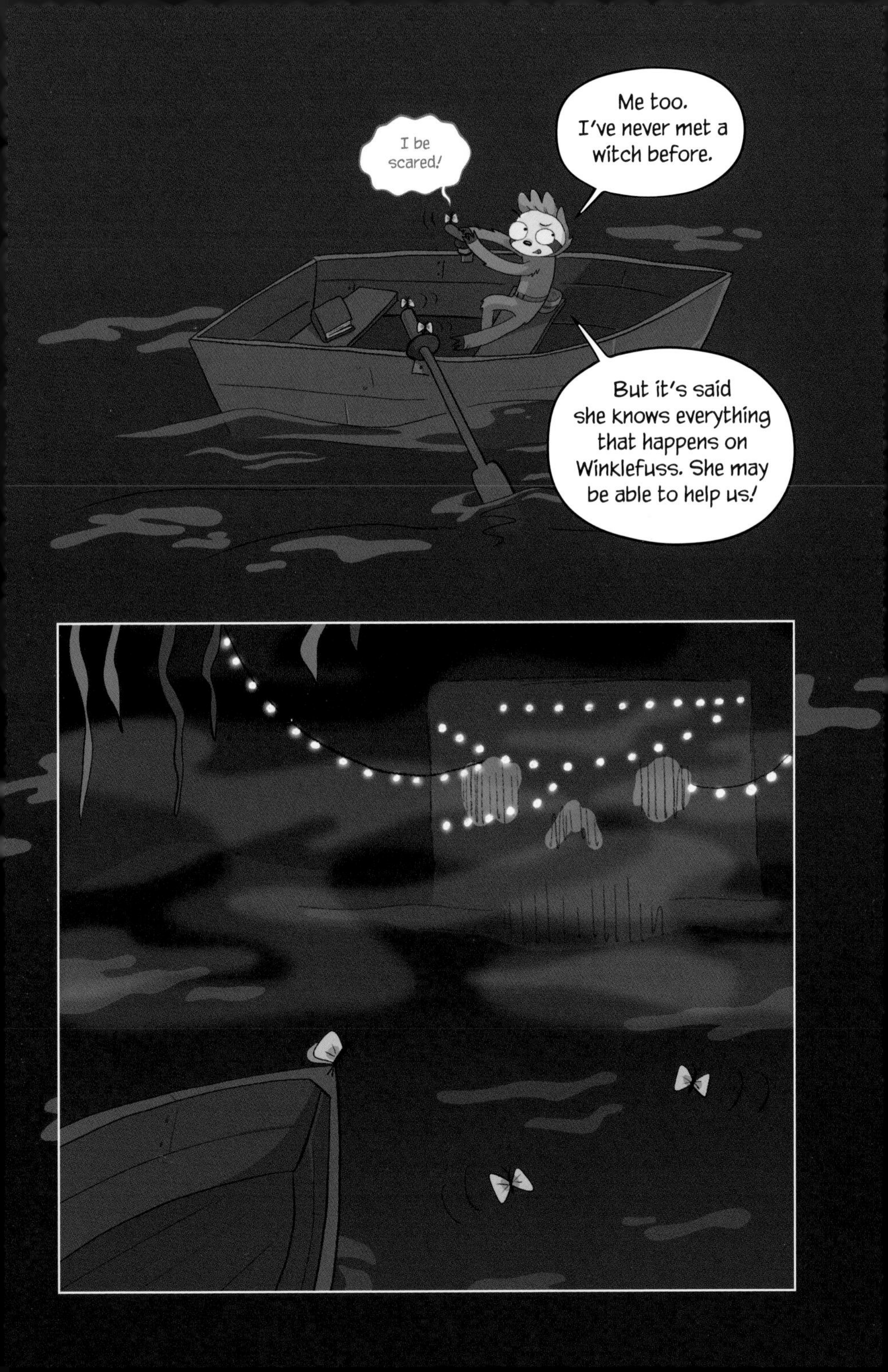
I be scared!
Me too. I've never met a witch before.
But it's said she knows everything that happens on Winklefuss. She may be able to help us!

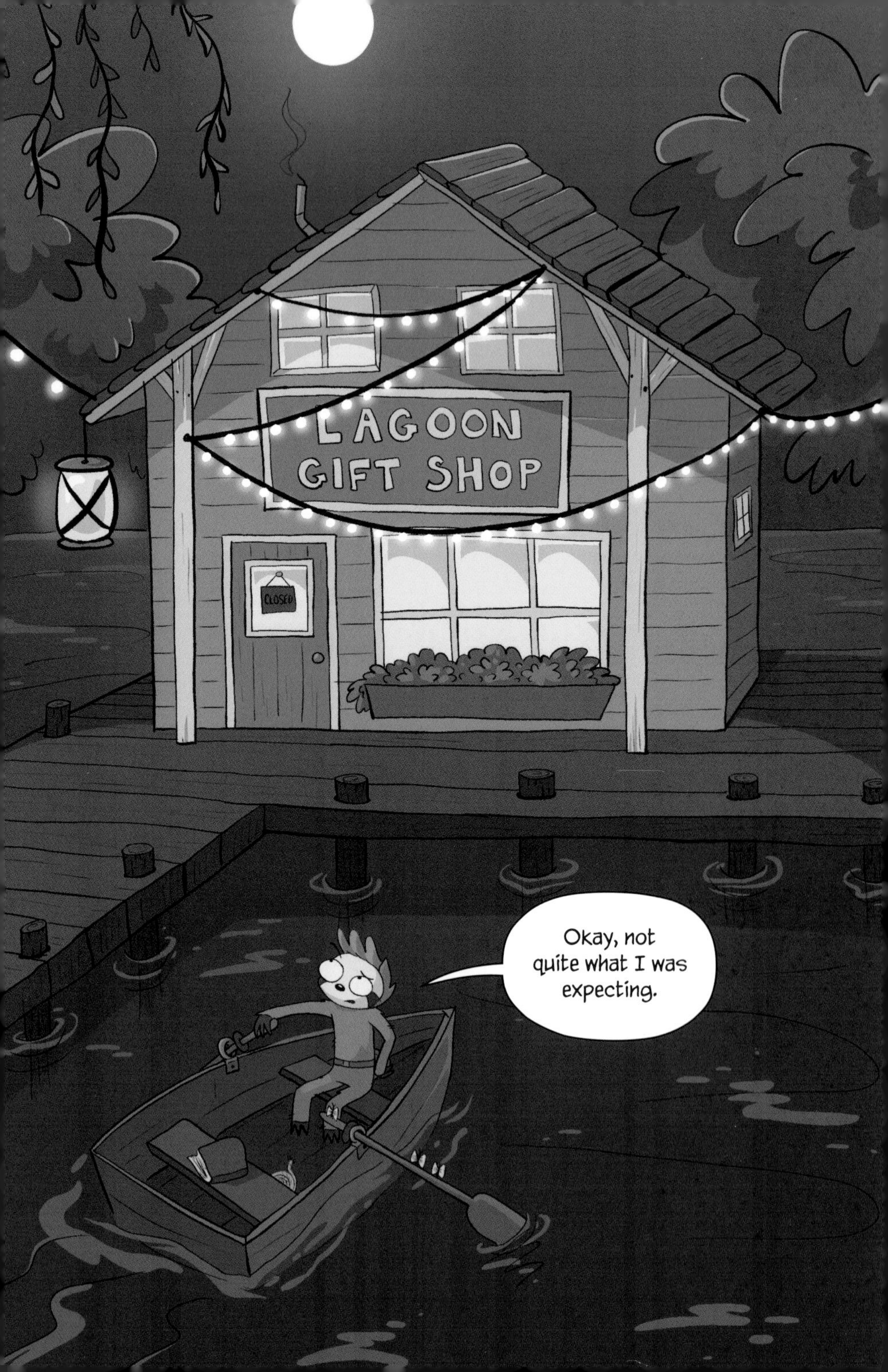
LAGOON GIFT SHOP
CLOSED
Okay, not quite what I was expecting.

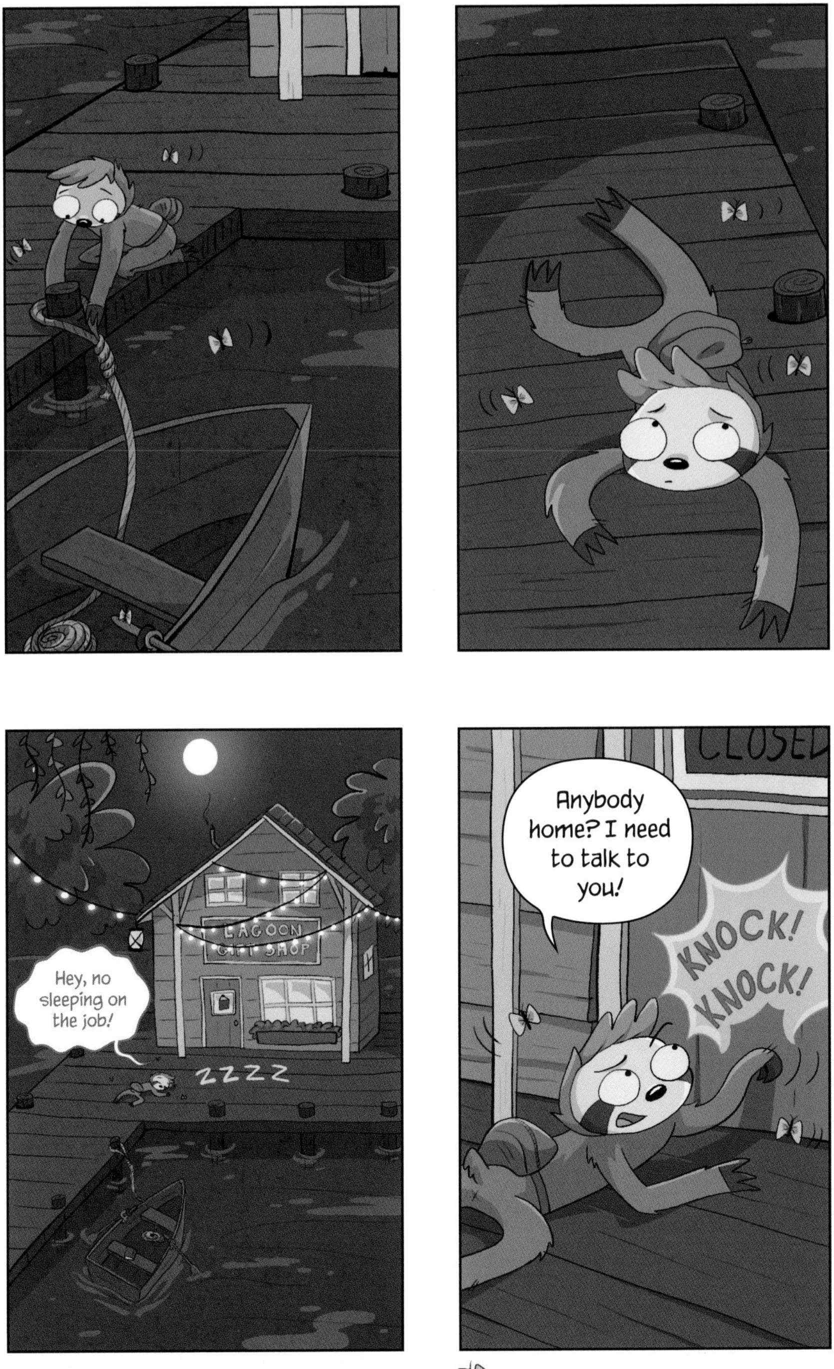
LAGOON GIFT SHOP
Hey, no sleeping on the job!
ZZZZ
CLOSED
Anybody home? I need to talk to you!
KNOCK! KNOCK!

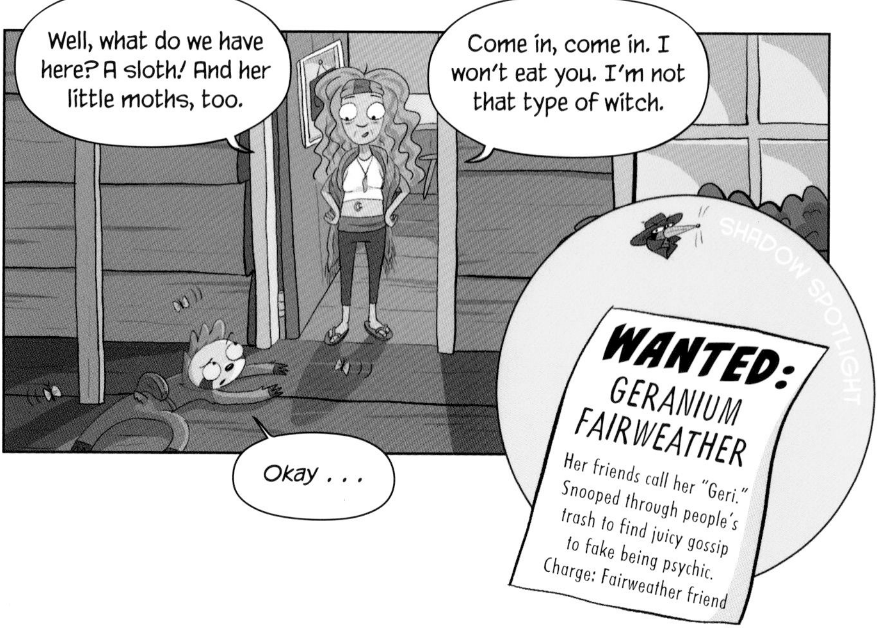
Well, what do we have here? A sloth! And her little moths, too.
Come in, come in. I won't eat you. I'm not that type of witch.
Okay . . .
SHADOW SPOTLIGHT
WANTED:
GERANIUM FAIRWEATHER
Her friends call her "Geri." Snooped through people's trash to find juicy gossip to fake being psychic.
Charge: Fairweather friend

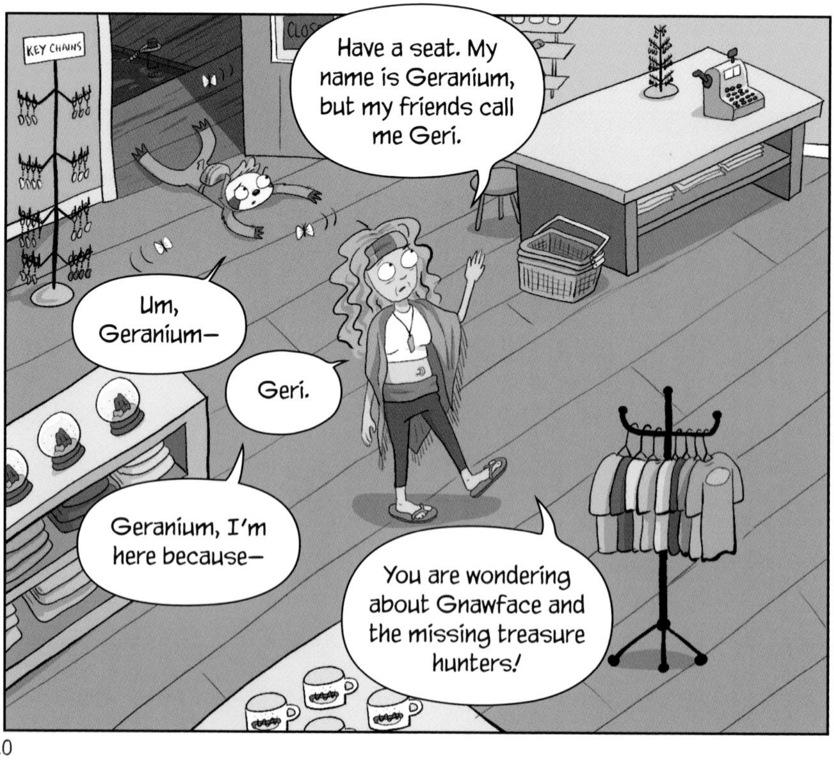
KEY CHAINS
Have a seat. My name is Geranium, but my friends call me Geri.
Um, Geranium—
Geri.
Geranium, I'm here because—
You are wondering about Gnawface and the missing treasure hunters!

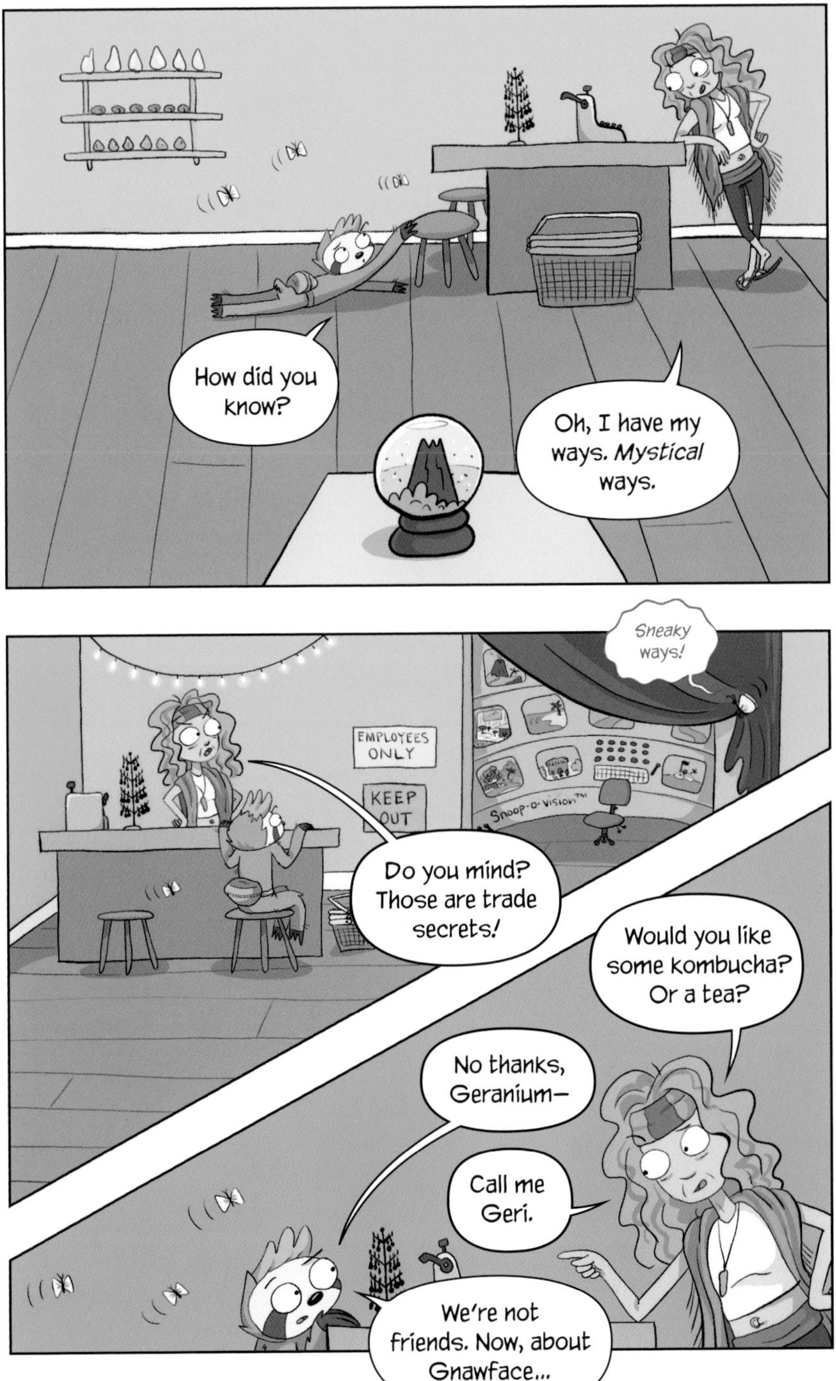
How did you know?
Oh, I have my ways. *Mystical* ways.
Sneaky ways!
EMPLOYEES ONLY
KEEP OUT
Snoop-o-vision™
Do you mind? Those are trade secrets!
Would you like some kombucha? Or a tea?
No thanks, Geranium—
Call me Geri.
We're not friends. Now, about Gnawface...

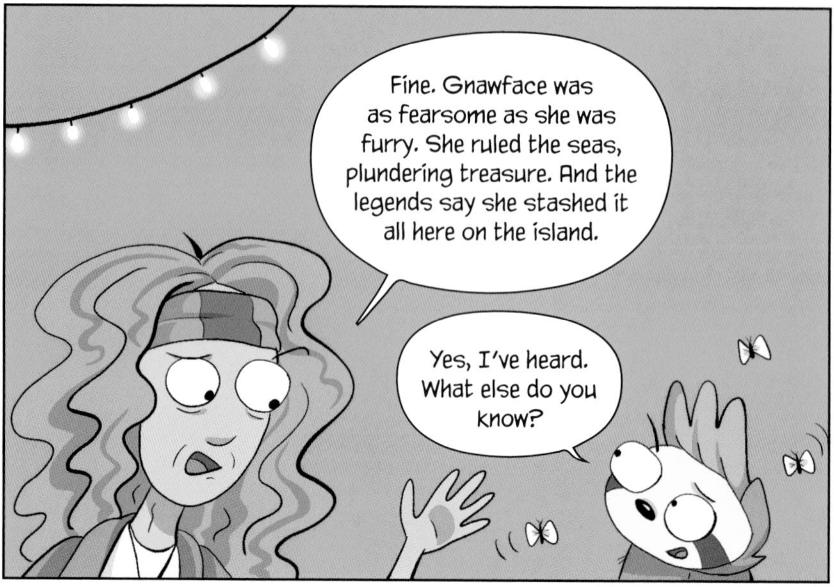
Fine. Gnawface was as fearsome as she was furry. She ruled the seas, plundering treasure. And the legends say she stashed it all here on the island.
Yes, I've heard. What else do you know?

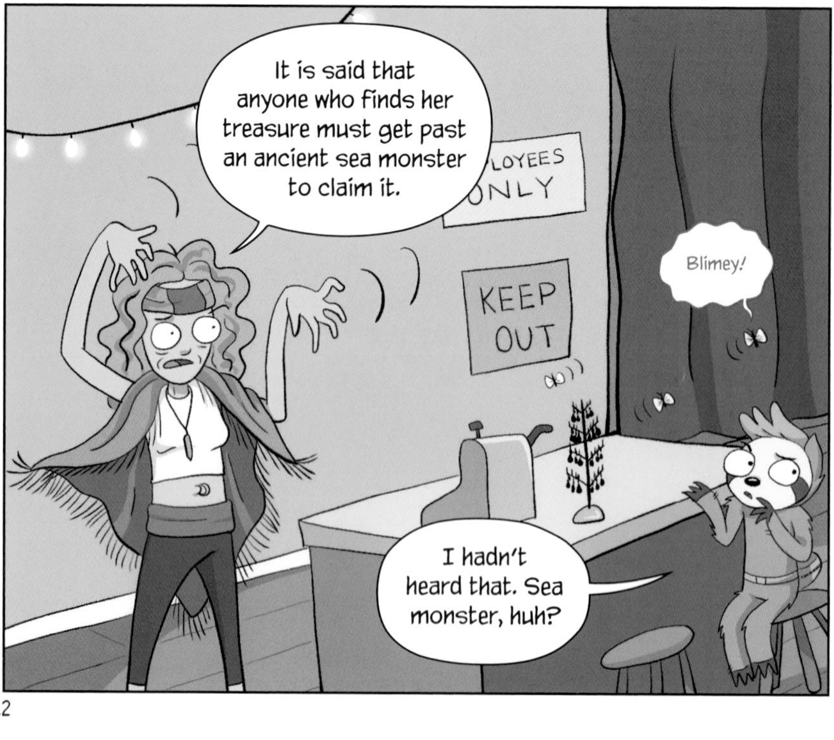
It is said that anyone who finds her treasure must get past an ancient sea monster to claim it.
LOYEES
ONLY
KEEP OUT
Blimey!
I hadn't heard that. Sea monster, huh?

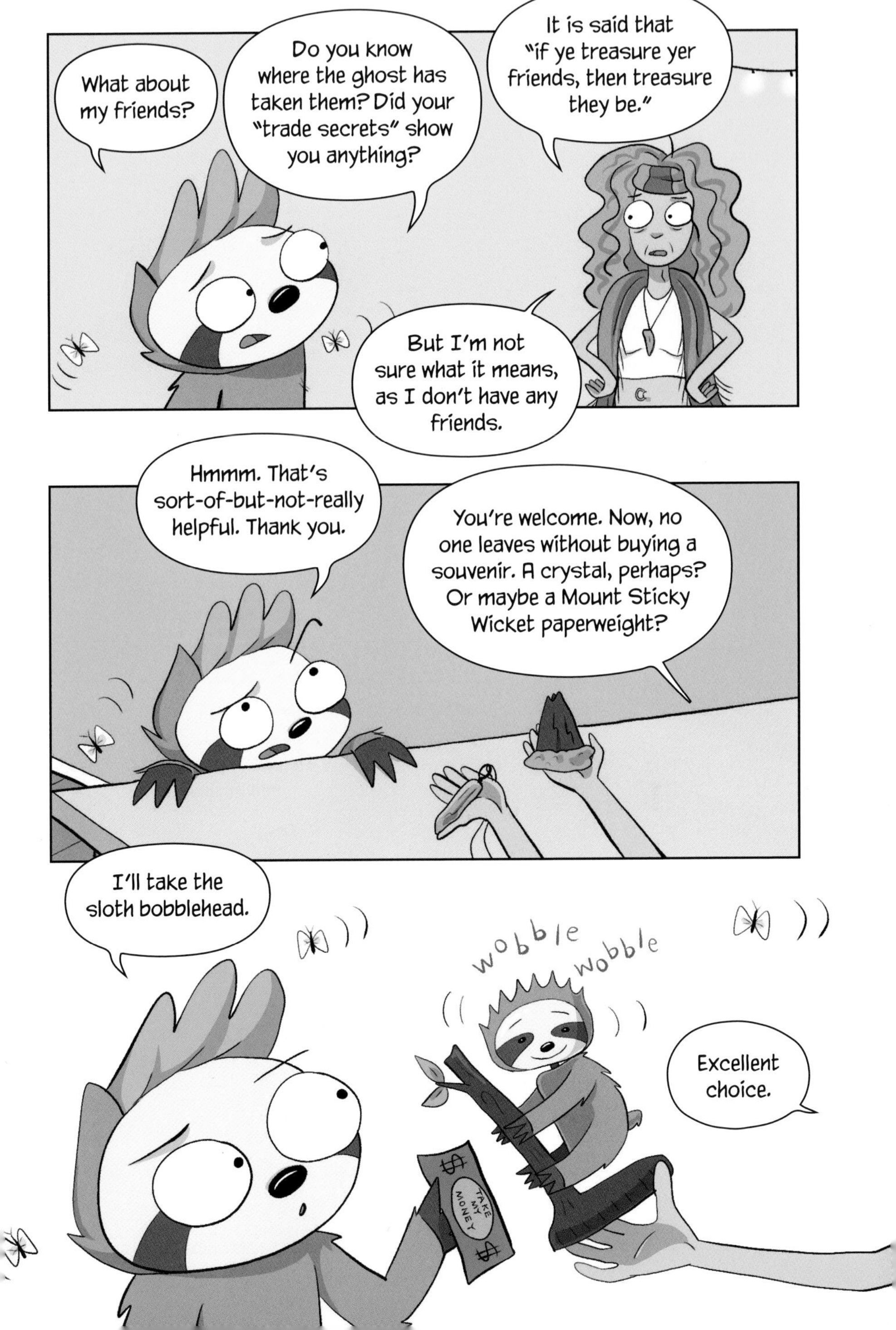
What about my friends?
Do you know where the ghost has taken them? Did your "trade secrets" show you anything?
It is said that "if ye treasure yer friends, then treasure they be."
But I'm not sure what it means, as I don't have any friends.
Hmmm. That's sort-of-but-not-really helpful. Thank you.
You're welcome. Now, no one leaves without buying a souvenir. A crystal, perhaps? Or maybe a Mount Sticky Wicket paperweight?
I'll take the sloth bobblehead.
wobble wobble
TAKE MY MONEY
Excellent choice.

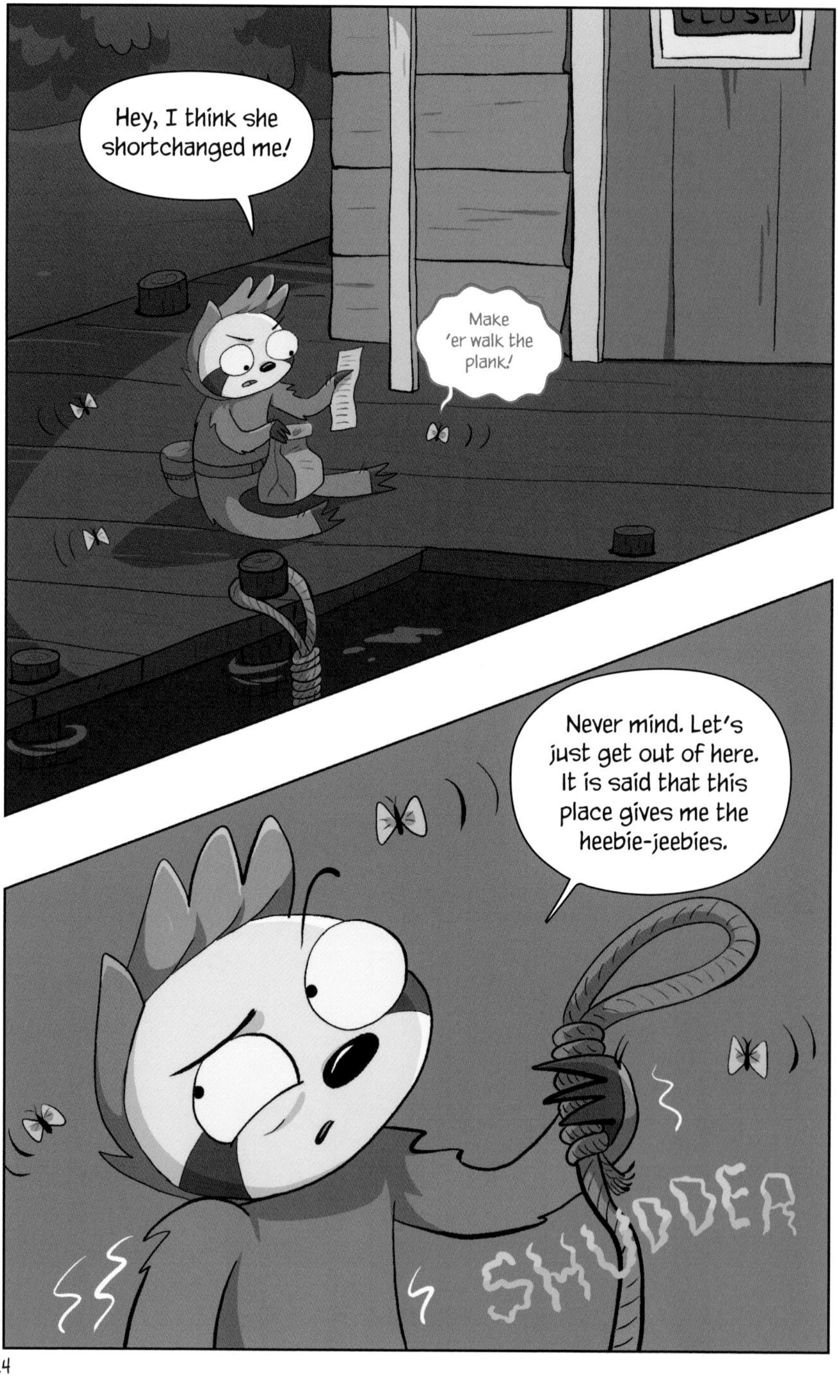
CLOSED
Hey, I think she shortchanged me!
Make 'er walk the plank!
Never mind. Let's just get out of here. It is said that this place gives me the heebie-jeebies.
SHUDDER

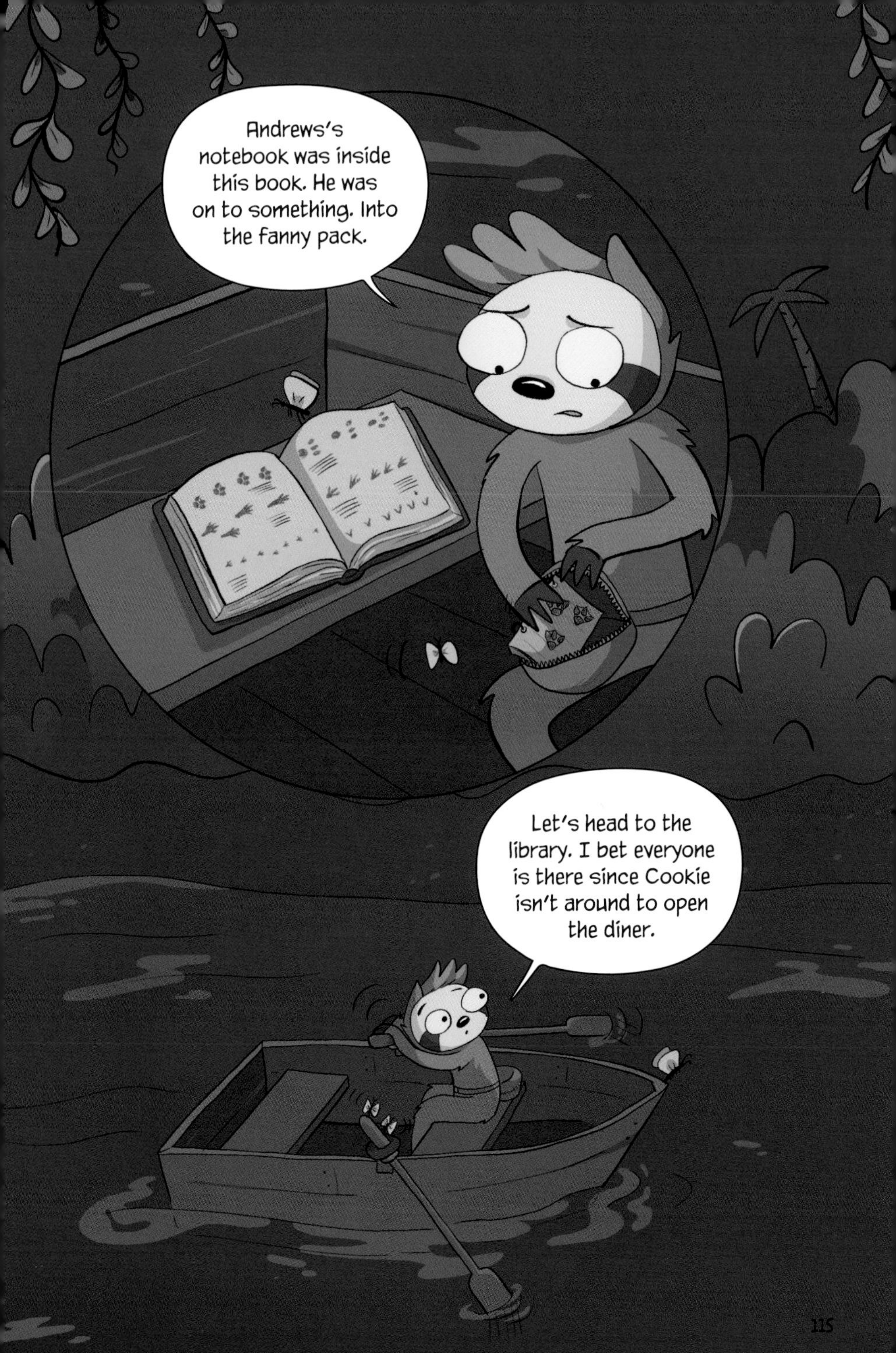
Andrews's notebook was inside this book. He was on to something. Into the fanny pack.
Let's head to the library. I bet everyone is there since Cookie isn't around to open the diner.

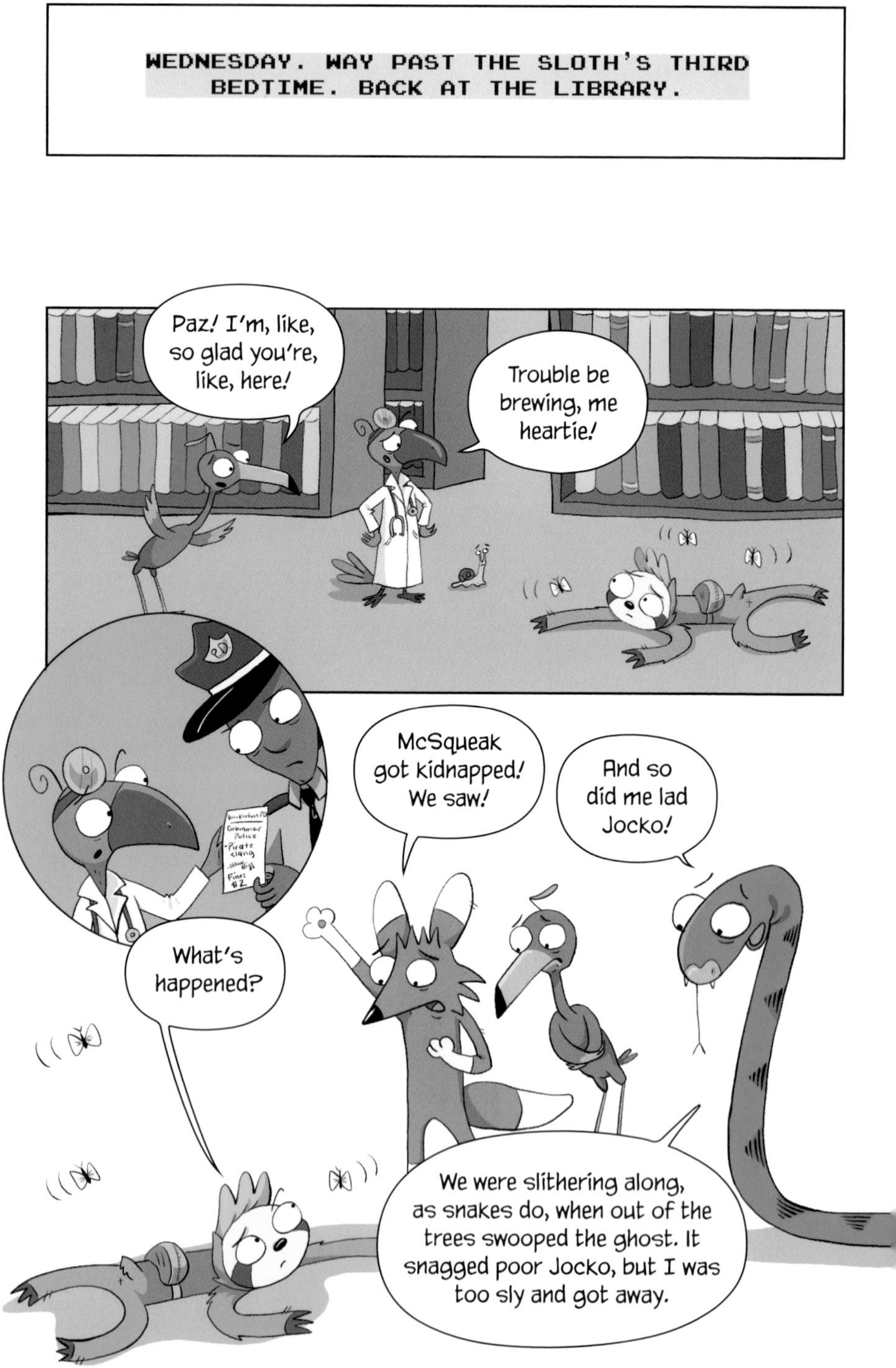
WEDNESDAY. WAY PAST THE SLOTH'S THIRD BEDTIME. BACK AT THE LIBRARY.
Paz! I'm, like, so glad you're, like, here!
Trouble be brewing, me heartie!
What's happened?
McSqueak got kidnapped! We saw!
And so did me lad Jocko!
We were slithering along, as snakes do, when out of the trees swooped the ghost. It snagged poor Jocko, but I was too sly and got away.

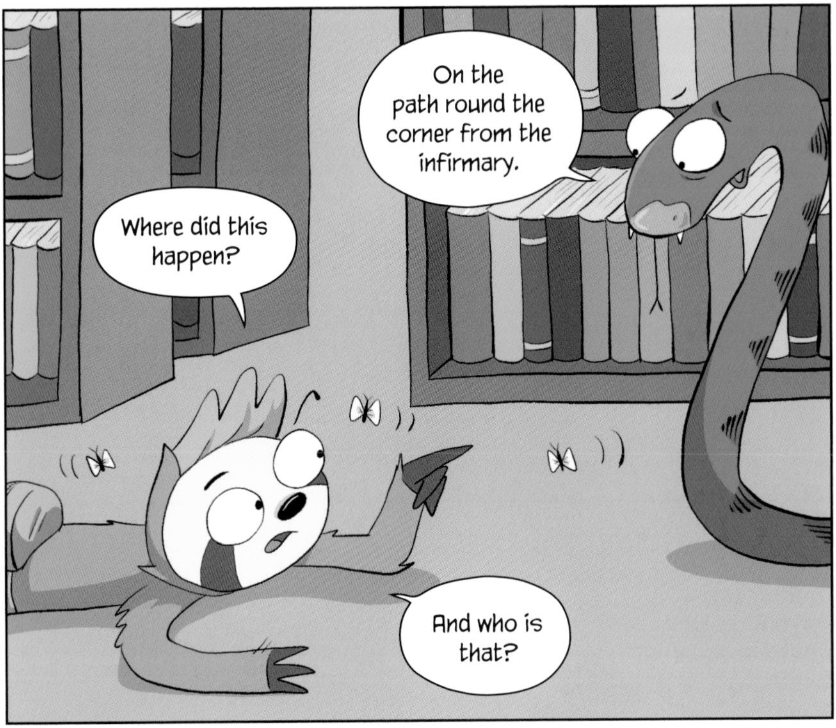
Where did this happen?
On the path round the corner from the infirmary.
And who is that?

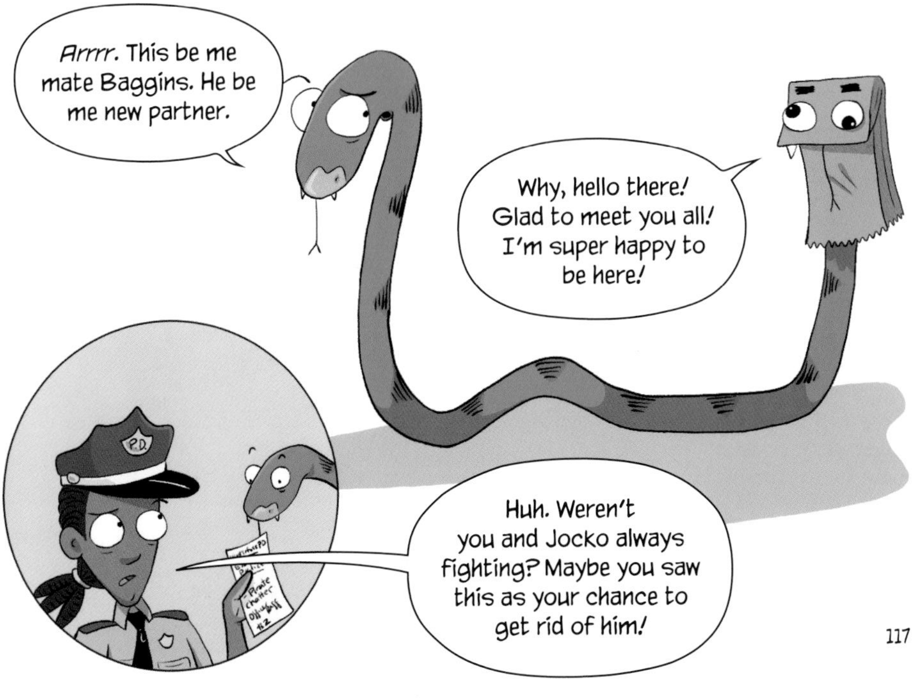
Arrrr. This be me mate Baggins. He be me new partner.
Why, hello there! Glad to meet you all! I'm super happy to be here!
Huh. Weren't you and Jocko always fighting? Maybe you saw this as your chance to get rid of him!

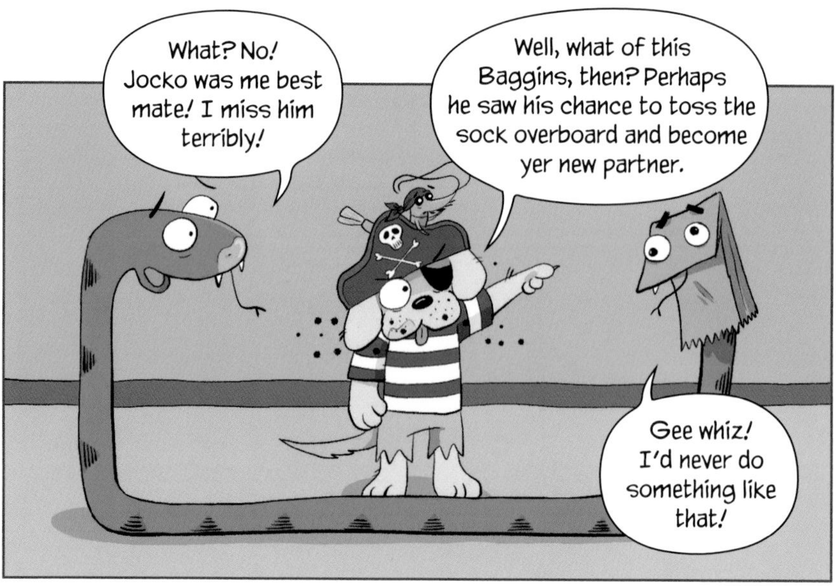
What? No! Jocko was me best mate! I miss him terribly!
Well, what of this Baggins, then? Perhaps he saw his chance to toss the sock overboard and become yer new partner.
Gee whiz! I'd never do something like that!

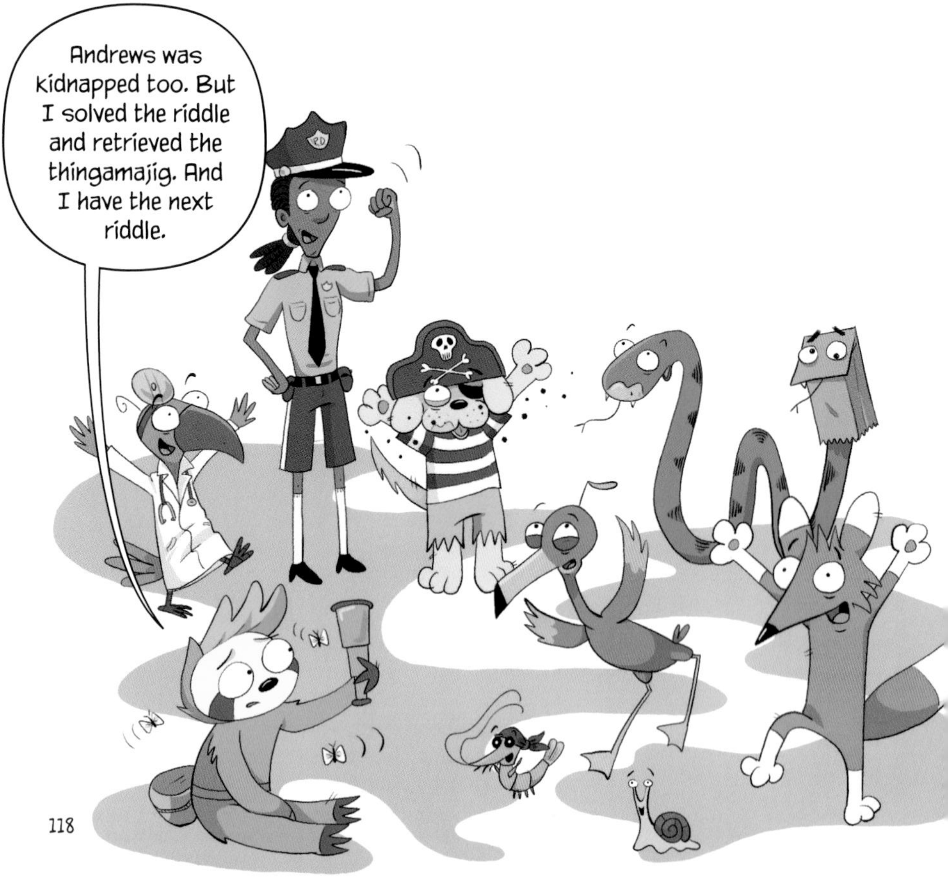
Andrews was kidnapped too. But I solved the riddle and retrieved the thingamajig. And I have the next riddle.

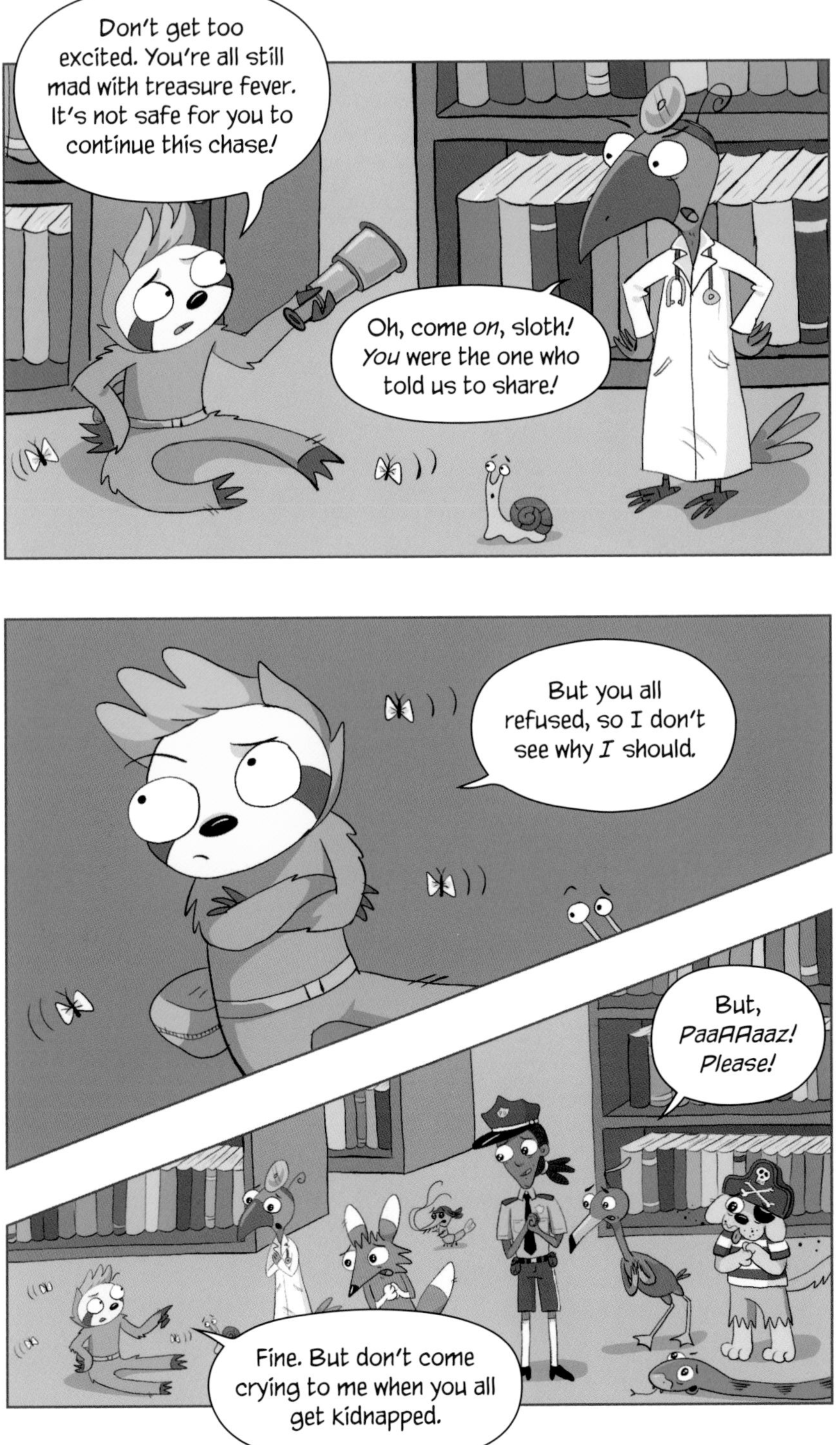
Don't get too excited. You're all still mad with treasure fever. It's not safe for you to continue this chase!
Oh, come *on*, sloth! *You* were the one who told us to share!
But you all refused, so I don't see why *I* should.
But, *PaaAAaaz! Please!*
Fine. But don't come crying to me when you all get kidnapped.

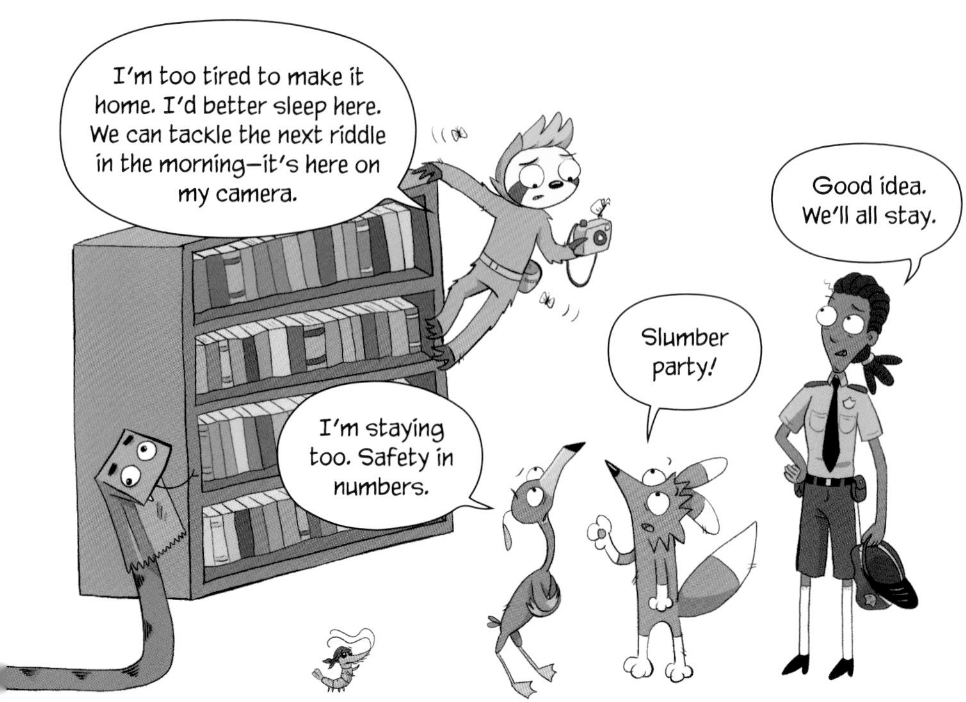
I'm too tired to make it home. I'd better sleep here. We can tackle the next riddle in the morning—it's here on my camera.
Good idea. We'll all stay.
Slumber party!
I'm staying too. Safety in numbers.

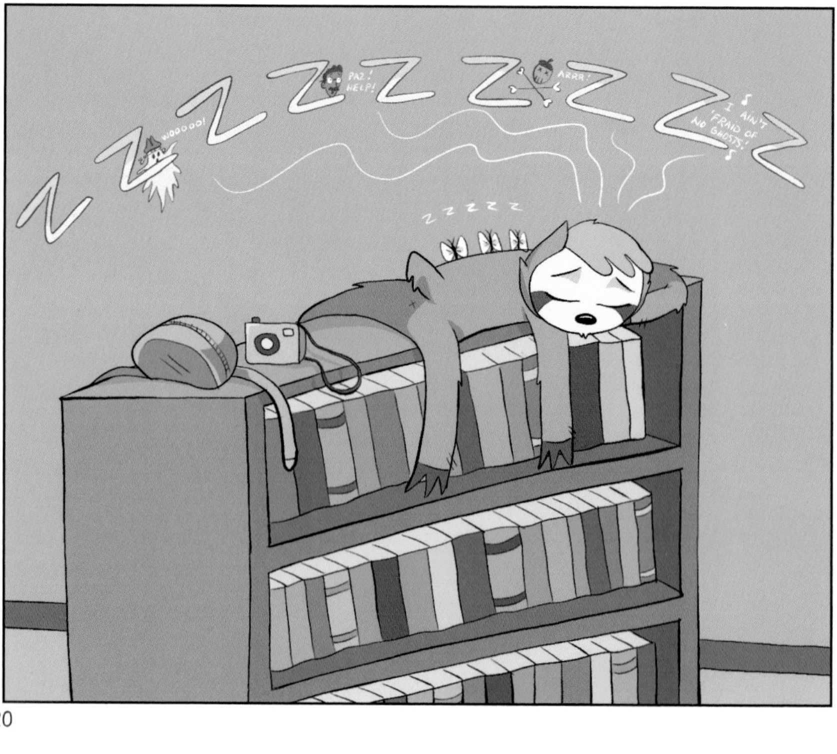
WOOOOO!
PAZ! HELP!
ARRR!
I AIN'T 'FRAID OF NO GHOSTS!

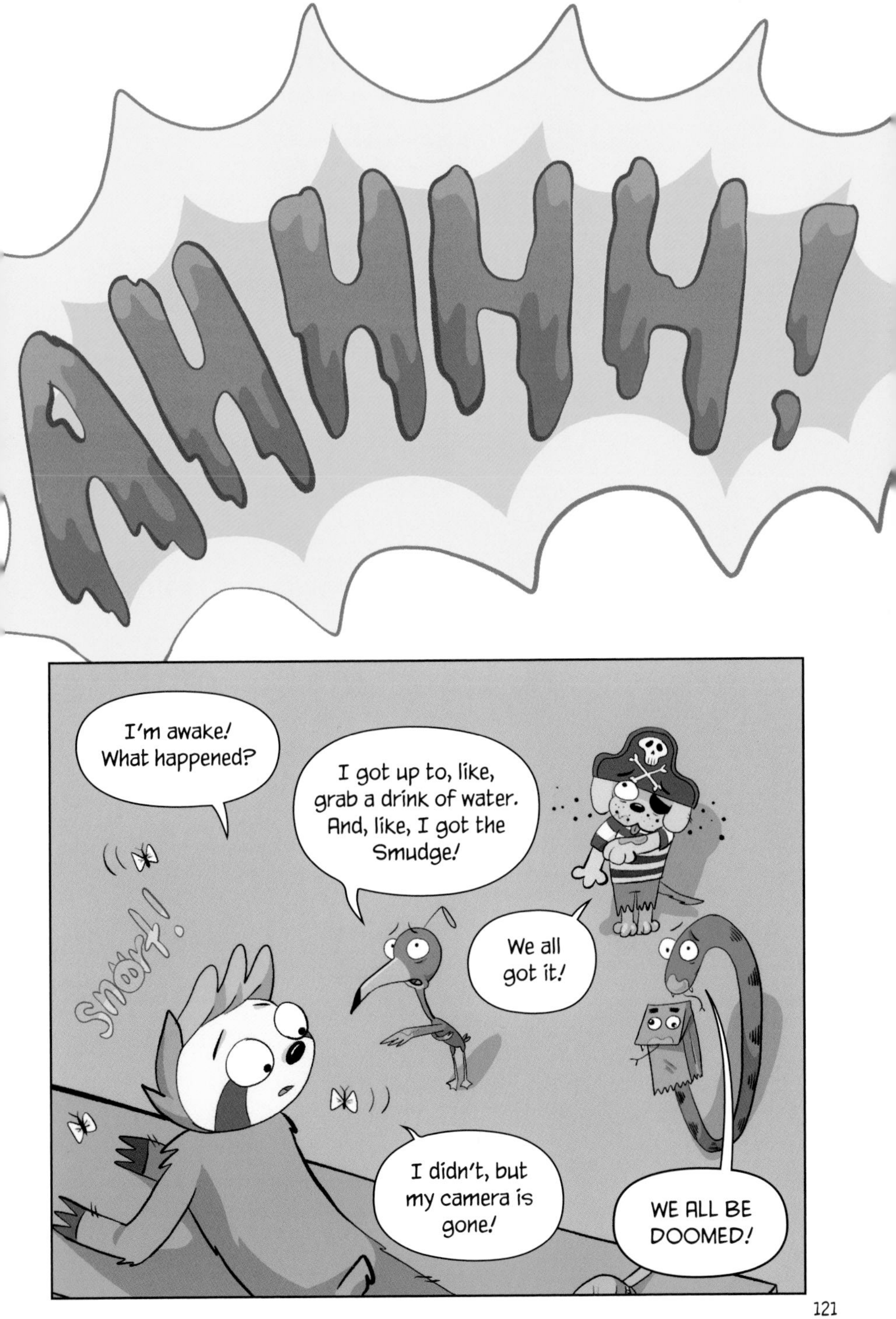
AHHHH!
I'm awake! What happened?
I got up to, like, grab a drink of water. And, like, I got the Smudge!
Snort!
We all got it!
I didn't, but my camera is gone!
WE ALL BE DOOMED!

CHAPTER 7

THURSDAY. EARLY MORNING.
IN THE LIBRARY AFTER A SCARY NIGHT.

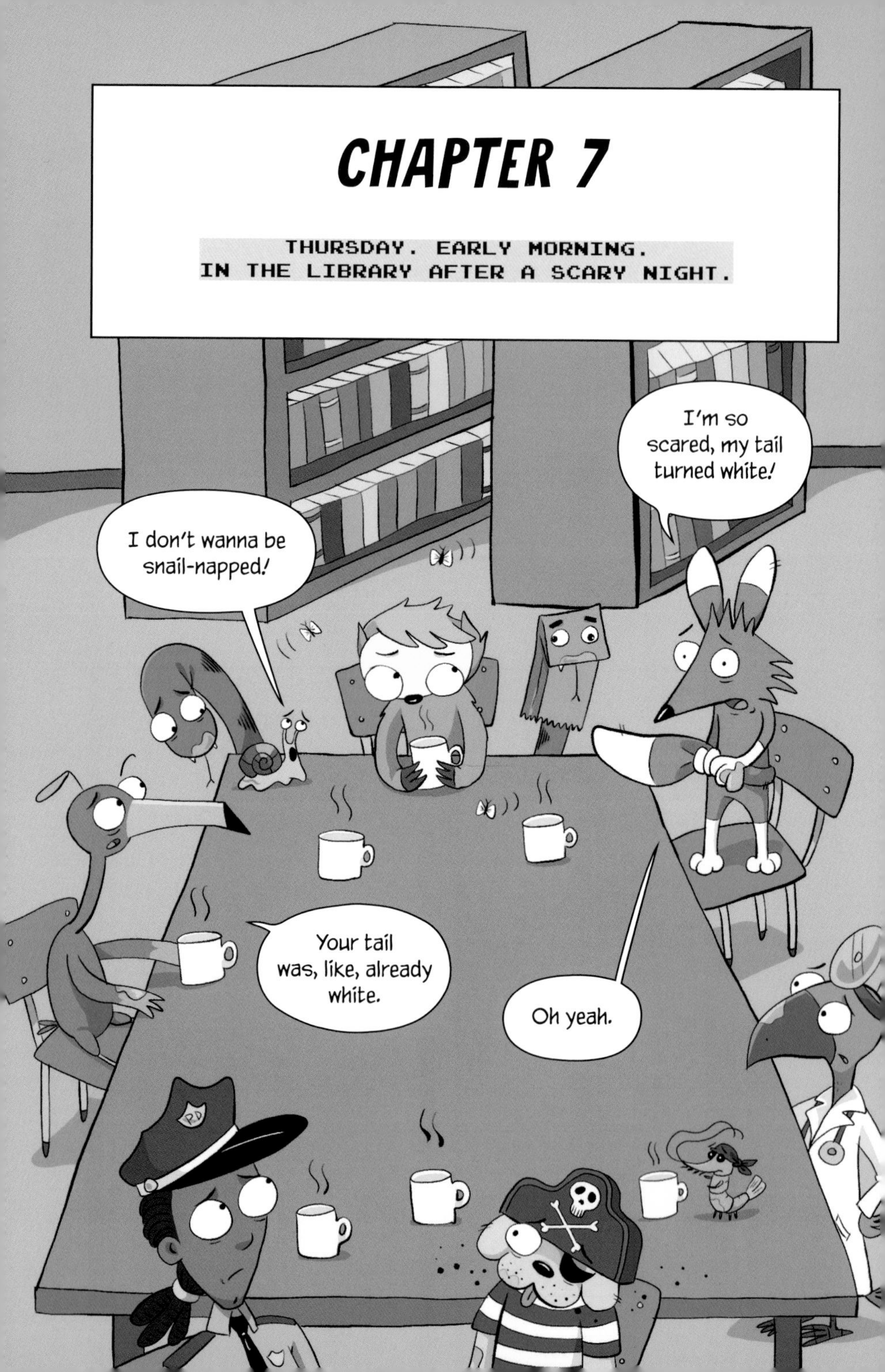
I'm so scared, my tail turned white!
I don't wanna be snail-napped!
Your tail was, like, already white.
Oh yeah.

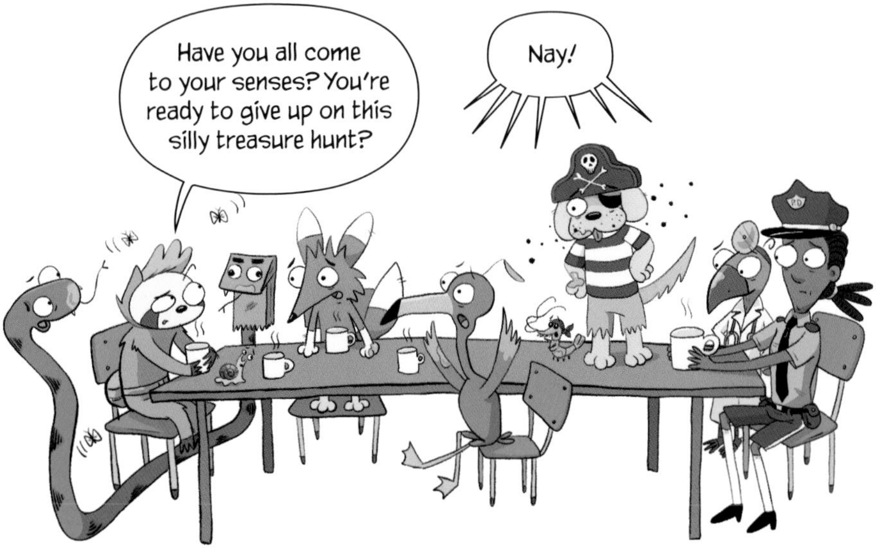
Have you all come to your senses? You're ready to give up on this silly treasure hunt?
Nay!

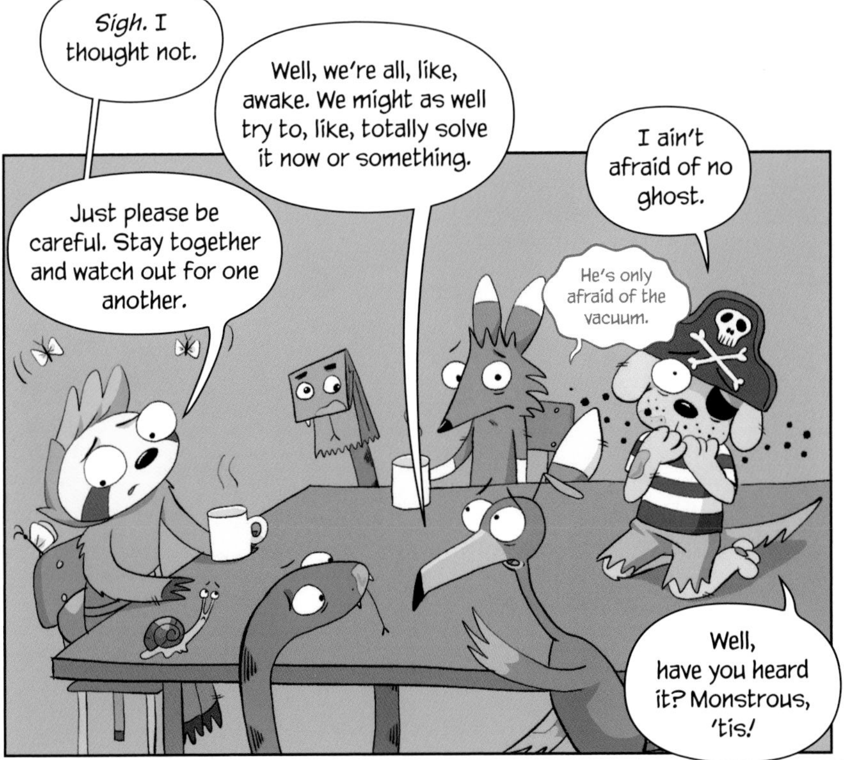
Sigh. I thought not.
Well, we're all, like, awake. We might as well try to, like, totally solve it now or something.
I ain't afraid of no ghost.
Just please be careful. Stay together and watch out for one another.
He's only afraid of the vacuum.
Well, have you heard it? Monstrous, 'tis!

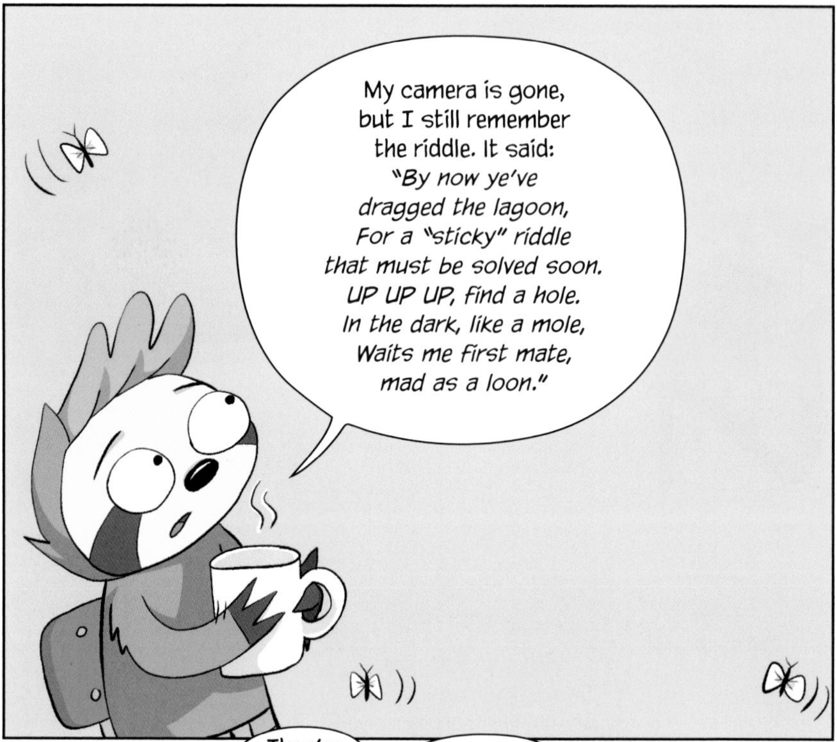
My camera is gone, but I still remember the riddle. It said: *"By now ye've dragged the lagoon, For a "sticky" riddle that must be solved soon. UP UP UP, find a hole. In the dark, like a mole, Waits me first mate, mad as a loon."*

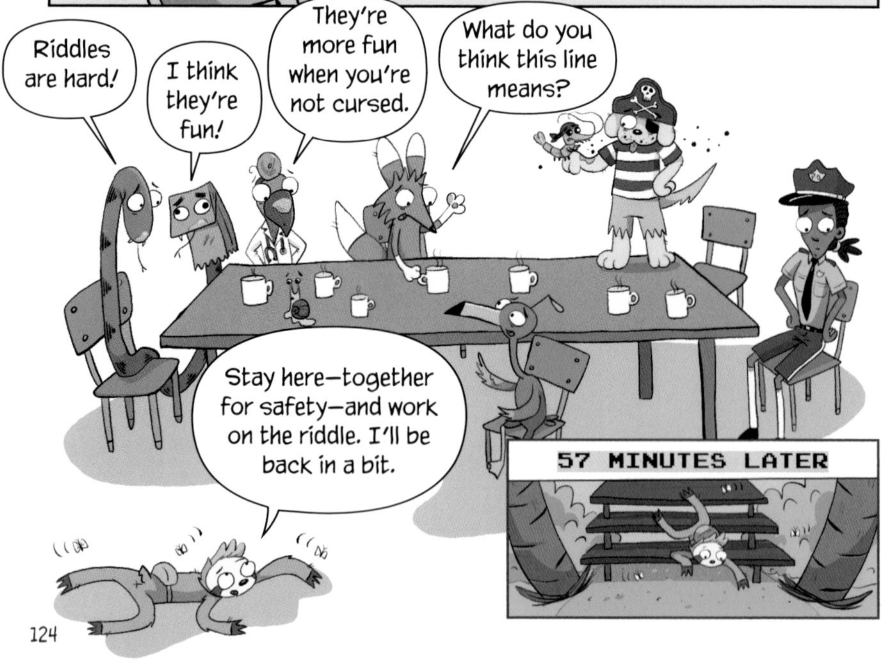
Riddles are hard!
I think they're fun!
They're more fun when you're not cursed.
What do you think this line means?
Stay here—together for safety—and work on the riddle. I'll be back in a bit.
57 MINUTES LATER

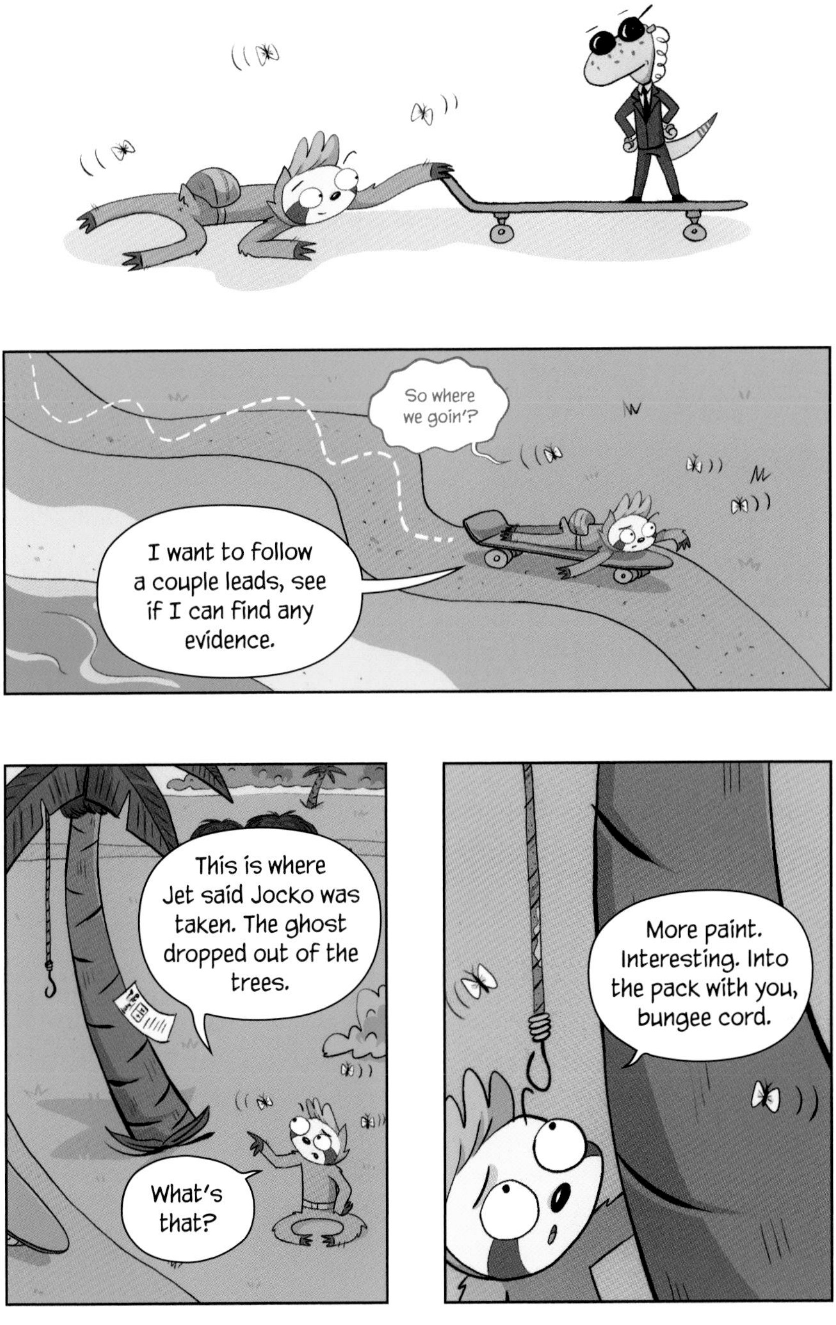
So where we goin'?
I want to follow a couple leads, see if I can find any evidence.
This is where Jet said Jocko was taken. The ghost dropped out of the trees.
What's that?
More paint. Interesting. Into the pack with you, bungee cord.

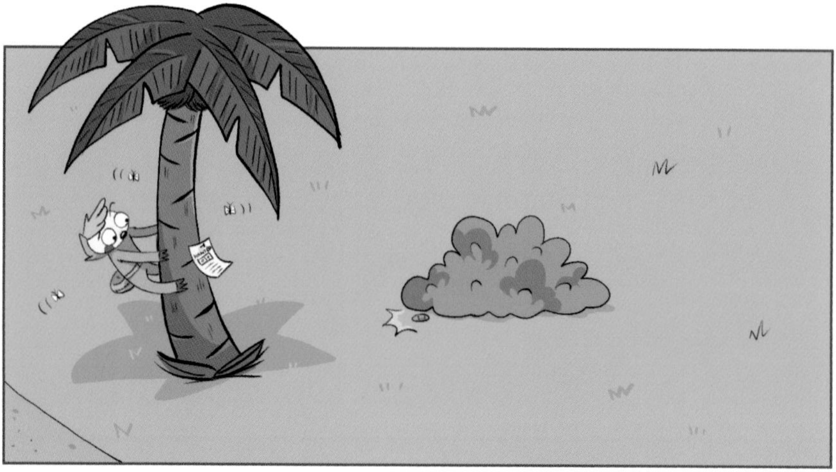

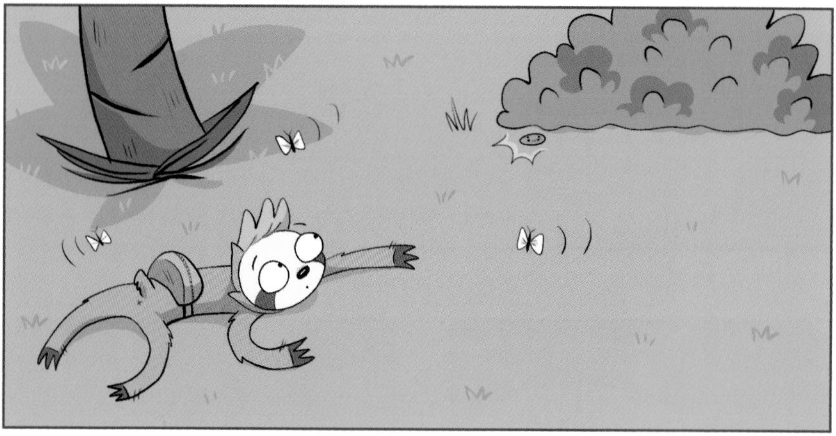

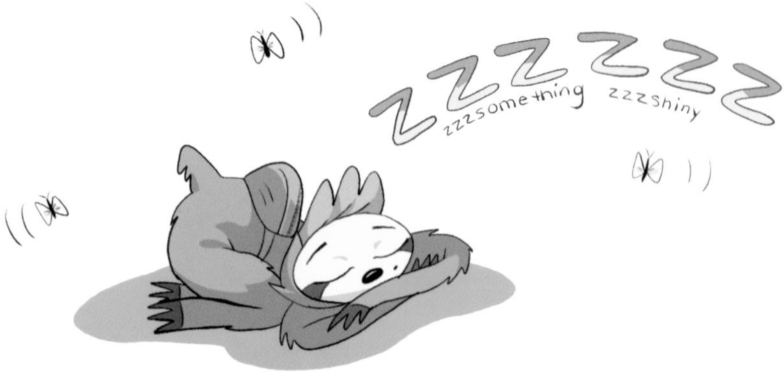
ZZZZZZZ
zzzsomething zzzshiny

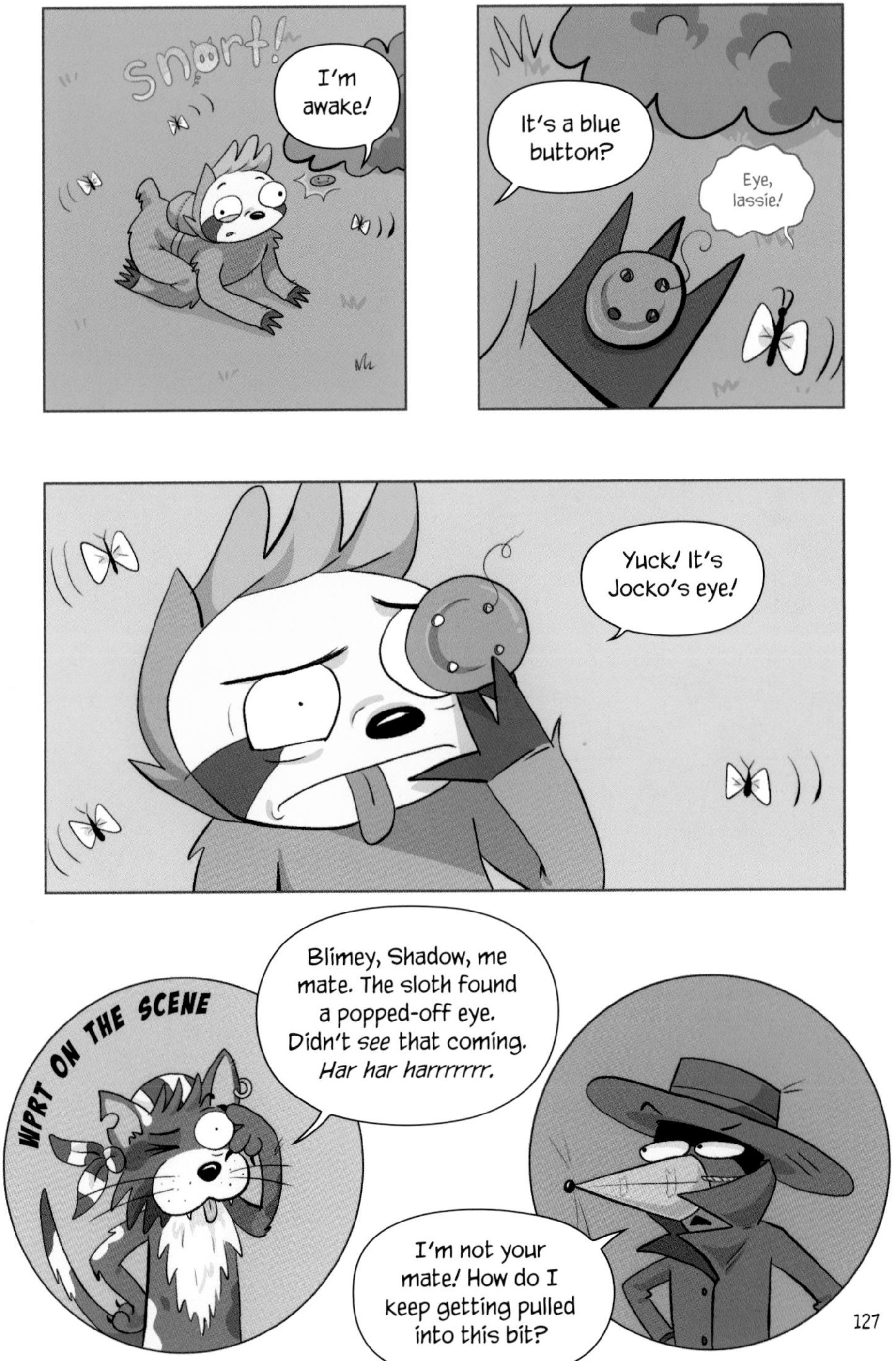
snort!
I'm awake!
It's a blue button?
Eye, lassie!
Yuck! It's Jocko's eye!
WPRT ON THE SCENE
Blimey, Shadow, me mate. The sloth found a popped-off eye. Didn't *see* that coming. *Har har harrrrrrr.*
I'm not your mate! How do I keep getting pulled into this bit?

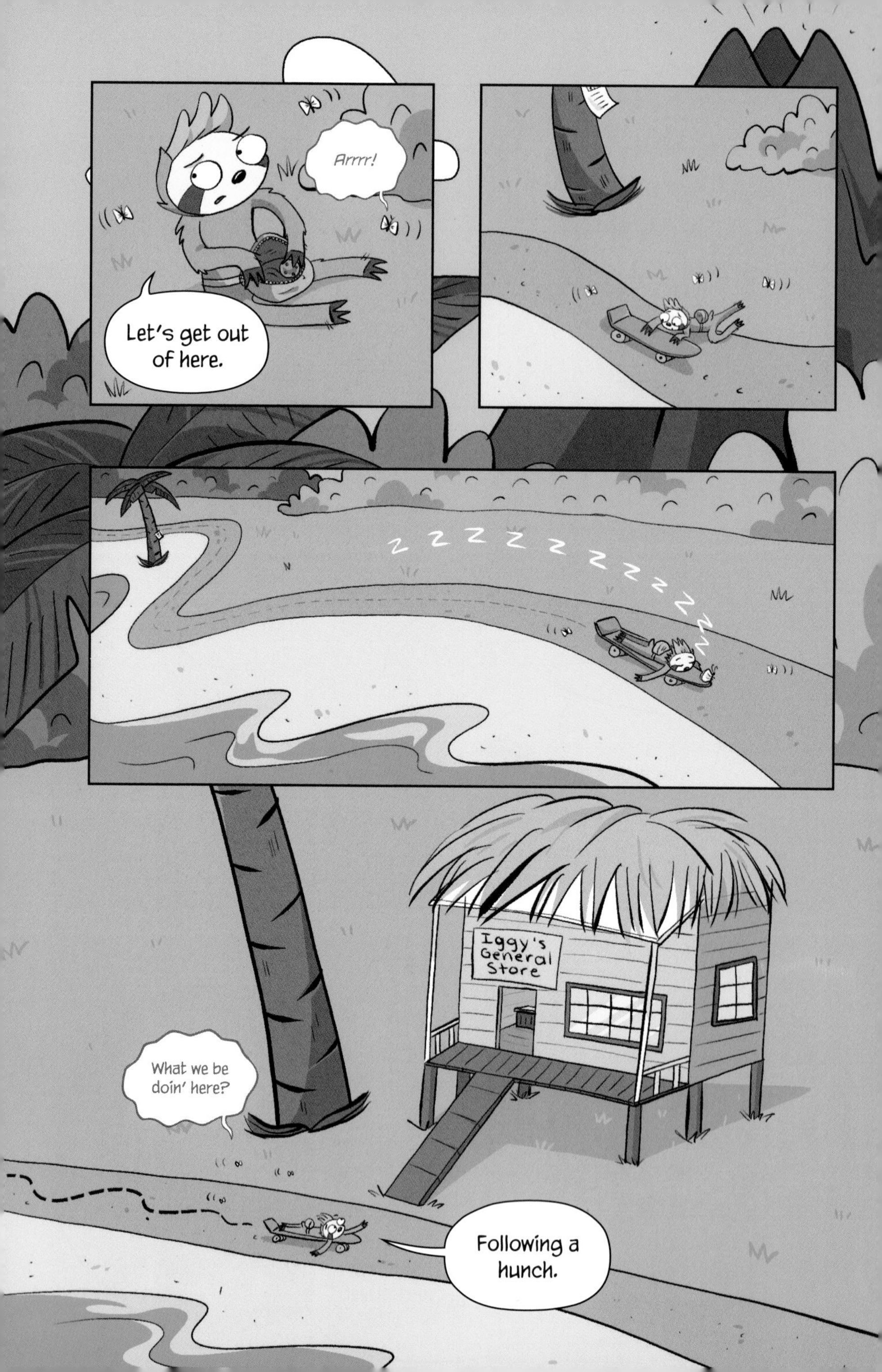
Arrrr!
Let's get out of here.
Z Z Z Z Z Z Z Z Z Z Z Z
Iggy's General Store
What we be doin' here?
Following a hunch.

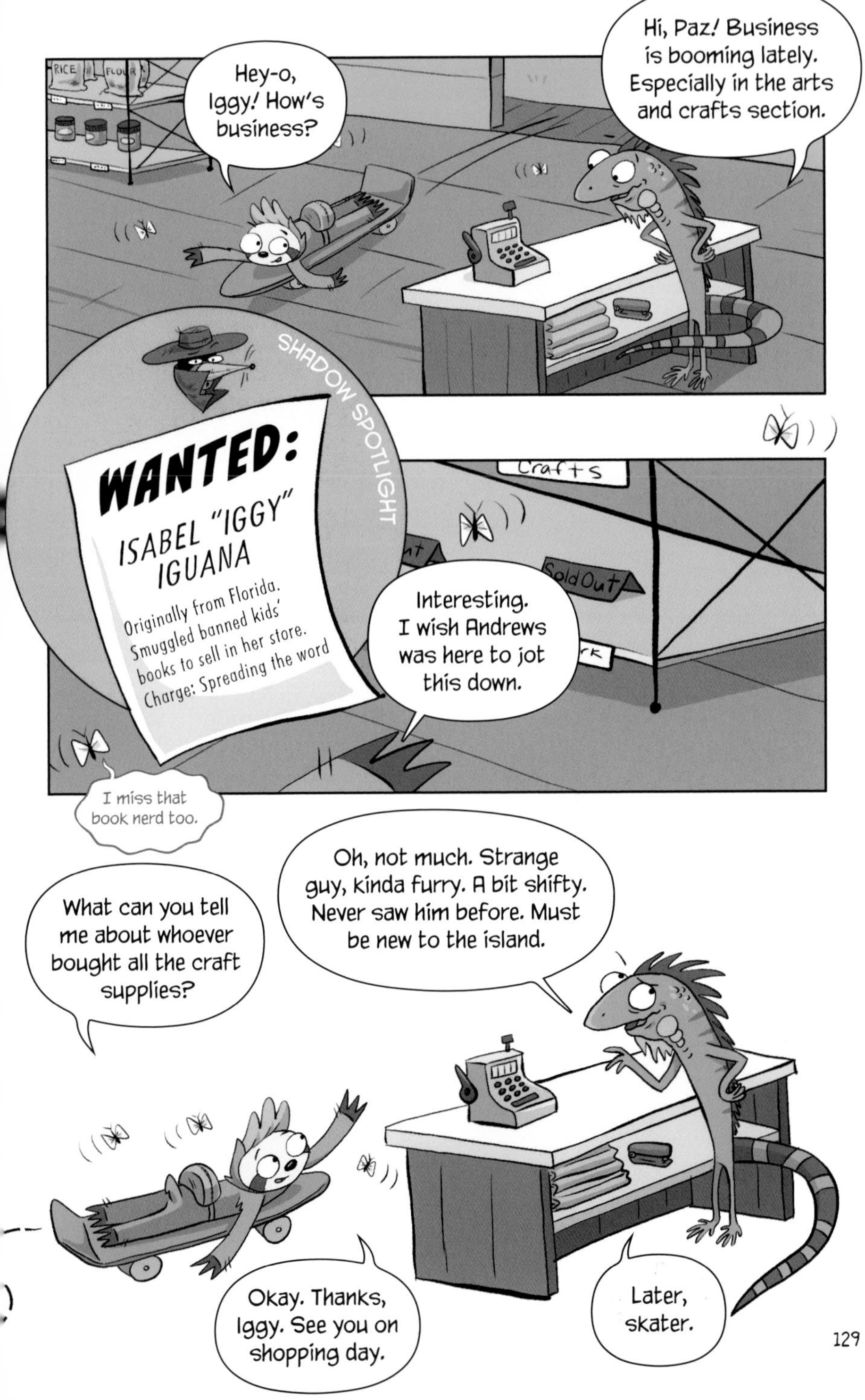

Hey-o, Iggy! How's business?
Hi, Paz! Business is booming lately. Especially in the arts and crafts section.
RICE
FLOUR
SHADOW SPOTLIGHT
WANTED:
ISABEL "IGGY" IGUANA
Originally from Florida. Smuggled banned kids' books to sell in her store. Charge: Spreading the word
Crafts
Sold Out
Interesting. I wish Andrews was here to jot this down.
I miss that book nerd too.
What can you tell me about whoever bought all the craft supplies?
Oh, not much. Strange guy, kinda furry. A bit shifty. Never saw him before. Must be new to the island.
Okay. Thanks, Iggy. See you on shopping day.
Later, skater.

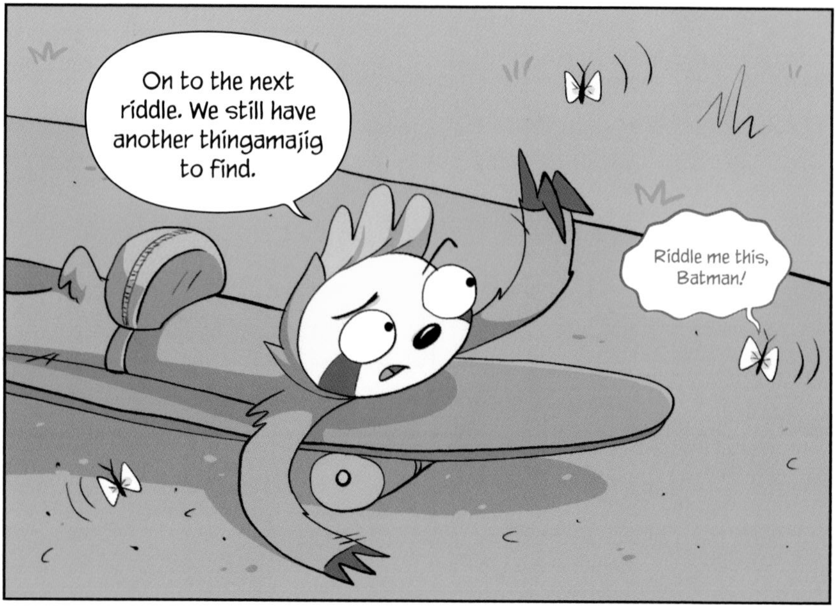
On to the next riddle. We still have another thingamajig to find.
Riddle me this, Batman!

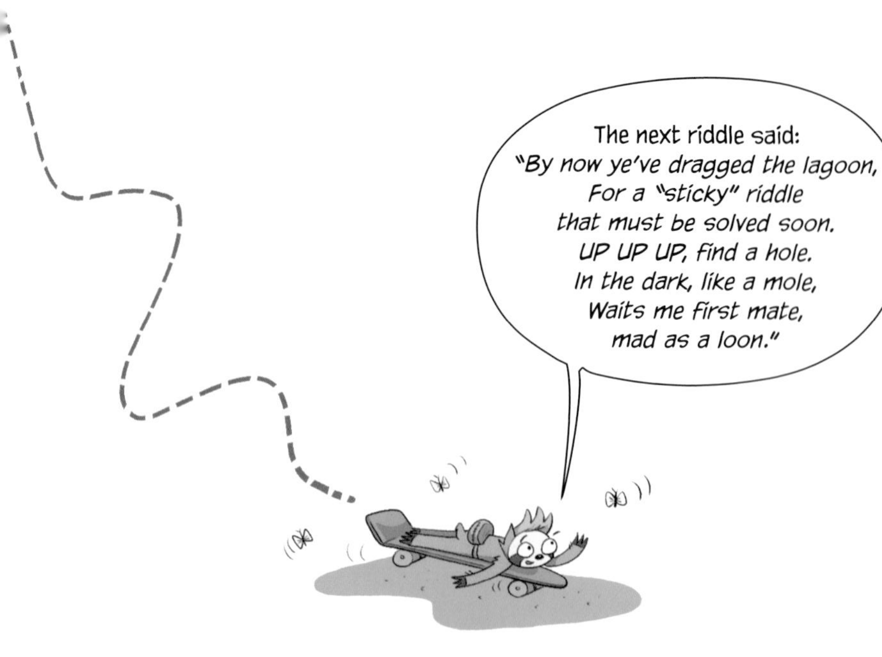
The next riddle said:
"By now ye've dragged the lagoon,
For a "sticky" riddle
that must be solved soon.
UP UP UP, find a hole.
In the dark, like a mole,
Waits me first mate,
mad as a loon."

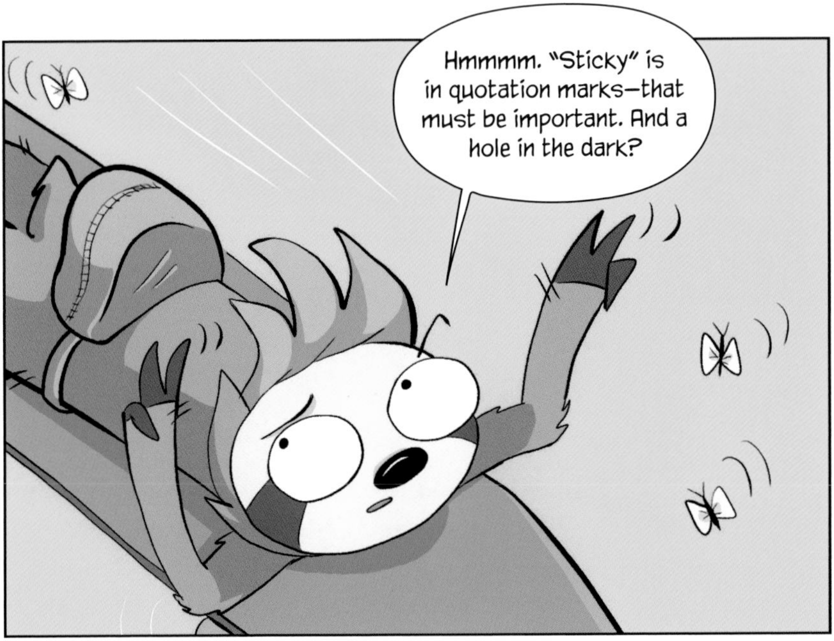
Hmmmm. "Sticky" is in quotation marks—that must be important. And a hole in the dark?

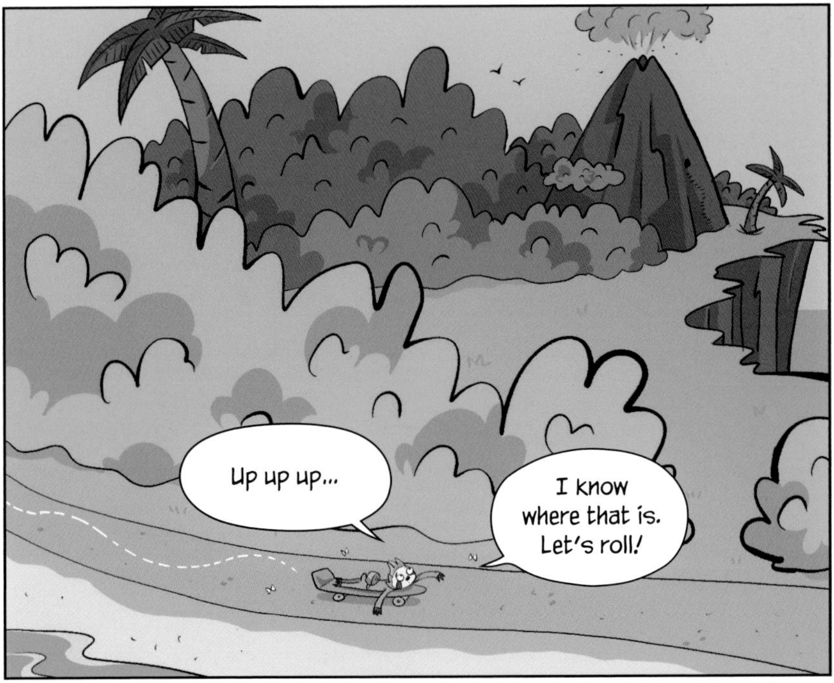
Up up up...
I know where that is. Let's roll!

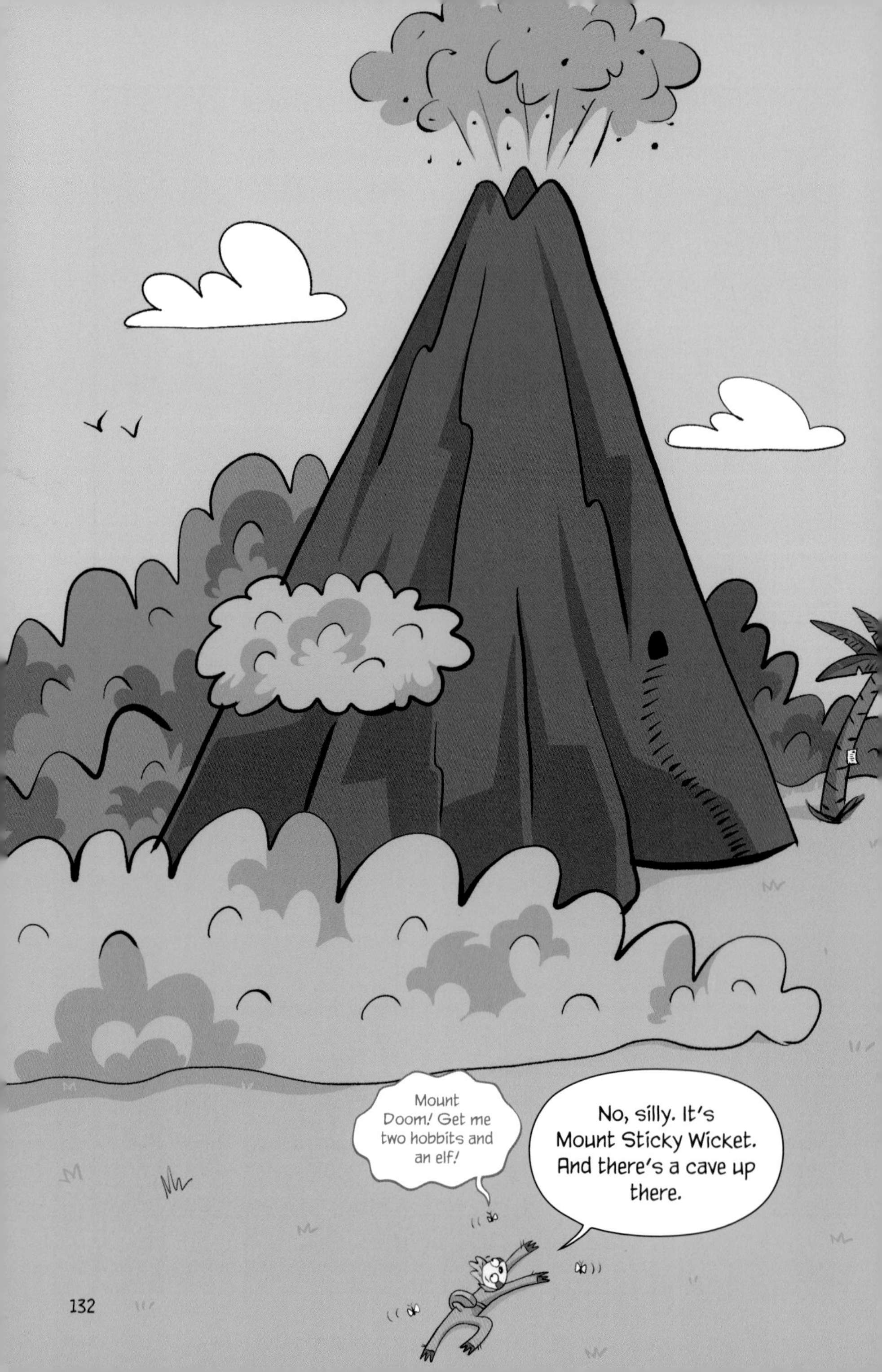
Mount Doom! Get me two hobbits and an elf!
No, silly. It's Mount Sticky Wicket. And there's a cave up there.

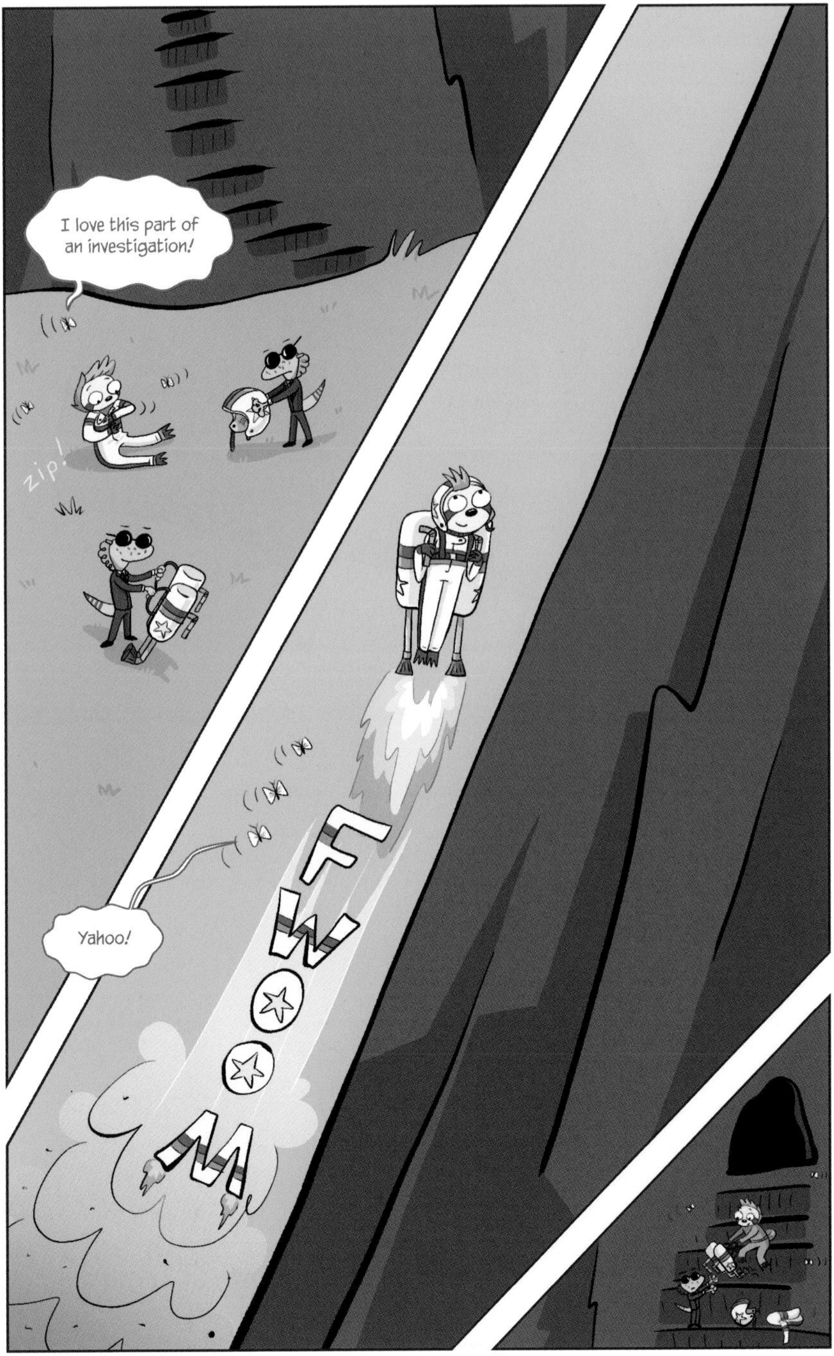
I love this part of an investigation!
zip!
Yahoo!
FWOOM

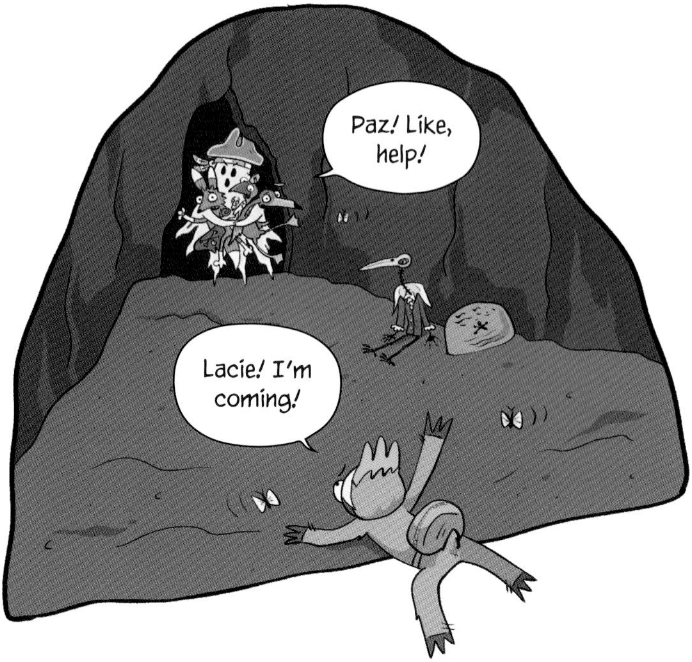
Paz! Like, help!
Lacie! I'm coming!

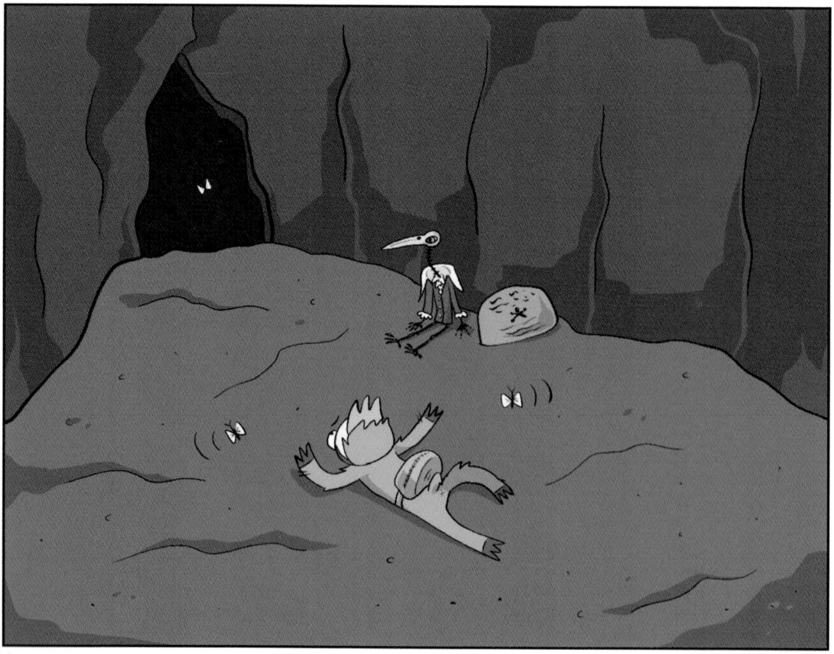

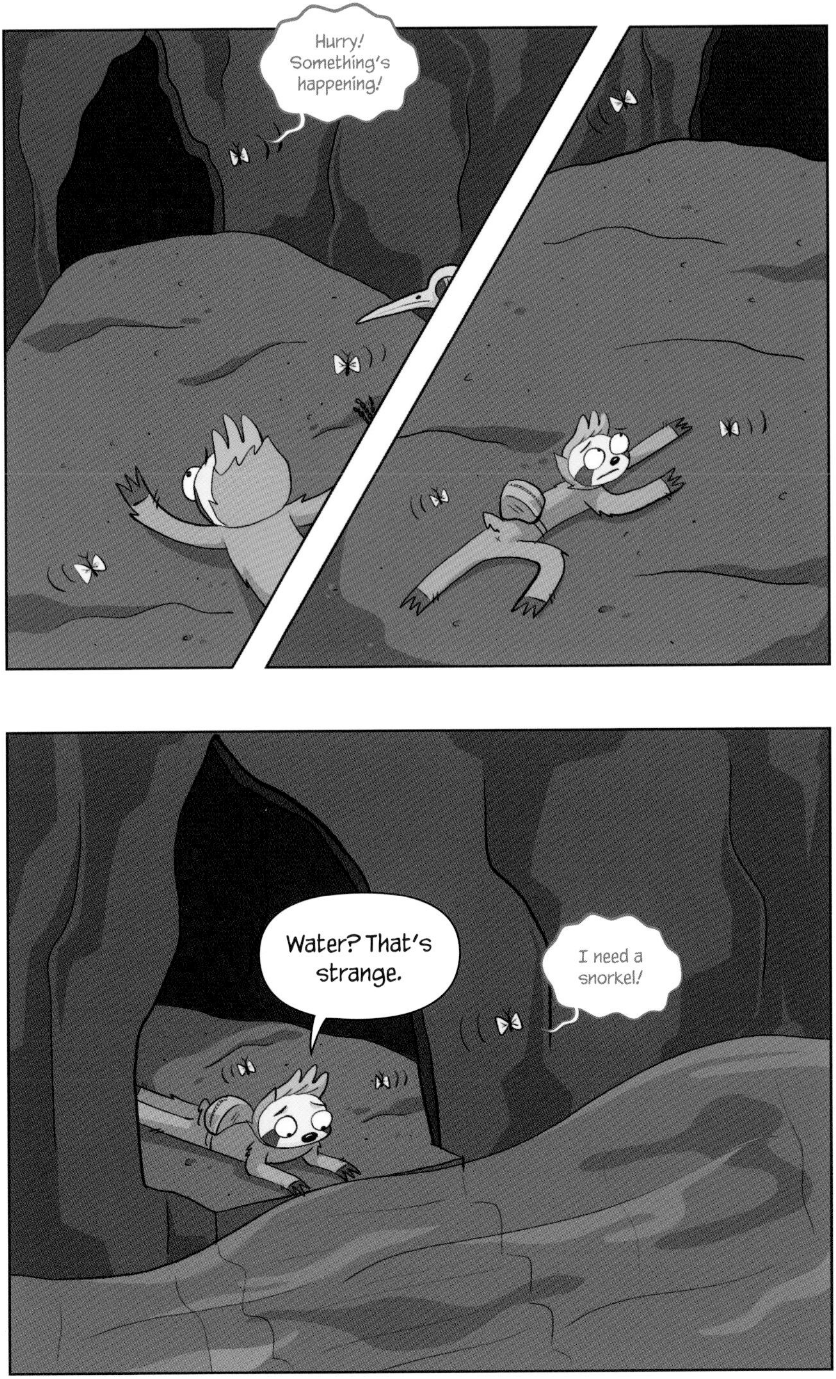
Hurry! Something's happening!
Water? That's strange.
I need a snorkel!

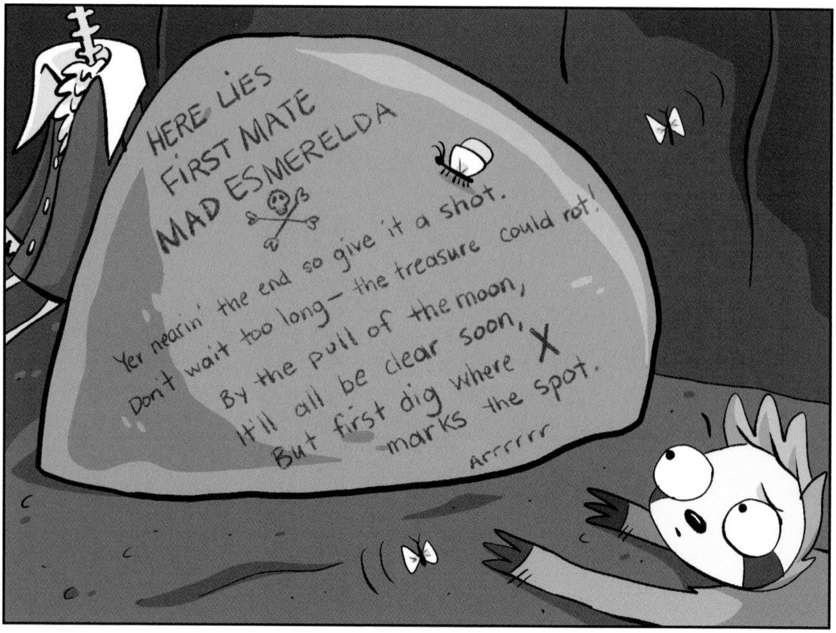
HERE LIES
FIRST MATE
MAD ESMERELDA
Yer nearin' the end so give it a shot.
Don't wait too long— the treasure could rot!
By the pull of the moon,
It'll all be clear soon,
But first dig where X marks the spot.
Arrrrrr

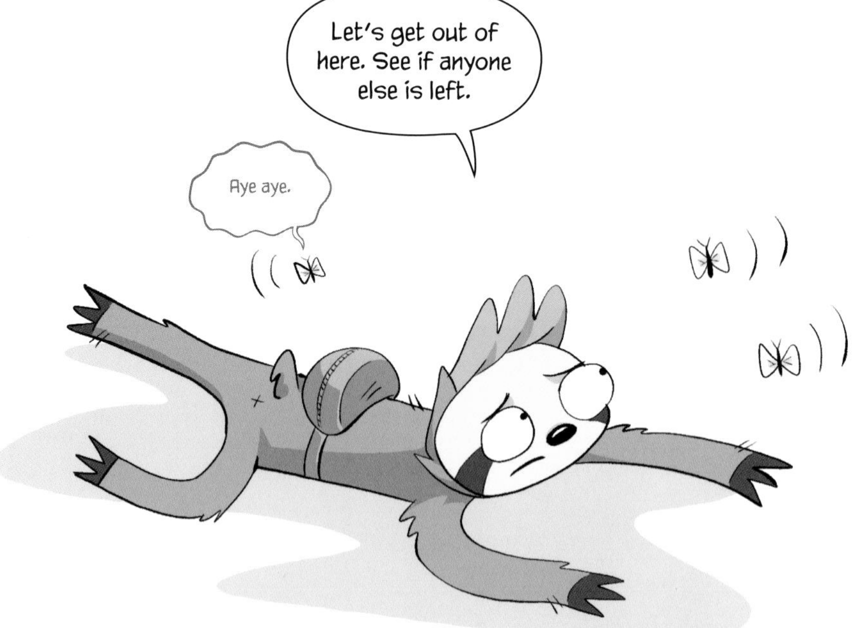
Let's get out of here. See if anyone else is left.
Aye aye.

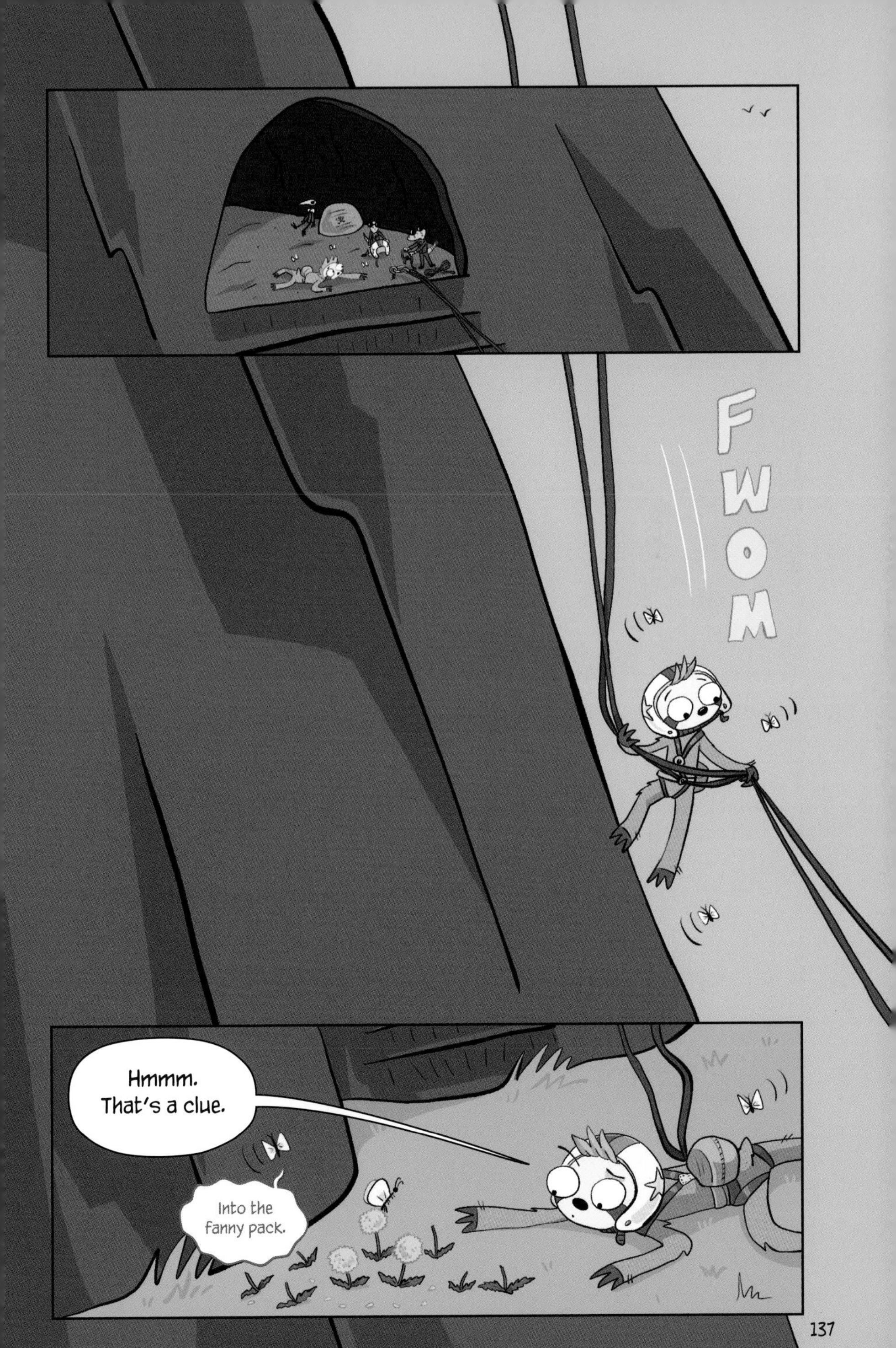
FWOM
Hmmm. That's a clue.
Into the fanny pack.

THURSDAY. LATE AFTERNOON;
WAY PAST NAP TIME. BACK AT THE LIBRARY.

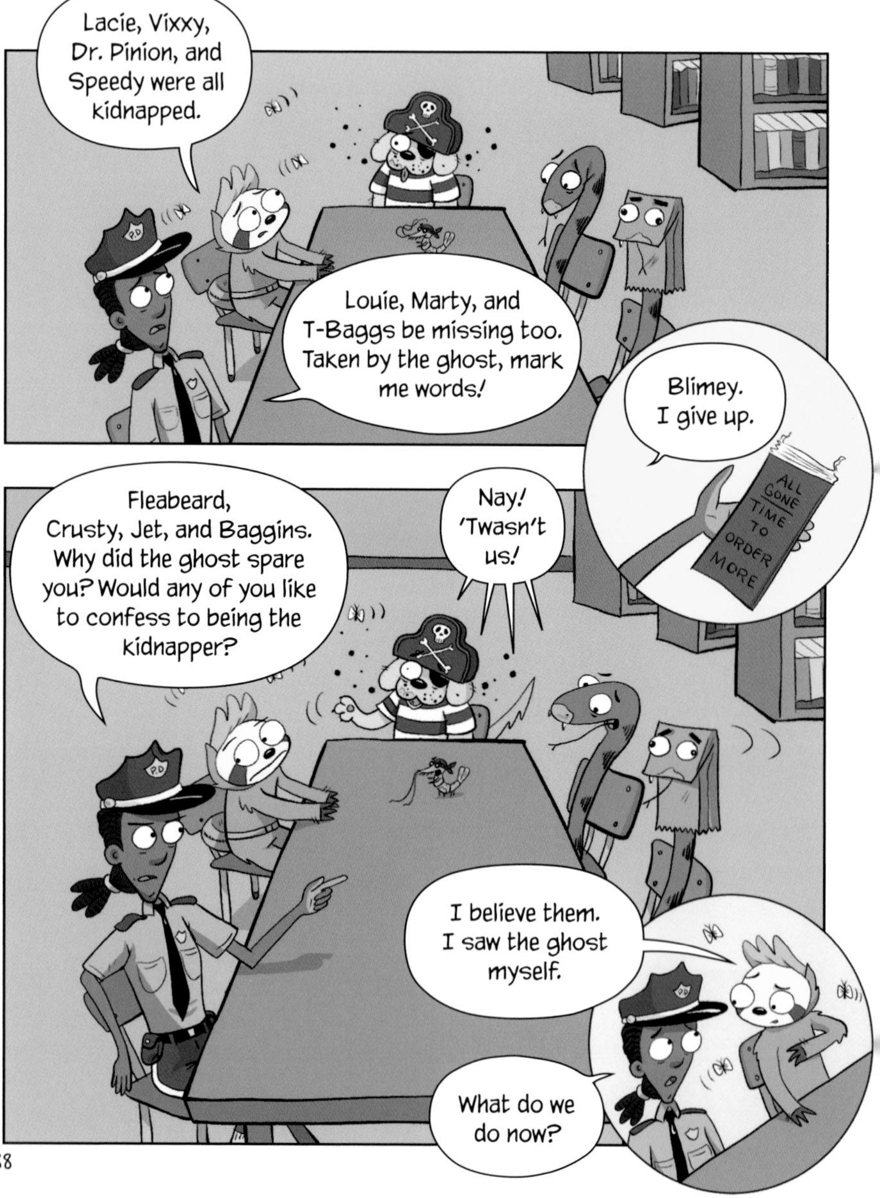
Lacie, Vixxy, Dr. Pinion, and Speedy were all kidnapped.
Louie, Marty, and T-Baggs be missing too. Taken by the ghost, mark me words!
Blimey. I give up.
ALL GONE TIME TO ORDER MORE
Fleabeard, Crusty, Jet, and Baggins. Why did the ghost spare you? Would any of you like to confess to being the kidnapper?
Nay! 'Twasn't us!
I believe them. I saw the ghost myself.
What do we do now?

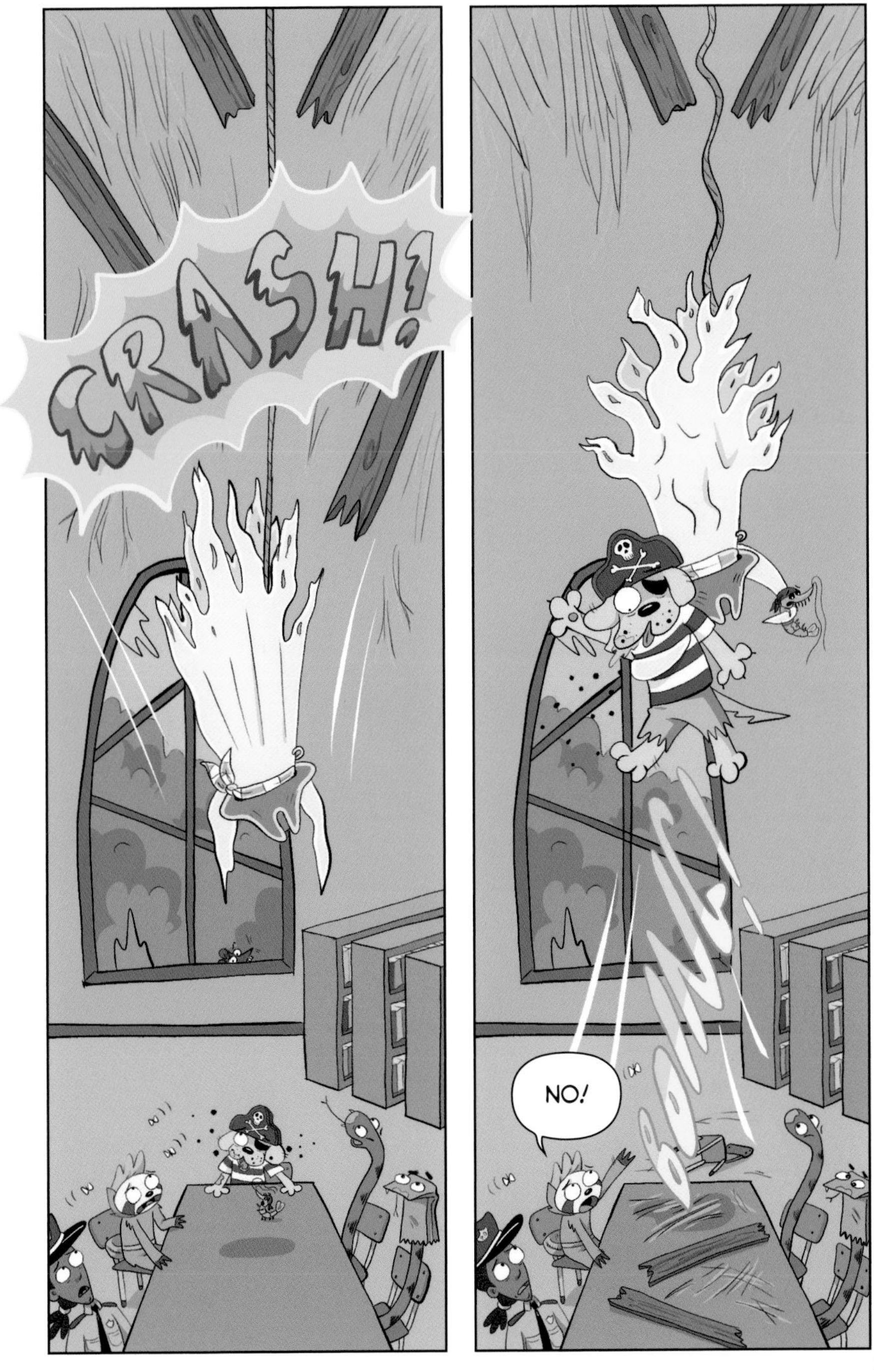
CRASH!
NO!

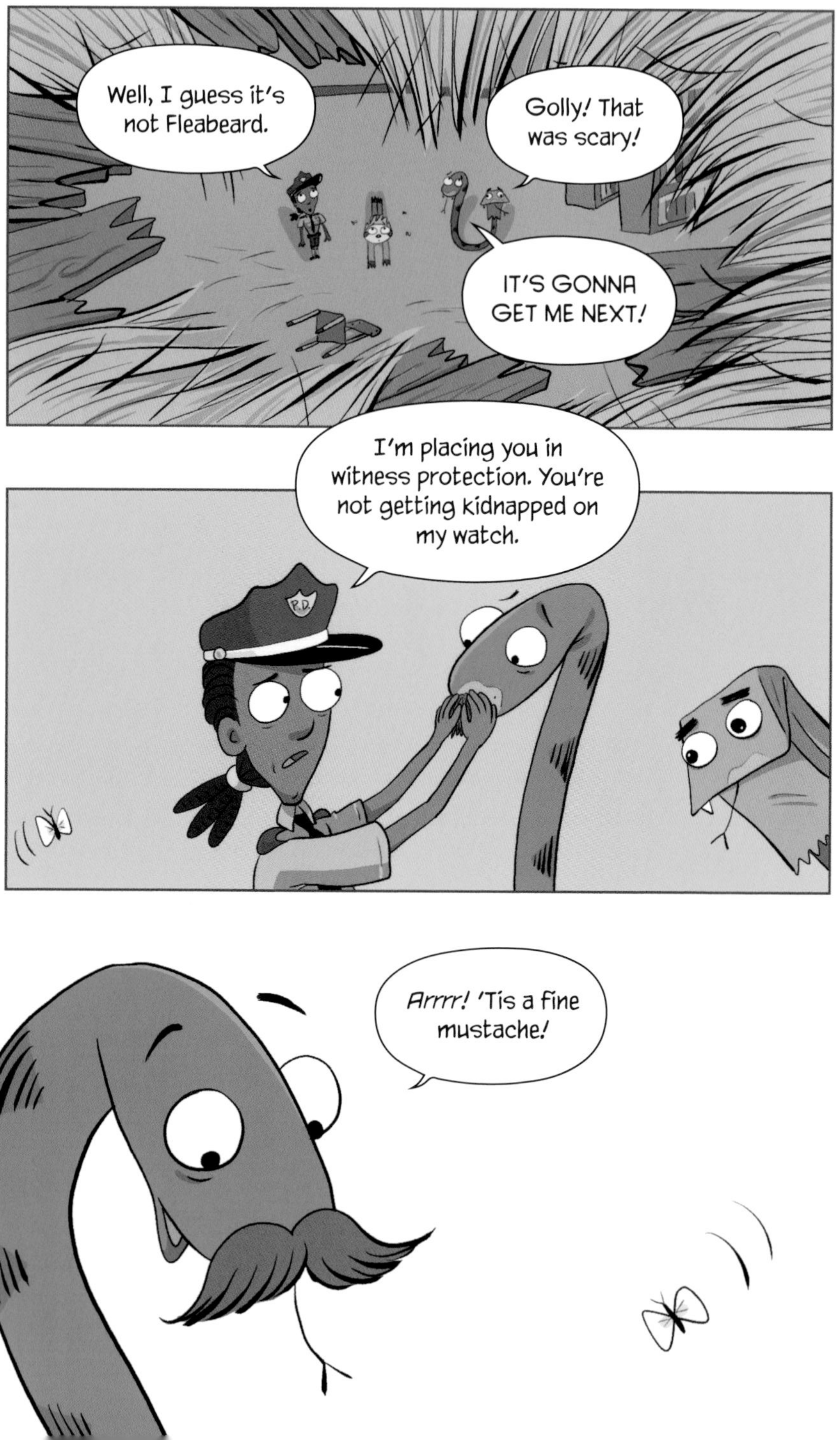
Well, I guess it's not Fleabeard.
Golly! That was scary!
IT'S GONNA GET ME NEXT!
I'm placing you in witness protection. You're not getting kidnapped on my watch.
P.D.
Arrrr! 'Tis a fine mustache!

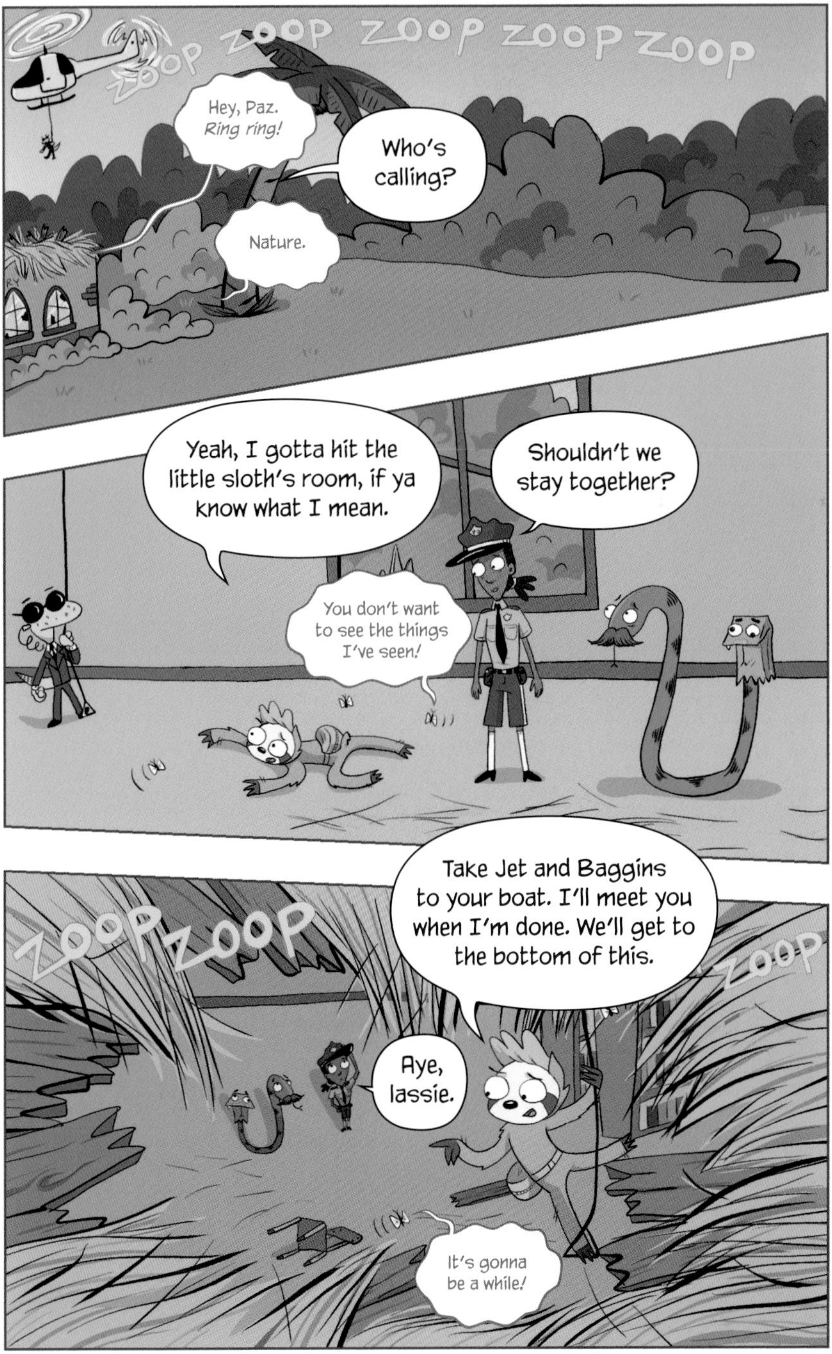
ZOOP ZOOP ZOOP ZOOP ZOOP ZOOP
Hey, Paz. *Ring ring!*
Who's calling?
Nature.
Yeah, I gotta hit the little sloth's room, if ya know what I mean.
Shouldn't we stay together?
You don't want to see the things I've seen!
ZOOP ZOOP
Take Jet and Baggins to your boat. I'll meet you when I'm done. We'll get to the bottom of this.
ZOOP
Aye, lassie.
It's gonna be a while!

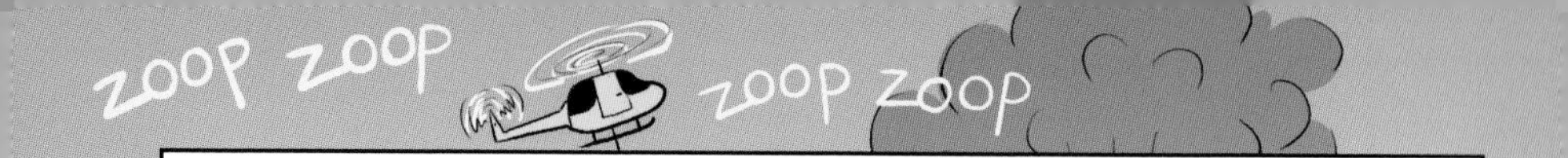
zoop zoop
zoop zoop

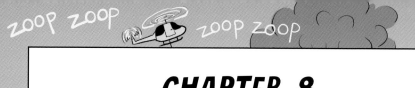

CHAPTER 8

THURSDAY. EARLY EVENING.
APPROACHING THE POOPER.

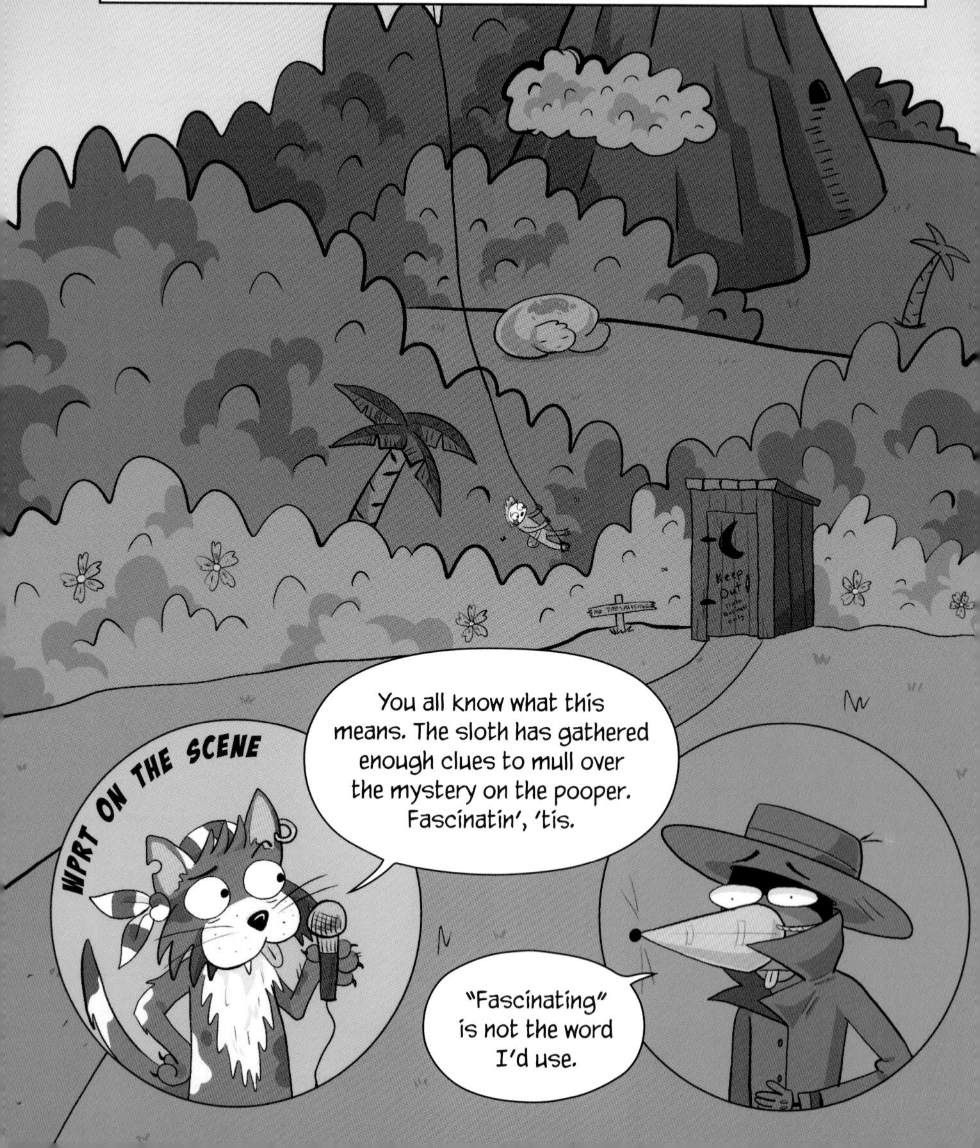
Keep Out!
WPRT ON THE SCENE
You all know what this means. The sloth has gathered enough clues to mull over the mystery on the pooper. Fascinatin', 'tis.
"Fascinating" is not the word I'd use.

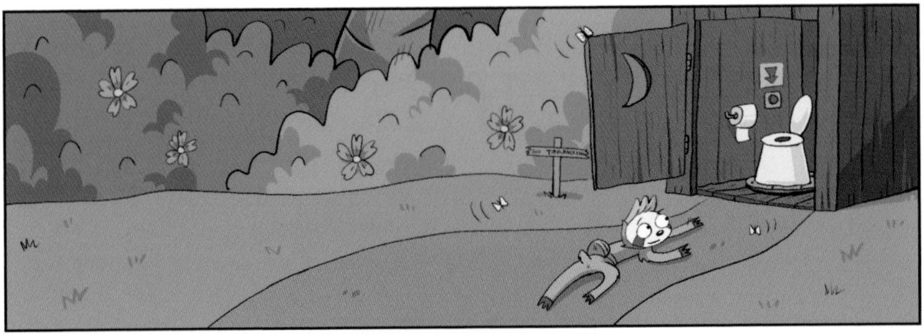

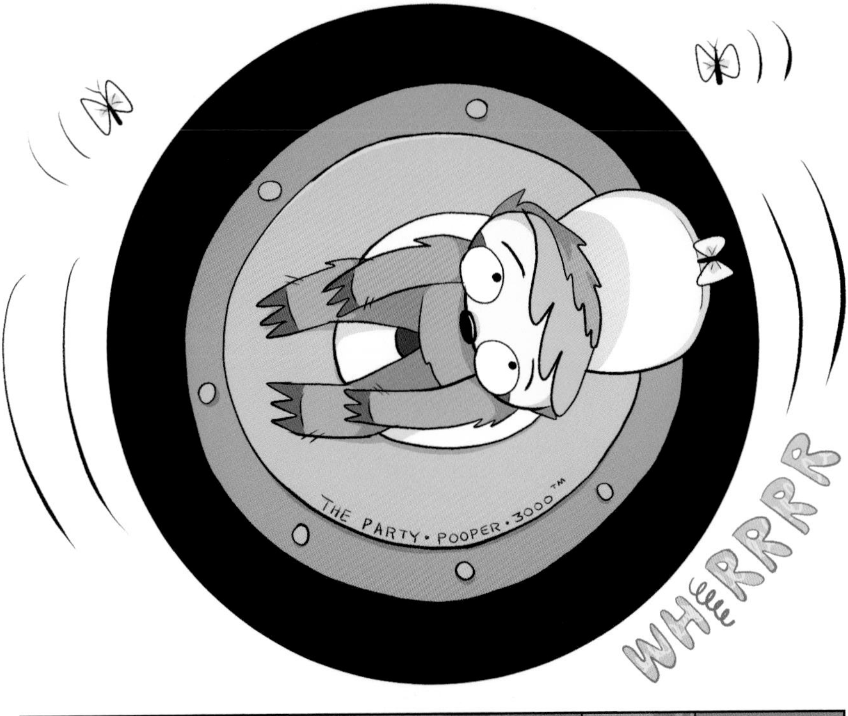
THE PARTY • POOPER • 3000™
WHeeeRRRR

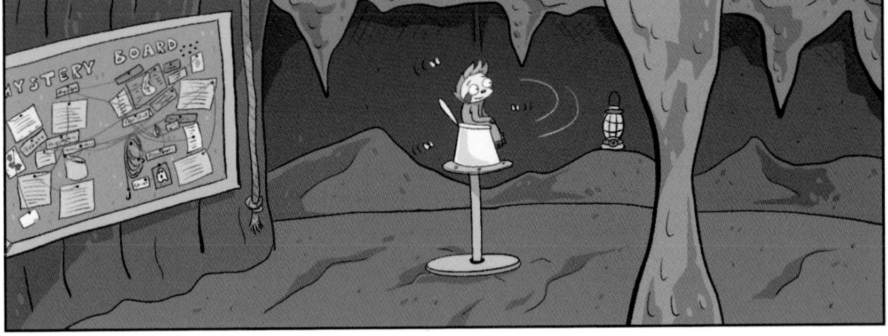
MYSTERY BOARD

CHAPTER 9

THURSDAY. WHEN MOST PEOPLE ARE WATCHING *WHEEL OF FORTUNE*. ON THE POOPER, SORTING OUT THE EVIDENCE.

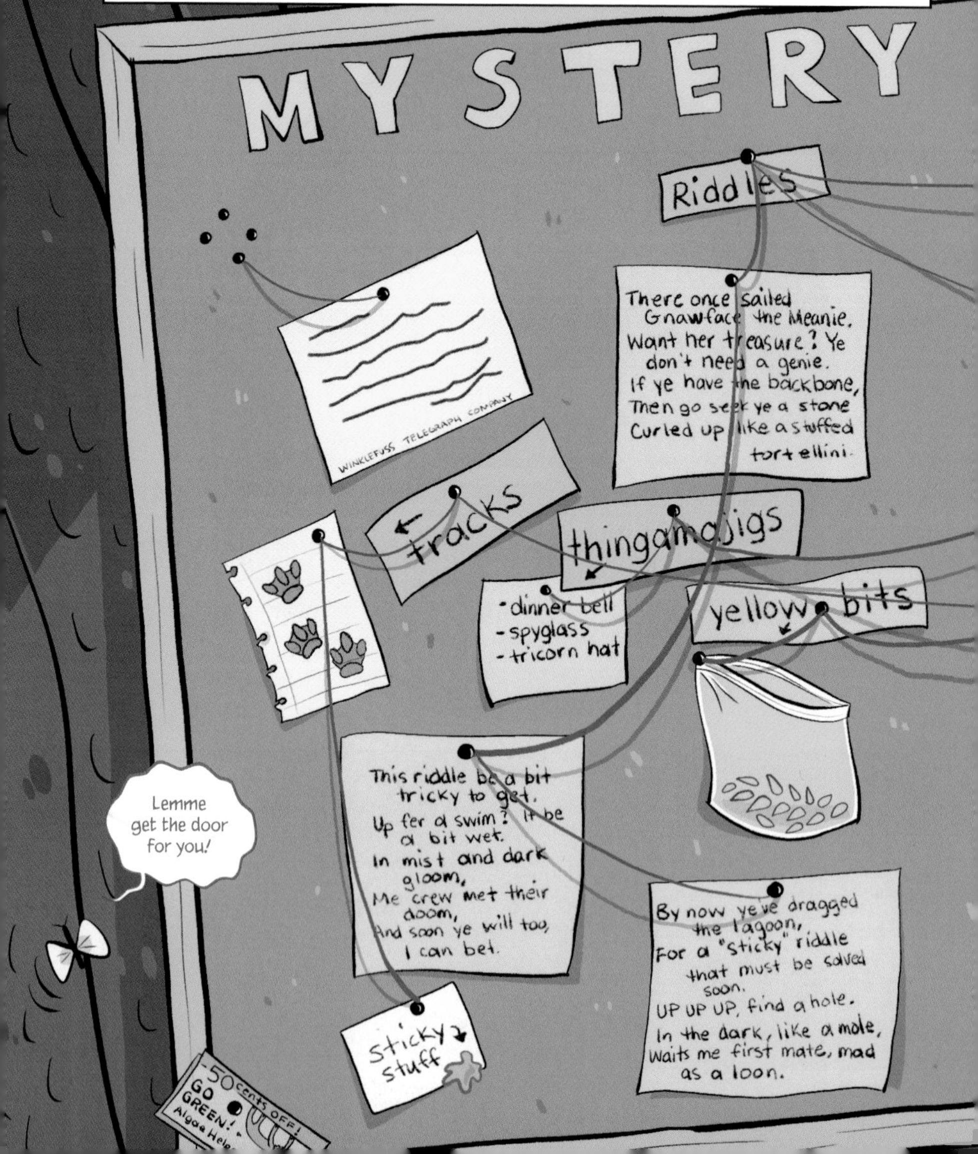
MYSTERY
Riddles
WINKLEFUSS TELEGRAPH COMPANY
There once sailed Gnawface the Meanie. Want her treasure? Ye don't need a genie. If ye have the backbone, Then go seek ye a stone Curled up like a stuffed tortellini.
tracks
thingamajigs
- dinner bell
- spyglass
- tricorn hat
yellow bits
This riddle be a bit tricky to get. Up fer a swim? It be a bit wet. In mist and dark gloom, Me crew met their doom, And soon ye will too, I can bet.
By now ye've dragged the lagoon, For a "sticky" riddle that must be solved soon. UP UP UP, find a hole. In the dark, like a mole, Waits me first mate, mad as a loon.
sticky stuff
Lemme get the door for you!
50 cents OFF!
GO GREEN!

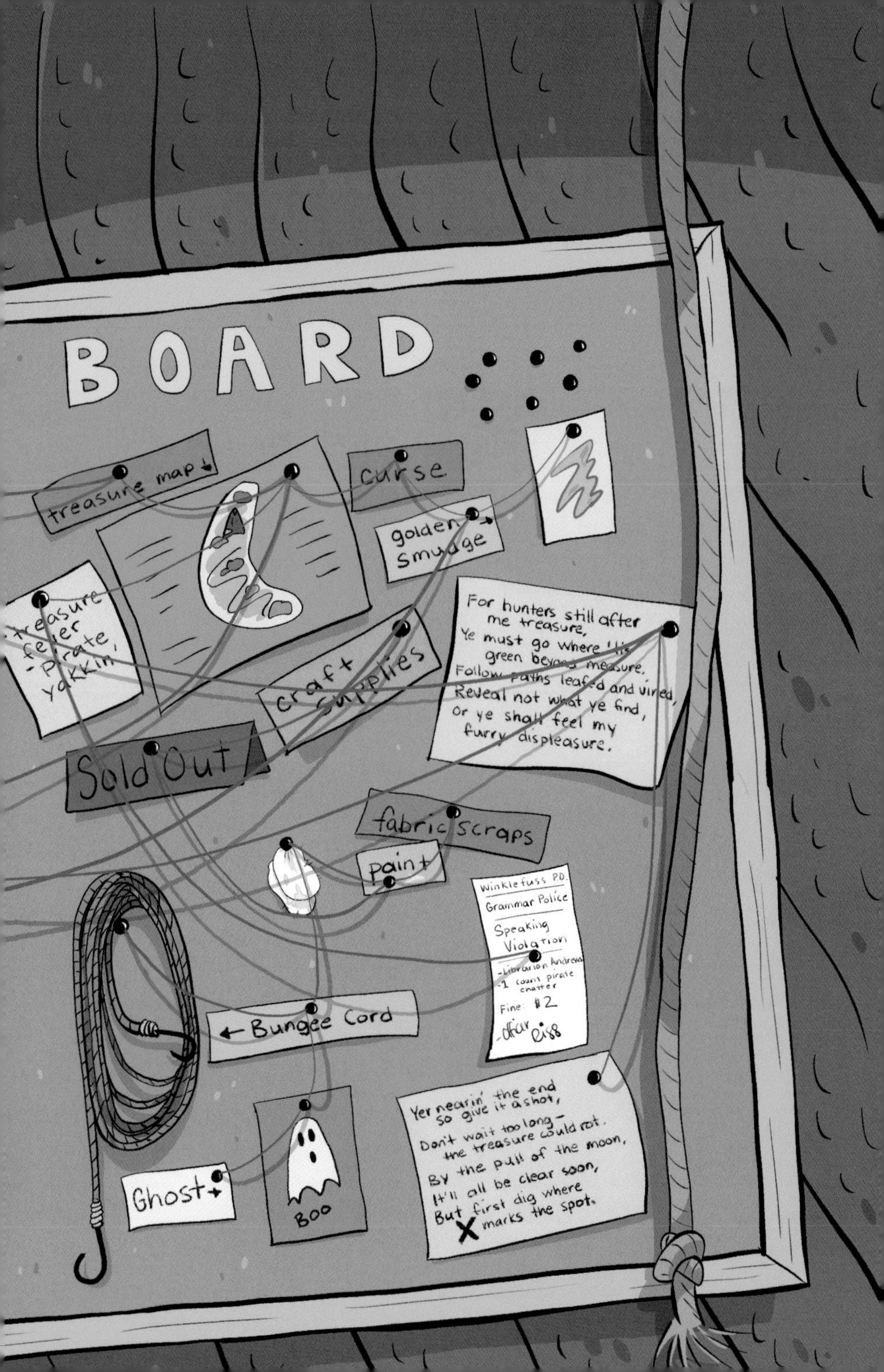
BOARD
treasure map↓
curse
golden smudge
treasure fever -Pirate Yakkin
craft supplies
Sold Out
For hunters still after me treasure,
Ye must go where 'tis green beyond measure.
Follow paths leafed and vined,
Reveal not what ye find,
Or ye shall feel my furry displeasure.
fabric scraps
paint
Winklefuss P.D.
Grammar Police
Speaking Violation
-Librarian Andrews
-1 count pirate chatter
Fine: $2
-Officer Riss
← Bungee Cord
Ghost
Boo
Yer nearin' the end so give it a shot,
Don't wait too long— the treasure could rot.
By the pull of the moon,
It'll all be clear soon,
But first dig where X marks the spot.

CHAPTER 10

THURSDAY. LONG AFTER PRIME TIME.
FINISHING UP SOME BUSINESS.

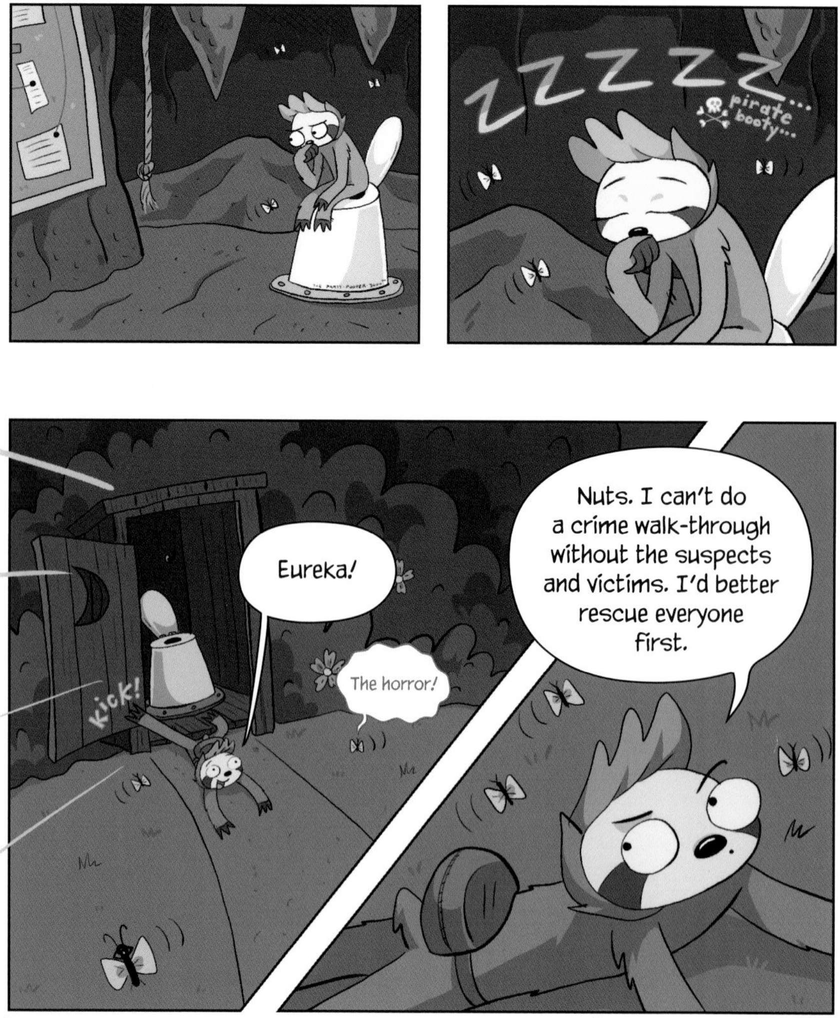
ZZZZZZ...
pirate booty...
KICK!
Eureka!
The horror!
Nuts. I can't do a crime walk-through without the suspects and victims. I'd better rescue everyone first.

CHAPTER II

THURSDAY. IN THE MOONLIGHT.
EMPTY AND RARING TO GO.

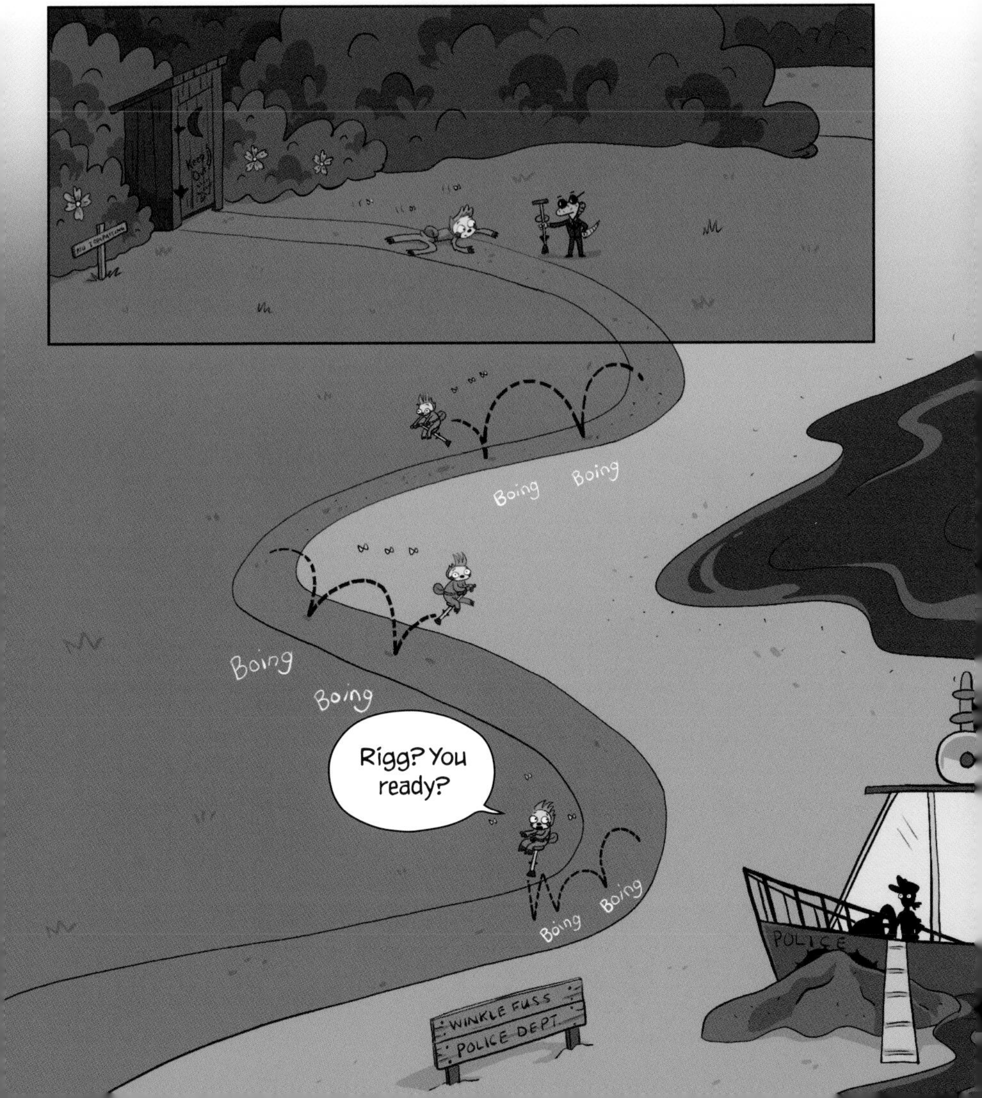
Boing
Boing
Boing
Boing
Rigg? You ready?
Boing
Boing
POLICE
WINKLE FUSS
POLICE DEPT.

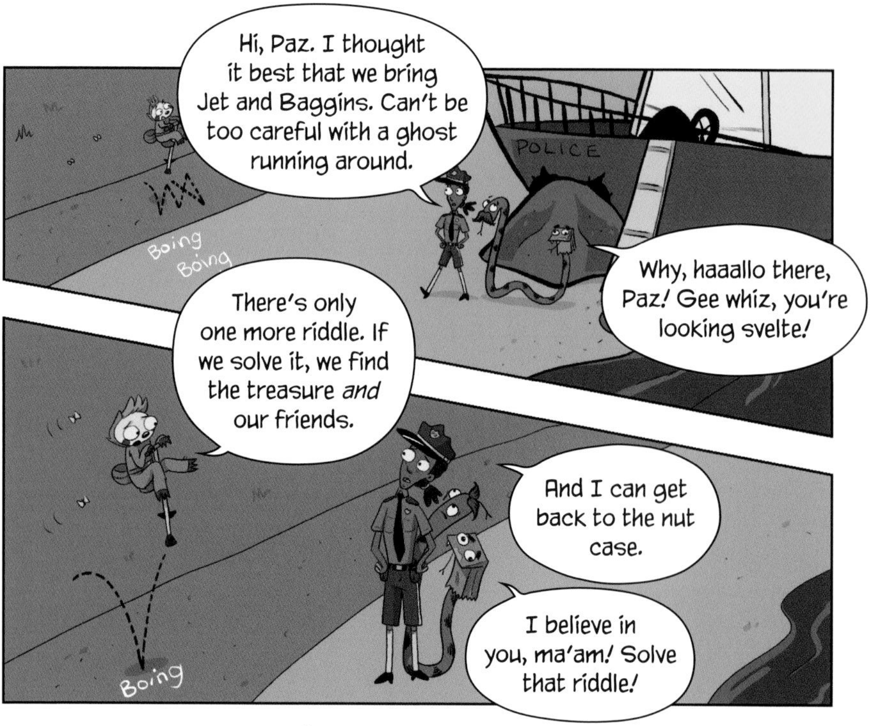
Hi, Paz. I thought it best that we bring Jet and Baggins. Can't be too careful with a ghost running around.
POLICE
Boing Boing
Why, haaallo there, Paz! Gee whiz, you're looking svelte!
There's only one more riddle. If we solve it, we find the treasure *and* our friends.
And I can get back to the nut case.
I believe in you, ma'am! Solve that riddle!
Boing

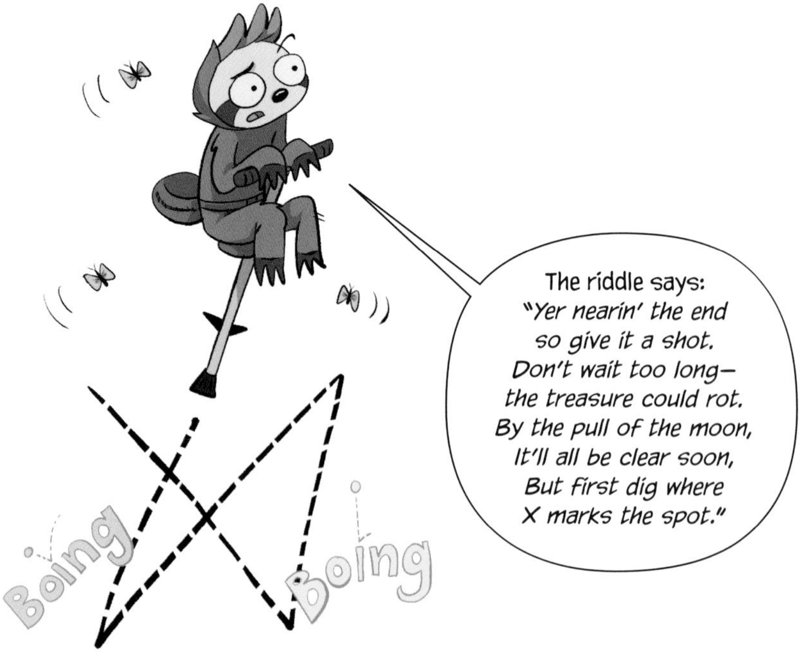
The riddle says:
"Yer nearin' the end so give it a shot. Don't wait too long— the treasure could rot. By the pull of the moon, It'll all be clear soon, But first dig where X marks the spot."
Boing
Boing

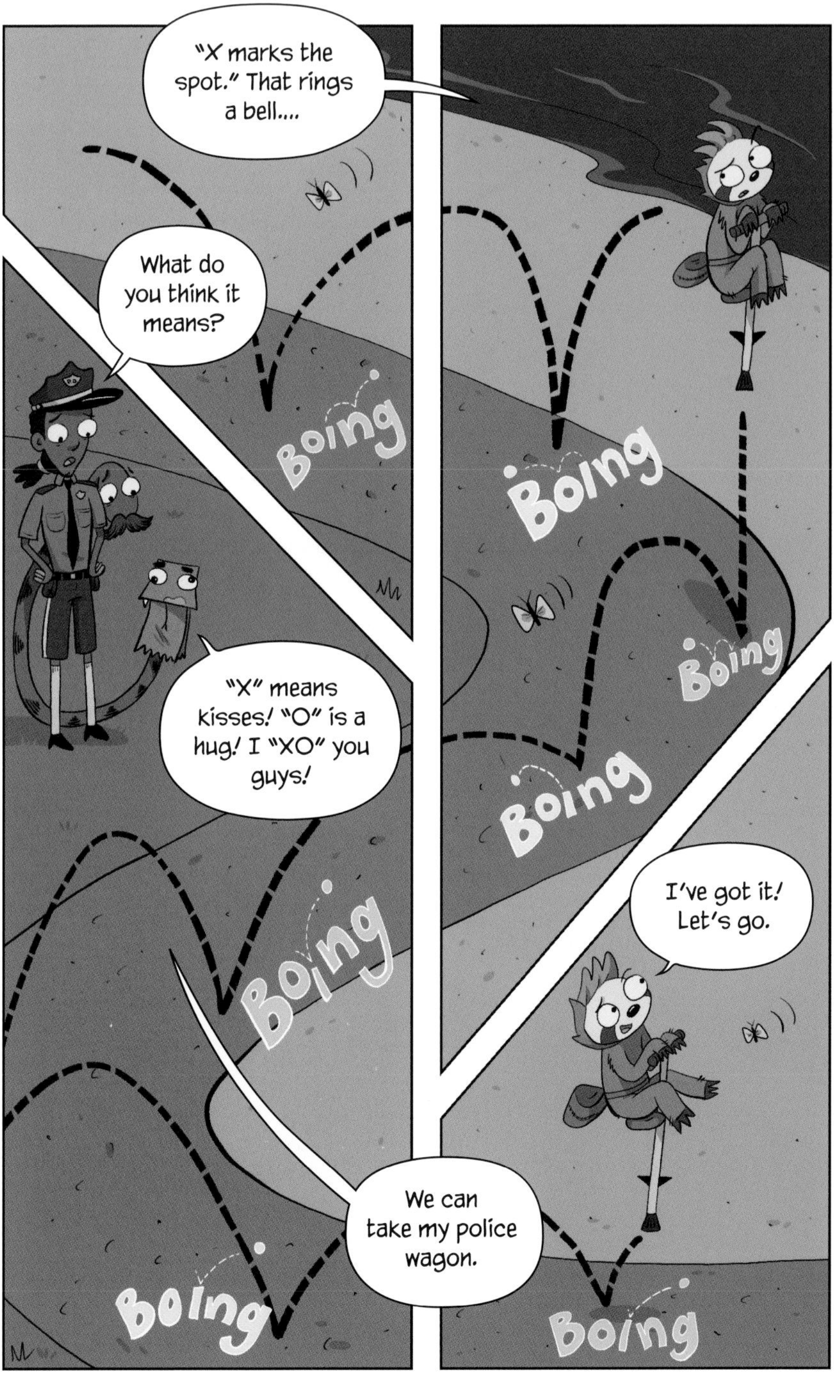
"X marks the spot." That rings a bell....
What do you think it means?
Boing
"X" means kisses! "O" is a hug! I "XO" you guys!
Boing
Boing
Boing
Boing
I've got it! Let's go.
We can take my police wagon.
Boing
Boing

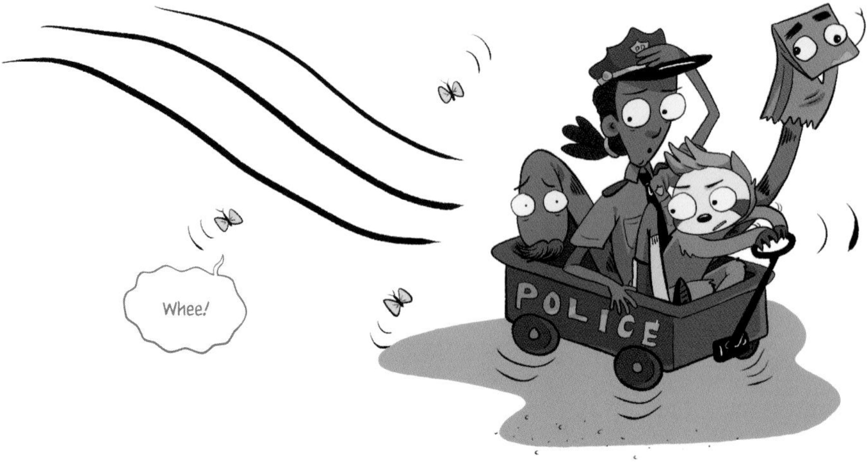
Whee!
POLICE

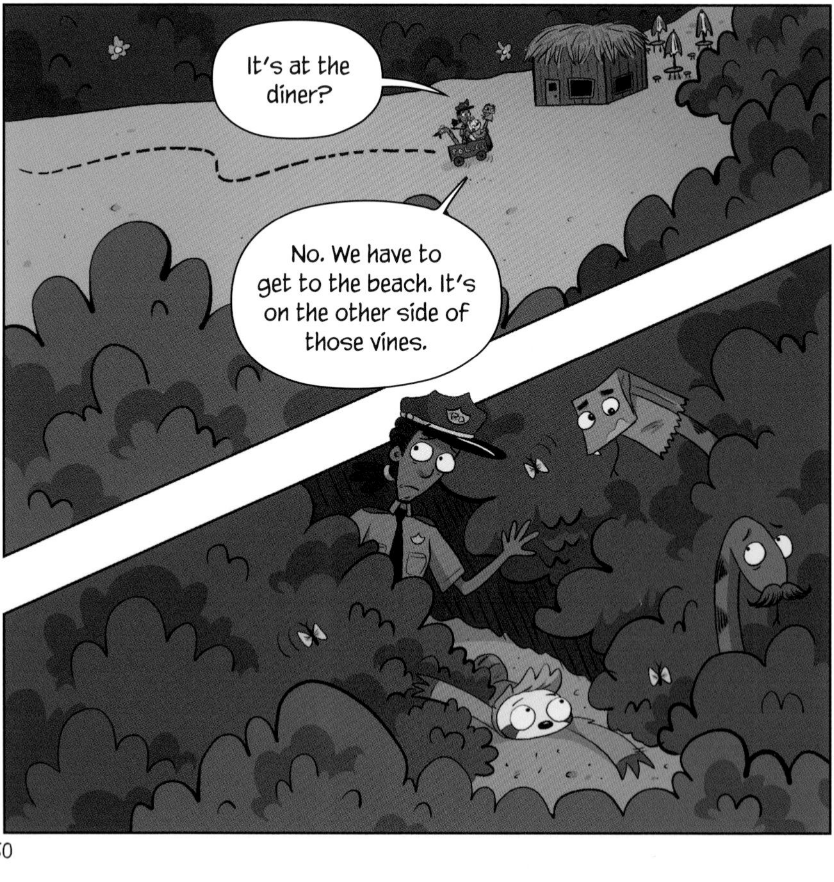
It's at the diner?
No. We have to get to the beach. It's on the other side of those vines.

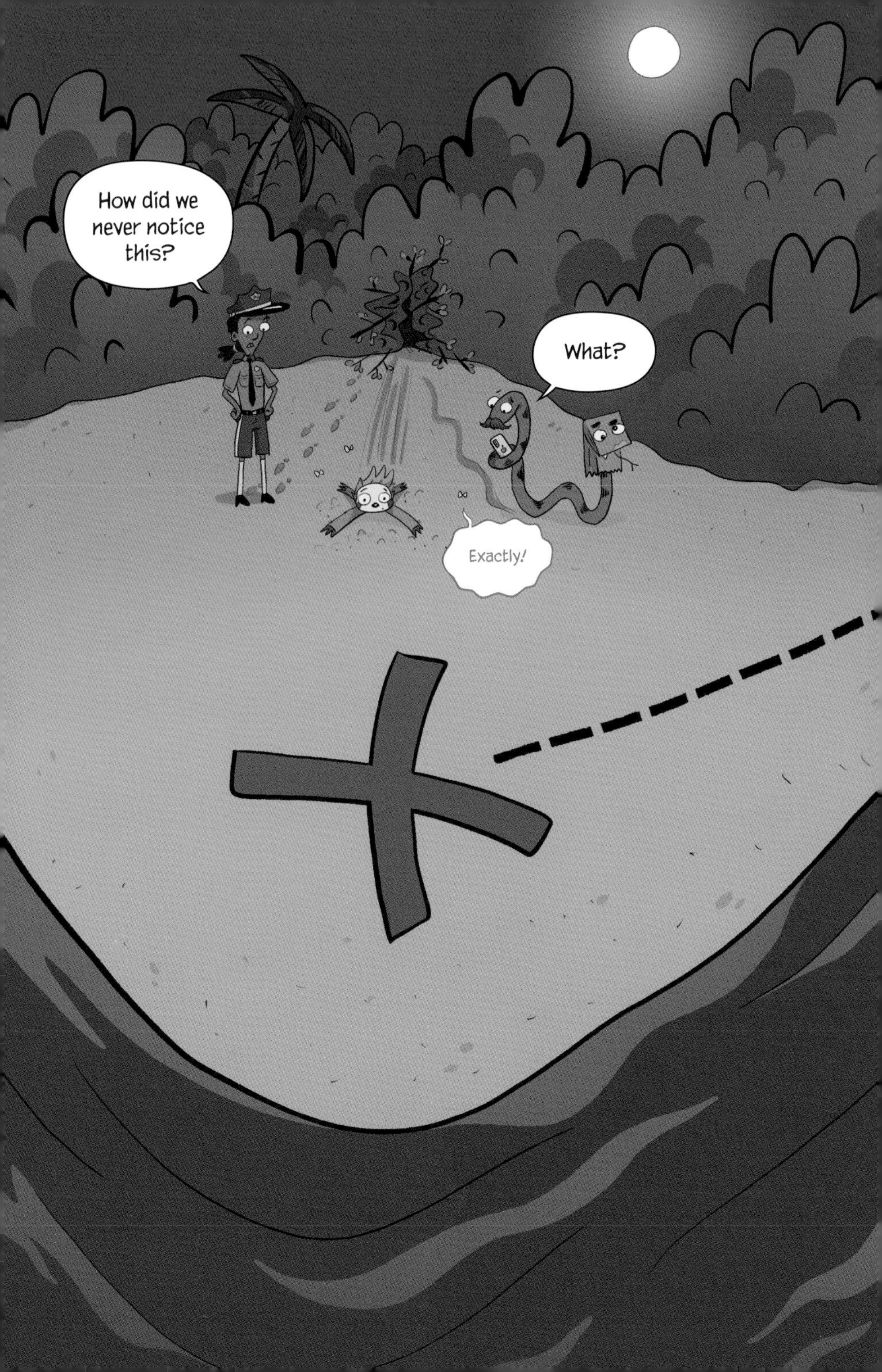
How did we never notice this?
What?
Exactly!

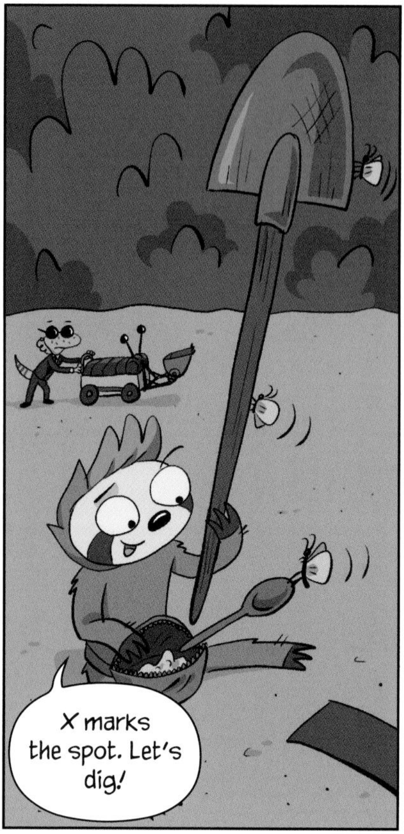
X marks the spot. Let's dig!

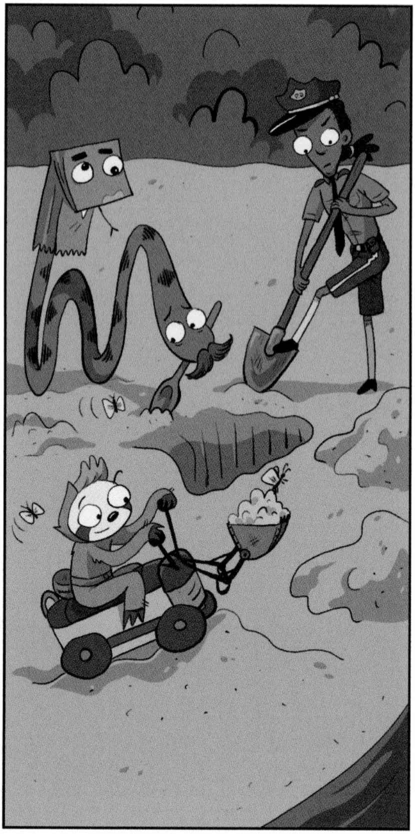

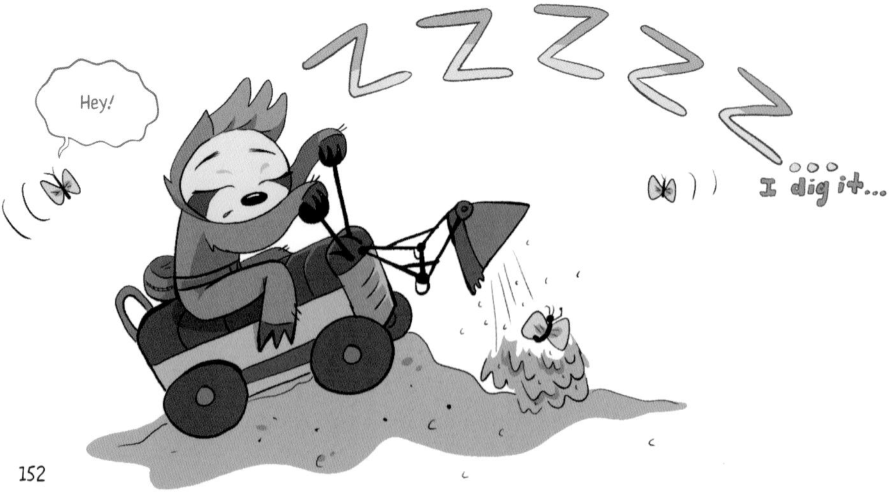
Hey!
ZZZZZ...
I dig it...

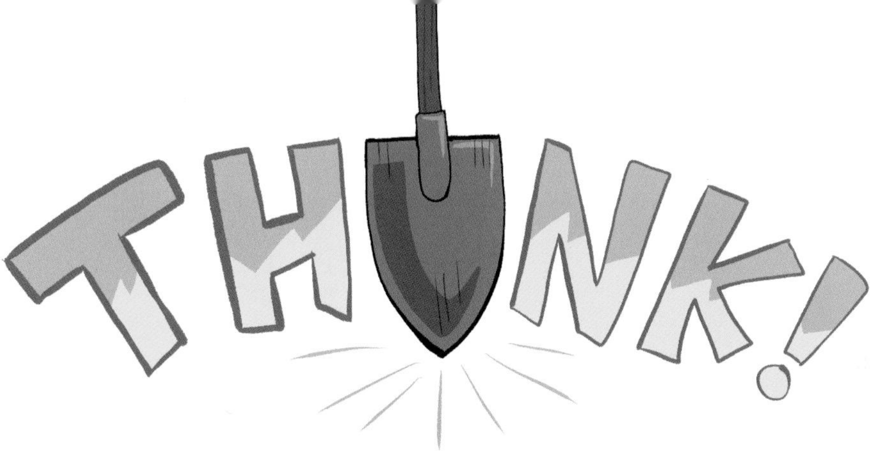
THUNK!

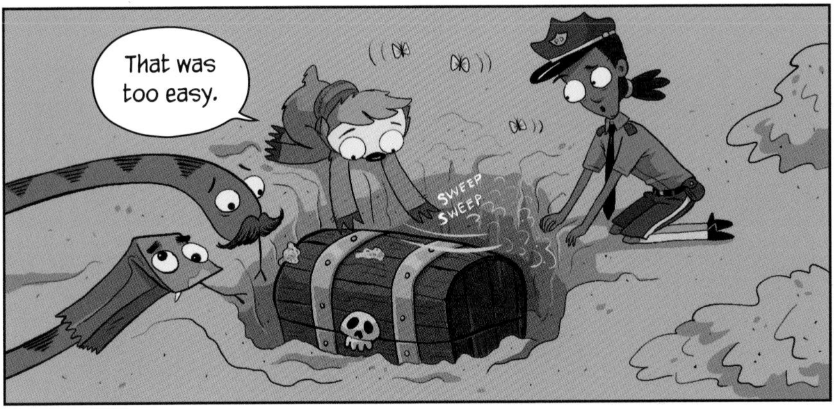
That was too easy.
SWEEP SWEEP

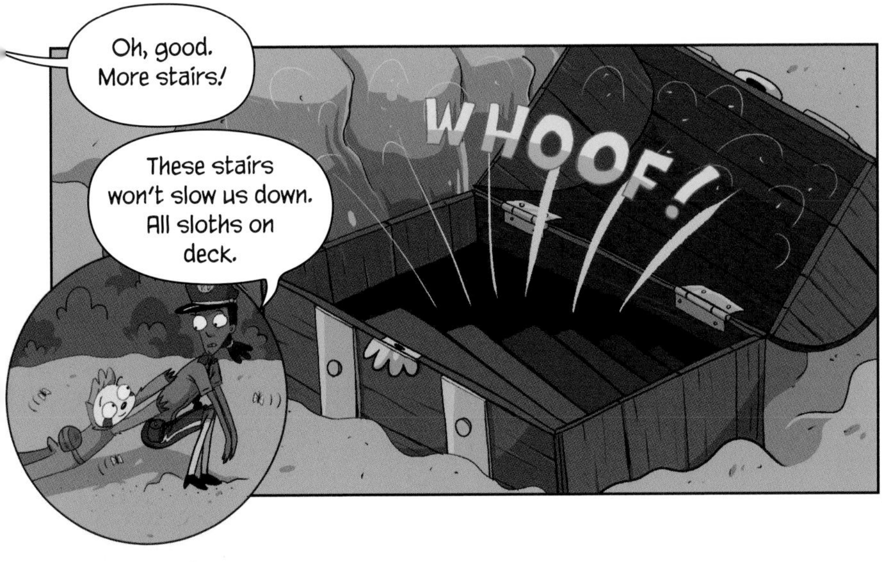
Oh, good. More stairs!
WHOOF!
These stairs won't slow us down. All sloths on deck.

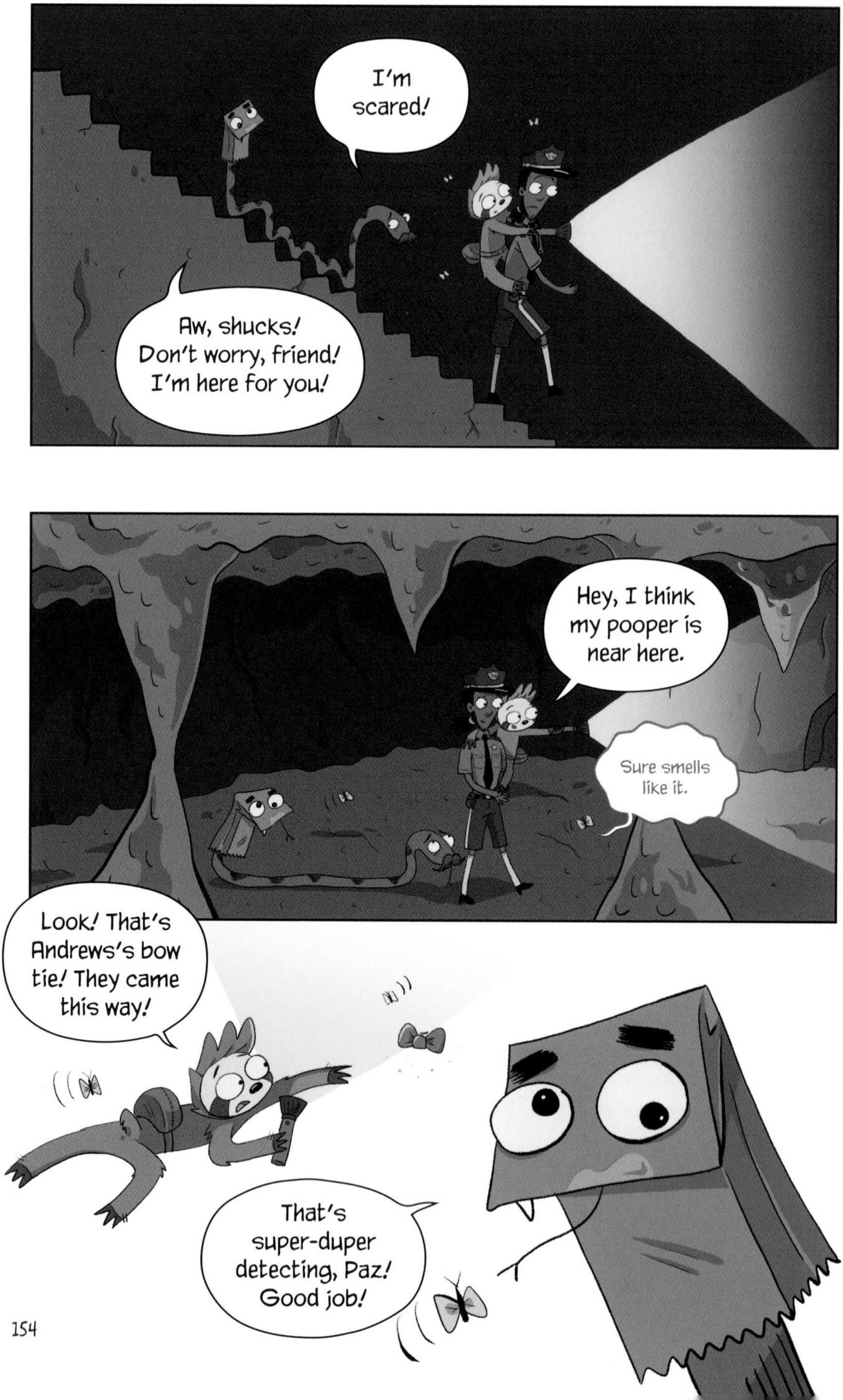
I'm scared!
Aw, shucks! Don't worry, friend! I'm here for you!
Hey, I think my pooper is near here.
Sure smells like it.
Look! That's Andrews's bow tie! They came this way!
That's super-duper detecting, Paz! Good job!

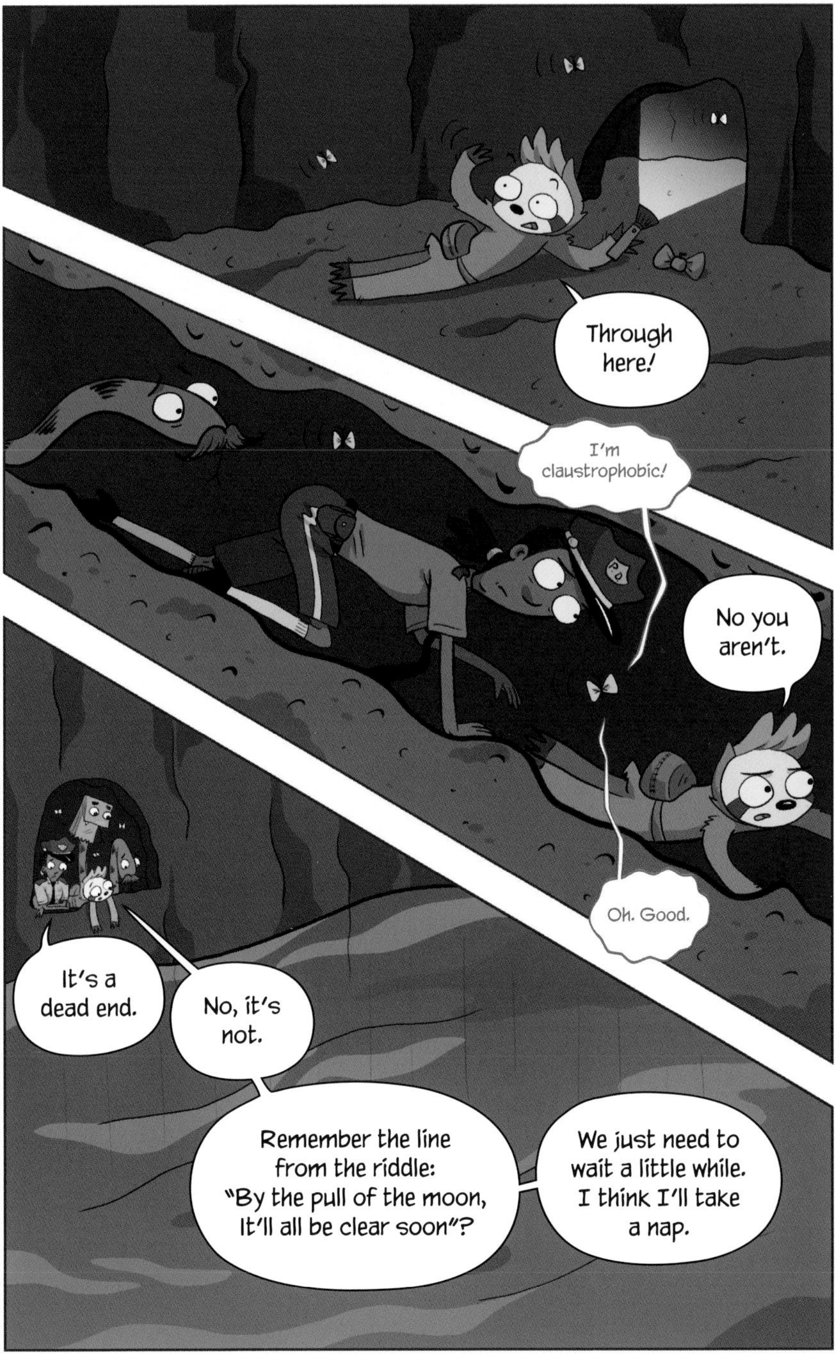
Through here!
I'm claustrophobic!
No you aren't.
Oh. Good.
It's a dead end.
No, it's not.
Remember the line from the riddle: "By the pull of the moon, It'll all be clear soon"?
We just need to wait a little while. I think I'll take a nap.

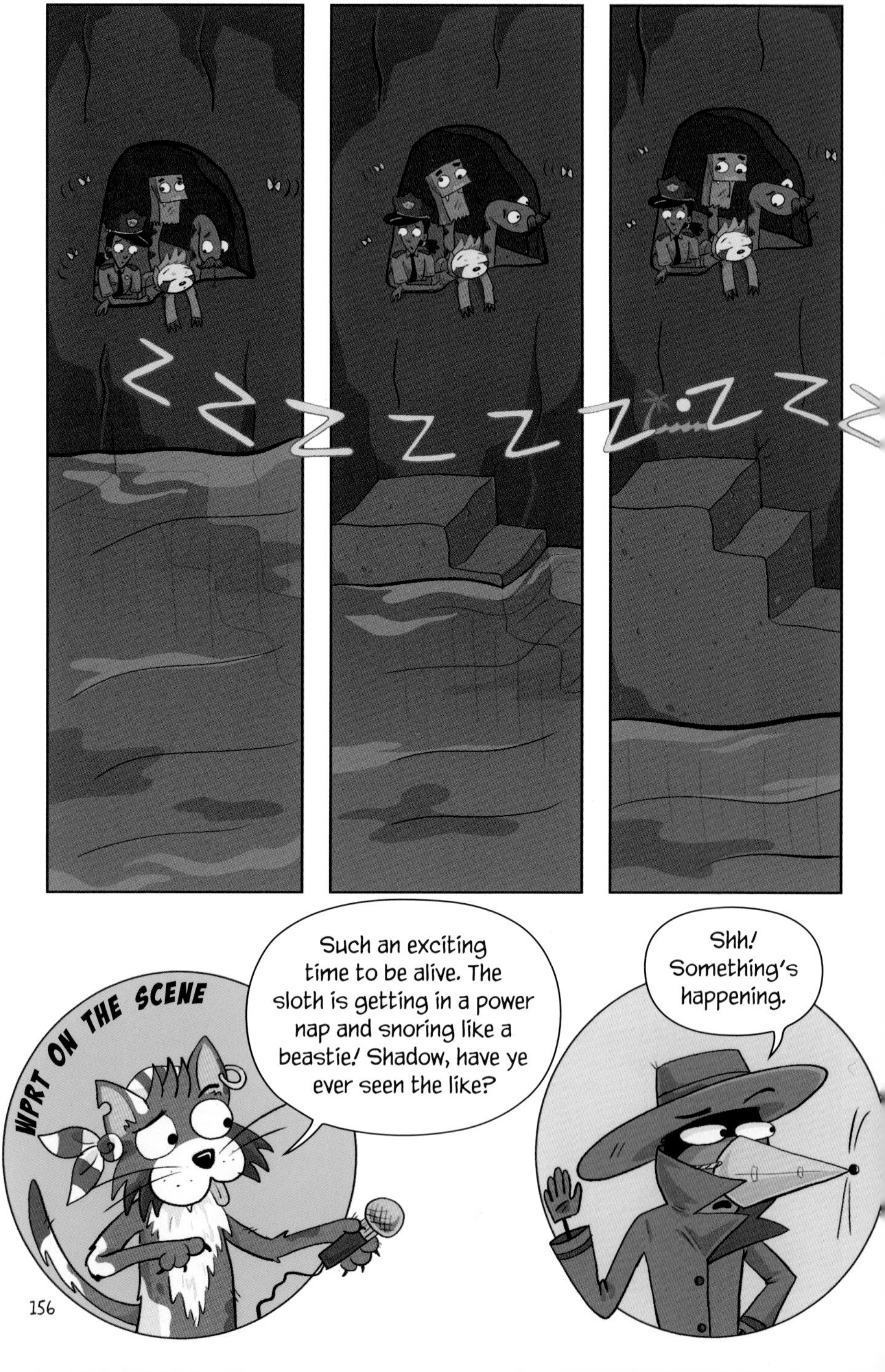
WPRT ON THE SCENE
Such an exciting time to be alive. The sloth is getting in a power nap and snoring like a beastie! Shadow, have ye ever seen the like?
Shh! Something's happening.

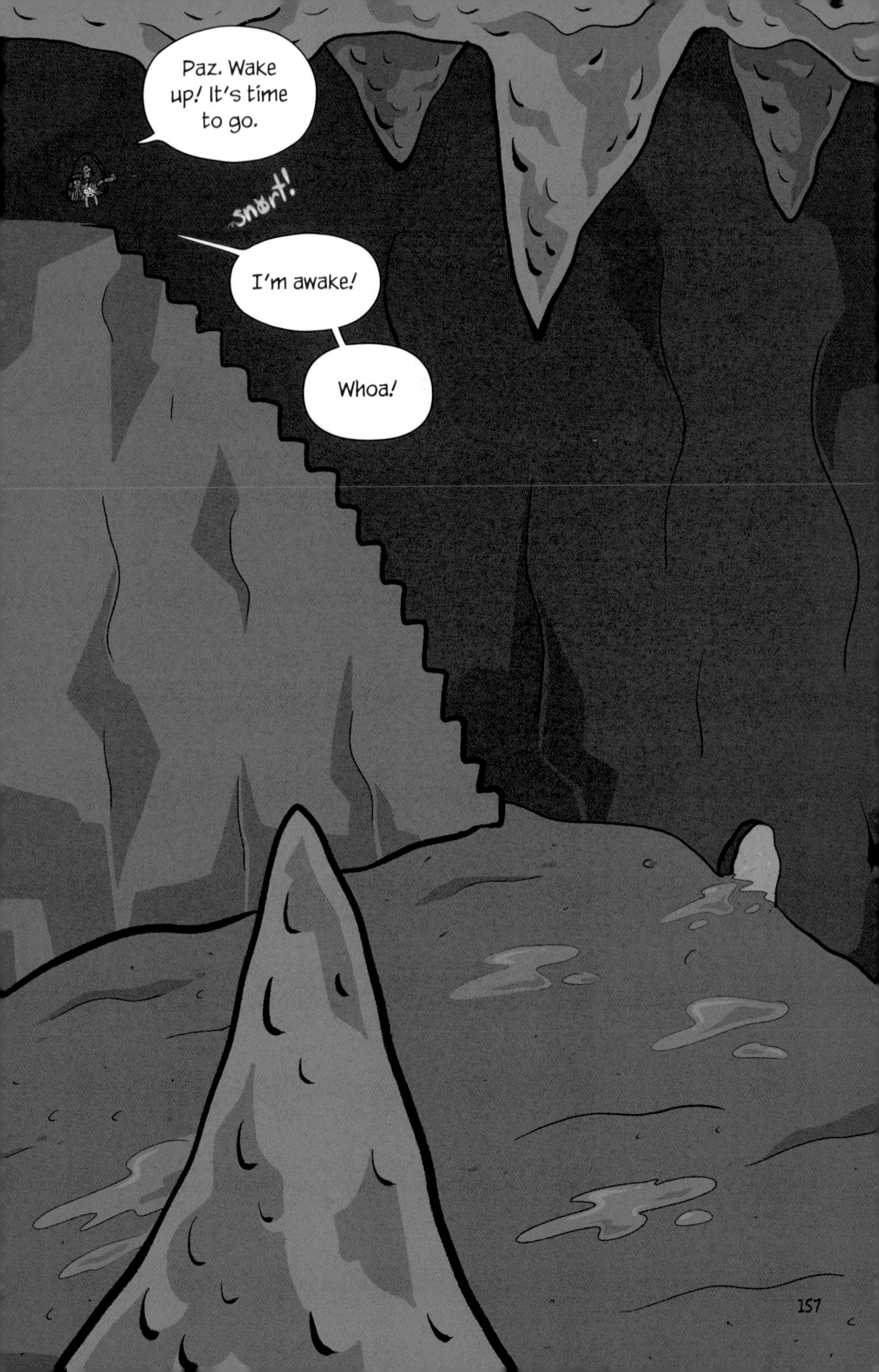
Paz. Wake up! It's time to go.
SNORT!
I'm awake!
Whoa!

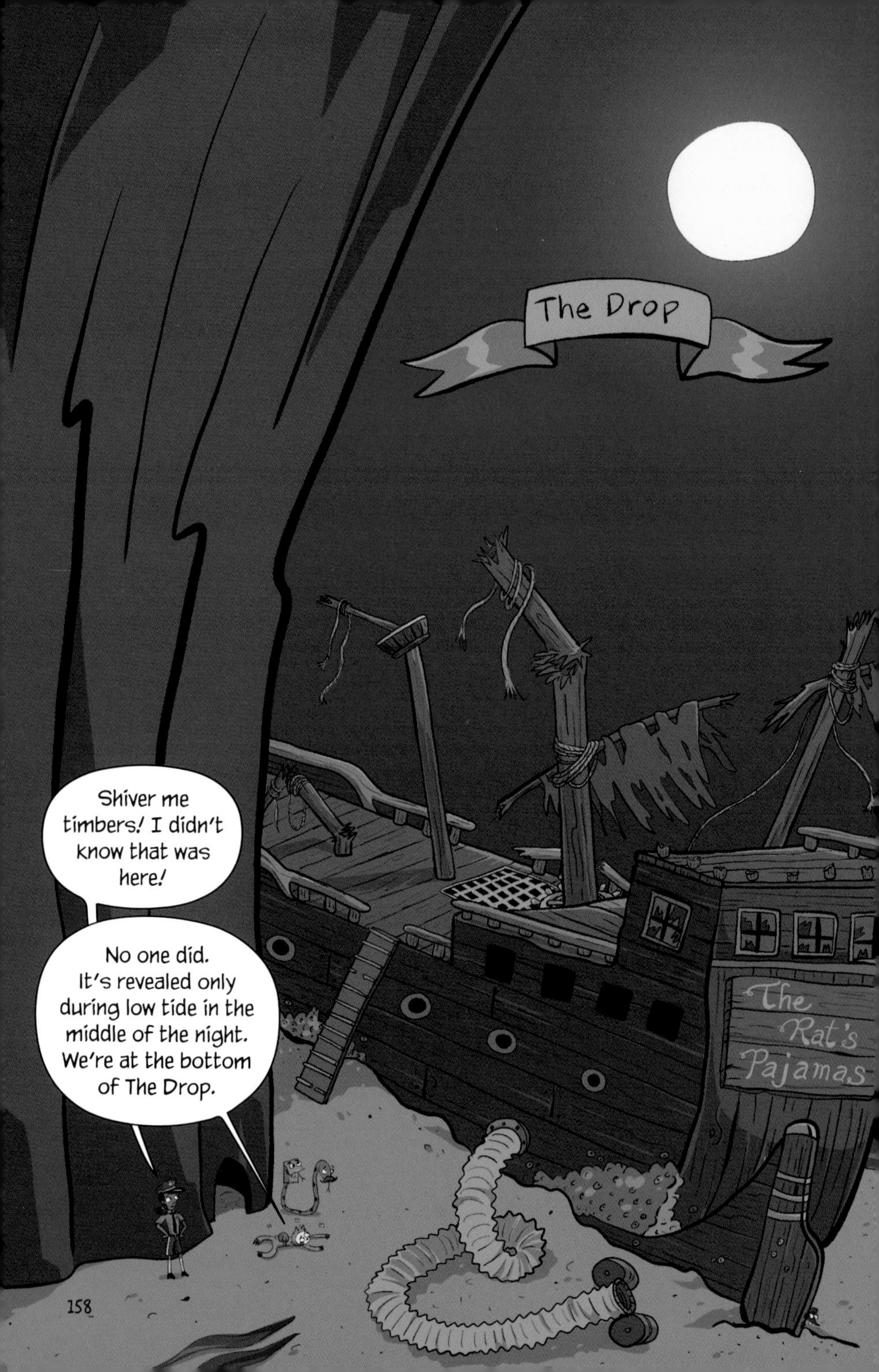
The Drop
Shiver me timbers! I didn't know that was here!
No one did. It's revealed only during low tide in the middle of the night. We're at the bottom of The Drop.
The Rat's Pajamas

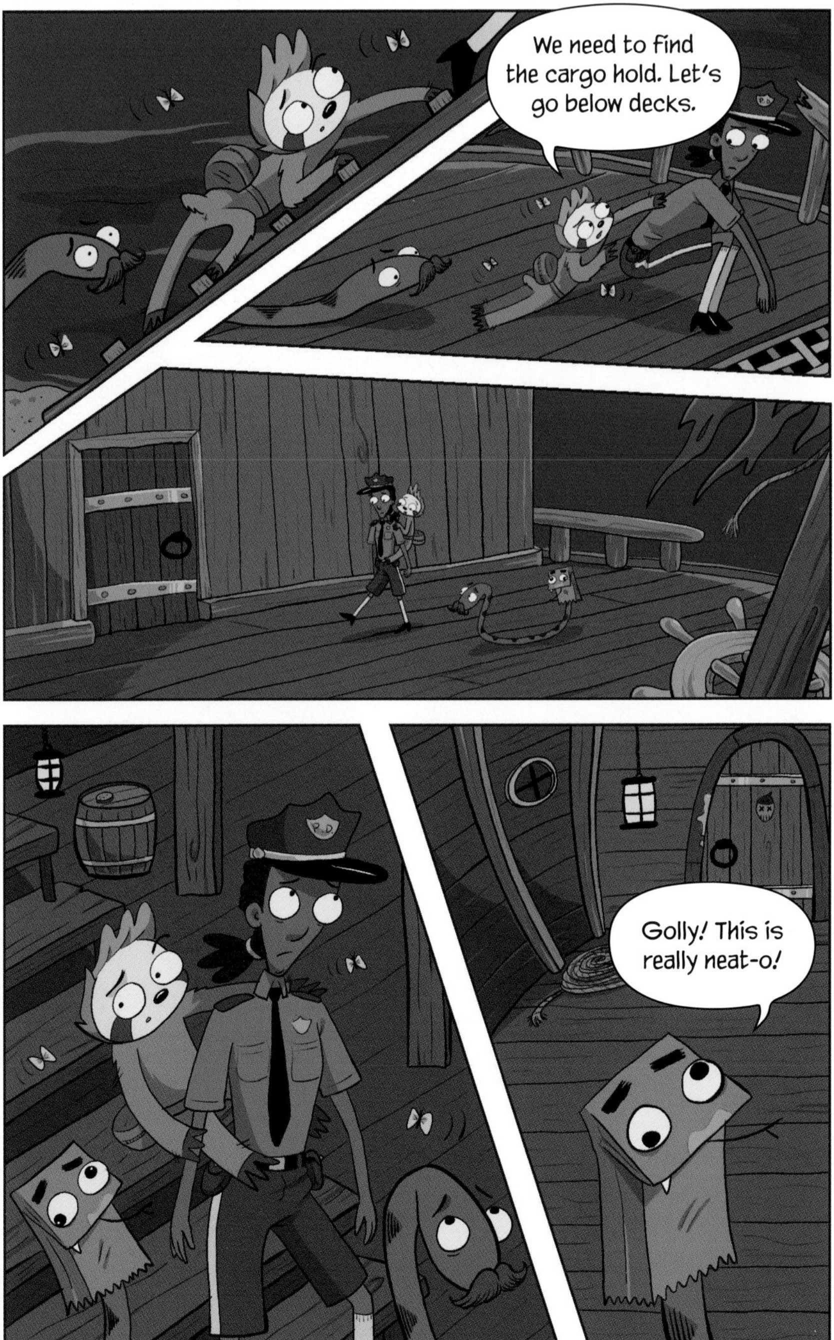
We need to find the cargo hold. Let's go below decks.
Golly! This is really neat-o!

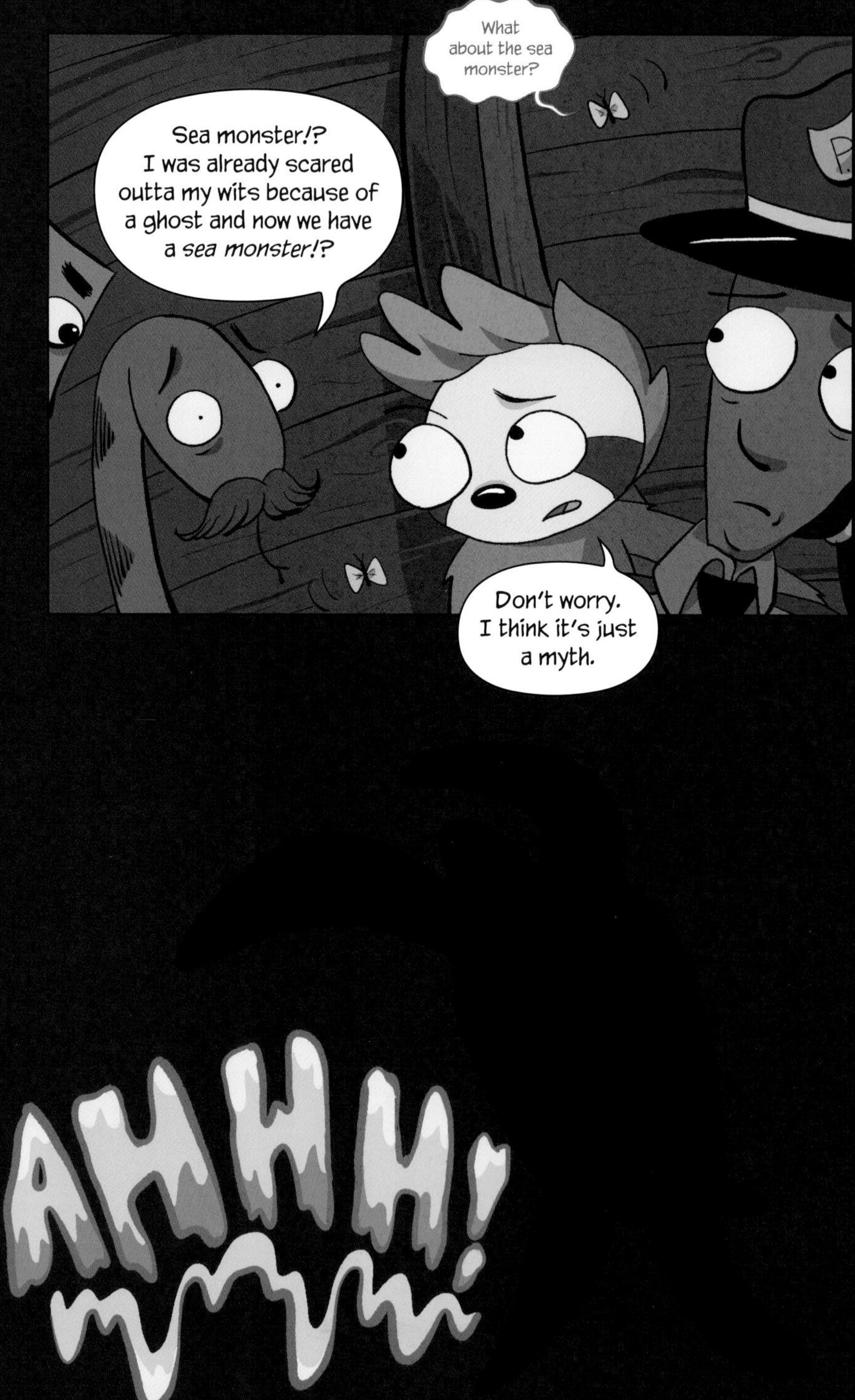
What about the sea monster?
Sea monster!? I was already scared outta my wits because of a ghost and now we have a *sea monster!?*
Don't worry. I think it's just a myth.
AHHH!

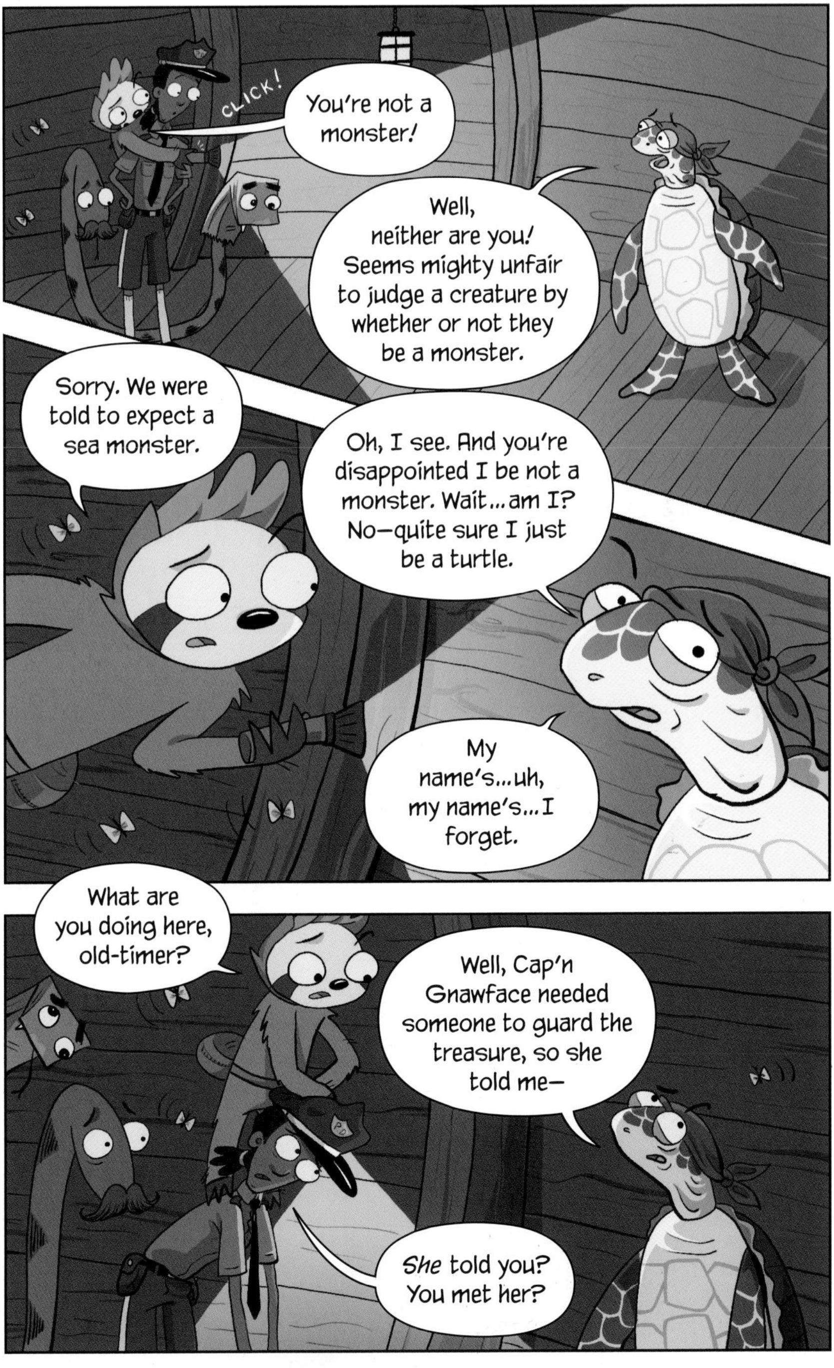
CLICK!
You're not a monster!
Well, neither are you! Seems mighty unfair to judge a creature by whether or not they be a monster.
Sorry. We were told to expect a sea monster.
Oh, I see. And you're disappointed I be not a monster. Wait...am I? No—quite sure I just be a turtle.
My name's...uh, my name's...I forget.
What are you doing here, old-timer?
Well, Cap'n Gnawface needed someone to guard the treasure, so she told me—
She told you? You met her?

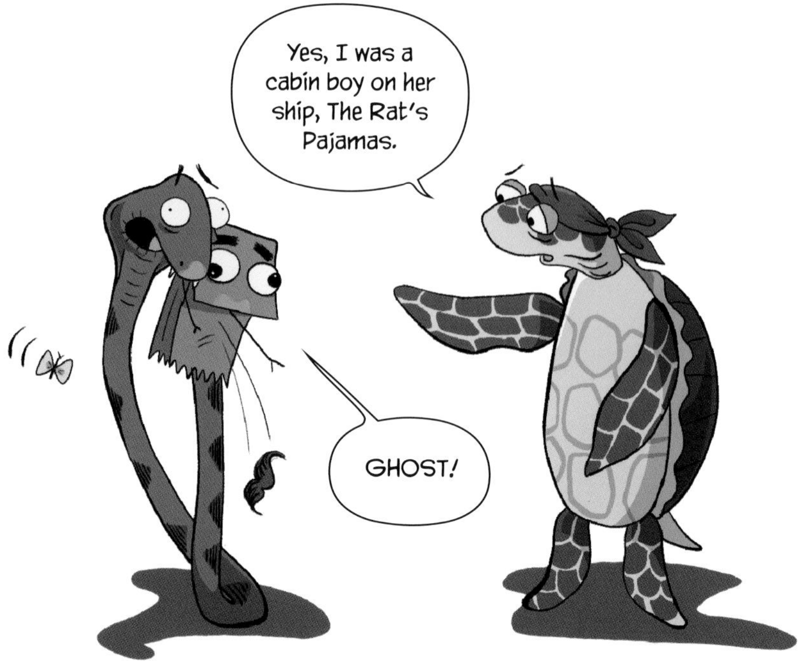
Yes, I was a cabin boy on her ship, The Rat's Pajamas.
GHOST!

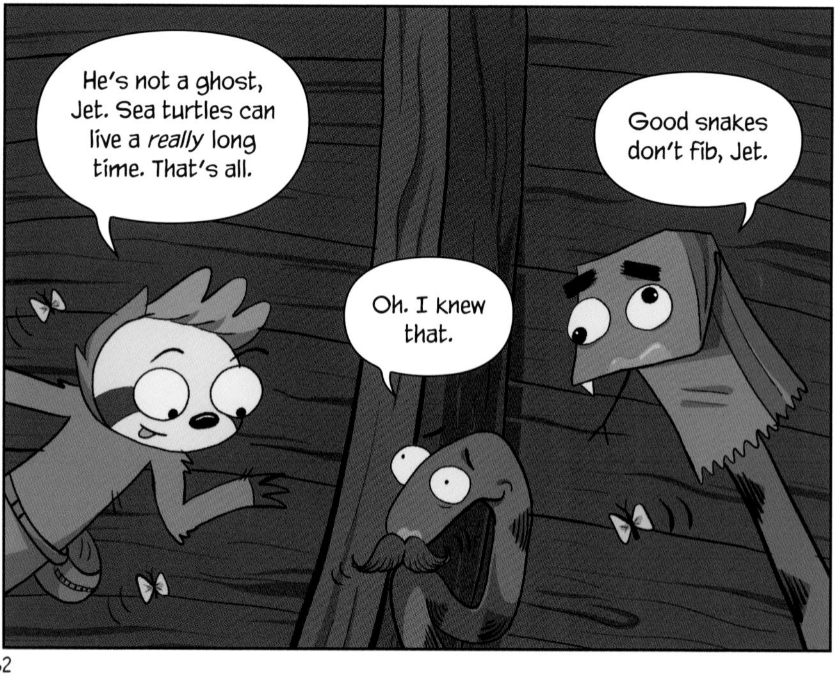
He's not a ghost, Jet. Sea turtles can live a *really* long time. That's all.
Good snakes don't fib, Jet.
Oh. I knew that.

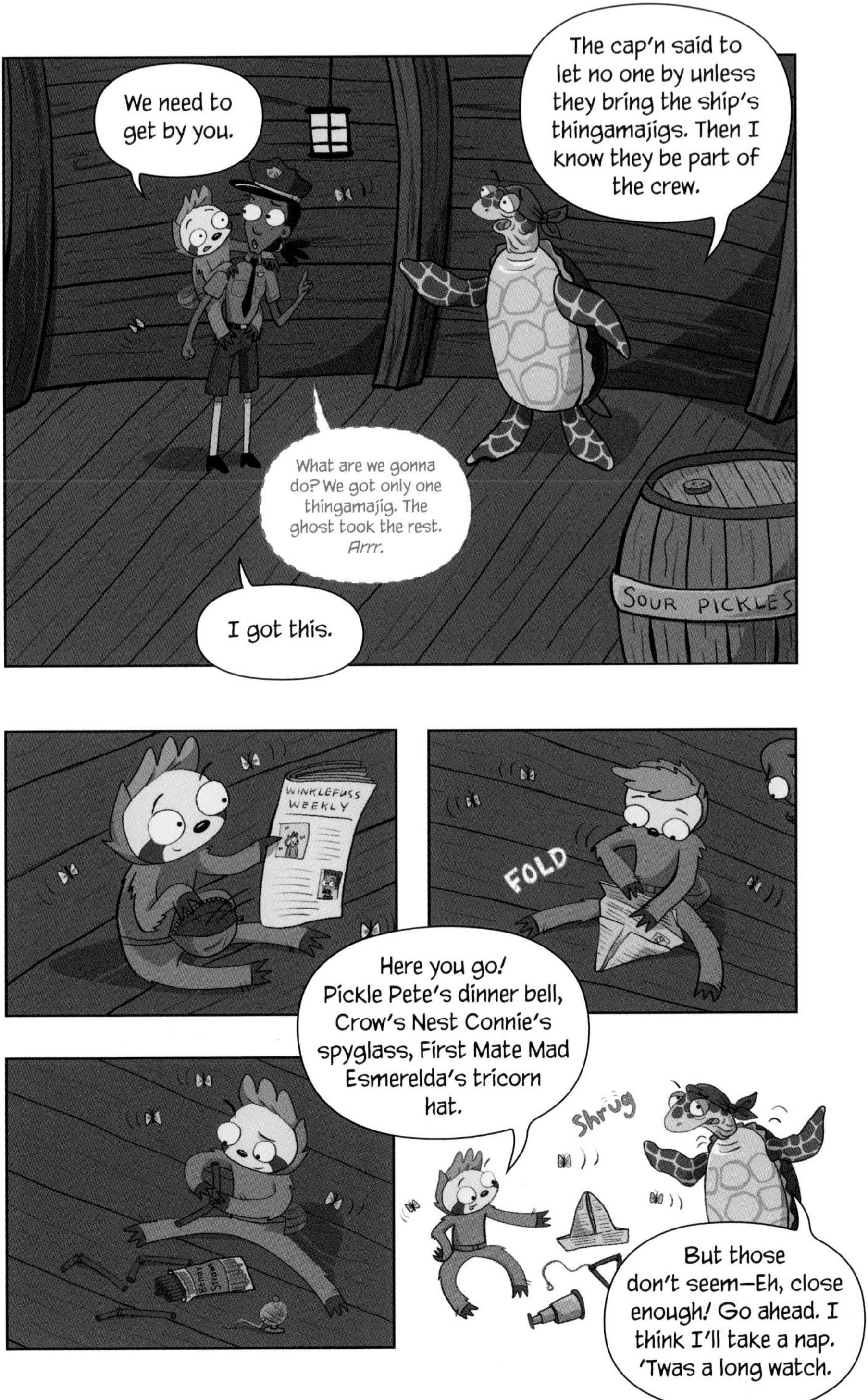
We need to get by you.
The cap'n said to let no one by unless they bring the ship's thingamajigs. Then I know they be part of the crew.
What are we gonna do? We got only one thingamajig. The ghost took the rest. *Arrr.*
I got this.
SOUR PICKLES
WINKLEFUSS WEEKLY
FOLD
Here you go! Pickle Pete's dinner bell, Crow's Nest Connie's spyglass, First Mate Mad Esmerelda's tricorn hat.
Shrug
But those don't seem—Eh, close enough! Go ahead. I think I'll take a nap. 'Twas a long watch.

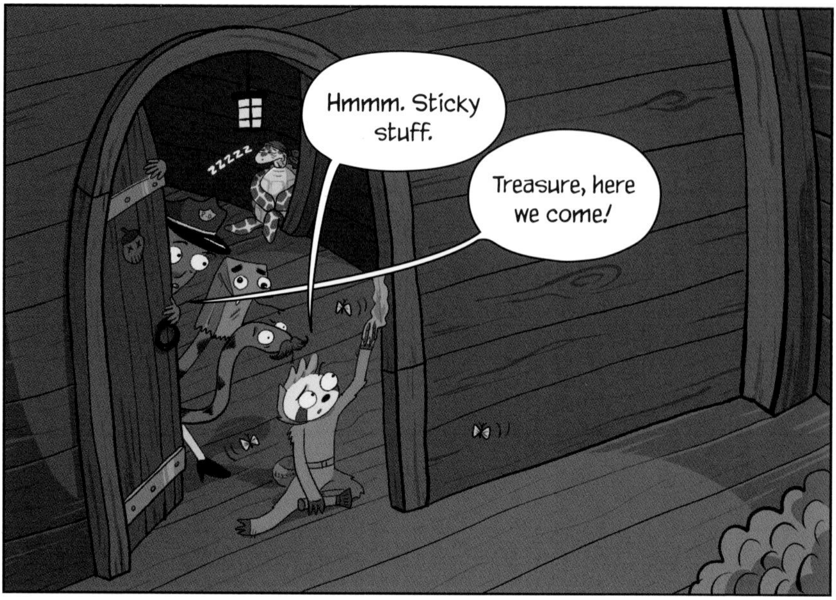
zzzzz
Hmmm. Sticky stuff.
Treasure, here we come!

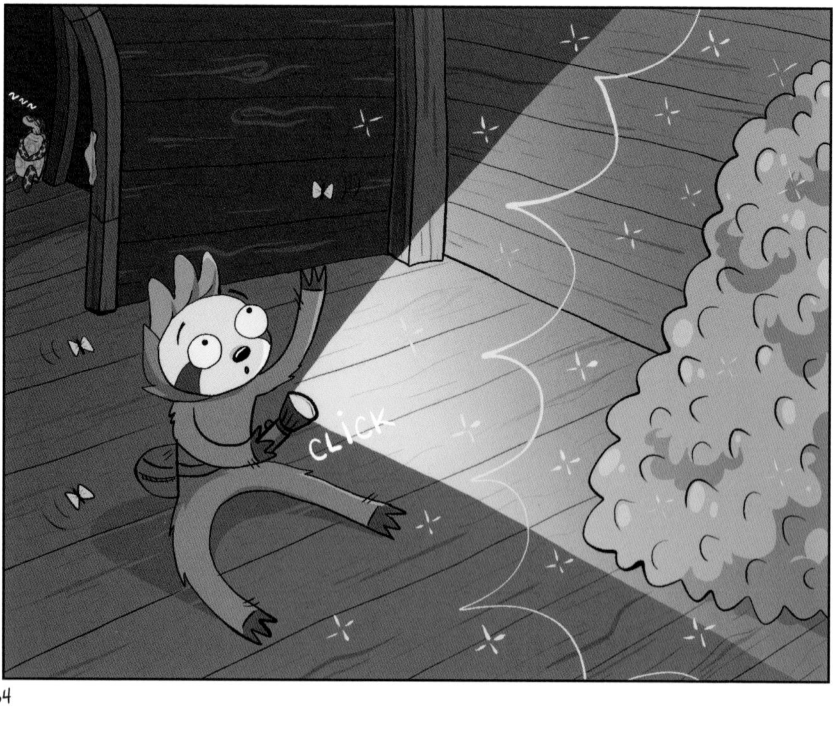
CLICK

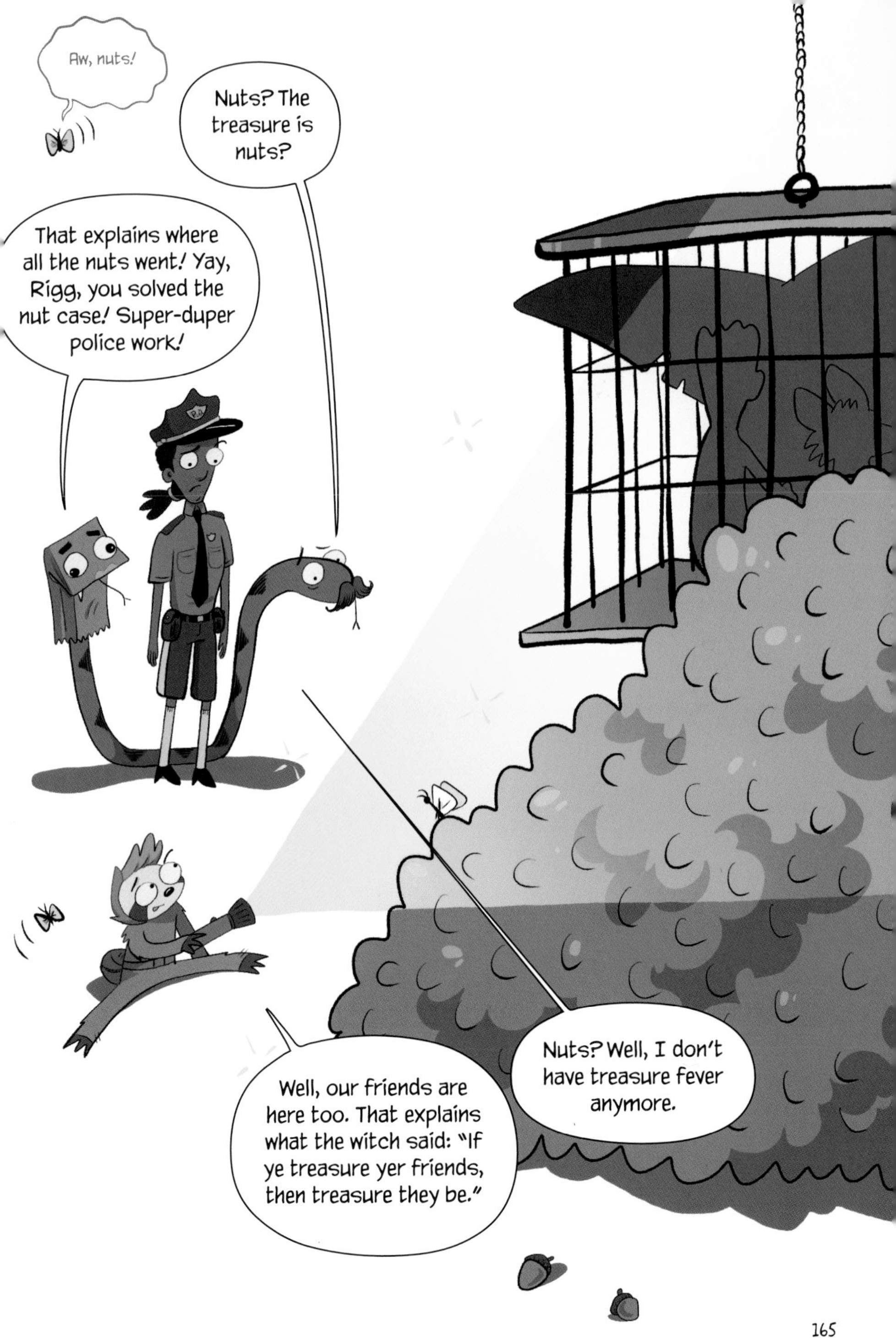
Aw, nuts!
Nuts? The treasure is nuts?
That explains where all the nuts went! Yay, Rigg, you solved the nut case! Super-duper police work!
Nuts? Well, I don't have treasure fever anymore.
Well, our friends are here too. That explains what the witch said: "If ye treasure yer friends, then treasure they be."

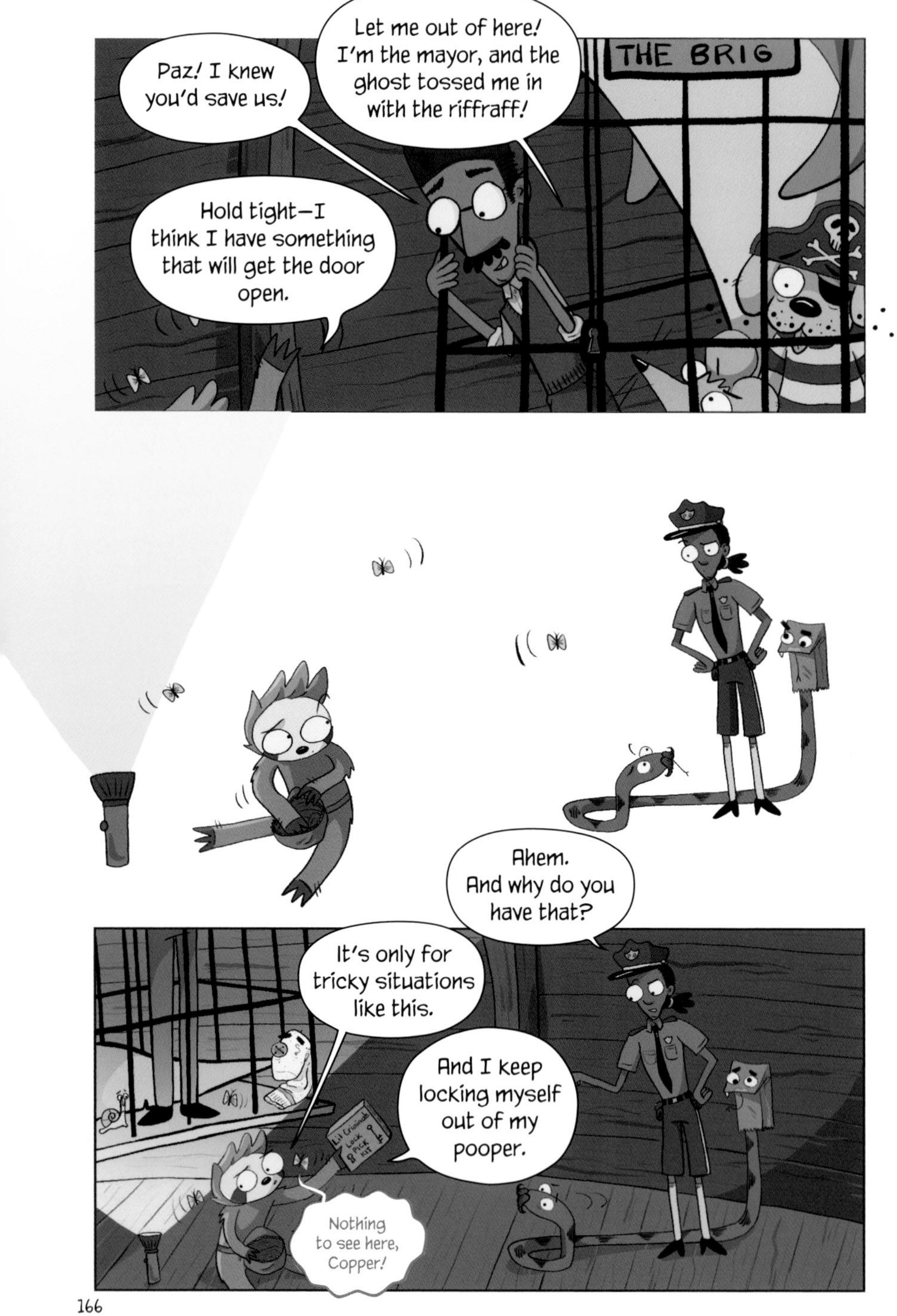
THE BRIG
Paz! I knew you'd save us!
Let me out of here! I'm the mayor, and the ghost tossed me in with the riffraff!
Hold tight—I think I have something that will get the door open.
Ahem. And why do you have that?
It's only for tricky situations like this.
And I keep locking myself out of my pooper.
Nothing to see here, Copper!

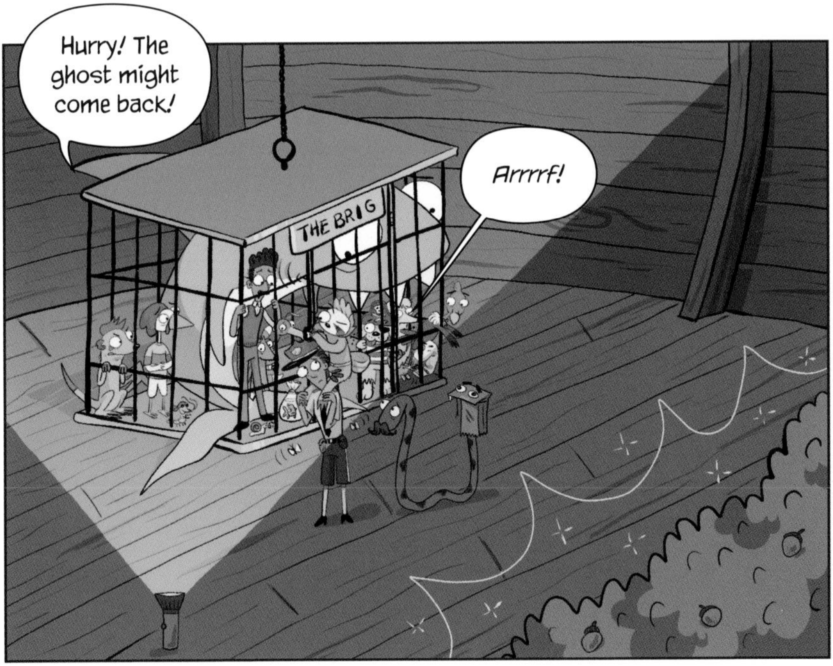
Hurry! The ghost might come back!
THE BRIG
Arrrrf!

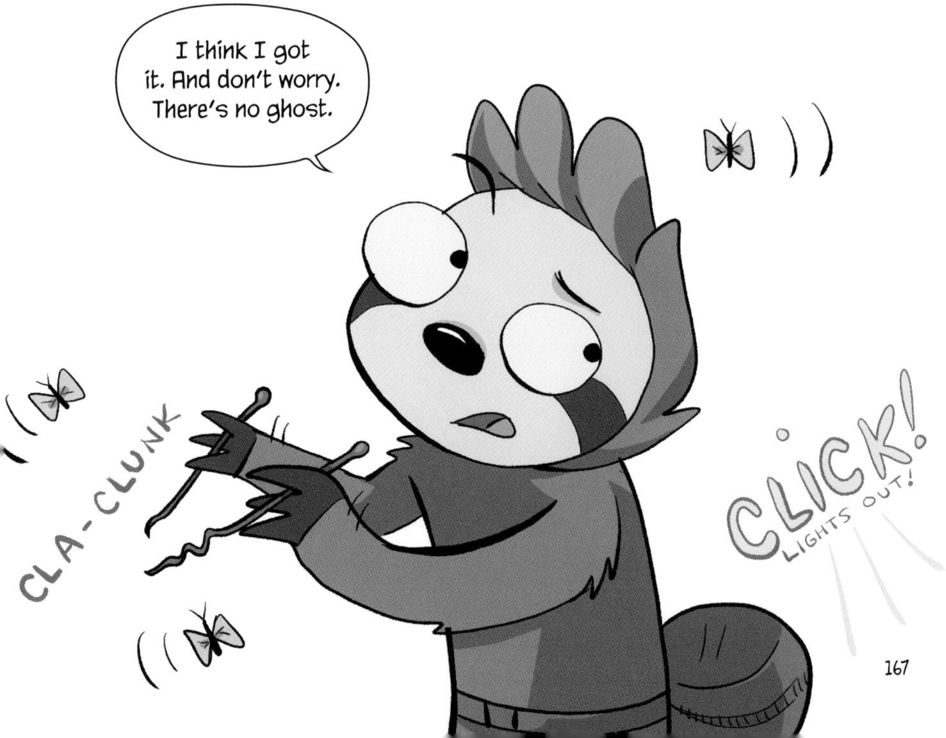
I think I got it. And don't worry. There's no ghost.
CLA-CLUNK
CLICK!
LIGHTS OUT!

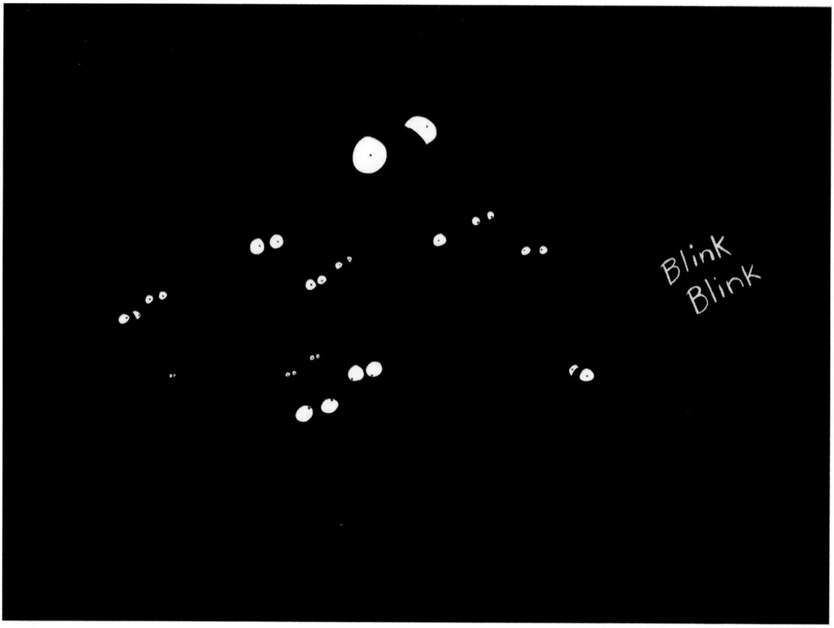
Blink
Blink

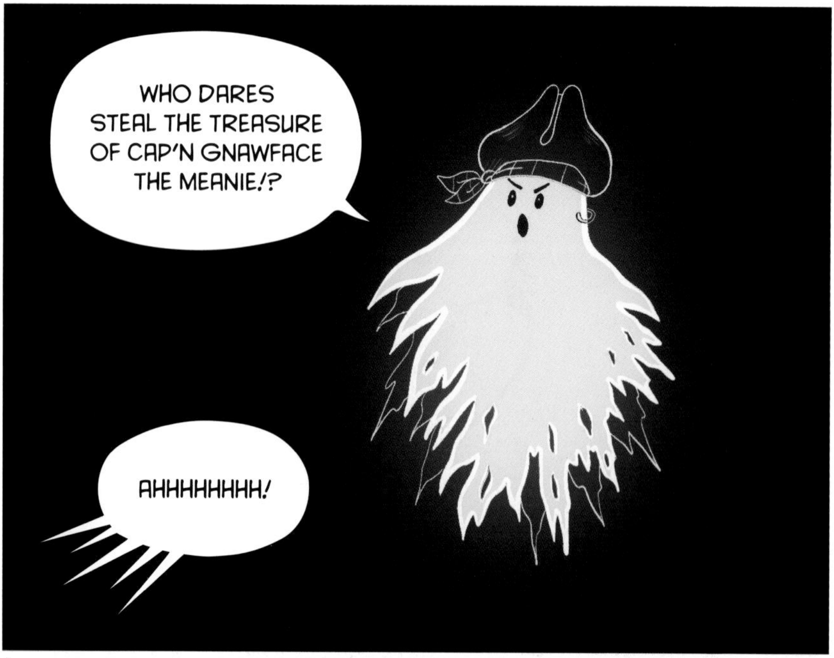
WHO DARES STEAL THE TREASURE OF CAP'N GNAWFACE THE MEANIE!?
AHHHHHHHH!

CHAPTER 12

FRIDAY. A FEW HOURS BEFORE DAWN.
IN THE HOLD OF A HAUNTED PIRATE SHIP.

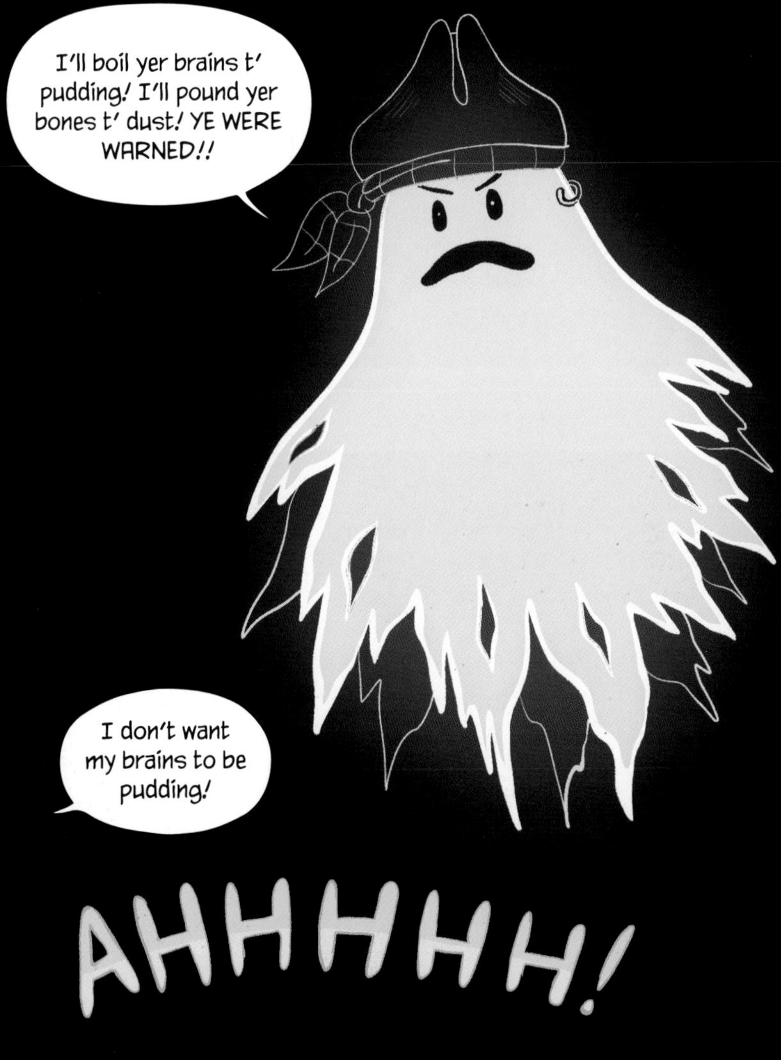
I'll boil yer brains t' pudding! I'll pound yer bones t' dust! YE WERE WARNED!!
I don't want my brains to be pudding!
AHHHHH!

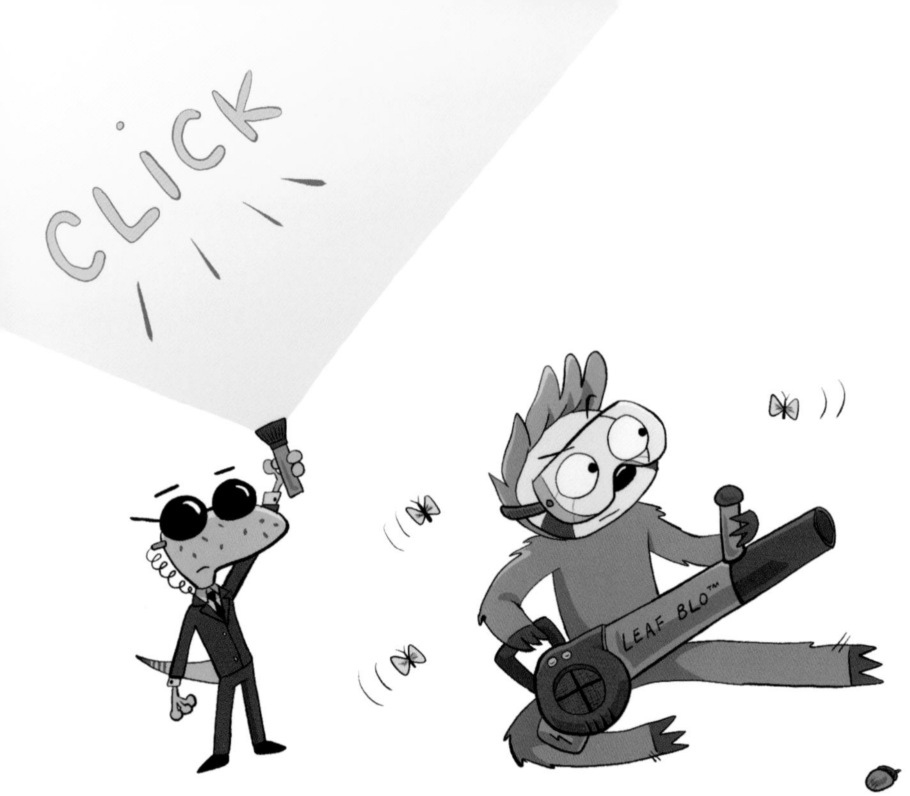
CLICK
LEAF BLO™

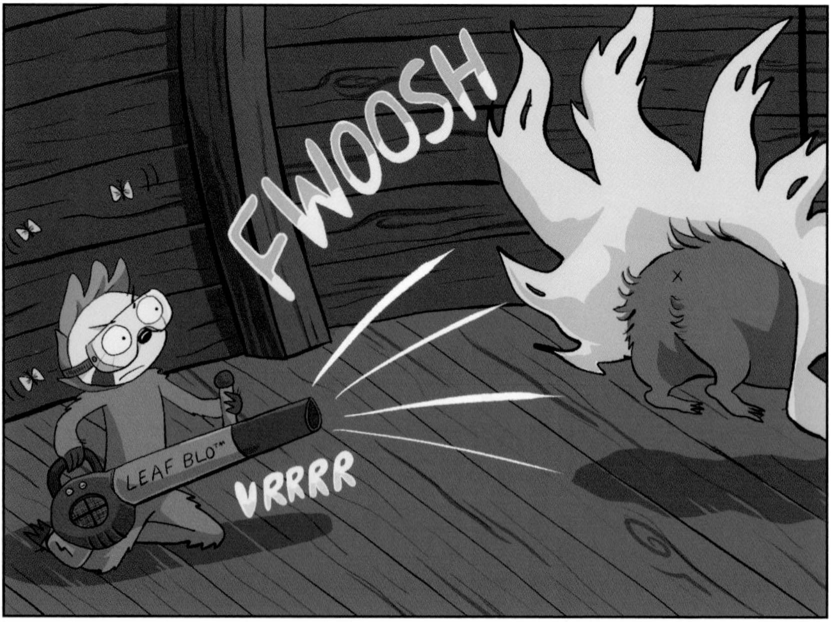
FWOOSH
LEAF BLO™
VRRRR

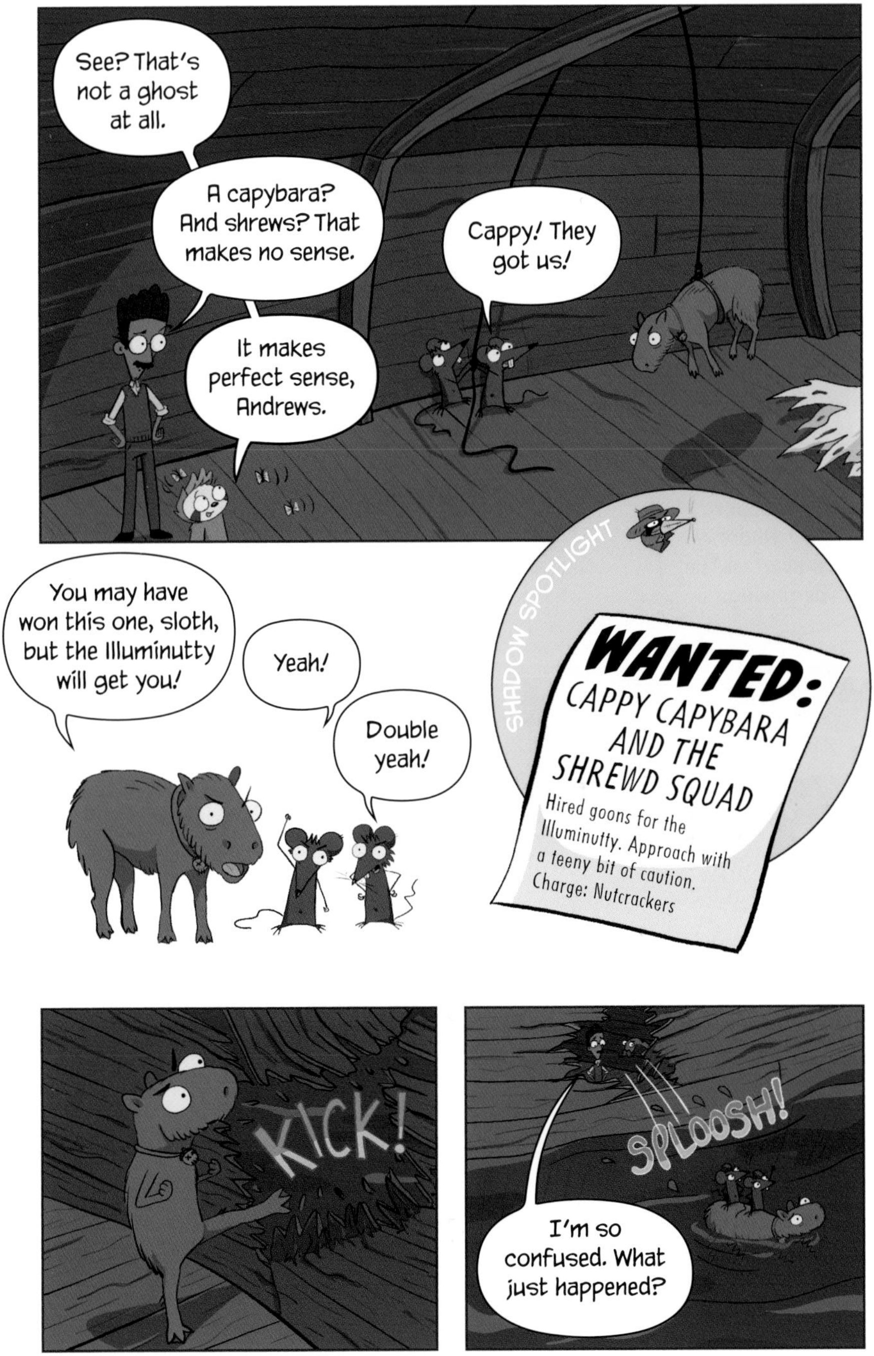
See? That's not a ghost at all.
A capybara? And shrews? That makes no sense.
It makes perfect sense, Andrews.
Cappy! They got us!
You may have won this one, sloth, but the Illuminutty will get you!
Yeah!
Double yeah!
SHADOW SPOTLIGHT
WANTED:
CAPPY CAPYBARA AND THE SHREWD SQUAD
Hired goons for the Illuminutty. Approach with a teeny bit of caution.
Charge: Nutcrackers
KICK!
SPLOOSH!
I'm so confused. What just happened?

"What just happened?" I rescued you. You really need to pay more attention, Andrews.

I mean, the whole thing. So, the ghost wasn't real? How did you know?

The evidence, my dear Andrews! Let's start at the beginning.

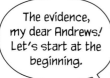

WHOOSH

Puff Puff

The first clue was found on The Crumb. When Not-So-Jolly Roger read the riddle on the radio, he alerted the Illuminutty that their nut horde was in danger of being found.

They had to stop the treasure hunt.

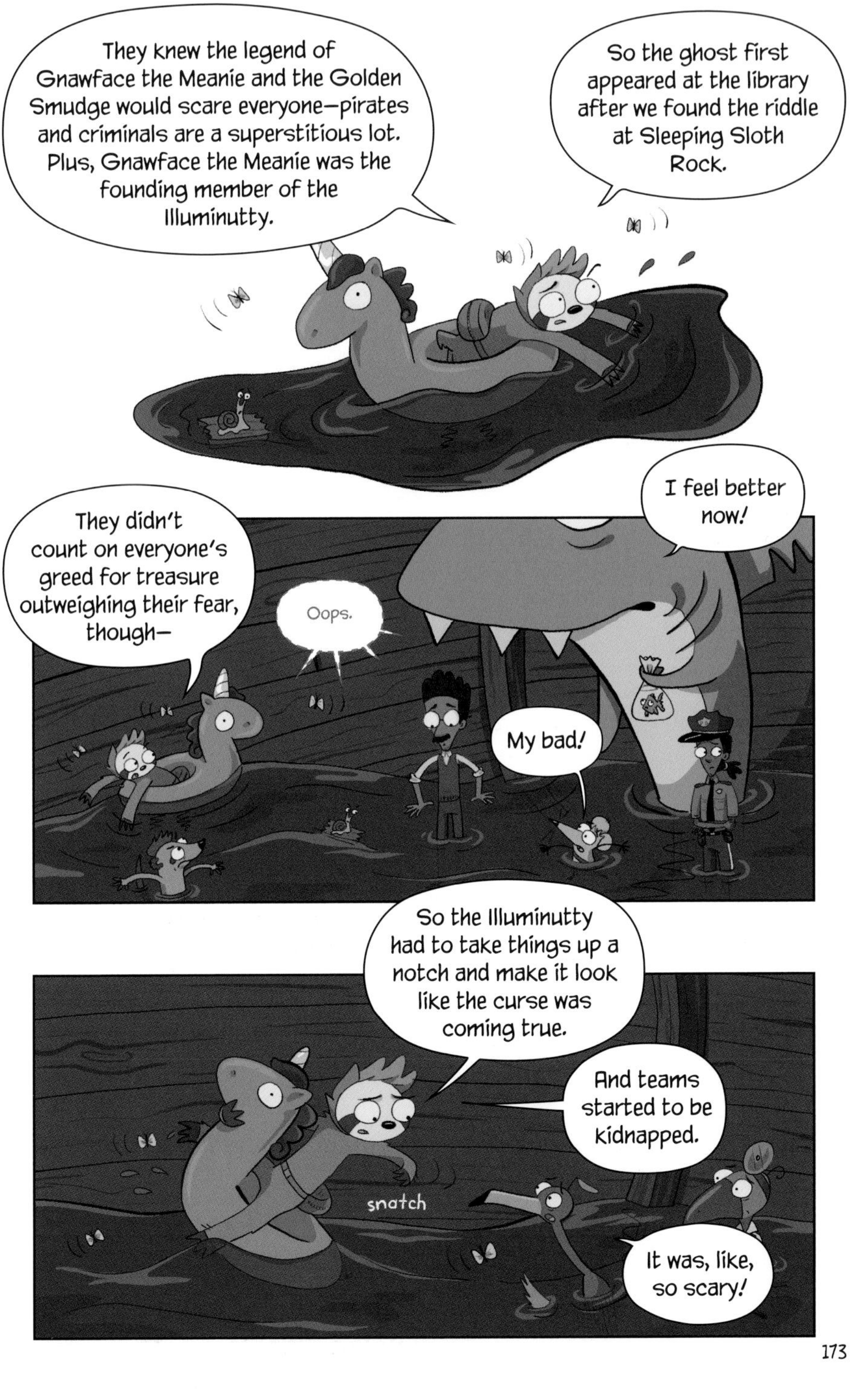
They knew the legend of Gnawface the Meanie and the Golden Smudge would scare everyone—pirates and criminals are a superstitious lot. Plus, Gnawface the Meanie was the founding member of the Illuminutty.
So the ghost first appeared at the library after we found the riddle at Sleeping Sloth Rock.
They didn't count on everyone's greed for treasure outweighing their fear, though—
Oops.
I feel better now!
My bad!
So the Illuminutty had to take things up a notch and make it look like the curse was coming true.
And teams started to be kidnapped.
snatch
It was, like, so scary!

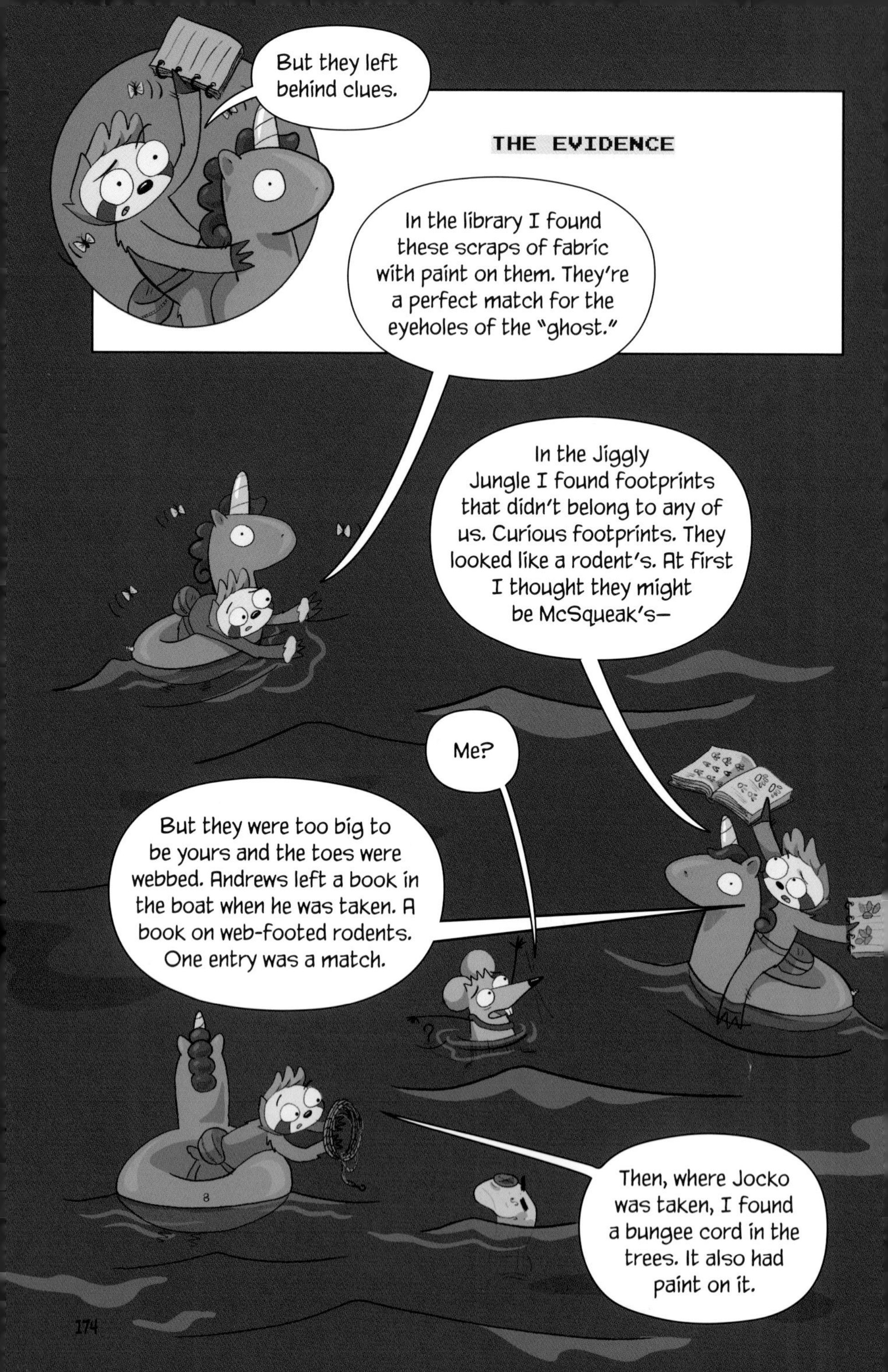

But they left behind clues.
THE EVIDENCE
In the library I found these scraps of fabric with paint on them. They're a perfect match for the eyeholes of the "ghost."
In the Jiggly Jungle I found footprints that didn't belong to any of us. Curious footprints. They looked like a rodent's. At first I thought they might be McSqueak's—
Me?
But they were too big to be yours and the toes were webbed. Andrews left a book in the boat when he was taken. A book on web-footed rodents. One entry was a match.
Then, where Jocko was taken, I found a bungee cord in the trees. It also had paint on it.

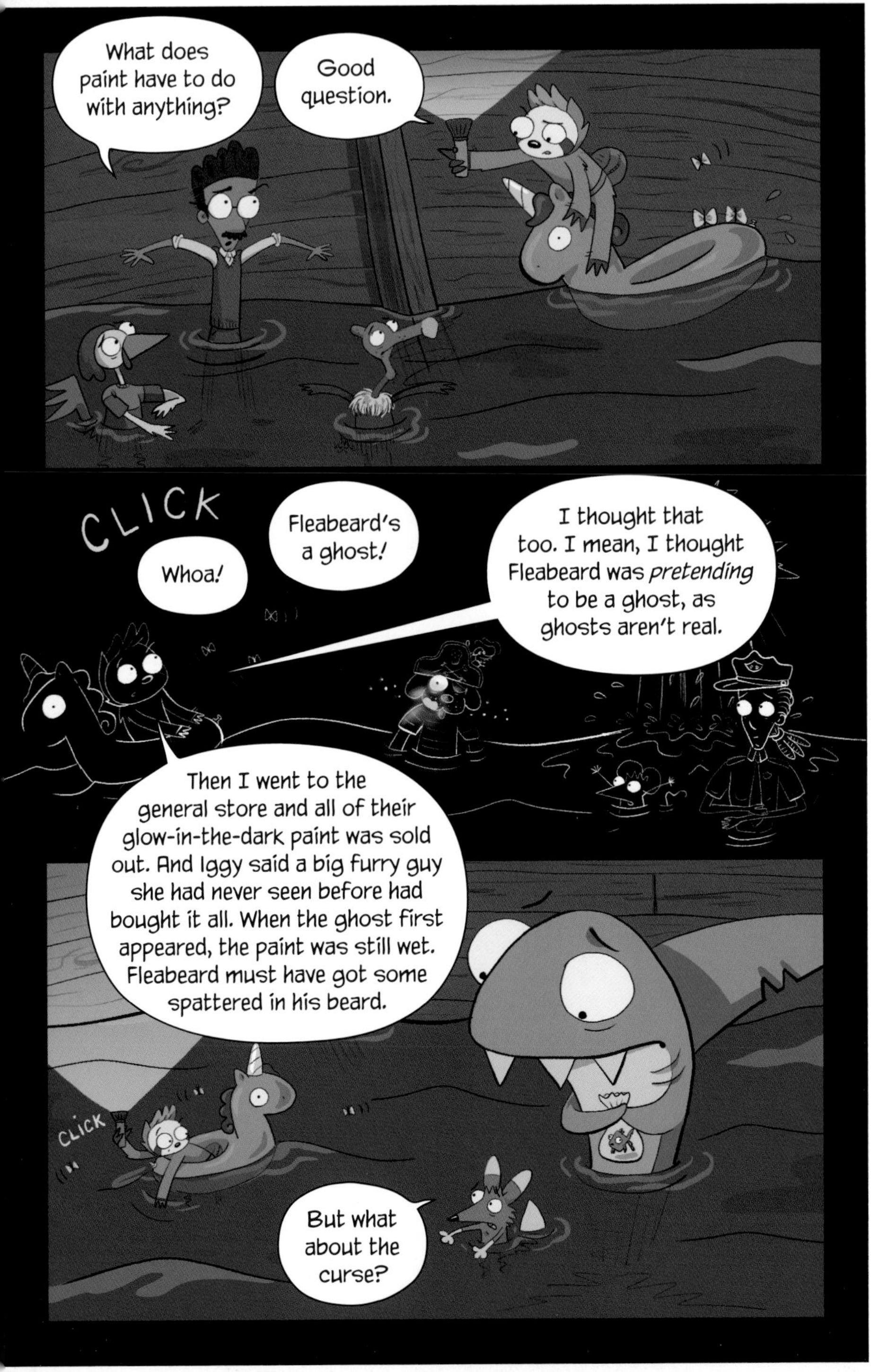
What does paint have to do with anything?
Good question.
CLICK
Whoa!
Fleabeard's a ghost!
I thought that too. I mean, I thought Fleabeard was *pretending* to be a ghost, as ghosts aren't real.
Then I went to the general store and all of their glow-in-the-dark paint was sold out. And Iggy said a big furry guy she had never seen before had bought it all. When the ghost first appeared, the paint was still wet. Fleabeard must have got some spattered in his beard.
CLICK
But what about the curse?

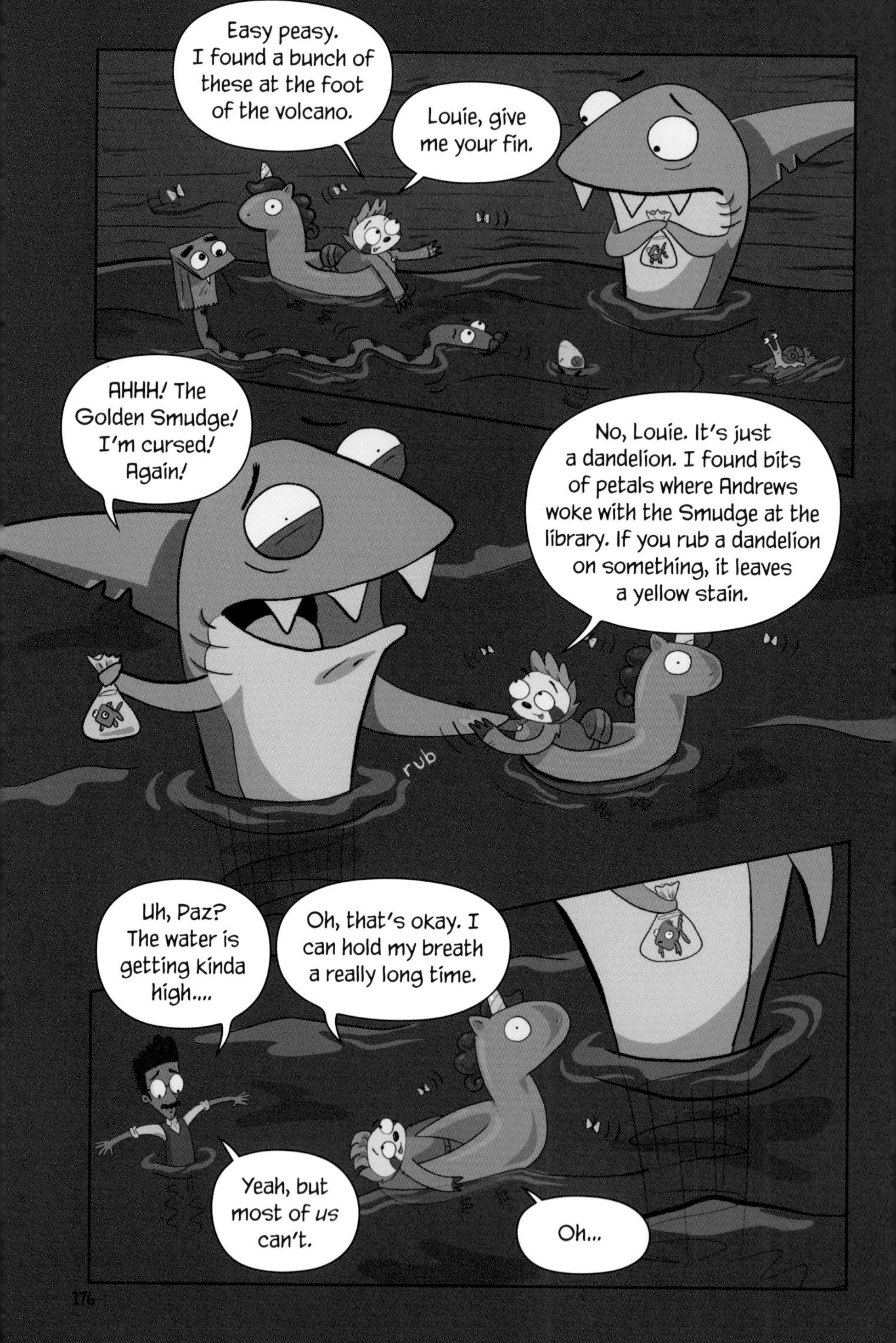
Easy peasy. I found a bunch of these at the foot of the volcano.
Louie, give me your fin.
AHHH! The Golden Smudge! I'm cursed! Again!
No, Louie. It's just a dandelion. I found bits of petals where Andrews woke with the Smudge at the library. If you rub a dandelion on something, it leaves a yellow stain.
rub
Uh, Paz? The water is getting kinda high....
Oh, that's okay. I can hold my breath a really long time.
Yeah, but most of *us* can't.
Oh...

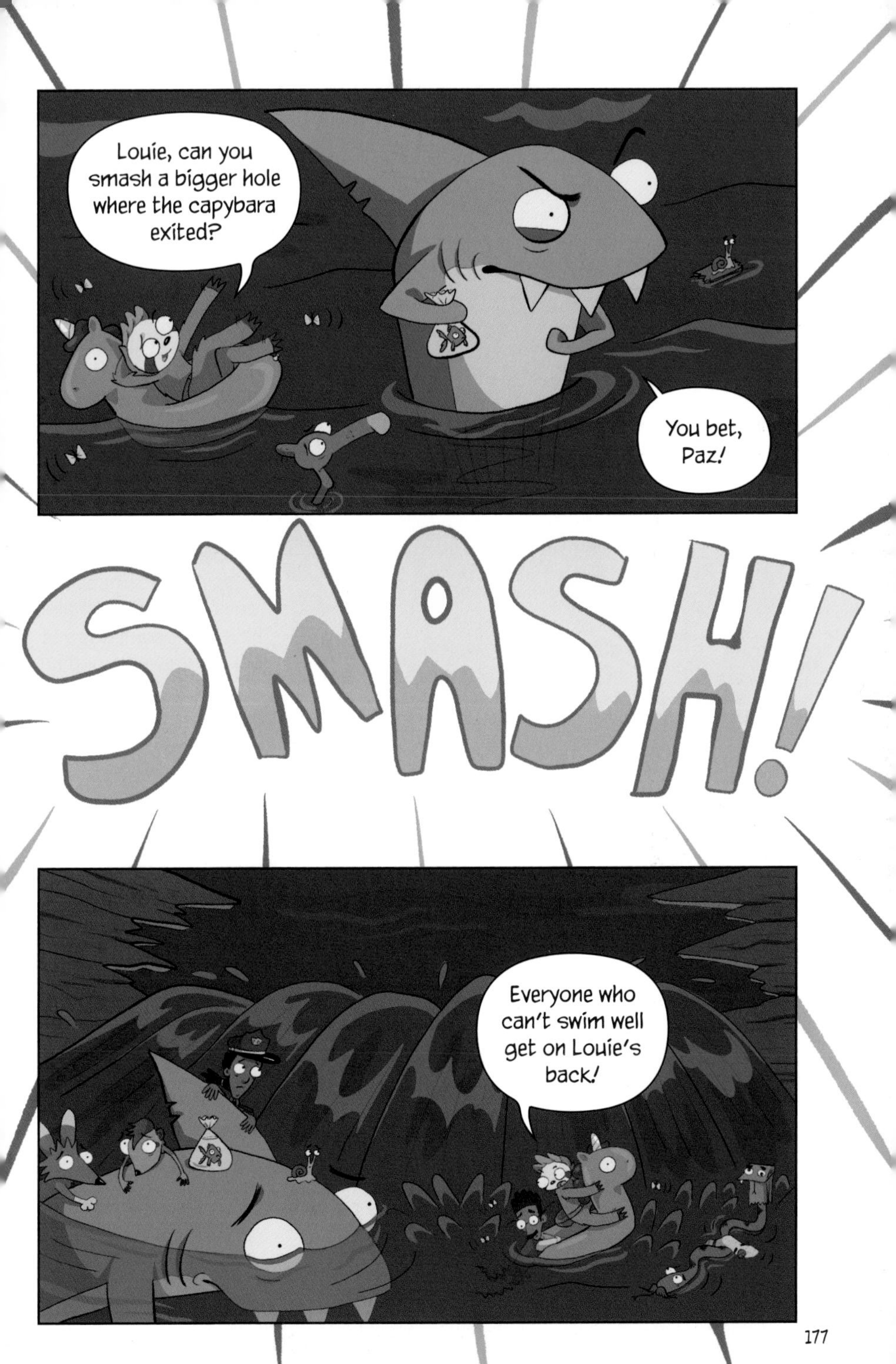

Louie, can you smash a bigger hole where the capybara exited?
You bet, Paz!
SMASH!
Everyone who can't swim well get on Louie's back!

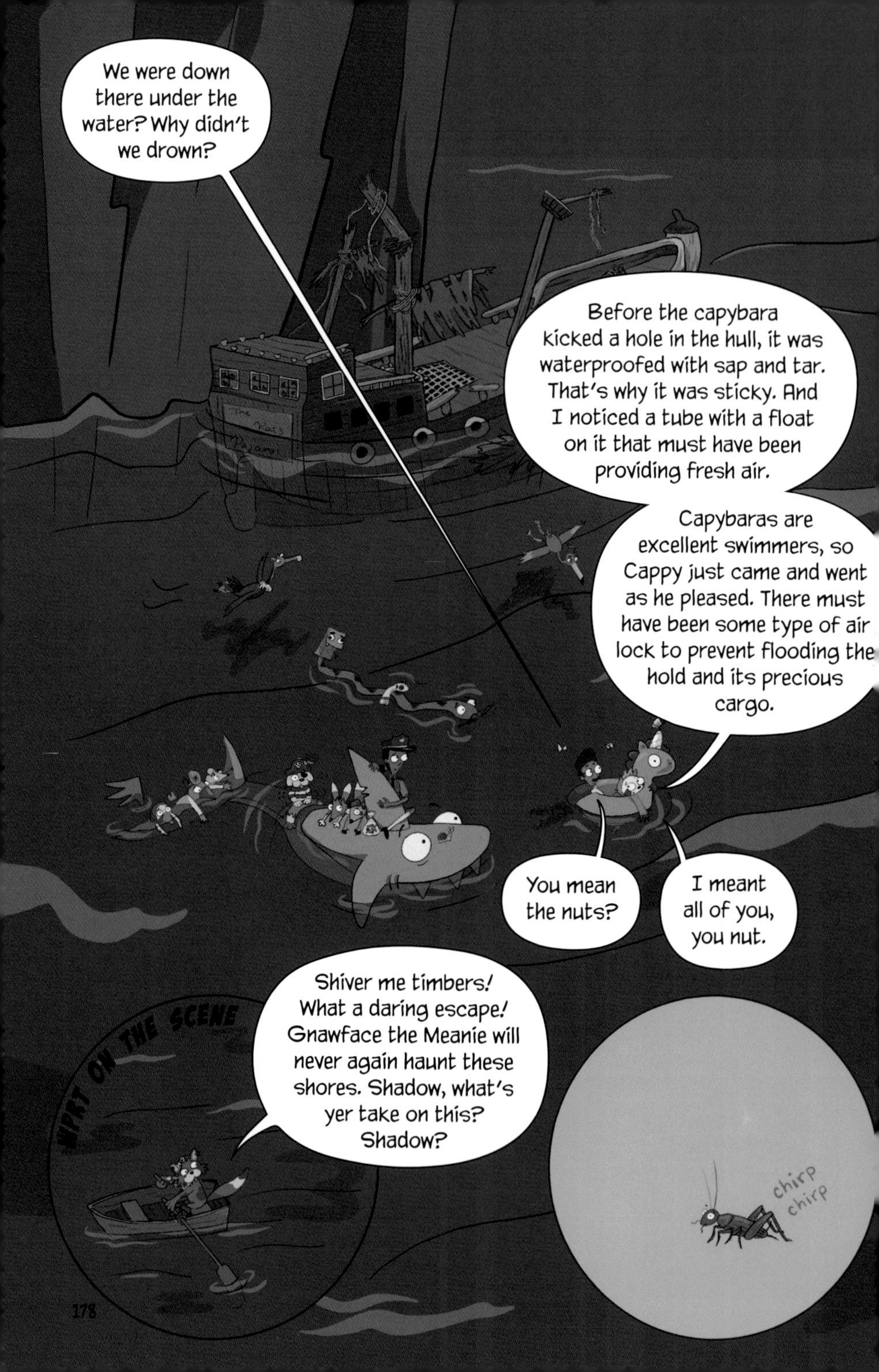
We were down there under the water? Why didn't we drown?
Before the capybara kicked a hole in the hull, it was waterproofed with sap and tar. That's why it was sticky. And I noticed a tube with a float on it that must have been providing fresh air.
Capybaras are excellent swimmers, so Cappy just came and went as he pleased. There must have been some type of air lock to prevent flooding the hold and its precious cargo.
You mean the nuts?
I meant all of you, you nut.
WPRT ON THE SCENE
Shiver me timbers! What a daring escape! Gnawface the Meanie will never again haunt these shores. Shadow, what's yer take on this? Shadow?
chirp chirp

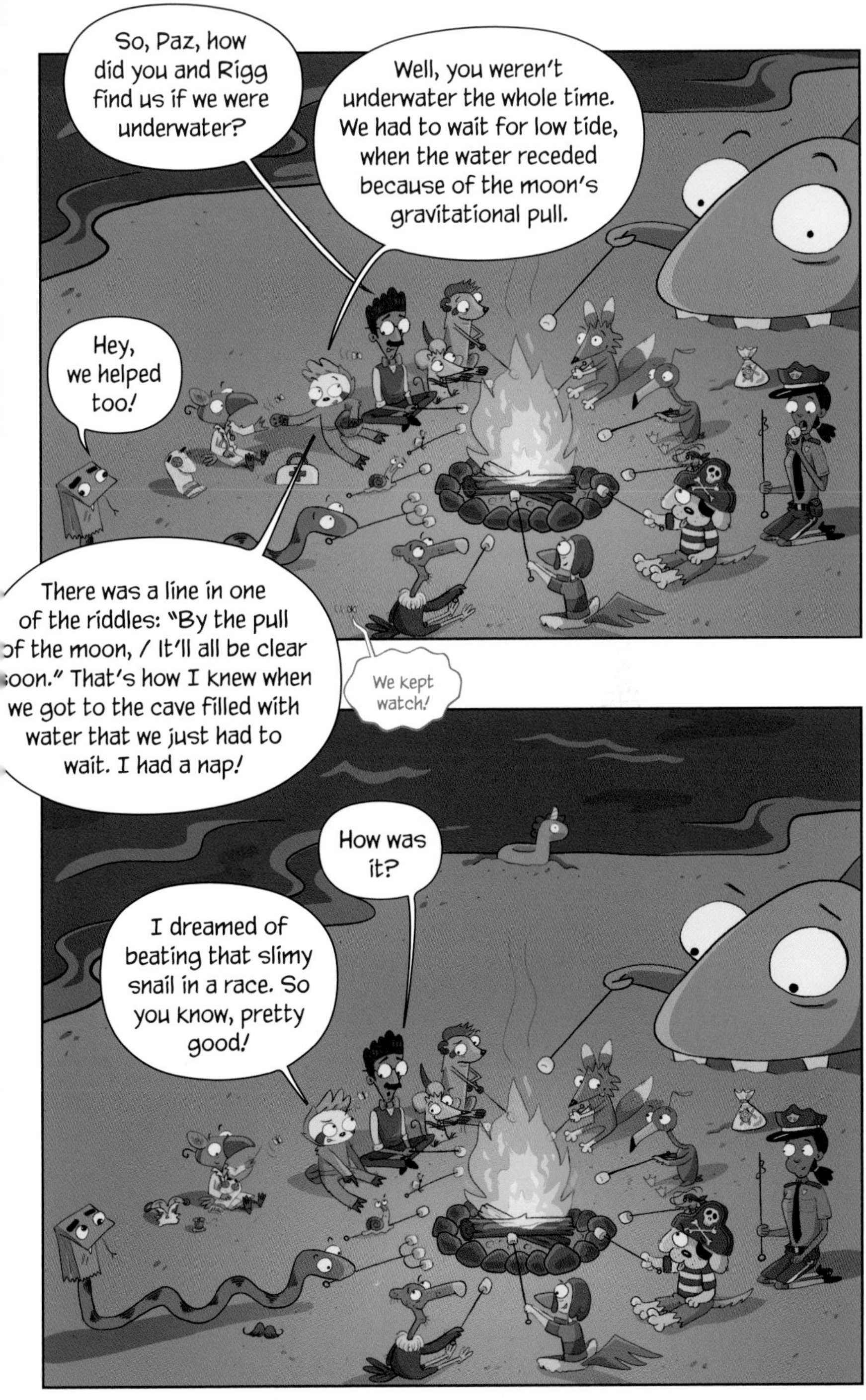

So, Paz, how did you and Rigg find us if we were underwater?
Well, you weren't underwater the whole time. We had to wait for low tide, when the water receded because of the moon's gravitational pull.
Hey, we helped too!
There was a line in one of the riddles: "By the pull of the moon, / It'll all be clear soon." That's how I knew when we got to the cave filled with water that we just had to wait. I had a nap!
We kept watch!
How was it?
I dreamed of beating that slimy snail in a race. So you know, pretty good!

POSTSCRIPT

FRIDAY. A BIT PAST NOON. SLEEPING IN AFTER A VERY LATE NIGHT OF RESCUING.

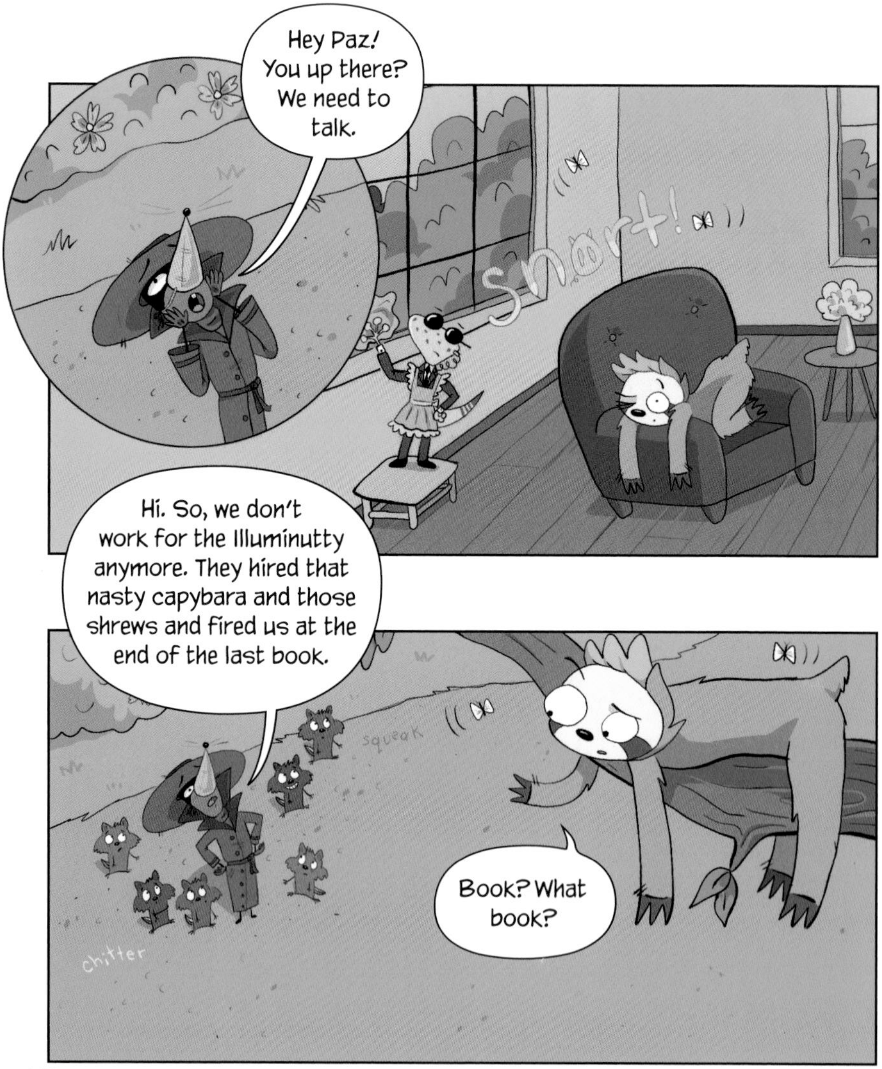
Hey Paz! You up there? We need to talk.
snort!
Hi. So, we don't work for the Illuminutty anymore. They hired that nasty capybara and those shrews and fired us at the end of the last book.
squeak
chitter
Book? What book?

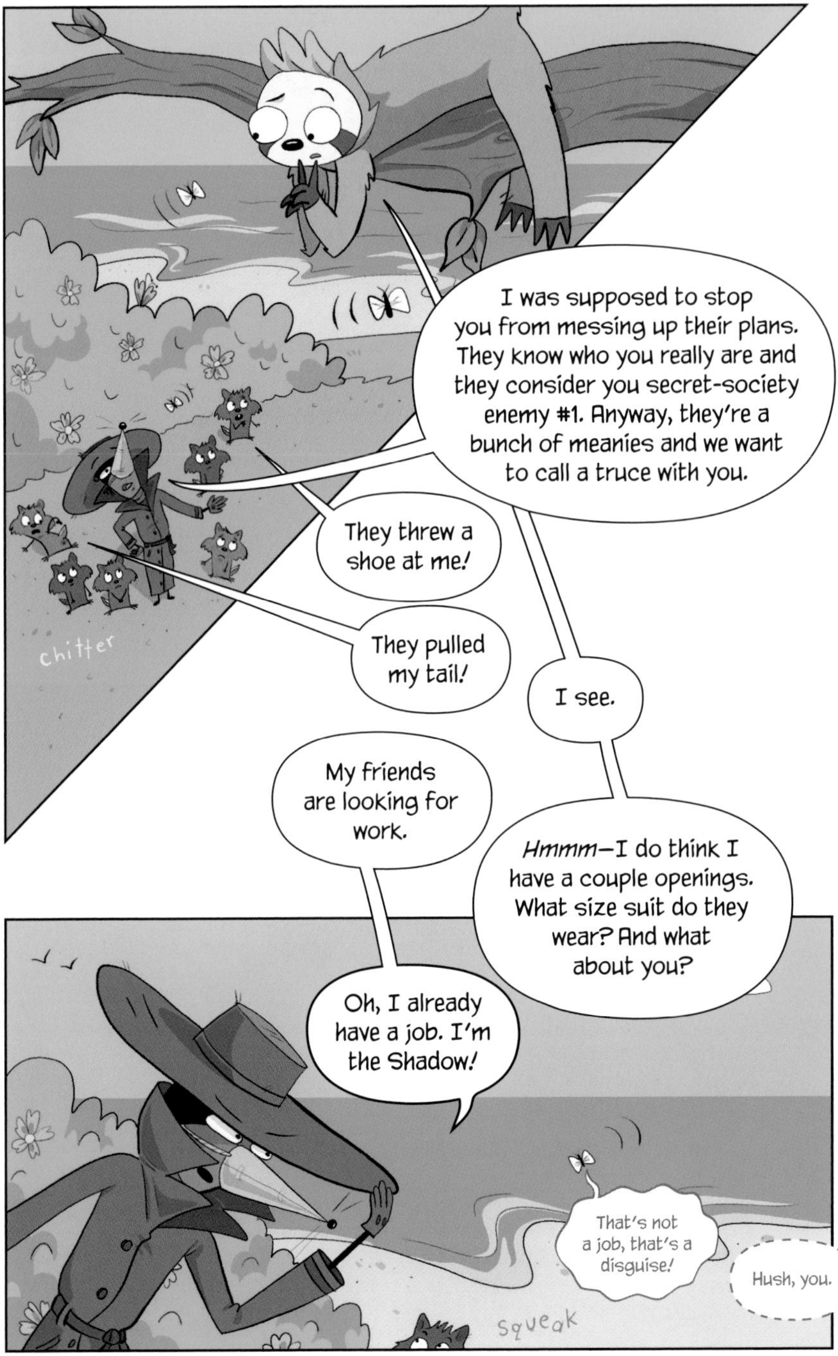
I was supposed to stop you from messing up their plans. They know who you really are and they consider you secret-society enemy #1. Anyway, they're a bunch of meanies and we want to call a truce with you.
They threw a shoe at me!
They pulled my tail!
chitter
I see.
My friends are looking for work.
Hmmm—I do think I have a couple openings. What size suit do they wear? And what about you?
Oh, I already have a job. I'm the Shadow!
That's not a job, that's a disguise!
Hush, you.
squeak

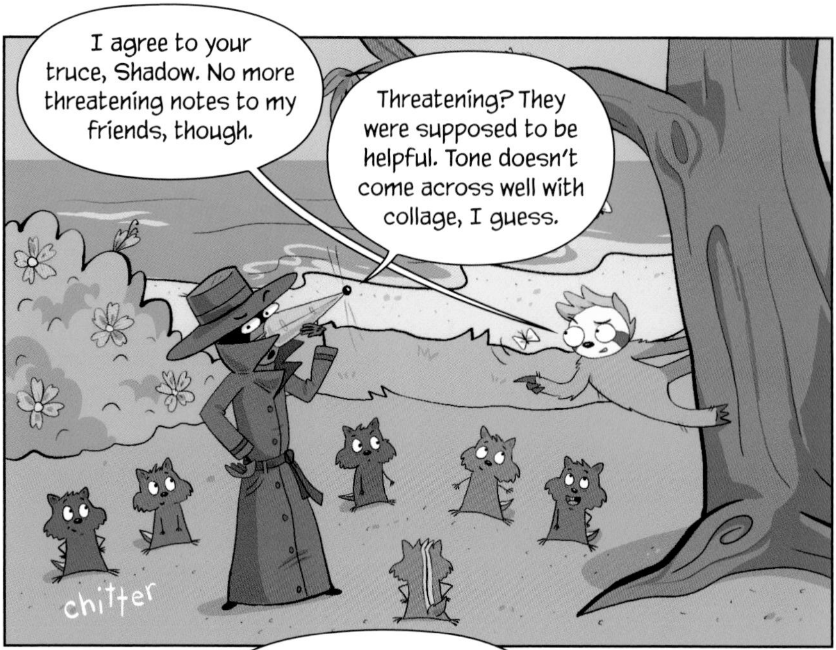
I agree to your truce, Shadow. No more threatening notes to my friends, though.
Threatening? They were supposed to be helpful. Tone doesn't come across well with collage, I guess.
chitter

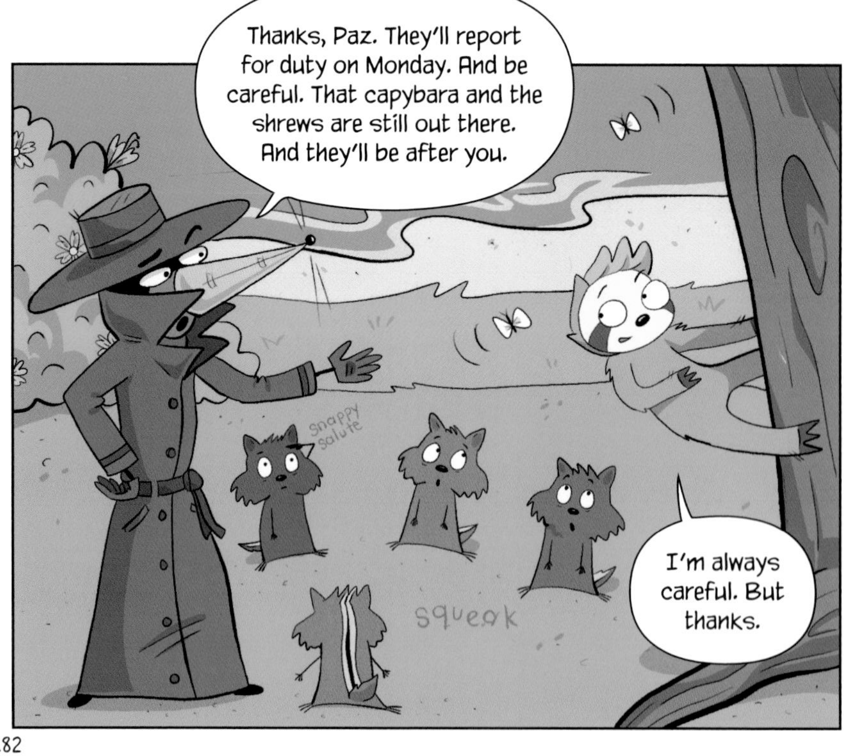
Thanks, Paz. They'll report for duty on Monday. And be careful. That capybara and the shrews are still out there. And they'll be after you.
snappy salute
squeak
I'm always careful. But thanks.

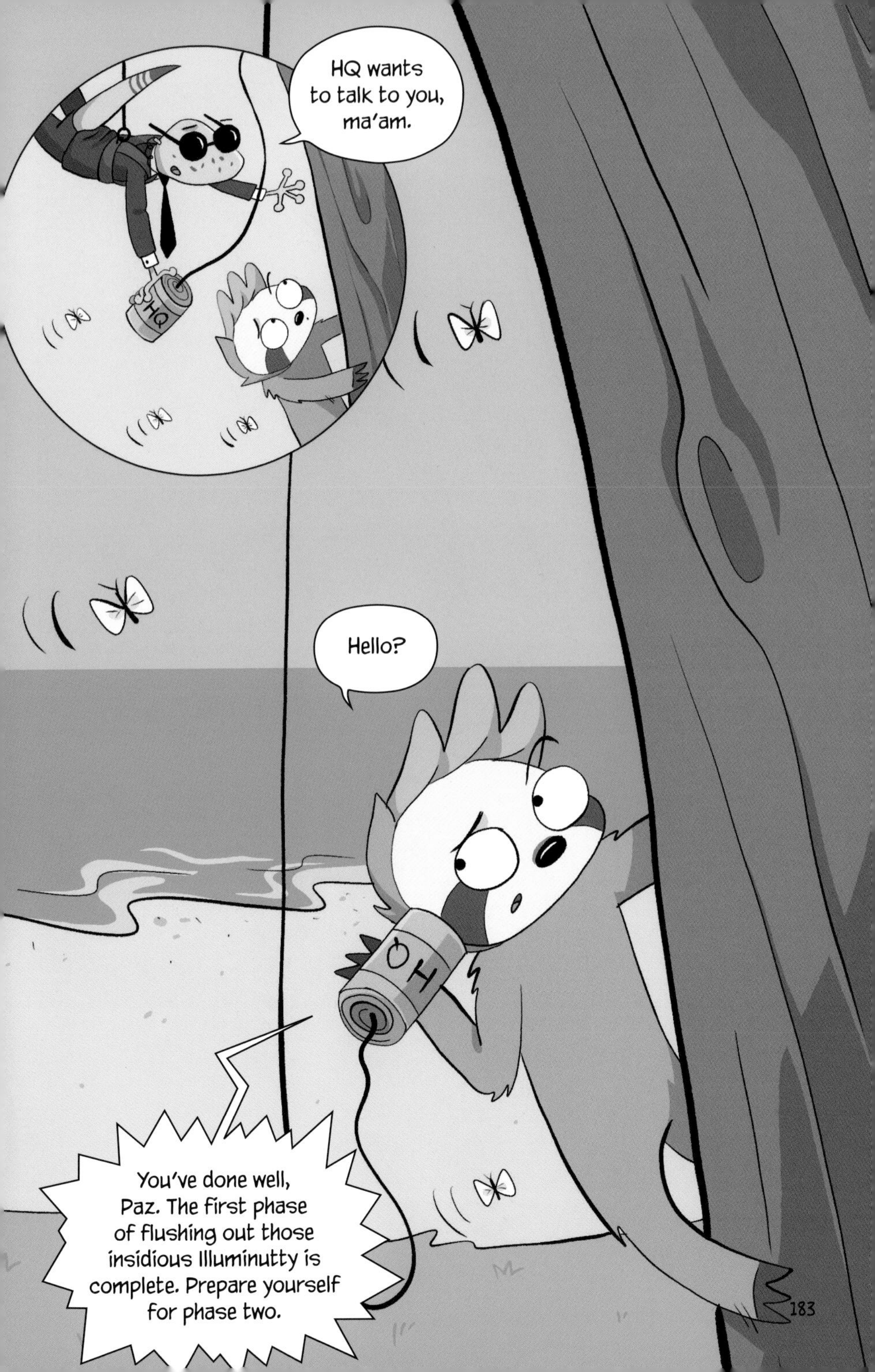
HQ wants to talk to you, ma'am.
HQ
Hello?
HQ
You've done well, Paz. The first phase of flushing out those insidious Illuminutty is complete. Prepare yourself for phase two.

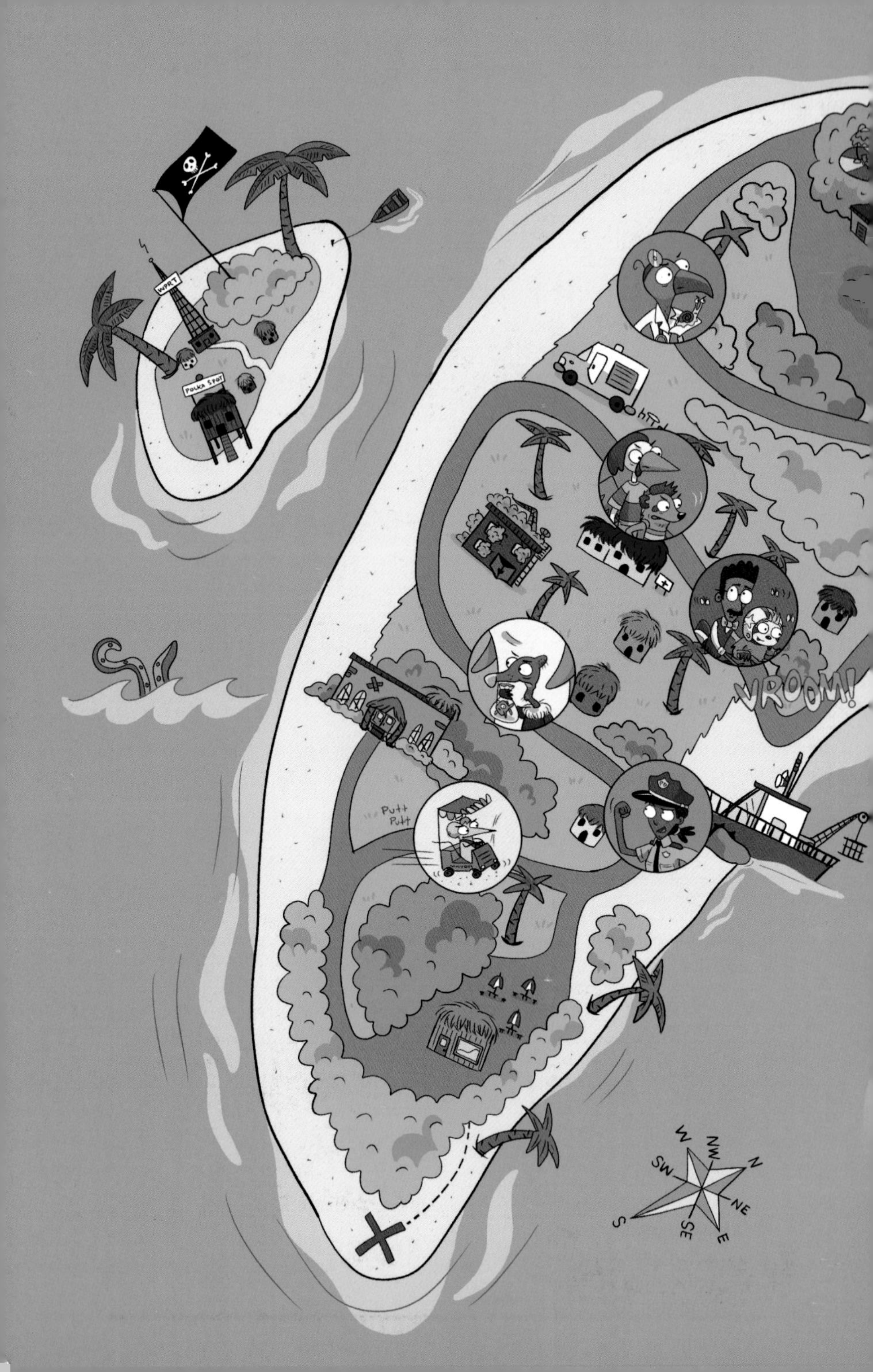
WPRT
POLKA SPOT
VROOM!
Putt
Putt
W
NW
N
SW
NE
S
SE
E